Know No Evil

D1638294

Know No Evil

Graeme Hampton

hera

First published in the United Kingdom in 2019 by Hera Books

This edition published in the United Kingdom in 2022 by

Hera Books
Unit 9 (Canelo), 5th Floor
Cargo Works, 1-2 Hatfields
London, SE1 9PG
United Kingdom

Copyright © Graeme Hampton 2019

The moral right of Graeme Hampton to be identified as the creator of this work has been asserted in accordance with the Copyright, Designs and Patents Act, 1988.

All rights reserved. No part of this publication may be reproduced or transmitted in any form or by any means, electronic or mechanical, including photocopy, recording, or any information storage and retrieval system, without permission in writing from the publisher.

A CIP catalogue record for this book is available from the British Library.

Print ISBN 978 1 80032 853 2
Ebook ISBN 978 1 912973 12 5

This book is a work of fiction. Names, characters, businesses, organizations, places and events are either the product of the author's imagination or are used fictitiously. Any resemblance to actual persons, living or dead, events or locales is entirely coincidental.

Look for more great books at www.herabooks.com

Printed and bound in Great Britain by Clays Ltd, Elcograf S.p.A.

1

In memory of my mother, Margaret, who loved to read.

Prologue

Then

It's gone midnight when we leave the club. The muffled thuds of a techno beat echo down the street. It begins to drizzle. We're wearing our best party gear: short skirts and high heels. We're not dressed for rain.

I hurriedly scan the street for a taxi. Bex looks like she's going to throw up.

I didn't want the night to end like this.

It had started off well enough: both of us celebrating the end of school and our new-found freedom. It had ended with a couple of shaven-headed bouncers asking us, politely, to leave one of Brixton's dodgier nightclubs. Bex had started a fight with another girl. Inevitably it had been about something and nothing, but it was enough to get us chucked out the club.

'I want another drink,' Bex says. She sways unsteadily in her stiletto heels and tries to pull the collar of her expensive new leather jacket up around her neck. It's almost cute, and I have to suppress an urge to giggle.

'I think we should get you home,' I say.

But Bex is too pissed to listen to reason. 'Let's go somewhere else,' she says. 'There's a new club just opened near the tube station.'

'It's miles away,' I argue.

'I don't care. *I don't care!*' Bex shouts, attracting disapproving looks from a passing couple. But she revels in the attention. 'Who's going to buy me a drink? *I want a drink.*'

There's a group of teenage lads standing outside the KFC on the corner by the church. They watch us, and eat their takeaways with their eyes narrowed and their voices low.

A taxi rounds the corner and I wave it down.

'I don't want to go home,' Bex says, tears smearing her mascara. 'Why do you always behave like you're my *mother*?'

The taxi pulls up beside us. I push Bex towards it with one hand and open the door with the other.

'She isn't going to chuck her guts up?' the driver asks, nodding at Bex. He looks pissed off, as though it's already been a long and trying night.

'No,' I lie. 'She'll be fine. I just need to get her home.'

Another argument ensues. 'I'm not going home! I want another *drink*.'

Bex pushes me away and ambles down the street in the direction of the watching lads, stumbling in her too-high heels, trying to pull her new denim skirt over her bare thighs. She passes the lads amid a cacophony of cat calls and jeering. One of them says something and his mates laugh.

Bex pulls a face at them and staggers onwards. A piece of deep-fried chicken hits her on the shoulder, leaving a greasy smear down the back of her cream leather jacket.

With my hand still on the taxi door, I have to make a quick decision. I shout 'Bex!' but she ignores me.

The rain is heavy now: icy daggers stinging my face and neck.

The taxi driver grumbles, 'Are you going to get in? If not, close the fucking door and piss off!'

I climb into the back of the taxi and ask the driver to take me home.

As the taxi pulls away, I glance out the rear window, watching as Bex totters into the night.

Then the taxi turns into a side street and my best friend disappears from view.

The next day, the following article appeared in the *London Echo*:

BERMONDSEY RIPPER'S LATEST VICTIM?

The body of an eighteen-year-old woman was discovered by a dog-walker in undergrowth in a park near East Dulwich station earlier this morning. She'd been beaten and strangled.

Police are so far refusing to comment on whether the young woman could be the latest victim of the so-called 'Bermondsey Ripper', who has been terrorising women in and around south London for the past year. Detective Inspector Ken Walters, who is leading the investigation into the murders, said it was 'unhelpful to speculate at this early stage'. He denied the police were struggling to make progress with the investigation, insisting there had been a number of breakthroughs in recent days.

The police have come in for continued criticism over their handling of the 'Bermondsey Ripper' case, which has so far seen six women viciously murdered in and around south London.

Chapter One

Now

Matt Denning reversed his Ford Focus into the narrow space between a Volvo estate and a concrete bollard. He shut the door and locked the car with a double bleep. In front of him, Haggerston Park shimmered in the sticky heat of an unusually hot London summer.

Denning slipped on his Ray-Bans, trying his best to look cool and unflustered.

Inside the park, a group of children hovered near some swings, looking bored and fractious. They eyed Denning with a mix of curiosity and suspicion as he passed. A couple of dog-walkers were engaged in an animated conversation as they watched the events unfolding in front of them.

Beyond the children's playground, a wooded section of the park had been cordoned off with a thin band of blue and white police tape, which hung limply in the stilted air. A couple of uniformed officers were talking to another group of children, some of whom looked like they were crying. A young officer, with dark, damp circles showing through his crisp white shirt, stood beside the path that led into the wood. Behind him Denning spotted half a dozen white-suited figures weaving between the trees and shrubbery, their faces obscured by masks. He could just about make out the distinctive shape of a forensic tent poking through the greenery.

Denning flashed his ID and the young constable nodded him past the temporary barrier.

It was slightly cooler inside the wooded area, but not much. Tall trees and their wide branches offered a modicum of protection from the sun's searing heat. Shards of daylight filtered through the foliage, dotting the ground with speckles of white.

As Denning approached the forensic tent, the smell hit him like a fist in the face. It made him think of curdled milk and rotting meat. He felt his stomach tighten.

A white-clad figure emerged from inside the tent. She walked over to him, dropped her mask and proffered a gloved hand. 'Sheila Gorton. I'm the crime scene manager. You must be DI Denning.' Her voice had a faint trace of a Canadian accent.

Denning shook her hand. 'Guilty as charged.'

'The boy wonder, so I hear.'

Ignoring her, he jerked his head in the direction of the tent. 'What's the story?'

Gorton was in her late forties and filled her forensic suit. 'Young woman. Late teens or early twenties. Beaten and strangled.' A couple of flies buzzed around her face as she spoke. She batted them away with a flick of her right hand. 'The bruising to the face is sufficiently extensive to suggest the beating was both sustained and brutal.'

'Has the pathologist had a look at her?'

She gave a light snort. 'The Home Office still haven't allocated one after Dr Chambers left, so we're waiting for UCL to send someone over from their pathology department. Should be here sometime today.'

One of the CSIs appeared and handed Denning a forensic suit. 'Any sign of sexual assault?'

'Possibly. The pathologist will be able to say for certain when he gets her on the table.'

Denning slipped a leg into the white suit. He looked at the near Elysian scene around him: a park in the middle of Hackney had initially struck him as somewhat incongruous; he'd always thought of east London as one vast urban conurbation, with nothing to break up the hard edges. 'Who found her?' he asked.

'Some kids,' she said. 'It's the start of the school holidays and I expect they were looking for something to do. They wanted to build a den, apparently. Poor little sods. Not exactly the best of starts to the holidays.' She looked at Denning. 'I'd better warn you; it isn't pleasant.'

'Is it ever?'

Stuffing his Ray-Bans into his top pocket, Denning zipped up the forensic suit, slipped the elasticated booties over his designer shoes and covered his face with a protective mask. Then he followed Gorton into the tent.

Amid the foliage, the body of a young woman lay on her back in a shallow grave. Her face was an abstract mask of red and purple, and there were marks around her throat. Her shoulder-length blonde hair was matted with dried blood. Sightless eyes stared back at him. Her mouth was half open, as though she was about to speak.

Denning knelt on the bone-dry earth to examine the body more closely. She was wearing a strapless grey sleeveless dress, which had been ripped from the shoulder to the hem. There were lacerations scored into her right hand and lower arms, as well as her forehead, along with what looked to Denning like teeth marks.

The grave was actually a natural hollow in the land. It had been partially camouflaged with twigs and leaves in an attempt to conceal the body.

Denning looked at Gorton and nodded. He headed out of the tent, Gorton following behind.

'Has the forensic photographer been?' he asked, removing his mask.

'Left about ten minutes ago.'

Denning climbed out of the forensic suit. 'Was there any ID on the victim?'

She shook her head. 'Nothing.'

'No phone? Bag?'

'Like I said – nada, zilch. Nothing.' She cocked her head to one side as she spoke. 'Sorry, I realise I'm not being very helpful.'

Denning shot her a reassuring smile. 'Not your bad.' He looked over his shoulder at the wooded copse; *the corpse in the copse*, he thought to himself, and had to bite back a wry smile at a naff pun. 'I'm guessing she wasn't killed here?' he said.

'The lack of blood surrounding the body would suggest she was killed elsewhere and the body dumped here. The pathologist should be able to confirm it, but I'd say she's been here less than twenty-four hours. In this heat, any longer and she'd have started going putrid.'

Denning suspected putrefaction may have already begun, but he wasn't going to question Sheila Gorton's professional opinion.

'What were those marks on her body? They look like lacerations, or bites?' He handed her his forensic suit.

'Foxes, I'd say. The area is home to a lot of wildlife. And there's the city farm on the other side of the park.'

Denning winced at the thought. 'The big question,' he said, as they walked back towards the main part of the park, 'is: how did she get here?'

'I would have thought the "big question" was who killed her, but I get your point.'

'Any idea about time of death?'

'Not really my area of expertise. You should really be aiming that one at the pathologist.' Her eyes twinkled. 'But I guess you don't want to hang around until we get one, so I can take a professional punt and estimate sometime yesterday evening.'

'Any chance you could be a bit more specific?' He offered her his best impression of a warm smile. 'I would appreciate it.'

'Judging by the early state of decomposition and rate of rigour mortis, I'd say twelve hours ago, give or take.'

Denning nodded his acknowledgment. 'So, we're saying sometime between midnight and 1 a.m.?'

7

Gorton nodded. 'Obviously the PM will be able to give you a more accurate timescale, but that would be my best guess.'

The cool shade of the wooded area had now given way to the blinding sunlight of the main park. Denning hurriedly slipped his sunglasses back on and wiped his forehead with the back of his hand.

He spotted a casually dressed young man approaching from the direction of the police incident van, which was now parked just beyond the main gate leading into the park.

As soon as the man saw Denning and Gorton, he sauntered over to join them.

Denning greeted him with a curt smile. 'Sheila Gorton, DS Neeraj. I'm guessing you two know each other?'

DS Deepak Neeraj was a year or two older than Denning. He was dressed in a pair of beige chinos and a chocolate brown and black checked shirt. His thick, jet-black hair was gelled into a neat quiff. Neeraj and Gorton nodded professionally at one another.

'Deep, what's happening?'

'A couple of the PCs have spoken to them kids what found the body,' he said. 'They can't tell us much though.' He kept his hands in his pockets as he spoke. 'We're going to get someone to take them home. They're pretty shook up.'

His focus was on Denning when he spoke, as though Gorton wasn't there. If he smiled more, Denning thought, he could have passed for attractive.

'Understandable,' offered Gorton. She aimed her words at Neeraj. 'Can't be every day you chance upon a dead body in your local playground.'

'Round here,' Neeraj replied, his hands still in his pockets, 'I wouldn't be too sure.'

They both looked at Denning. He was gazing around the park, taking in the scene: people stood around observing the proceedings, while others sunbathed on the yellowing grass trying to affect a lack of interest. A couple of pensioners sat on a bench immediately beyond the cordon, eating ice cream and watching the police activity as though it were live telly unfolding before them. A wiry terrier frolicked in a flower bed.

After a moment Denning became aware that a silence had fallen. Gorton and Neeraj were looking at him, expecting a reply. 'Of course,' he said. 'Get someone to take them home. We'll take a formal statement from them later, once family liaison have been in touch.'

Gorton said, 'I'll email you the PM results as soon as I can.' She touched his elbow gently, offered him a half smile, then returned to join the other CSIs in the wooded area.

Denning turned to Neeraj. 'Any other witnesses?'

Neeraj shook his head. 'The plods have spoken to everyone who was in the park this morning, but there's nothing useful.'

They walked in the direction of the mobile police unit.

'Has anyone checked the CCTV?'

'Sorry...?'

They stopped. Denning pointed at the park's main gate. 'There must be CCTV at the various entrances to the park. Has anyone checked them?'

'Not yet.'

'Well, can you do that? The CSM believes she was killed sometime after midnight, then dumped here. So check times from around 12 a.m. onwards.'

Neeraj seemed to give the matter some thought before replying. 'OK. I'll get someone on to that.' He walked towards the mobile unit, hands still in his pockets.

Chapter Two

Standing in the car park at the back of Dalston police station, Detective Sergeant Molly Fisher lit her second guilty Silk Cut of the day.

She turned her face towards the sun, feeling the warm rays prickle her pale skin. Distracted by the sound of a door closing behind her, she glanced over towards the entrance to the custody suite and saw DC Trudi Bell weaving her way across the car park, packet of B&H in one hand, mobile phone in the other; her tight-fitting black top and grey pencil skirt emphasising her curves.

'All right, babe? How's things?' Trudi asked, removing a cigarette from the packet.

Molly offered Trudi a light. 'You know: same old, same old.'

Trudi took the lighter and lit her cigarette. She inhaled deeply, before blowing out a long plume of smoke and letting her shoulders drop. 'Christ, I needed that.' She handed Molly back the lighter. 'I thought you'd given up?'

'I did,' said Molly. 'For about a day.'

Trudi laughed. 'Well, you've got to die of something.' She looked up at the sky and screwed her eyes. 'Christ. A day like this, we should be sunning our arses on a beach, not stuck in this shit hole.'

Molly smiled her agreement. 'I know. It's just heaven.' She'd spent her childhood in Australia, where hot summers weren't even worthy of comment. Days like these made her yearn for the Sydney lido. 'How's life in the glamorous world of MIT?' she asked.

'A young woman has been found strangled and battered to death in Haggerston Park. And in the middle of summer too; some people have no consideration.'

Molly pulled a face. 'Shit. Nasty.' She flicked some ash into the metal cigarette bin on the wall beside the door to the custody suite. 'Any leads?'

Trudi kept her face pointed at the sun. 'Not sure yet. Apparently the new boy's calling the shots.'

'New boy?'

Trudi took another long drag on her ciggie. 'DI Matthew Denning. You must have seen him around?' She cocked her head in Molly's direction. 'He looks like a frigging ad for Hugo Boss.'

'I can't say I have, but you lot in MIT are slightly aloof from the rest of us humble drones in regular CID.'

Trudi let out another coarse laugh. A couple of uniformed officers looked over at them, wrinkling their brows as they passed. 'Yeah, that's us all right. Aloof!'

'So what's he like then, this Denning bloke?'

'Well, I reckon you wouldn't chuck him out of bed.'

They both laughed this time.

'What does he think?' Molly asked, making it sound casual.

Trudi took another long drag on her cigarette. 'Early days. I just had a quick word with Deep Neeraj and he reckons it's the work of a psycho.' She paused, looking at the cigarette in her hand. 'Well, actually he told my cleavage, but you get the picture.'

Molly remembered DS Neeraj from a DI's leaving do at Easter: he'd fancied his chances almost as much as he fancied himself. 'What else did he say?'

'He told me it's pretty nasty.' She waved her cigarette at Molly. 'Denning's about to call a briefing, so I thought I'd grab some fresh air first.'

'You and me both.'

Trudi flicked ash onto the bonnet of a squad car. 'What about you? How's it going on the drugs case?'

Molly tucked a loose strand of hair behind her ear. 'Adam Sloane? Poor kid's still in a coma. Doctors reckon it was a dodgy E. Mummy claims he must have been tricked into taking it, but there's no greater denial than a mother's blindness.' She looked at Trudi and frowned, then added: 'They don't know if he'll pull through.'

Trudi shook her head. 'Do you know who supplied the gear?'

'Oh, we know all right, we just can't prove anything.'

'Usual suspects?'

'Yup.' Molly pulled a face. 'Gregor Kane's gang have been supplying kids all over the Ashbrook Estate, not to mention half the schools in east London. Maybe if we had more resources, we might actually be able to do something about it. As it is, we're pissing against a hurricane. And Kane knows it.'

'How come?'

'Kane's a bottom feeder: he's not a big enough player to attract the attention of the big boys in Trident, so we're left to clean up the mess with all the limited resources of an over-stretched CID.'

Trudi took a last, deep draw on her cigarette. She slowly exhaled the smoke in a long thin stream.

'Kane isn't bulletproof,' she said 'No matter what he or his scumbag family think.' Trudi dropped the cigarette butt onto the tarmac and twisted it under the heel of her shoe.

'I dunno. So far the only witness – the boy's best mate – is keeping tight-lipped. Kane isn't stupid. He knows how to cover his arse.'

'He's had enough practice.' Trudi put a hand on Molly's arm. 'Word of advice: don't take this crap so seriously. The minute you let it get to you here,' she jabbed her thumb against her temple, 'you're fucked.'

Molly tried to smile. 'I know you're right. It's just...' She paused. 'Perhaps I need a night out to remind me that there's life beyond the grind.'

Trudi was about to say something when her phone beeped. She glanced down at a text message, squinting slightly as the sun gleamed off the screen. 'I need to get back up there, briefing's about to start. We'll catch up over a pint this weekend, yeah?'

'Sure.' She watched Trudi head back towards the door to the custody suite. She keyed in the security code, pulled open the heavy metal door and disappeared inside the building.

Molly took her time finishing her ciggie. It had been her New Year's resolution to give up smoking, as it had been the previous year, and the year before that...

She ground the stub against a wall and dropped it into the metal bin. Despite the heat, she shivered.

Trudi's words danced round her brain like a dervish: *a young woman... strangled and battered to death... in the middle of summer too...* A horrible image flashed into her head, bleak and vivid.

She closed her eyes and tried to block the mental picture from her head.

Chapter Three

'Close the door.' DCI Liz McKenna's office was small but tidy. It was separated from the main MIT room by half-glassed walls and grubby venetian blinds. A desk fan whirred rhythmically from the top of a filing cabinet, circulating warm air around the room. Behind the fan a sad-looking cyclamen gasped for breath.

Denning felt a thin bead of sweat gather on his forehead. As he sat down opposite McKenna, his right temple started to throb.

He had just finished briefing his team; filling them in on what they knew so far. What little they knew... He had been on his way back to his desk when McKenna had appeared and jerked her head in the direction of her office.

McKenna didn't seem to notice the heat. She was dressed in a crisp, black and white striped blouse and faded grey jeans. A battered leather biker's jacket hung on a peg on the back of her office door. Her face was heavily lined, making her look closer to sixty than fifty, though Denning reckoned she was probably somewhere in between.

'I won't fanny about, Matt,' she said. 'I know you're new, both to this particular MIT and the rank of inspector. I won't lie and say you were my first choice for the job, but you're here, you're bright and you've got a solid track record: your work with South East MIT at Lewisham clearly impressed all the right people in the right places, and I'm told you get the job done with little fuss and flannel. All of which are major points in your favour as far as I'm concerned.' McKenna's rasping voice was like a rusty nail on a broken harpsichord. Denning spotted an unopened packet of cheroots on her desk, next to a cracked mug, which smelt faintly of Glenmorangie. 'However, your old boss at Lewisham did express concerns about you not being a team player. This job *is* teamwork, Matt. I can't stress that enough.'

'I appreciate that I might have come across like that before, but that isn't the case any more. I've learned about teamwork, and I accept it's part of the job.' In the past two years he'd been on so many team-building exercises he reckoned he could almost build a catamaran from Lego blindfolded.

'Whatever the case, I like to give people the benefit of the doubt,' she continued, 'until they persuade me otherwise.'

Most of what Denning knew about Liz McKenna came courtesy of hearsay and office gossip. Someone had told him she originally hailed from Motherwell and had cut her teeth in one of the roughest parts of Glasgow, allegedly making headlines when she'd stopped an armed robbery in a betting shop with nothing more than a baton and sheer nerve. At some point in her illustrious career she'd gained the nickname Betty Taggart.

'Thank you for the vote of confidence, ma'am.'

McKenna winced. 'Don't call me "ma'am", I'm not Helen Mirren.' Her accent was a curious hybrid of Glaswegian and estuary English; it sounded oddly mellifluous. 'This is your chance to show us what you can do. Don't let me down.'

'I don't intend to,' he said coldly. 'I expect this to be a relatively straightforward case.'

McKenna fixed him with a gimlet stare. 'In my experience, murder is rarely as straightforward as it first appears.' He could feel her eyes boring into him, almost willing him to challenge her. 'Try adopting a more open-minded approach and don't make too many assumptions. And, let's be blunt, until we can ID the victim, we're pissing in the dark.'

Denning felt the throbbing in his temple grow more pronounced. His former boss at Lewisham MIT had often warned him against appearing over confident. *Was he coming across as too over confident now? Arrogant even…? Would a note of humility strike a better chord?*

'I've asked DS Neeraj and DC Bell to get onto Missing Persons,' he said. 'Somebody has to be missing our victim. She's *someone's* daughter.'

McKenna let his comment hang in the heavy air. 'Identification has to be our priority at this stage,' she said after a moment. 'We need to catch this bastard quickly. I've called a media briefing for this afternoon. As Senior Investigating Officer, I'll be handling all media liaison, but I'll ensure you stay up to speed with everything. At this stage, we'll stick to the basic facts, nothing more. Convince them we've got a lead, even if that isn't the case.' She paused. 'As far as the press is concerned, we're all over this like a dose of the clap.' He watched her eyes flick from him to the unopened packet of cheroots on the desk, then back to him. 'One more thing, Matt. I want DS Neeraj to deputise you.'

'Sorry, but I'm not sure…'

'Look, I know Deep can be a bit of a knob, but he's a good officer, and he knows his way around a murder inquiry.'

'With respect, I don't think Neeraj and I have the greatest working relationship.' Denning looked at her, trying not to focus on the pain in his temple. The bead of sweat on his forehead was in danger of turning into a trickle. 'I get the impression he resents me.'

McKenna smiled, showing uneven teeth, yellowing and slightly feral. 'It's no secret he put in for the inspector's job. He's been here eight years, he's done the leg work and even shown initiative on the odd occasion. I reckon he thought the job was a shoo-in.' She sat back in her chair and steepled her hands under her chin. 'You've been parachuted in over his head because these days the Met has a thing for fast-tracked graduates with flashy degrees in psychobabble.' She leant forward, placing her palms on the desk. 'Diversity may be terribly fashionable, but we all know what really helps get a leg-up in this game is being white and having a dick.'

Denning swallowed the temptation to point out McKenna had done all right for herself, despite only ticking one of the diversity boxes, perhaps two if you pushed it... But she was being unfair. He'd joined the Met straight after university and after six months on their training programme had been promoted to DS. At thirty-three he was aware that he was probably one of the youngest DIs in the Met, but he'd earned his promotion, and nobody could claim otherwise.

'I'm not going to apologise for my background.'

'Keep your tights on, son. I'm not asking you to *like* Neeraj, just work with him. Maybe you could learn something from each other.'

There was a knock on the door. Trudi Bell stuck her blonde-bobbed head into the office. 'Sorry to interrupt, boss, but we've got a name from MisPer. A Leanne Wyatt was reported missing by her mum, Susan Wyatt, about twenty minutes ago – it's only just come up on the system. She's twenty-one years old, slim-build and dyed blonde hair. Lives on the Beaverbrook estate in Hackney. It fits our girl, boss.'

McKenna drummed her nicotine-stained fingers on the unopened packet of cheroots. 'Leanne Wyatt... Why does that name ring a bell, DC Bell?'

Trudi twitched back a grimace, then said, 'Leanne Wyatt is, *was*, the girlfriend of Gregor Kane.'

McKenna stopped the finger drumming. She sat back in her chair again and gave a throaty sigh. 'Fuck, that's all we bloody need!'

Chapter Four

'Gregor Kane is a right piece of shit.' Neeraj was chattier now, but Denning could sense there was still an edge about him. He'd spent most of the journey to Susan Wyatt's house filling Denning in on office gossip and refusing to make eye contact. Denning wanted to say something, apologise perhaps, for having taken a job that Neeraj had evidently assumed was going to be his. But another part of him refused to see why he should feel the need to apologise for being good at his job. Instead, he simply nodded, smiled and concentrated on the road ahead.

Despite the air conditioning being on full blast, it was still uncomfortably warm in the car.

Neeraj popped an Extra Strong Mint into his mouth, without offering Denning one. 'You must have heard of his old man, Alfie Kane? King Alfie, as he likes to be known.'

Denning had heard stories about the Kane family, none of them good, and certainly nothing that could ever be put before a jury. Rumours and hearsay, but Kane was always clever enough to hide his tracks.

Neeraj snorted and noisily crunched the mint. 'Alfie Kane runs a haulage business based out in Braintree, but he's from round here originally. The business is supposedly all legit. We've never managed to nail him for anything, and probably never will. He's smart... shrewd, in a cunning dog sort of a way.' He crunched the mint some more, before continuing. 'There was a rumour he was using the lorry business as a cover to smuggle illegals into the UK, but nothing could be proved. If you ask me, he's just a player with an ego but he's earned himself a reputation.'

'A reputation...?' Denning slowed for a red traffic light.

'A rival firm went bust a few years back. Their premises were torched in what looked like an insurance job, only the insurance company wouldn't pay out. Alfie Kane took over most of their contracts.'

'Coincidence?'

'Could be. Naturally enough nothing could be linked to Kane, at least not officially. But there were rumours.'

There were always rumours when it came to men like Alfie Kane. Denning had met numerous Alfie Kanes over the years. Men like Kane attracted rumours: a combination of jealousy and urban myth. However, rumours didn't prove he was a criminal. 'What about Gregor Kane?'

Denning turned off Balls Pond Road and headed down a narrow street lined with tall Victorian houses on one side and a block of modern Lego-like flats on the other. A notice attached to one of them advertised the starting prices at just under a million. 'Ideal for first-time buyers,' it stated, without any sense of irony.

'Gregor is the baby of the family. Alfie's missus had him when she was well over forty,' Neeraj continued. 'His first arrest was five years ago for assaulting a kid in a McDonald's. The kid lost an eye. Nearly lost his life too. Apparently he'd "disrespected" Kane in front of some girl. The case was dropped after the kid's family withdrew the complaint. Since then Kane's been in and out of trouble. Mostly GBH, intimidation, that kind of thing.' He finished eating the mint. 'He keeps himself busy these days selling drugs to local schoolkids; got quite a racket going by all accounts. But just like his old man, the shit never sticks.'

—

Susan Wyatt lived on the ground floor of a square, concrete four-storey block in Dalston. Denning guessed it had been built sometime in the 1970s: an era when functionality took precedence over style. To her credit, she'd made some effort to keep the exterior neat, with a bright basket hanging beside the front door and a couple of cheery tubs by the doorstep. As he rang the bell, Denning was sure he saw neighbours' curtains twitching.

The door was opened by a woman in her mid-to-late forties, with a trendy hairstyle that trimmed a few years off her age, but a heavily lined face that put them back on despite a generous application of make-up. She offered them a cautious look, as though she half-expected trouble to come knocking from time to time.

Denning and Neeraj flashed their warrant cards and explained who they were.

She showed them into a compact but pleasantly furnished living room; there were over-sized knick-knacks everywhere, cheap and tasteless but somehow managing to make the place seem homely. A chintzy sofa and two matching armchairs were positioned around a large, flat-screen television. 'Can I get you some tea?' she asked. Her jumpy body language suggested she already knew how the scene was going to play out, despite clinging to some faint hope she was wrong.

They declined the offer. Neeraj sat on the low chintzy sofa without waiting to be asked. He was still wearing his jacket.

'You reported your daughter missing, Mrs Wyatt,' Denning said.

She nodded. 'Yes. She was supposed to pick Charlie up this morning, but she never showed up. It's not like her. Her whole life revolves around little Charlie. She'd never let him down.'

'Charlie?' Denning enquired.

'Her little boy. He was staying with me last night. Leanne said she was meeting a friend, so I said I'd have him. She said she'd come round this morning and pick him up first thing. Well, she hadn't appeared by lunchtime, so I began to worry. I phoned her mobile a few times, but there was no answer. I left a couple of messages on her voicemail, and phoned her neighbour. She knocked on Leanne's door, but there was no one in. Then I phoned some of her friends. No one had seen her last night.'

Denning asked, 'Is it possible she could have stayed over with someone last night and simply lost track of time?'

She shook her head. 'It's really not like her to stay out and forget about Charlie.'

'How old is Charlie?' Neeraj asked.

'He'll be five in October.'

'Where is he now?' asked Denning.

She jerked her head towards the living room wall. 'He's next door, playing with my neighbour's grandkids. I didn't want him here when you called round.'

'Does Leanne often leave her son with you while she goes out drinking?' Neeraj asked.

'No. Leanne's not the sort to go out boozing night after night, if that's what you're thinking. In fact, ever since Charlie came along, she's hardly been out at all. It's a shame for her, really. She works in a hair salon on Kingsland Road. Sometimes she'll join the other girls for a drink after work, but she's a good mother: she always puts Charlie first.'

'I'm sure my colleague wasn't implying anything,' Denning said, shooting a sharp look in Neeraj's direction, which he either failed to notice, or chose to ignore. 'Do you know who she was with last night, or where they were going?' he asked.

Susan shook her head. 'She didn't say. Just said it was a friend and they were going out for a drink, possibly a meal.'

'And you have no idea where?'

She lifted her face and looked over at Denning. 'Like I told you, she doesn't go out much these days, and I don't like to pry into her private life. We've had arguments about that before now.' She shook her head wearily, then shot Denning a worried look. 'Has something happened? Is that why you came round here so quickly?'

'Do you have a recent photo of Leanne?' Denning asked, keeping his voice level.

She blinked a couple of times, as though she was trying to keep tears at bay. Despite the make-up and half smiles, there was a hardness about her face that suggested she'd experienced more than her fair share of life's knocks. 'Yes.' Her eyes flicked from one officer to the other for a moment, then she stood up and walked over to an MDF shelving unit next to the television.

'This was taken last summer.' She handed them a silver-framed photograph showing a young woman smiling at the camera. Leanne was wearing a t-shirt with 'Girl Power' emblazoned across the front. A cute-looking child sat in her lap staring benignly at the camera. Denning assumed this was Charlie, the as yet unseen child, currently playing next door, unaware his entire life was about to change forever.

It was sunny when the picture was taken and both mother and son were squinting at the camera.

Denning took the photo from Susan Wyatt and looked closely at Leanne before passing it over to Neeraj. It was impossible to say whether the smiling, carefree girl in the picture was the same person he'd seen a couple of hours earlier, battered beyond recognition and half-buried in a park. However, the age and general description matched, and from what her mother was telling them, it seemed out of character for Leanne Wyatt to just disappear.

'Leanne had a flat on the Beaverbrook Estate, is that right?' asked Denning.

She nodded. 'Yes, she's been there about three years now.'

'We'll need to search her flat. We'll be as careful as possible.' He noticed she was staring straight at him, almost *through* him. 'Do you have a key to her flat?'

It was like she was in a trance, and not fully taking in what they were saying. 'Yes,' she said after a minute. 'I'll get it for you.' She headed through to the kitchen, reappearing a couple of minutes later with a silver Yale key, which she handed to Denning, along with a yellow Post-it note with an address scribbled on it in slightly shaky handwriting: 29 Tressell House,

Keir Hardy Way. 'It's just off Hackney New Road,' she said, in case they didn't know where it was. Though of course they did. Every copper in east London knew of the Beaverbrook Estate, by reputation if nothing else.

'I'll need a list of all Leanne's friends and colleagues. Also, do you know if Leanne had a regular boyfriend?' Denning asked. It was a loaded question; they had to get onto the awkward subject of Gregor Kane and Leanne Wyatt's relationship with him.

Susan Wyatt was staring at the blank TV screen. Denning could sense how her brain was working: making connections and assumptions; not wanting to believe what was screaming at her. 'Not any more,' she said, after a moment. 'She was seeing someone, but they split up about three or four months ago.

'Something has happed, hasn't it? That's why you're here. That's why they sent plain clothes officers and not uniformed police.' Her voice was calm, any hint of hysteria kept at bay by a steely determination and a need to know what had happened to her little girl. 'You might as well tell me.'

'We've found a body, Mrs Wyatt,' Denning began. 'Earlier this morning, in Haggerston Park. The body of a young woman that fits Leanne's description.'

She was silent for second, then let out a single, audible sob.

Neeraj shuffled his feet awkwardly and looked at Denning.

'I'm very sorry, Mrs Wyatt. We will need you to formally identify the body.' Denning paused, he wanted to reach out and hold her, tell her everything would be all right, but it would be both inappropriate and a lie. 'Is there anyone we can contact? A family member? A friend? Leanne's father?'

She sniffed back the tears. 'He pissed off when she was six. I haven't seen him in years.' She wiped her nose with her hand, struggling to compose herself. 'No. No, I'd rather do this by myself.'

'I'm sorry, but I need to ask you some more questions,' Denning said softly. 'You said Leanne split up from someone a few months ago? Can you confirm the name of the person she was seeing?'

'A lad called Gregor Kane,' she said quietly. 'I never liked him. I always thought he was trouble and would end up getting Leanne into trouble. She met him at a friend's party while she was still at school. I mean, I knew about the family's reputation – everyone round here knows the Kanes – but I always tried to give him the benefit of the doubt.'

'How serious was the relationship?' asked Denning.

She half smiled at him. 'He isn't Charlie's dad, if that's what you're wondering. The relationship was very on and off.'

'Who ended the relationship?' It was Neeraj's turn this time, and his manner was as direct and blunt as before.

Susan Wyatt thought for a moment. 'It was Leanne. She decided she'd had enough. He used to treat her like rubbish. I think she believed deep down that if she threatened to leave him, he'd change his ways. But leopards don't change their spots. Besides, I don't think he felt the same way about her as she felt about him. Well, it's different for men, isn't it?' She eyed the two officers coolly. 'It's more about sex than love, especially at that age.'

'Who *is* Charlie's dad?' Neeraj asked.

Susan stared at Neeraj. For a brief second Denning thought she was going to tell him to piss off. He wouldn't have blamed her if she had. 'She never told me. Just said he was someone she knew from school. Whoever he was, he's never had anything to do with Charlie. Leanne brought him up by herself. With some help from me, of course, and her nan when she was still with us, God rest her.'

'What was Gregor Kane like around Charlie?' Denning asked.

She nodded, but was now speaking through tears. 'Good. Yes, Gregor might be a vicious bastard at times, but he was good with Charlie.' She flicked away tears with the back of her hand. 'I sometimes wondered if he really was Charlie's dad, and

Leanne just didn't want to say. I did once think about doing one of those DNA tests, try and get a lock of his hair or something, but what would have been the point? It wouldn't have changed anything, only caused another argument.'

Susan Wyatt sobbed and shook her head. 'What am I going to say to Charlie? He'll want to know what's happened to his mummy.'

'If necessary, we'll appoint a Family Liaison Officer to look after you, and a child psychologist will be available to help Charlie come to terms with what's happened.'

Denning explained that a couple of uniformed officers would call round and take her to the mortuary to identify the body. There wasn't much else he could tell her. There were the usual promises about catching whoever had done this, the suggestion of bereavement counselling and turning to family and friends for support. But it would all mean nothing in the end if she had just lost her only daughter and they could offer up little more than empty platitudes.

Chapter Five

They found Gregor Kane in his favourite haunt: the Henley Castle, an un-gentrified pub on Dalston High Road.

The pub had seen better days. The interior was bedecked in varnished pine, with peeling photos of sport stars of yesteryear stuck to the walls and harsh strip lighting overhead. A couple of the lights didn't work and grim shadows pooled on the faded bottle-green and shit-brown carpet, which was pockmarked with beer stains and decade-old fag burns. An old-fashioned juke box sat in a corner by the gents and blasted out a tinny din.

Neeraj pointed Kane out as soon as they walked in. He was playing pool near the bar with a group of mates. Most were dressed identically in faded jeans and hoodies. Someone grunted when Denning and Neeraj approached, accompanied by a hail of laughter from his mates.

'Gregor Kane?' Denning asked.

'Minute,' Kane replied, poised to pot a red.

Denning pulled the pool cue from his hand. '*Now*, if you don't mind, Mr Kane.'

Kane was better dressed than his mates, his designer shirt and expensive jeans confirming his place as head of the pack.

His mates made various ooh and ahh noises; someone, possibly the same one as before, offered up another porcine grunt. Kane took a deep breath through his nose and then stood to his full height. He wasn't particularly tall, a little over five feet six inches, but he had the lithe muscle tone of a regular gym-goer. Denning noticed a small diamond stud in his left ear.

'What do you want?' Kane's accent momentarily caught Denning off guard. It was educated, rather than the guttural tones he had expected, and seemed strangely incongruous.

'I'm Detective Inspector Denning,' he said, flashing his warrant card. 'And this is Detective Sergeant Neeraj.' Denning nodded towards Neeraj, who stood silently a pace behind him. 'I need to ask you some questions about Leanne Wyatt.'

Behind him, Denning heard someone say 'slag'.

'I understand you and Leanne used to be friendly.'

There was more laughter from behind him. 'Leanne's a silly little bitch, if you'll pardon my French. And I wouldn't go believing a word she tells you.' Kane spoke smugly, with the confidence of knowing they were on his turf: his territory meant his rules, and as long as his smirking, laughing crew were there to back him up, there was little chance of him letting his guard down.

'When did you last see her?'

'Me and her haven't spoken for months. Why? What's she been saying about me now?'

Denning was curious as to what he meant by 'now'. Had Leanne made a complaint about Kane in the past? 'She hasn't said anything, Mr Kane.'

'Then what's this about? Because I'm a busy man.' The polished accent ricocheted round the shabby pub like designer shrapnel.

'The body of a young woman was found in Haggerston Park earlier today, and we have grounds to believe it's Leanne Wyatt.'

The cat-calls from Kane's posse stopped. Kane, however, gave nothing away. His gaze remained fixed on Denning. After a moment he asked, 'What happened?'

There was a fetid, sickly smell emanating from somewhere in the pub; possibly caused by blocked drains, or sour beer, or more likely a combination of both. Denning felt his stomach twist. He didn't want to spend any longer in this grotty dive than he had to.

'We believe she was murdered and then dumped in the park.'

'Fuck. Well, cheers for telling me. But, you know, Leanne kind of brought shit on herself.'

Denning wasn't sure if this swagger was for his mates' benefit, or if Gregor Kane really cared so little for someone who once had feelings for him. Either way, he could feel his intense dislike of Kane growing by the second.

'Can you tell me what you mean by that?'

Kane squared up to Denning, looking him in the eye like a feral dog marking its ground. People like Gregor Kane, Denning reminded himself, had self-assurance bred into them from birth. 'I dunno why you're asking me all this shit. Me and Leanne finished way back. She'd moved on to some other twat after me. And probably another few after him.'

'A young woman's dead, Mr Kane. A young woman who was also a mother. I think she demands a bit more respect than you seem to be showing her.' Denning's voice was composed, though he could feel his left temple starting to throb again.

Kane looked to his mates, but they stayed silent. He raised his chin in Denning's direction. 'Look, I'm sorry she's dead, but Leanne never really fitted in round here. She was always on the lookout for some muppet to support her and her brat. As far as she was concerned, if I flashed the cash she was happy to keep me sweet. But I've got nothing to do with her being murdered, and unless you have any proof to the contrary, I suggest you and your little friend do one before I put in an official complaint for harassment. Now, if you don't mind, I've got a game to finish.' He grabbed the pool cue from Denning and stood in front of him, smiling his defiance at the two officers. 'Is there anything else?'

'Where were you?'

Kane potted another red before answering. 'What time?'

'Just answer the question, Mr Kane.'

He was silent for a moment, not thinking up an excuse, but rather, Denning reckoned, trying to see how far he push them.

'I was at the Cat in the Hat on Upper Street. It was a mate's birthday. I was there from around nine until gone one. Ask anyone who was there. Now, is there anything else?'

Denning looked over to Neeraj, who was staring at his feet. They were in danger of going round in circles, with Kane knowing the rules too well to give anything away. 'That's all for now, Mr Kane. If there is anything else, then we'll certainly be in touch.'

Denning and Neeraj turned to leave. They'd almost reached the door when Kane said: 'You want to have a word with Daryl Bailey. If anyone had a reason for offing Leanne then it was probably him. And next time you want to talk to me, you'd better have a good reason.'

Chapter Six

'Daryl Bailey! That little fucker Kane is talking out of his arse.' Neeraj was crunching another mint, this time even more noisily than before, animated now, in contrast to his frigid silence in the Henley Castle. 'OK, Bailey was a bit of a lad back in the day, but it's bollocks to suggest he's in any way involved with this caper.'

They were driving back to the station. Denning was listening as Neeraj ranted about Kane but then offering up comment on Daryl Bailey. Neeraj, it seemed, had been something of a fan. 'He used to play for West Ham when I was a kid,' Neeraj explained. 'I met him once. He signed my programme. I've still got it somewhere. I mean, I know there were rumours about him, but I don't believe he'd be involved with a kid like Leanne Wyatt. It's just not his style.' He finished crunching the mint and swallowed it, before picking at his teeth. 'Kane, on the other hand, looks like he'd be capable of anything, including murdering some girl just 'cos she looked at him the wrong way.'

'Rumours...?' Denning asked, when Neeraj finally paused for breath. Denning had little interest in football. Rugby was his game, and had been ever since he'd played for his school first eleven.

'What?' Neeraj looked over at Denning, a pissed-off expression nailed to his face.

'You said there were rumours about Daryl Bailey. What were they?'

Neeraj pinched his nose then shook his head. 'I can't remember the exact details now. It was ages ago.'

'OK. A rough indication would do.'

Neeraj was silent. He stared out the window at the passing urban landscape; the same desultory look on his face as before. Denning pulled over and stopped the car. He turned to face his moody passenger.

'Deep, I'm sorry it's me heading up this case and not you. That's not my call. You put in for the job and didn't get it. I did. It's shit, but it's life.'

Neeraj continued to gaze out the window. A woman was walking along the pavement half walking, half dragging a child behind her. The child began to scream, but the mother remained oblivious. 'None of this matters, Deep. What does matter is that I need a team I can depend on. I can't do this job without the support of you and every other fucker in MIT. If you and me can't work together then one of us is going to have to put in for a transfer, and it isn't going to be me. Off the record, you're not my first choice as a co-pilot on this case, but McKenna wants us to work together, so I'm prepared to give it a go. Maybe you could try to.'

There was silence from the passenger seat. The woman and screaming child had disappeared into a newsagent's. After a moment, Neeraj turned to face Denning. His face was impassive, his eyes reluctantly meeting Denning's. 'Off the record, I think you're a smarmy dickhead who only got this job because you talk posh and you've got a degree in nothing special.' His face contorted into an attempt at a smile. 'But I admire your honesty. And it'd take a braver man than me to get on the wrong side of Betty Taggert.'

They laughed, ice broken. Denning started up the car, indicated, and pulled out into the traffic.

'Apparently some little tart claimed he tried it on with her,' Neeraj said. 'The rumours, about Daryl Bailey.' He looked over at Denning. 'It was all lies of course, and nothing was ever proved, but it cost him his job.'

'He was sacked?'

'As good as. He'd left West Ham by then. He was playing for some crap team up north. Had to give up professional football though.'

'When was this?'

Neeraj shrugged. 'Not sure exactly. A few years back. Anyway, why does it matter? Kane's just trying to throw us off the scent. I'd put money on that little fucker having done Leanne. That's just his style.'

Denning kept his thoughts to himself. Kane was certainly arrogant, probably capable of demonstrating ruthlessness whenever he felt he had to, but he couldn't help thinking that a lot of what they'd just witnessed was Kane's bravado, put on for the benefit of his gang. Get Kane on his own and they'd likely be playing a very different game. 'What's with the accent?'

'What do you mean?' Neeraj was still staring morosely out of the car window.

'Why does Kane talk like Little Lord Fauntleroy?'

There was a momentary pause, during which Neeraj presumably tried to work out what Denning was getting at. 'Oh yeah, you mean, why's he sound like a posh boy?' He gave a dry laugh. 'His old man sent him to St Joseph's, you know: the posh school for rich bastards in Islington. But at the end of the day, you can't polish a turd.' Neeraj laughed at his own joke.

Denning knew of St Joseph's: an eight-grand-a-term repository where parents with large wallets sent their offspring to be cushioned from the wilder realities of life. But then his own parents had paid for him and his brother to attend private school, so who was he to judge?

They'd arrived back at the station now, the sun beating down on them as soon as they stepped out the car.

The MIT suite was buzzing with life when they entered. DC Bell looked up from her desk when she saw Denning. She raised her hand in acknowledgement. The Metropolitan Police's Homicide and Serious Crime Command consisted of eighteen Major Investigation Teams, known as MITs. Their team was based in Stoke Newington and covered east London.

Denning headed over to his desk at the far end of the room, next to the water cooler.

Unlike his colleagues', his desk was clutter free. The only personal touch was a silver-framed photograph of his wife, Sarah, which she'd given to him on his promotion to inspector just over a month ago. Otherwise, he liked to keep his personal life private. He glanced at the photo, which had been taken during their honeymoon in Mauritius. That was four years ago, and he couldn't believe so much had happened in the past four years. Here he was, now leading a murder inquiry with a team of detectives under him who would be looking to him for leadership and guidance, and a hatchet-faced DCI above, who would be waiting for him to fail...

'Boss?'

He looked up to see DC Bell standing next to him; a piece of A4 paper in her hand.

'Sorry, Trudi. What is it?'

She perched on the end of his desk. He could smell her perfume; something familiar, which he couldn't quite name...

'I've made a list of all Leanne's friends and work colleagues. I've put a tick next to the ones I've spoken to. I've left messages with the others to call me back ASAP, but I expect it'll be tomorrow before I hear from them now.'

Denning glanced at the clock on the wall – it had gone four; unless anything major came in now, the team would start winding down for the day. From tomorrow onwards the pace would accelerate significantly. Before they knew it, they be eating, drinking and dreaming about this case.

'Ryan Cormack and Dave Kinsella have spoken to Leanne's neighbours, but I don't think they got much: usual wall-of-silence stuff.'

It sounded depressingly familiar. Everyone wanted a police force who could provide justice: safe streets and bad people locked away to protect the good and the innocent. But when it came to playing their part, the great British public was more than willing to turn a blind eye whenever it suited them.

'Thanks for this.' He took the paper and placed it on his desk, briefly scanning the list of names. Trudi was about to return to her own desk when he suddenly asked, 'Can you do a PNC check on a Daryl Bailey? Specifically, see if there's anything about a sexual assault claim dating back a few years.'

'Daryl Bailey?' Her voice was half an octave higher than normal. 'The footballer?'

Denning smiled at her. 'The very same.'

She headed back to her desk. He was sure he'd seen DS Dave Kinsella's head twitch at the mention of Bailey's name.

Denning headed over to Kinsella's desk. It was messy with Post-it notes and scraps of paper littering the desktop. Kinsella had several photos of his children on his desk. Denning knew he was divorced, and probably only saw his kids every other weekend. He sympathised with his plight.

'Dave. How's it going?'

Kinsella was pushing fifty and balding, with a bushy moustache and a beer gut that would see him fail any routine medical. Despite his length of service, he had neither the ambition nor the talent to reach beyond the rank of Detective Sergeant. Kinsella was old school; the kind of diehard detective that was all but extinct in the Met these days. The face of British policing was changing and a dinosaur like Dave Kinsella just didn't belong any more.

Kinsella nodded an acknowledgement. 'Not bad, boss. How did you get on with that little turd Gregor Kane?' There was sweat lining the bottom of Kinsella's thick moustache. *Christ* thought Denning, *he even looks like a seventies throwback…*

'He's an arrogant little shit, and he's probably got motive. But he says he's got an alibi.' He stood next to Kinsella's desk, trying to look relaxed and friendly. Denning tried hard to get along with most people, but with Dave Kinsella, it always felt like he was making an effort. 'You've been around a while, Dave. What's your take on Kane?'

Kinsella sucked air in over his teeth and sat back in his seat. A faint smell of BO came off him. 'You've got the arrogant little shit bit right. He's been arrested more times than I've had hot dinners, but his old man gets him off the hook every time. But murder... It's a bit of a leap, even for him.'

'What about his old man, Alfie Kane? Is he capable?'

Kinsella looked blank for a moment. 'Probably. But this isn't his style. If he wanted someone out the way, we'd be looking at a missing person inquiry, not a murder. And why would Alfie Kane kill a kid like Leanne Wyatt?'

'To protect his son, maybe? If she had something on Gregor, threatened to grass him up? Or maybe he was worried she might get her claws into him, saddle his precious boy with a child when he's little more than a kid himself.' He threw Kinsella a half smile. 'Look, it's all speculation at this stage. Let's keep an open mind.' He changed tack. 'I understand you and DC Cormack had a chat with the neighbours. Anything useful?'

'Nothing much. An old bag on the next landing said she looked after Leanne's kid from time to time, but other than that – nada.'

'Does the "old bag" come with a name?'

Kinsella shuffled through some papers on his desk and unearthed a ringed A5 notepad containing illegible scrawl. 'A Mrs Nelson. Didn't give her first name. Lives at 22 Tressell House. Seemed friendly enough, offered us tea and cake. Probably belongs to the generation that still respects the police.'

'There has to be some of them still out there,' Denning said with a wry grin. He glanced over at Ryan Cormack's desk: he was typing away at his computer, probably writing up his notes from today and then putting them onto the shared drive so the whole team could access them. 'Go on.'

'She had no idea if Leanne had a boyfriend, but she did say she'd seen Leanne being dropped off by some bloke in a posh car a few times. Didn't know the make of the car, and couldn't give me a description of the driver, but she seemed to think he was an older man. Older than Leanne, I mean.'

'Anything else?'

Kinsella stared blankly at his notes, probably trying to decipher his scribbles. 'Said she and Leanne hardly spoke, just "please" and "thank you" whenever she dropped the brat off and then picked him up again. 'Fraid that's all, boss.'

Denning nodded his thanks to Kinsella then returned to his desk. Trudi Bell had pinged an email across to him: *Nothing on Daryl Bailey – clean as a whistle!*

Denning sighed. Things weren't getting off to a brilliant start. As soon as the body had been confirmed as being Leanne Wyatt, they would go after Kane. They would go after him hard and fast.

Chapter Seven

Jon Cavanagh was lying half asleep on an ancient chaise longue in the cluttered living room at the back of the north London terraced house they shared when Molly Fisher returned home. Radio Four was chattering noisily in the background, and a tangy whiff of dope hung pungent in the air.

He raised a lazy hand when she entered the room. The wooden floor was littered with folders and papers and dozens of out-of-date copies of the *NME*. A couple of squashed beer cans poked out the top of the overflowing waste paper basket like crushed tin corpses. Despite the sunny evening, the velvet curtains were drawn over the French windows. Thin shafts of light poked thought the gaps, bathing the room in a muted amber glow.

'Back already? I didn't realise it was so late.'

She kissed him on the forehead and sat on the edge of the couch, knocking his feet out the way with her hand. The chaise longue had once belonged to one of the Mitford sisters, or so Jon claimed. A missing leg had been replaced with a couple of bricks, and ancient horsehair spewed out of a gash in the faded upholstery. Molly fantasised about one day chucking it in a skip.

'Have you done anything today?' she asked.

He sat up, massaging grit out of tired eyes with his massive fists. 'Of course I have. I ain't been lying here all day, if that's what you're thinking.'

He arched his back and stretched his muscles, bones noisily clicking into place. 'It's this fucking *heat*.' he said, rubbing a paw over his unshaven muzzle. 'How is anyone expected to function in this *heat*...?' He padded over to the French windows, threw back the heavy curtains and thrust open the glass doors. Warm air and birdsong filled the room.

'Why don't I make us something to eat?' Molly offered. 'We can have it in the garden.'

He didn't answer, just stared out the French windows, hands gripping the frame, breathing in the sultry air.

Molly headed into the kitchen, where a pile of dirty dishes sat defiantly in the sink. She was sure they'd been there when she'd left for work that morning. A fly buzzed noisily around a pot on the stove. She lifted the lid and sniffed two-day-old pasta, instantly screwing up her face and wrinkling her nose. She removed the pot from the stove and carefully scraped its contents into the bin.

It had been almost two years since she'd moved in with Jon, and all attempts to instil domestic order had been met with stubborn resistance. Jon liked mess. He claimed it made the house feel homely.

And it *was* Jon's house after all, bought after the breakdown of his second marriage twenty years ago. She had tried to imprint her mark on it, tried to introduce a note of feminine charm into the hard, stale fabric of the place, but mostly without success.

She opened the kitchen window to let in some fresh air and shoo away the buzzing fly, then rummaged in the fridge hoping to find some vegetables that hadn't yet turned to mush.

She could hear Jon clattering around the living room. Radio Four had been replaced with Aerosmith's 'Dream On', the volume turned up full blast.

Her mind briefly flitted back to the conversation with Trudi Bell earlier in the day. A young woman murdered, her body left in a park... A half-buried nugget of memory flickered like a broken light in the back of her brain... *reckon it's the work of a psycho...* It was such a random phrase; cops used it all the time to describe everything from granny bashings to serial murder. And yet it spoke of something more than another run of the mill domestic murder. A psychopathic killer... *a young woman... strangled and battered to death... in the middle of summer too...* Leaving a body in a park... Images kept dancing in her head and she struggled to blink them away.

She tried to focus on dinner. There wasn't much in the fridge: some cherry tomatoes, a withered lettuce and half a cucumber sweating in its wrapper. She found some pre-cooked barbeque chicken thighs that were still just the right side of their sell-by date and a bottle of vinaigrette dressing she'd bought the week before last, and a bottle of Pinot Grigio in the fridge door. She placed the food and wine, along with a couple of dusty glasses, onto a tray and took it all outside.

The back garden was dense with untamed shrubbery, brown and parched in the arid heat. A rusting wrought-iron table and two chipped chairs sat on a tiny patch of patio just outside the French windows. Molly placed the tray on the table. The sun was thinking about setting now, throwing up a welcome patch of shade between the side of the kitchen and the neighbour's wall.

Jon appeared, looming large in the French windows. 'Looks grand.' He gave a watery smile. 'I'm sorry, but I'm not hungry.'

Molly poured out two glasses of wine and took a sip from one of them, enjoying the chill liquid as it washed down her throat.

'Have you eaten anything today?'

He sat down opposite her and shrugged. 'I had some crisps and a pasty at lunchtime. At least I think it was lunchtime. I kind of lose track of the hours some days.'

Molly suppressed a sigh. She wanted to light up a cigarette, but she'd already exceeded her quota for the day. 'Jon, you need to sort yourself out. You're in danger of wasting your life.'

'Not another lecture, please.'

She winced. She knew Jon was in a bad place, and had been since he'd lost his job as political editor with the *London Echo* almost a year ago. His dark moods had struck before, but were usually short-lived. This time, however, it seemed like the black dog was permanently at his heels. She worried that he might go off the rails. But she also worried that her patience was in danger of running thin. 'Sorry,' she said. 'I didn't mean to sound like a nag. I just worry.' She threw him a conciliatory smile. 'What about the book? Did you do any more work on it today?' Since losing his job with the paper, he was supposedly writing a book about the political elite and media corruption. He had yet to get beyond chapter one.

'Some. Not much. I just can't seem to focus.' He placed his hand on hers and held it there for a few moments. 'Bad day at work, was it?'

She laughed and shook her head. 'Is there any other kind these days?'

He reached out and touched her arm, stroking it tenderly and giving her a brief glimpse of the old Jon, the one she'd fallen in love with.

They ate in silence for a while. The sun was about to disappear behind the spire of a nearby church, before beginning its lazy descent below the horizon. Although lacking the searing potency of earlier, it was still warm, but pleasantly so rather than uncomfortably.

Molly finished her wine and poured another glass. She took a sip and looked over at Jon. He was toying with a cherry tomato on his plate. She decided to take a punt and pick his brains.

'Do you remember a series of murders, about twelve years ago?' she asked. 'The Bermondsey Ripper? It was all over the papers at the time.'

Jon scratched his bald head. He decided to abandon the tomato and instead poked his fork at a grey slab of chicken. 'Strange conversation to bring up over dinner.'

She took another sip of Pinot Grigio; it washed away the taste of dry chicken and wet salad. 'Just… do you remember? The *Echo* must have covered it.'

He continued to jab at the chicken. 'Yeah. Vaguely. A guy called Anthony Ferguson. He murdered a load of women. He was a nutter. Why do you ask?'

She wasn't sure how much to tell him. She wasn't even sure there was anything *to* tell beyond some crazy thoughts chewing her brain. 'No reason. I just wondered if you remembered much about the case.'

Jon laughed. 'This has got nothing to do with your obsession with murderers, has it? I mean this was all years back. Ferguson was found guilty, sentenced to life. He's still inside, as far as I know.' He put his fork down and stared quizzically at Molly. 'Seriously, Mol, what's this all about? Has some new evidence come to light or something?'

'No. I was just… curious.' She toyed with her wine glass, unconsciously twisting the stem between her thumb and forefinger. 'A young woman was found murdered in a park earlier today and it got me thinking about those murders.'

Jon wrinkled his brow. 'It's a bit random, not to mention morbid. Has this got something to do with your ongoing ambition to join the murder squad?'

She gave a slightly forced laugh. 'Like I said, it's just idle curiosity, that's all. Nothing sinister.' She drank some more wine. 'And I do not have an obsession with murderers. Unless it's with seeing them locked up.'

He smiled at her and rubbed her leg with his foot. 'Look, I know you're a good detective, and I don't doubt you'd be an asset to any murder squad, but you've got to be patient. Your time will come. Let's forget about Anthony Ferguson; he was a sicko. Let's just enjoy the evening.' He clinked his wine glass against hers and took a glug of wine, before turning his face towards the cooling sun.

Molly threw a smile back at him. She tried to chase the thought from her head, but somehow it just wouldn't disappear. 'I've always wondered if he really did commit those murders,' she said, almost sotto voce.

'Sorry?' Jon looked at her, puzzled.

She smiled at him, not realising she'd said it out loud. 'Nothing,' she said. 'You're right. Let's forget about murder and enjoy the evening.'

Chapter Eight

It was just after seven when Denning arrived home. He and Sarah lived in a large, open-plan warehouse conversion at the point where the fringes of the City of London begin to merge into the East End. Trendy Shoreditch had been her idea and not his, but as it was her income that paid the rent, he wasn't in much of a position to argue.

Sarah was washing and slicing vegetables in the kitchen area off the main living room. The heady scent of her perfume filled the room. Classic FM was playing an aria from Act Two of Mozart's *Marriage of Figaro*.

He threw his jacket over one of the linen sofas, headed into the kitchen and took a beer from the fridge, giving Sarah a peck on the cheek as he brushed past her. 'I thought I said I'd cook tonight?'

She gave a light laugh. 'I couldn't wait for you to get back.' She finished chopping the vegetables and took a fillet of salmon from the fridge, placing it on a wooden board on the worktop. She then added some extra virgin olive oil to a steel wok on the stove, lighting the gas underneath.

'How was your day?' he asked.

'Hectic as always. You?'

'Yeah, good.' He opened the beer and took a sip straight from the bottle. 'I've been asked to head up a murder investigation.'

'Murder?'

He recounted the events of the day without going into detail.

She added the vegetables to the wok, stirring them around the hot oil with a wooden spatula.

'Yes, there was something on the local news about that. Tragic. What a waste of a life.'

'Mmm.' He took another sip of beer and headed into the living area. The doors to the balcony were open, letting in a cool evening breeze.

He went out onto the balcony, and stood leaning against the railing, sipping his beer and appreciating the breeze on his cheeks. The setting sun suffused its golden glow over the jagged landscape, and in the near distance he could make out the overground line snaking its way north towards Dalston on a series of Victorian brick viaducts. To the east of Hoxton station lay Haggerston Park. He tried hard not to think about a young woman lying strangled and battered in her shallow grave, and now lying cold and dead on a mortuary slab. He tried even harder not to think that a little boy might be growing up without a mother.

Half closing the balcony doors behind him, he headed back into the living area and sat down on one of the over-sized sofas that occupied the vast room. There were a couple of estate agent's brochures on the coffee table. He picked them up and flicked through the glossy photos of expensive properties in leafy suburbs. 'I thought we could look at the Finchley house this weekend,' Sarah shouted from the kitchen. 'That's assuming you're not working.'

He threw the brochures back on the table and took another sip of beer. 'I've got Jake this weekend, remember?'

Sarah appeared from the kitchen and stood at the end of the sofa, the wooden spatula still in her hand. 'Sorry, I forgot to say: Claire phoned earlier. She said she tried your mobile but couldn't get an answer. She didn't want to leave a voicemail. She's asked if you could make it next weekend.'

He rubbed a hand over his eyes. 'She's changed the arrangements again? That's the second time this month.' He looked over at the photo of his son that sat on the bleached-wood sideboard at the far end of the living area. He'd taken the

44

photo on his phone during a trip to Alton Towers on Jake's last birthday. His son was smiling, something he hadn't been doing a lot of lately.

Sarah scrunched her face into a half smile, punctured with a nasal sigh. 'Don't shoot the messenger.'

'Sorry. It's just... I was looking forward to taking him bowling.'

'Matt, you always take him bowling. Either that or it's the cinema. Why not take him to the Science Museum or the Planetarium? He might enjoy it and learn something at the same time.'

'He's an eight-year-old boy, Sarah. He's got school for education. Weekends are for fun.'

She perched on the arm of the sofa, and placed a reassuring hand on his shoulder. 'I know I don't have any right to interfere, but it won't do him any good in the long run if you keep indulging him all the time. I'm sure Claire would agree with me.'

Denning doubted if his ex-wife would agree with Sarah on anything, especially the welfare of their only child. 'Maybe.' So much of his life was spent treading a fine line; always trying to keep everyone else happy. Sometimes he thought it would be nice to take his son somewhere far away and never come back. 'I can ask him,' he said.

'Great. And at least think about that house. We can easily afford somewhere bigger now. Preferably somewhere with a garden. Jake would like that.' She rubbed his shoulder and headed back into the kitchen.

Denning glanced at the brochures on the coffee table. 'I thought you liked living round here. And do we really want to commit ourselves to a massive mortgage?' He bristled at the prospect of years and years of debt hanging over their heads.

'Why are you always worrying about money?' Sarah shouted from the kitchen. 'I should get a decent bonus this year, and there's the extra money you're bringing in now you've been promoted. We might as well plan for the future.'

Money seemed to occupy so many of their thoughts these days, but for different reasons. He suspected Sarah was unaware of just how little he earned as a detective inspector, while her annual bonus as a portfolio manager with a major investment bank could have easily paid for a third car.

Then there were the maintenance payments for Jake. Not that he resented that: it was important for his son to have stability in his life, and being a parent was a full-time commitment, irrespective of how rarely he actually saw his son.

He looked over at the picture of Jake. He hadn't been himself the last couple of times they'd gone out. Maybe Sarah was right: perhaps it was time to try somewhere different for their irregular father and son outings. Maybe he needed to work harder at being a better dad.

Chapter Nine

Molly booted up Jon's laptop. She was sitting at the desk in the tiny office at the back of the house, which overlooked the garden. Jon was downstairs, watching a football match he'd recorded on Sky Plus, two cans of Stella Artois for company.

If she'd told him what she was doing he would have accused her of being obsessed, and it was just possible he might have a point.

But if nothing else, this would quench her curiosity.

She typed the name 'Anthony Ferguson' into the search box and hit the return key. The screen instantly filled with a list of over a dozen websites, mostly news sites, but also a couple of discussion forums and a website devoted to the celebration of the world's most notorious serial killers.

Molly clicked on the BBC news website.

She was already familiar with the basic facts of the case: seven women had been dragged off the street at night and brutally murdered. The oldest was thirty-four, the youngest was fifteen. The police had initially underplayed any links between the first few killings before eventually having to admit they were the work of the same man: Anthony John Ferguson, twenty-eight; a loner who lived with his elderly grandmother in New Cross.

She read on.

The victims had all been sexually assaulted, beaten and strangled. The level of violence had suggested the perpetrator was deranged and dangerous. The press had dubbed him 'The Bermondsey Ripper', though his killing spree had quickly extended beyond Bermondsey to other areas of south east London.

Within days of the last murder, Ferguson had been arrested and charged.

At his trial, the judge labelled him the very embodiment of human depravity, and handed him a full-life tariff, meaning Ferguson would never be released. The press speculated that he'd acted out of a deep-rooted hatred of women. He had shown no remorse for his actions, and had never expressed any pity for his victims or their families. Two psychiatrists had declared Ferguson as being of sound mind with no history of mental illness, though one suggested there was some indication of psychopathy in Ferguson's personality, and noted that he had a below-average IQ.

Ferguson had launched an appeal with the Court of Appeal six months after his conviction; no longer claiming his innocence, but challenging the full-life tariff. However, as the tariff had been set by the trial judge rather than a politician, the appeal was rejected and the sentence upheld.

Molly remembered the trial. It was just before she'd gone back to Oz to stay with her dad and his new wife for a couple of years of dodging arguments and trying to sort her life out.

At the bottom of the BBC page there were links to several online articles and news stories about Ferguson. She clicked on a couple of them. The coverage of both the crimes and the man who carried them out bordered on salacious. Ferguson was variously described as a 'monster', a 'beast' and 'the devil in human form'. His grandmother had been forced to move house after an online vigilante group published her address. She died the following year from a heart attack. The brother of one victim was quoting as saying that he hoped Ferguson would 'rot in hell'. There were the usual demands to bring back the death penalty for Ferguson and people like him.

A couple of stories focused on Ferguson's background, trying to uncover a reason for his behaviour, and asking if people like Anthony Ferguson were born evil, or whether upbringing played a part.

But it was the final article that prickled her interest. It was written by a freelance journalist who questioned certain aspects of the Ferguson case, hinting at a possible miscarriage of justice.

Molly re-read the article a couple of times. The story was little more than speculation, with nothing to substantiate its claims beyond idle conjecture.

She noted the name of the journalist, Magda Kilbride, and a contact email address. The article had been written two years ago to mark the tenth anniversary of the killings so it was likely the email address would still be active. She started to draft an email, thinking carefully about what she wanted to say. It would be better if she didn't mention being a police officer, as that would imply her enquiry was in some way official. At this stage it wasn't even an enquiry, just casual curiosity. Or was it something more; a niggling doubt that had refused to go away...?

She looked at the decade-old photograph of Anthony Ferguson: dead eyes framed in a pockmarked face. She didn't believe it was possible for a person to look evil but, innocent or guilty, there was something about Ferguson that made her skin crawl.

Chapter Ten

'We've got the preliminary results of the post mortem through,' Denning announced to his team next morning. They were gathered together in the MIT suite on the fifth floor. The air conditioning was still off, and the room already felt hot and oppressive. 'We also now have confirmation that our victim is Leanne Wyatt.'

Denning stood at the front of the room next to a large whiteboard. He had the beginnings of a headache, no doubt caused by lack of sleep and exacerbated by the heat.

He looked around the room. He was at least four officers short of the number ideally needed to competently conduct a murder investigation. A combination of biting cuts to police budgets and a couple of officers on long-term sick leave meant he was already starting this investigation on the back foot.

A blown-up aerial photograph of the park dominated the right hand side of the whiteboard: a circled cross in red marker indicating the area where the body had been found. The map was surrounded by photographs of the crime scene, including several pictures of the victim, graphic and bloodied; enough to turn all but the strongest of stomachs.

'Results confirm Leanne Wyatt was strangled and beaten by a blunt instrument, most likely a hammer. There was evidence of vaginal bruising, suggesting she'd been raped.' He pointed to the photograph of Leanne taken during the post-mortem. Her face had been cleaned up but was pale and empty, like a bleached waxwork.

'What are those scratch marks on her body?' DC Ryan Cormack asked.

'Foxes, apparently,' Denning said. 'According to the PM report, some of them are quite deep.'

'The mark on her forehead looks a bit like a cross,' Ryan added.

Denning looked more closely at the photo. Ryan had a point: the scratch marks on the victim's forehead did faintly resemble a cross, but equally, they also looked like random scratch marks.

'Best not to jump to any conclusions just yet,' Denning said calmly. 'Let's stick to the bare facts for now.' He read the PM report. 'Time of death is given at around midnight on the evening of July 23rd. There were high levels of alcohol in her system and traces of amphetamines, but no evidence of Rohypnol or any other drugs associated with rape. We're still waiting for the forensic report,' he said, making a mental note to chase up Gorton. 'Obviously our priority at this stage is to find out where the murder took place and who was responsible.'

'So we round up all known sex offenders,' Kinsella said.

'That's certainly a possibility, Dave, but most sex attacks are opportunistic: the attacks usually occur where the bodies are found. This is different. It feels like there's been an element of planning here.'

Kinsella made a noise Denning couldn't quite hear. He ignored it and continued, 'CCTV picked up a white Ford Transit van parked near the eastern entrance to the park around midnight yesterday. Unfortunately, the park's CCTV is analogue rather than digital, so the images aren't sharp enough to get any clear details. We're going to get the boys and girls in the tech team to digitally enhance the picture quality. Hopefully this will give us a registration number, and then we can run it through the Automatic Number Plate Recognition system. Tech have also got Leanne's laptop which, with a bit of luck, should throw up something useful. Her mobile phone is still missing, and it's possible her killer has it, maybe even kept it as a souvenir. We'll contact her service provider and try and get a trace. Even if it's switched off, they'll be able to give us an approximate location, which we can then narrow down. In the meantime, we'll continue with door-to-door and speak to people who knew our victim. However, it seems Leanne kept herself to herself and didn't have many friends. Perhaps this was because she had a small child and couldn't get out much, but it's also possible she was shy and didn't make friends easily. As we speak to more people who knew her, we should build up a better picture of who she was and why someone might want to kill her.'

'My money's still on Gregor Kane for this. He knew the victim, he's got previous for assault, and he's nasty. He fits the bill to a tee.' Kinsella shared his wisdom with the team. He was sitting on his desk, arms folded over his barrel of a chest, wearing the same sweat-stained shirt he'd been wearing the previous day.

'Despite having an alibi, Kane remains a person of interest,' Denning said. 'However, until we can disprove his alibi, we're going to have to handle Kane with kid gloves.'

'Don't we always.'

Denning watched as Kinsella rolled his eyes. He didn't doubt Kane was certainly capable of this, but Kane was nobody's fool: if he had killed Leanne, he would have covered his tracks well. If they were going to go after the likes of Gregor Kane and his slippery father, they would need to be one hundred per cent sure of their facts.

'What about DNA?' Ryan Cormack asked.

'I'm going to chase up forensics, as soon as I've finished this briefing, so hopefully we'll get their report ASAP. Once we have it, we can cross-match anything with the DNA database and see if we get a match.'

Denning turned to the whiteboard. Taking a marker pen, he scribbled another name on the board: Daryl Bailey.

A murmur of whispering passed between various members of the team, then Kinsella asked, 'How exactly does Daryl Bailey fit into this?'

'His name came up when we were questioning Kane.'

'You're not going to take Gregor Kane's word for it?' asked Neeraj. 'He's just trying to get himself off the hook.'

'One of Leanne's workmates confirmed that she seeing an older man,' Denning explained. 'She didn't give a name, but the description fits Daryl Bailey. Either way, we need to speak to him, to eliminate him or otherwise.' He cleared his throat and continued. 'In the meantime, I need someone to check out an allegation, or *possible* allegation of sexual assault that may or may not have been made against Mr Bailey around ten years ago.' He looked at Neeraj, who just sat there impassively, staring blankly back at Denning. Denning turned to DC Bell. 'Trudi, can you look into that? Get in touch with Bailey's old clubs. Find out all you can about what he got up to when he played for them. See if there's any hint of scandal, any suggestion of impropriety, especially if it involved young women.'

Trudi nodded and scribbled the details in her notebook.

Denning turned back to the whiteboard. 'Our first priority at the moment is to locate where Leanne was killed. Let's start by finding out where she was on the evening of the twentieth and who she was with. Her mother said she was meeting a friend that night. Her clothing suggests she was dressed for a night out, so where did she go? Who did she meet?' He looked round the room at a sea of nodding faces. 'This could turn out to have been a random attack, but we have to explore the possibility that Leanne knew her killer. We need to examine every aspect of her life: who were her friends? Was she seeing anyone other than Gregor Kane? Kane seemed to imply that she was. I accept that Gregor Kane may not be the most reliable of individuals, but we have to explore the possibility he's telling the truth in this instance.'

'What about her son?' Kinsella asked.

'I don't think he did it, Dave. He's only five,' Trudi said, earning a cacophony of laughs and sniggers from the team.

'I mean, do we know who the father is?' Kinsella said, shooting an angry look in Trudi's direction. 'That might be relevant to all this.'

'Gregor Kane is the obvious choice,' Neeraj offered.

'Whoever he is, he's definitely worth speaking to,' Kinsella said.

'Susan Wyatt claims Leanne insisted Kane wasn't the father, and this seemed to be backed up by what Kane said yesterday. However, that doesn't entirely rule him out.' Denning recalled how Kane's apparent disregard for Leanne's son was at odds with Susan Wyatt's description of someone who was always good with little Charlie. One of them was lying, and his money was on Kane: a love of children wouldn't sit well with his macho bravado.

'Of course, it is just possible she never knew who the kid's father was.' Kinsella seemed to address the comment to the wider room rather than Denning directly. Denning flashed a sharp look at Kinsella, which went unnoticed.

'I'm not sure that's helpful, Dave. Let's work on the assumption that Leanne *did* know who Charlie's father is, in which case, yes, it would help to speak with him, so at the very least we can rule him out of our inquiries.'

'Assuming it isn't Gregor Kane,' said Kinsella. Denning caught sight of Neeraj smirking. He returned to the whiteboard.

'Okay, let's focus. This is a murder inquiry. We need to get results and sooner rather than later. We need to trace Leanne's movements on the night in question.'

Trudi said, 'If she was dressed for a night out, then I'd say she was meeting either a good friend, or a bloke.'

'Doesn't mean it was her killer though,' Ryan said.

'Maybe not,' said Denning, 'but if she was meeting someone, we need to find them. Let's speak to local bars and clubs, check their CCTV if necessary. Dave, I'm putting you and Ryan onto that. Get the uniforms to help you. Whatever Leanne Wyatt was doing and whoever she was doing it with, we need that information. I want a clear picture of her movements that night right up until she was last seen alive.'

Dave Kinsella guffawed into his coffee mug, 'Of course, we could always just cut to the chase and arrest Gregor Kane.'

There was a murmur of laughter from the group. Denning ignored both the comment and its reaction.

He glanced over in the direction of Betty Taggart's office. He was sure he could feel her watching him from behind the dusty blinds.

Chapter Eleven

Café Alberto could be found in a side street off the Charing Cross end of the Strand. It was quiet at that time of the day, except for a group of foreign students who sat near the entrance, staring at a map of London on a tablet, the remains of a leisurely breakfast scattered across their table. A flurry of commuters hurried by, their faces fixed on the ground beneath them, while trains rumbled noisily in and out of the nearby station.

Molly ordered a latte from the barista who stood smiling and eager behind the polished chrome and glass counter, and headed to one of the pavement tables outside.

She needed a cigarette.

It was early, but the sun was already high in the sky and the day showed all the signs of being another scorcher.

She was removing the cellophane wrapper from a new packet of Silk Cut when a tall, thin woman dressed in black, with magenta hair, and wearing a pair of expensive shades, suddenly appeared in front of her. She looked like a skinny man in drag.

'Molly…?' The woman removed her shades and eyed Molly quizzically, like a panther assessing a trapped fawn.

Molly blinked for a moment. 'Yes.'

The stranger sat down opposite her. 'Magda Kilbride.' She thrust a hand in Molly's direction.

Molly noticed her red-varnished nails and a silver thumb ring as she returned the handshake.

'Can I get you something to drink?' Molly asked.

'Americano, no milk,' she barked at the barista who'd just brought out Molly's latte.

Magda Kilbride wore black Levis, a black silk blouse, and a stylish man's jacket with a silver Celtic dagger brooch pinned to the left breast. Despite the sun, her face was deathly pale, devoid of make-up except for a splash of crimson lippy slashed across her narrow lips like a cut.

Molly offered her a cigarette, but Magda shook her head. Placing a bulky Prada handbag on the table, she removed a slim, black Samsung recorder from the depths of its interior. She put the recorder on the table and switched it on.

'I'd rather you didn't record this,' Molly said.

'Don't worry, DS Fisher, I'm happy to keep this strictly off the record. For now.' Her accent was polished, but with a hint of long-buried Mancunian.

Molly resisted the obvious temptation to ask how Magda had discovered she was a police officer, especially as she'd purposefully kept that piece of information to herself. She knew from Jon how journalists had the uncanny knack of uncovering truths people preferred to keep hidden.

Molly lit her Silk Cut and tried to keep her hand from shaking. She watched as Magda sat back on her chair, either deliberately trying to make herself look more relaxed or because she wanted to dodge Molly's cigarette smoke.

Magda fixed Molly with a hard stare.

'Thanks for agreeing to meet me.' Molly took a sip of her milky coffee, placing the cup back on the saucer with a slight clatter.

'Your email was pretty vague, but I have to admit I was intrigued.'

'Well, I was intrigued by your article on Anthony Ferguson. I thought it might be useful if we spoke to one another.'

Magda's thin, rouged lips snaked into a smile. 'The Bermondsey Ripper. I suspect a man came up with that particular sobriquet. They tend to have unoriginal minds, don't you think?' She cocked her head in Molly's direction. 'I take it our little tête-à-tête isn't in any official capacity.'

Molly glanced at the miniature recorder sitting on the table between them, like a spectre at the feast. If she listened carefully she was sure she could hear it whirring. A serving police officer talking to a journalist about a case, even a long-dead one, was a potentially sackable offence. If her governor found out, she'd have to be a contortionist to wriggle her way out of the trouble she'd be in. She reached over and switched off the recorder.

'No, this isn't official,' she said. 'And I still don't want our conversation recorded.' She looked at Magda, willing the journalist to challenge her.

Magda continued to stare at Molly for a few moments. The barista returned with her coffee and placed it on the table. Magda's gaze remained fixed on Molly. Her eyes were dark and unfriendly, just like Anthony Ferguson's, and for the briefest of seconds, Molly wondered if they could be related. Eventually Magda spoke. 'You say this isn't official. Why, then, are you asking about a case from twelve years ago? I would have thought you had better things to do with your time.'

It was a good question. Molly had tried to think up a credible lie on the way there, but she suspected Magda Kilbride's bullshitometer was finely tuned.

'It's just possible there could have been a miscarriage of justice,' Molly said, sticking to a half truth and hoping it would pass muster. 'I've come into some information that, if true, would at the very least raise some serious questions about Ferguson's conviction.'

'Then tell your bosses.'

'I can't go to a senior officer without something concrete, that's why it has to stay unofficial at this stage.'

Magda's poker face remained impassive. 'Why come to me?'

'Your article implied that there may have been doubts about the case. Doubts that were never made public at the time.'

Magda let out a raucous laugh that lay somewhere between a donkey's bray and a witch's cackle. 'Are you asking me if there could have been a police cock-up over a serious murder inquiry, DS Fisher? That's quite an allegation.'

Molly wondered if Magda Kilbride was playing her. It was just possible she knew jack shit about Anthony Ferguson's conviction, and the article had been nothing more than her casting a stone into the ocean to see how far the ripples spread. But there was something about Magda that made Molly want to take her seriously. She *was* being played, Molly was sure of that, but only in as much as Magda wanted to get more information out of Molly than she was willing to offer up in return. It was a game Magda Kilbride had clearly played before.

'No. I just want to know if you can tell me anything that might help.'

'Ken Walters,' said Magda, 'the detective who investigated the Ripper murders. He retired shortly after the case went to trial, pensioned off early, or so the rumours went. The *official* reason is because the case had left him "emotionally scarred".' She mimed quotation marks around the last two words.

'The unofficial reason...?'

Magda traced a manicured finger round the rim of her coffee cup. There was a bright red stain where her brutal lipstick had left its mark on the china. '*Unofficially*, it was rumoured that he had expressed concerns about the way the case was handled. Concerns which were ignored at the time, by both his senior officers and by the prosecution team at Ferguson's trial. It was all hushed up, naturally. Your lot are proven experts when it comes to burying your own shit in the sand.'

'What kind of concerns?'

Magda shrugged her slender shoulders. 'You'd best talk to Walters about that.'

Molly made a mental note of the name: Ken Walters should be easy enough to trace, even if he was now retired.

'How did you get to hear about this?'

Again that laugh, perhaps leaning more towards a cackle than a bray this time. 'Let's just say you're not the first detective sergeant I've shared an early morning coffee with.'

'You must have believed there was something in those rumours; why else would you write that story?' She looked at Magda, gazing into those dark, soulless eyes. 'Do *you* think Anthony Ferguson is innocent?'

'It doesn't matter what I think. It's what you want to believe. If this mysterious information that's suddenly come your way has any credibility, then sure, go for it. Fight for the poor bastard's innocence.' She offered Molly her wiry smile again. 'I'm happy to come along for the ride. It'll make a great story if nothing else.'

Molly finished her cigarette and ground the stub into an ashtray. She took another sip of her latte; it was still warm, just. 'Is there anything else you can tell me? Anything useful?'

Magda toyed with her coffee cup. 'Speak to Walters,' she said. She lifted the cup to her ruby lips as though to drink it, then changed her mind. Placing the cup back on the saucer, she looked Molly in the eye and said, 'Does Jon know about any of this?'

Molly tried to hide her surprise. 'Jon…?'

Magda smiled again. 'I did a stint on the *London Echo*, yonks ago. Your boyfriend was quite the *grande fromage* back then. What's he up to these days?'

The foreign students ambled out of the café and blinked into the sun. One of them said something Molly didn't understand, then they headed off in the direction of Embankment tube station.

'Jon's writing a book.' She just about managed to keep her voice even. 'Should I mention you to him?'

Another gurgling laugh. 'If you like, though I doubt he'd remember me. It was a very long time ago.' She took a card out of her jacket pocket and placed it on the table in front of Molly. 'Get in touch after you've spoken to Walters. You never know, he might say something that jogs my memory.' She put the mini recorder back into the cavernous void of her handbag and got to her feet. 'Cheers for the coffee. We'll be in touch.'

She swung the massive bag onto her skinny shoulder, placed the shades back over her morbid eyes and walked off towards the Strand. A minute later she'd disappeared into the throng of commuters pouring out of Charing Cross station to become just another anonymous face in the crowd.

Molly picked up the card. Staring at it, she debated whether to keep it or tear it up and drop it in the ashtray. Magda Kilbride hadn't been able to tell her much, and she had definitely been holding something back. Then there was the mention of Jon. A pointed mention, aimed, she was sure, to provoke a reaction. And she suspected her face had betrayed exactly the kind of reaction Magda had been hoping for.

After a moment she slipped the card into the top pocket of her shirt. Despite the heat, she felt a sudden chill: she had a horrible feeling she hadn't heard the last of Magda Kilbride.

Chapter Twelve

Daryl Bailey was about to head to the gym when Denning and Neeraj knocked on the door of his substantial semi-detached house in one of north Finchley's leafier streets.

'Can I help you?' he enquired, a harassed look on his face; a sports bag slung over his shoulder.

Denning flashed his ID, followed, a moment later, by Neeraj. 'Daryl Bailey?'

Bailey nodded, eyes jumping from one copper to the other in quick succession.

'Can we have a word with you about Leanne Wyatt?' Denning asked.

Bailey gave a heavy sigh. 'I've got a squash game booked in a half an hour. Is there any chance you could come back later?'

Denning stood on the doorstep, trying hard to smile. 'No, Mr Bailey. I'm afraid we can't come back later. We're investigating a murder.'

Reluctantly, the door swung open to reveal a smart tiled hallway, with a set of deeply carpeted stairs heading to the first floor.

Bailey showed them into a large but characterless sitting room. The room was painted in shades of cream and pale grey, and decorated with modern, tasteless furniture. An enormous television clung to the wall above the space where the fireplace would once have been. Denning guessed Bailey lived alone.

They sat on an uncomfortable metal-framed sofa, their knees almost touching their chins. Bailey sat opposite them on an egg-shaped swivel chair.

Neeraj was looking round the room with a mixture of awe and envy. The walls were awash with photographs of Bailey in his football kit; mementos of the glory days. A small, silver trophy sat on a table in the corner by the large bay window.

'Should I offer you tea or coffee, or something?' Bailey was making an effort to appear at ease with the situation; trying hard to suggest that a visit from the police was as unfamiliar as it was unwelcome.

Denning shook his head. 'I think it might be better if we get straight to the point, Mr Bailey.'

Daryl Bailey was in his late thirties, but could have passed for younger in a good light. His dark blond hair was just starting to thin on top, but he was still in good shape, no doubt helped by those regular exertions on the squash court.

'I believe you used to be a professional footballer,' said Denning. 'What do you do now?'

Bailey's mouth hung open for a moment before he spoke, as though he was trying to work out the significance of the question. 'I'm a coach for a couple of local youth clubs,' he said after a pause. 'I also do a bit of teaching at a secondary school in Hackney. PE mostly.' He looked from Denning to Neeraj. 'It pays the bills.'

'Did you know Leanne Wyatt?' Denning asked.

Bailey shifted awkwardly on his chair. 'She was a pupil at the school where I teach. At least she used to be. She left around five years ago.'

'Which school was that?'

Another pause. 'Dalston Academy on Queensland Road. I only taught her briefly. I mostly take the boys for sport and PE, but when one of the female PE teachers was on maternity leave, they didn't replace her, so everyone had to just muck in.'

'So your relationship with Leanne was purely professional…?' Denning let the question hang in the ether.

'Of course. What are you implying?'

'We're not implying anything, Mr Bailey. Leanne Wyatt has been murdered and your name came up during the course of our investigation, that's all.'

Bailey looked at Denning; a slight twitch briefly flickered on his left eyelid. 'Who gave you my name?' He looked indignant. 'Look, Leanne was a pupil at a school I teach at. One of thousands over the years. Are you speaking to anyone else from the school?'

'Not at this stage. Are you suggesting we should?'

'No. Why would I?' Another momentary twitch. 'What exactly is this about? Are you implying I had something to do with Leanne's death? Because if you are, then that's nonsense. I hadn't seen her for over a year.'

'I thought you said she left school five years ago.'

'Sorry?' He rubbed a hand over his forehead, a quick, almost unconscious movement. 'Yes. But I bumped into her just over a year ago.' Bailey looked over at Neeraj, who was scribbling notes in a pad. 'She called round to ask the deputy head for a reference and I saw her in the corridor. I asked her what she was doing and she said something about having just applied for a job in a hairdresser's. To be honest, I was on my way to a class and I didn't take too much notice of her.'

'Did you know she had a son?'

'A son? No, of course not. Why would I? I hardly knew the girl.'

'Why did you leave professional football, Mr Bailey?'

'Are you kidding me? Do you know anything about the game? Once you hit thirty you're already on your way out. I was lucky to last as long as I did. Look, I know what you're both thinking, but I'm happy with my life now. I don't miss the game, at least not at that level. I enjoy teaching kids. The next generation of England stars are out there somewhere, and with a bit of luck I can help find some of them. That's a hundred times more rewarding than being paid an inflated salary for kicking a ball round a football stadium.'

It sounded convincing, but Denning wondered if Bailey was trying to persuade himself as much as them. 'Are you sure it wasn't anything to do with an allegation of inappropriate behaviour that was made against you?'

Bailey stared at both men in silence for a moment before eventually dropping his gaze. 'That's crap.'

'Is it?' Denning refused to let it drop.

'I've never done anything "inappropriate" in my life. You can check police records if you don't believe me.'

The denial was so fulsome it defied challenge. Denning suspected Bailey knew they had no proof of any allegations; at this stage all they had was an unfounded rumour that possibly couldn't even be substantiated at all.

'We'll certainly be checking, Mr Bailey,' Denning informed him. 'In the meantime, is there anything else you can tell us about your relationship with Leanne?'

'I didn't have any sort of *relationship* with Leanne. I taught her a few times, apart from that I hardly even spoke to the girl.' He made a point of looking at his watch: a chunky Rolex, no doubt a souvenir from the good old days when money came all too easily. 'Unless you have any more dumb questions, I really do have to go.'

'Before you do, can you tell us where you were on Monday evening?'

Bailey momentarily opened and closed his mouth, like a sea lion awaiting a dead fish. 'I was at home watching television.' He glared at Denning. 'I'm afraid I don't have any witnesses.'

Denning smiled and said they'd be in touch if they had any more questions. Bailey showed them out.

–

Back in the car, Neeraj turned to Denning, 'Did you see those photographs on Bailey's wall?'

Denning pulled the Ford Focus onto Finchley Road, and headed south in the direction of Dalston. 'You were impressed with Daryl Bailey then?'

Neeraj rummaged in the pocket of his leather jacket and took out a packet of Extra Strong Mints. 'Yeah, the guy's got style. And class.' He popped a mint into his mouth, then made to put them back into his pocket; he paused and offered one to Denning. 'It's just a pity he was lying through his arse.'

Chapter Thirteen

Ever since her early morning meeting with Magda Kilbride, Molly had been twitchy. She'd fully expected the journalist to dismiss her claims about Anthony Ferguson with a derisory laugh. The fact she hadn't done so, told Molly that she just might be on to something.

She gave the mouse a shake and woke her computer from sleep mode then, using the Met's intranet, logged onto HOLMES2. Having started life as an advanced search tool which could instantly cross-reference data between different police forces, HOLMES2 had recently been upgraded to include full and comprehensive details on any ongoing major criminal investigations in the UK, including photos of relevant crime scenes.

Misuse of either HOLMES2 or the Police National Computer database was an instant disciplinary matter, and if someone were to check that she'd been accessing it for anything other than official police business, she'd be in serious trouble.

But she had to know if she was right.

She tapped in her access code and password and quickly brought up the appropriate file: Leanne Wyatt's murder case. DI Denning was clearly thorough and very organised: all the relevant information had already been uploaded onto the system, including scene-of-crime analysis; the post-mortem report and a note that the forensics report was to follow.

It was the post-mortem report she wanted.

She clicked on the relevant file and waited for the information to appear on the screen. There was a separate attachment which contained photographs from the crime scene as well as the post-mortem photographs. She clicked on the attachment, waited a few seconds for the file to download, then opened the file to examine the post-mortem photographs.

She stared at the pictures of Leanne Wyatt: her face had been cleaned up by the morticians, presumably for the benefit of whichever family member had been given the unfortunate task of having to identify her. Molly was looking at the face of a young girl, the life battered and strangled out of her. It was tragic and it was horrible and such a waste of life.

But she couldn't miss it. There in the middle of her forehead, almost dead centre, a couple of ugly red scratches in what distinctly looked like the shape of a cross.

–

The Fleur de Lys on Islington's Upper Street had been laid out with the same identikit fixtures and fittings that could be found in any generic pub chain; the walls decorated in shades of pale beige, on which were hung insipid prints of what looked like some kind of flower, before Denning realised they were Fleur de Lys.

A bored-looking cleaner pushed a Henry Hoover around a far corner trying his best to ignore them.

It had been Ryan Cormack who'd phoned it in: the manager had contacted them to say that someone fitting Leanne's description had been in the bar on Monday evening.

Denning slid a photo of Leanne Wyatt across the bar top. 'Was this the woman you saw on the evening of the 23rd?'

The manager, who had given his name as Jason Meredith, was in his mid-twenties with badly dyed blond spikey hair and piercings threaded along one earlobe. He was unshaven and looked like he hadn't slept; as though the evening shift and the morning shift had bled into one another without even pausing for breath. 'That's what I told one of your colleagues. I saw the news last night and I recognised her. She was in here on Monday night, sitting at the end of the bar chatting to some man. She was nicely dressed, and, you know, nice looking.' He pushed the photo back across the bar. 'It was nasty, what happened to her, like.'

'What about the man she was with?'

Meredith shrugged. 'Just some bloke. Bit older than her, but there was nothing strange about him. And they seemed to know each other; I mean she walked straight up to him as soon as she arrived.'

'When was that?'

'About eight, or thereabouts. I'm not sure what time he arrived. I only really noticed him after she turned up. We were quite busy for a Monday, so I didn't have much time to chat to the customers.'

'What about CCTV?'

'The CCTV in the bar area doesn't work. I've been on at the owners to get it repaired for weeks now, but you might as well speak to the back of your hand.'

'The bar area? Does that mean the CCTV is working elsewhere?'

'The one down by the toilets works. And by the entrance. It records straight onto a DVD.'

'We'll take any DVDs for the night in question, if you don't mind.'

'We only keep the DVDs for twenty-four hours, then they're recorded over.'

Denning was incredulous. 'What's the point of that?'

'Saves money. I mean, if there's been an incident, then we keep hold of any footage for evidence, like, but otherwise the DVDs just get reused.'

'It's just unfortunate there was an "incident" on Monday evening,' Denning offered.

'Yeah, but I didn't know one of our customers was going to get murdered, did I?' He folded his arms across his chest. 'You need to take it up with the owners if you've got a problem.'

'I might just do that,' said Denning. 'Can you describe the man she was with?'

'Late thirties, maybe slightly older. Well dressed, polite; chucking cash around like there was no tomorrow.'

'Did you recognise him?'

Meredith looked perplexed. 'Recognise…?'

'Had you seen him before?'

'No. He wasn't one of our regulars. I think *she's* been in here a couple of times, but I'd never seen her with him before the other evening.'

'I don't suppose you happened to hear what they were talking about?'

He shook his head. 'No chance. It was heaving in here. There was a band playing and you could barely hear yourself think.'

'Anything else?'

He looked blank for a moment, and rubbed a hand over his stubbly chin. 'Well…'

'Go on.'

'I can't be sure, mind, but it looked like she was crying at one point.'

'Crying?'

'Yeah. I mean I couldn't say for certain, but she did look like she was upset about something. It was possible they'd had an argument, but I might be wrong.'

Denning thought about this. 'Do you know what they were arguing about?'

Meredith unfolded his arms and leant on the bar. 'Like I said, I'm not even sure they *were* arguing. But whatever it was, they obviously kissed and made up at some point, because the next time I looked up, they were sat over there,' he pointed at one of the booths, 'and seemed quite chatty again.'

'What time did they leave?'

He shrugged. 'I couldn't tell you that, sorry.'

'OK,' said Denning, 'but I expect the CCTV could have helped there.'

'Yes,' Meredith replied coldly, 'I expect it would have been more helpful.'

–

Once they were back out on the street, blinking in the brilliant sunlight, Neeraj said, 'The description doesn't fit Gregor Kane.'

'No,' said Denning, 'but it does fit Daryl Bailey.'

'It could fit half the men in London, including me and you.'

'Perhaps...' Denning was staring down the street, towards the lower end of Upper Street, where it ran into Pentonville Road. 'Where did Kane say he was on Monday night?'

'The Cat in the Hat. It's a nightclub near the Angel tube station.'

'Yes,' said Denning. 'I know it is. It's also less than a five minute walk from this bar.' He turned to face Neeraj. 'Do you believe in coincidences, Deep? Because I don't.'

Chapter Fourteen

'Thanks for agreeing to see me,' Molly said. 'I'll try not to take up too much of your time.'

Kenneth Walters smiled and offered Molly a cup of tea. 'It's not often I get a visit from an attractive young lady, so please take as long as you like.'

Walters was in his mid-sixties, meaning he would have been in his early to mid-fifties at the time of Ferguson's killing spree. Too young to retire…?

The house was in a cul-de-sac off a quiet road in Hornchurch. Plenty of pictures of family were dotted around various tables and bookcases in the cosy living room. Large picture windows opened onto a well-tended garden. Judging by the immaculate state of the garden, Molly guessed this was how Ken Walters filled his days.

Walters had been easy enough to trace: Trudi Bell's dad had worked in the same nick as him back in the late nineties, and they had kept in touch via the occasional Christmas card.

Molly had told her DI she was following up a lead in the Gregor Kane drugs case. It was a lie, and she felt guilty telling it, but she needed to speak to Walters. If nothing else, he would be able to confirm or deny what Magda Kilbride had told her.

'Here we are.' Walters appeared from the kitchen carrying a tray heavy with tea and cake. He placed the tray on the coffee table and poured out a cup each for Molly and himself. 'Help yourself to milk and sugar.' He passed the cup to Molly, then sat on an armchair beside the patio doors. 'Would you like some walnut cake?' he asked. 'My wife made it yesterday.'

Molly felt it would be rude to refuse. There was something avuncular about Ken Walters: he was a couple of kilos over-weight, with a greying beard and sharp blue eyes that twinkled at her from behind the thick lenses of his gold-rimmed glasses. He looked like a kindly grandfather, which she imagined he probably was.

She balanced the cake on her saucer and tried not to spill anything. She desperately wanted another cigarette.

'You said on the phone that you wanted to ask me some questions about Anthony Ferguson, but you didn't say why. Has something happened?'

'No,' she replied, her mouth full of cake. 'No, this is strictly unofficial, Mr Walters.' She swallowed the mouthful of cake and wiped crumbs from her mouth. 'I'm hoping to join the homicide division, and I'm currently completing a module in forensic science as part of the Met's internal diploma certificate. I have to write an essay based on an actual murder inquiry, and I thought the Bermondsey Ripper investigation would make an interesting case study.' It worried her just how easily the lies came to her now. It would only take a phone call to an old colleague in the Met to prove she was talking bollocks; she was banking on Walters not taking that chance.

'Please call me Ken,' he said. 'We're all on the same side after all. And I think it's really wonderful that the Met offer these kind of schemes nowadays. Such things never existed in my day: it was sink or swim, and you'd surprised just how many people sank. Sometimes without a trace.' He gave a jovial laugh at his own joke.

Molly smiled back at him. She suspected Walters liked talking about his days on the force. She knew that many retired police officers felt a growing void where their purpose in life had disappeared overnight – a void they were unable to fill. It would be worse for Walters if his retirement had been forced on him, assuming Magda Kilbride had been telling the truth.

'I just want a bit of background about Anthony Ferguson,' she said. 'I know the basic details, but I'd like to know more about the specifics of the case. As you led the investigation I thought it would be useful to get your take on what happened.'

'Yes, yes, of course. I'd be happy to help.' Walters sat back in his armchair and closed his eyes, nodding slowly. When he spoke it was almost like he was in a trance. 'I can remember the case so vividly. Even after thirty years in the Met, there are some cases that never leave you.' He took another sip of tea, staring at the cup for what seemed like an eternity before placing it back on the table beside him. 'The first victim was found a short distance from a pub where she worked, in a car park just off Jamaica Road: she'd been raped, beaten and strangled. Then about a month later another woman was found in a park near the Old Kent Road, same MO, only more violence this time.' He gave a deep sigh. 'We didn't make a connection at first; assumed it was just coincidental. It was only after the third murder that we realised we were dealing with the same man. Nobody likes having a serial killer on their patch: they're always the worst kind. It becomes like a sick game for them; pushing us to see how much they can get away with before we finally catch them. One of our team had been a junior detective on the Sutcliffe murders in the eighties, so we knew what would happen if we didn't catch this monster: the press and the public would crucify us. And rightfully so. But we had very little to go on: no witnesses and very little DNA evidence to work with.' He removed his glasses and rubbed a hand over his eyes. 'As the murders progressed they became increasingly more brutal. I can never understand why someone would feel the need to use that level of violence. I mean, there's no reason for it, is there?'

He looked at Molly, as though this were a question he expected her to answer, but she just quietly shook her head.

'He scored a cross onto the forehead of some of the victims. Is that right?' she asked.

His face briefly registered a note of surprise, then he slowly nodded. 'That was what finally convinced us we were looking for the same man. Although that information was never made public just in case someone confessed, then we could use that knowledge to prove they weren't having us on. Also, the last thing we needed was a copycat killer thinking about doing something similar to try and throw us off the scent.'

'Why did he do it? The cross I mean, why?'

The old man shook his head 'Some killers like to mark their victims in some way. It's almost like a calling card. But as to why it was a cross, I don't know. Ferguson wasn't religious, so that didn't explain it. We asked him about it, of course, but he wouldn't say. But then he didn't say much.'

'How did you catch Ferguson?'

'We brought in a forensic psychologist. He described an insecure loner with poorly developed social skills. He suggested we were looking for a psychopath. Well, Anthony Ferguson comfortably fitted that description.' He gave a weary smile. 'Even so, it took months of painstaking detective work to finally nail him. As is so often the case, it was a lucky break that swung it our way. Ferguson was eventually arrested after getting into a fight at work – he was working for a building firm at the time and had a minor skirmish with a work colleague – his DNA was a direct match to two of the victims. From that we investigated him further and found out that he was a regular at the pub where the first victim worked, and CCTV placed him in the vicinity of another two. Initially he refused to tell us anything, offering up an endless stream of "no comments". He was a pathetic little runt of a man. I mean I know the types of men who commit these atrocious crimes are usually inadequate specimens, but even so, there was something particularly hopeless about Ferguson. Then there was this palpable sense of evil that came off him: it was almost tangible. I'm not a religious man, Molly, but when I looked at Anthony Ferguson I swear it felt like the devil was staring back at me.'

He paused for a moment as though the memories were so awful his brain needed a chance to cool down before it melted from the horrors it had been forced to revisit.

Molly finished her tea. So far everything he'd told her confirmed what she already knew. But if Magda Kilbride was to be believed — and that was still a big if — then where were the doubts Walters had expressed about the case?

'Did Ferguson give a reason for committing the murders?' she asked.

He shook his head. 'It was only when we presented him with the CCTV and DNA evidence that he started to talk, even then he didn't say much. He denied everything, as they always do. He claimed the evidence was faked, and the police were out to frame him.'

Molly waited before she asked her next question. 'Is it right that he had an alibi for one of the murders?' she asked.

Walters' brow wrinkled. 'You have been doing your research, detective.' He took a slow deep breath, then said, 'Ferguson mentioned something about having been with a friend on the night of the last murder. It was all rubbish, of course. It was the same during the trial: the defence put it forward but it was quickly dismissed. Besides, even though he protested his innocence, he couldn't explain away what evidence we did have against him. However, I think by then he knew the game was up.'

'I presume you checked out his alibi?'

He looked at her before he answered. 'We spoke to the friend, naturally.' Walters gave a deep chuckle. 'He was an alcoholic who could barely remember what he'd had for breakfast, never mind whether or not he'd been with Ferguson on the night in question. It was a complete waste of time. The prosecution made mincemeat of him at the trial.'

'Can you remember the friend's name?'

Walters stroked his beard and gave another shake of his head. 'Dennis, or Derek or something. I can't remember a surname.'

Dennis or Derek… no surname… It wasn't much but it was something.

She decided to grasp the nettle: 'Was there a chance he didn't do it? Anthony Ferguson: is there any possibility he could be innocent?'

Walters stared into his tea cup, then looked hard at Molly. 'Oh, Ferguson did it all right. Take my word for it. The man was pure evil.'

Molly didn't believe in moral absolutes like good and evil: it was too convenient. Even if Ken Walters believed in the existence of evil, it was neither a credible motive nor an indication of guilt. But Walters seemed a decent man. She suspected he'd done the best he could at the time: not cutting corners or accepting easy answers. Perhaps Magda Kilbride was wrong. Perhaps she'd deliberately stirred the shit pot in the hope of finding something that wasn't there.

However, despite Walters' apparent certainty, something didn't add up...

Molly asked: 'Apart from the assault at work, did Ferguson have any other convictions?'

Another shake of the head. 'No. There was nothing on the system. Of course, it's entirely possible he had committed other violent crimes and we just didn't know about them, or hadn't connected them to Ferguson.'

'But there was no previous history of violence, particularly sexual violence? Something must have happened to turn him into a rapist and murderer. It couldn't have come entirely out of the blue. What did the forensic psychologist think?'

'He said there was probably a trigger point: problems at home, death of a loved one, something like that. Only Ferguson knows the real reason, and I suspect he'll take that particular secret with him to the grave.'

Molly cocked her head at Walters and offered him a shy smile. 'Ken, I appreciate it must have been a difficult time for you, but I have to ask, did you ever have any doubts about the case?'

'No.'

'Even though he had an alibi for one of the murders?'

He stared at her, his eyes magnified by his thick lenses. 'As I've already told you, the right man is in jail for those crimes. And jail is the best place for him.'

She persisted, gently but with a look that said she wasn't going to give up easily. 'Are you absolutely certain there's nothing that in hindsight could have been missed? Something that may have seemed inconsequential at the time, but looking back now feels significant?'

He removed his glasses again and polished the lenses with the corner of his cardigan. 'I'm not sure what you're implying, Molly, but we conducted a thorough and detailed investigation at the time. Thousands of man hours were spent going over every little detail, examining whatever evidence had, poring over hours and hours of CCTV footage. I can assure you, nothing was missed.'

His tone had changed: the smiley benevolent granddad had become the hard-edged detective inspector from twelve years ago. 'Most of this information can be found on the Police National Computer, you know. Or even the internet for that matter. Perhaps you'd be better off looking there for help with your essay?' He replaced his glasses and sat back in his chair, arms folded over his chest.

The implication was clear: their conversation had come to a natural conclusion.

Molly smiled and thanked him for his time. He politely smiled back and showed her to the front door.

'If you do remember anything else, please get in touch,' she said, as he held the door open for her. 'You've got my mobile number.'

He held onto the front door, tightly enough for his knuckles to turn white. He said he'd give her a call if anything came back to him.

As she heard the door click shut behind her, she contemplated the long tube journey back to Dalston and the lies she'd told her boss. And not just her boss. She felt a twinge of guilt at misleading an old man who had earned peace in his retirement. Forcing him to dredge up memories he'd clearly wanted to confine to the dustbin of his own personal history had been a form of cruelty.

She was sure Kenneth Walters *was* a decent man, but she was equally sure he'd been holding something back. It wasn't that he'd lied to her, rather she suspected he simply hadn't told her the whole truth. An alibi, however weak… It was worth chasing.

Chapter Fifteen

It was a 1980s estate of narrow, mellow brick houses with short driveways and neat little gardens. A group of children playing on their bikes stared blankly at Denning as he drove past. An ice-cream van tinkled its merry tune somewhere in a nearby street.

11 Avonbrook Close was indistinguishable from its Surrey Quays neighbours. It hadn't changed much since he and Claire had purchased it eight years earlier. Except there was a smart new Lexus parked in the driveway, which Denning doubted belonged to his ex-wife.

He'd dropped Neeraj back at the station with instructions to get hold of Samantha Haddon, and to find out everything they could about Daryl Bailey. Denning hadn't bought that guff about Bailey preferring the benevolent altruism of school coaching over the giddy kudos of professional football. Something stank like rotting fish, and Denning was determined to uncover the truth behind Daryl Bailey's fall from glory.

Denning paused for a second before ringing the doorbell. He could hear voices inside the house, not raised but loud enough to be audible through the double glazing. One was Claire's, soft and mellifluous, if slightly highly pitched; the other he didn't recognise, but belonged to a man.

The voices stopped the moment the doorbell chimed. A few seconds later, his ex-wife answered the door, twitching her face into a tight smile. She was wearing a summery dress with primroses on the front and a pale blue belt tied smartly round the waist. Her strawberry-blonde hair was slightly dishevelled as though she'd just got out of bed. She blinked as the sun hit her face.

'What do you want, Matt?' Her voice only betrayed the faintest hint of annoyance.

'Can I come in?'

She stood in the doorway for a few seconds, blocking it with her slender frame, throwing a brief glance in the direction of her neighbours, before stepping aside to let him in.

He made his way into the kitchen/dining room at the back of the house, where the voices had been coming from. A tall, toned man with a heavy tan and a couple of days' worth of stubble round his chin was standing by the sink, sipping coffee out of what had once been Denning's favourite mug. He flashed an even-toothed smile, placed the mug on the worktop and extended a hand in Denning's direction.

'You must be Matt.' His firm handshake seemed to go with the beaming smile and the burnished features. He was dressed in an expensive D&G open-necked shirt and designer jeans; a silver Rolex, possibly fake, clasped to his wrist. 'Alan Marsden.'

Denning reckoned Marsden was in his late thirties, perhaps a well-maintained early forties. He oozed the kind of smarmy confidence that so often passed for charm. It was possible he'd popped round to sell Claire insurance, or a conservatory, or to read the electricity meter. However, Denning suspected Marsden's relationship with his ex-wife was of a more intimate nature.

Claire was standing by the kitchen door now; eyes jumping from Denning to Marsden and back again.

'I need to talk to you about Jake,' Denning said. 'Preferably in private.' Looking out the kitchen window, he saw his son chasing a football round the yellow lawn. Jake was young for his age; small and wiry, and prone to mood swings. Every time Denning saw him he was reminded of the fact he was only a part-time presence in his life.

Marsden nodded at Claire, the smile remaining a fixed feature on his face. 'I'll call you later, babe.' He reached out and kissed her on the mouth, then turned to Denning. 'Nice to finally meet you, Matt. Maybe we can chat over a beer sometime…?'

Denning nodded back at Marsden, then sat down at the kitchen table. He heard the front door click shut, followed a minute later by the sound of the Lexus reversing out of the driveway.

Claire headed to the sink and began rinsing Marsden's coffee mug under the tap. The kitchen stank of bleach and Cif. His ex-wife hated mess. It was one of the things that had irritated him during their eight-year marriage. These days he and Sarah employed a cleaner and let the mess take care of itself.

'When were you planning to tell me you were seeing someone?'

'That's really none of your business.' She dried the mug with a tea towel and placed it down on the worktop with a nervous thump.

'Is he staying here?'

'Now *that* really is none of your damned business.'

He took that as a yes. 'If it affects Jake, then it's my business.'

She fussed around the spotless kitchen, refusing to give him eye contact. 'My private life stopped being your business four years ago on the day you walked out on me and Jake. I don't ask questions about you and *her*, so why should I explain my private life to you?' She was wiping a cloth over the worktops, rubbing at an imagined mark beside the hob. This was Claire's coping mechanism: whenever she was upset or had to face confrontation, she would clean. Sometimes it was just dusting or emptying half-full wastepaper baskets; other times the vacuum cleaner would come out and any attempts at conversation would be drowned out by the din. 'Alan's just stopping here until his place is finished. He's got building work going on and it's all running behind schedule.'

Denning didn't care about Marsden's domestic problems, and he was determined to avoid a fight, but he was fully prepared to stand his ground.

'Look, I haven't got the time or the energy for another argument. I just wanted some clarity with regards to Jake. We agreed I would have him this weekend. I don't know how much free time I'm going to have over the next few weeks.' He didn't go into detail about the murder investigation; he doubted Claire would be interested if he did. 'Plus, it's important for Jake to have stability in his life.' He glanced out the window. Jake was still kicking the football around the compact garden, humming to himself as he played. 'He would have been looking forward to seeing me. It's not fair to disappoint him like that.'

Claire had her back to him now, scrubbing away at the stainless steel sink, obliterating invisible dirt. 'Alan said he'd take him to LazerWorld in Leicester Square. He told Jake before he checked with me, and we can't disappoint him now, can we? Besides, he never likes being around Sarah. She always makes him feel unwelcome.'

It was lie laced with a spice of truth: Sarah made an effort with Jake, but it was obvious she was making an effort and kids picked up on these things, especially kids as sensitive as Jake.

'He could go to LazerWorld next week.' He looked out of the kitchen window again. Jake was playing with a neighbour's cat now, stroking it far too hard and pulling on its tail. The cat, a fat ginger beast with white fluffy fur round its ears, didn't seem to mind.

'He's going with a couple of his friends. It's too late to change things now.' She stopped scrubbing the spotless sink and looked at him. 'I'm sorry, Matt. I realise it means messing you around, but Jake comes first. Besides, when I phoned Sarah, she didn't seem to think it would be a problem.'

'That's another thing. Why did you phone Sarah? If you can't get hold of me on the mobile, then leave a message.' He could feel the anger creeping into his voice. 'You only phoned Sarah because you knew she wouldn't kick up a fuss.'

'That's not true. I *wanted* to speak to you. I thought you'd have been home from work when I rang.' He knew she was lying. Claire hated confrontation, and Sarah would have given her a much easier time than he would have done. But he decided to let it lie; there was no point in provoking yet another argument. He'd learned by now which battles were worth fighting, and which ones he should just walk away from. 'How's he been lately?'

Claire stopped cleaning and rinsed the cloth under the tap before squeezing it dry and folding it neatly beside the taps. 'He's fine. He's always fine. The new medication is calming him down. He's even looking forward to going back to school next month.'

It had been over three years since Jake had been diagnosed with ADHD and autism spectrum disorder, after the five years of being fobbed off by doctors and teachers and told he was simply 'disruptive'. A child psychologist had pointed them in the direction of an accurate diagnosis, after which medicine and a change of school had helped turn Jake from a 'disruptive' child into a happier and much calmer one. That had been until recently. Having seen the super-smooth Alan Marsden standing in his ex-wife's kitchen, sipping coffee and oozing oleaginous charm, he began to see why Jake might be feeling a little unsettled of late.

'How does Jake get on with Alan?'

She sat down opposite him at the kitchen table. 'Jake likes him.' She twisted her lips into another smile. 'Alan's good with Jake. He never had kids of his own. His marriage ended badly, and now he wants to move on and build a new life for himself. And I can relate to that.' She smiled again, more warmly this time, her expression almost propitiatory, remembering perhaps the good times rather than the bad. 'You'll like Alan, if you get to know him.'

Denning had no plans to get to know Alan Marsden. He only wanted to know what his role was going to be in his son's life. 'How long have you been seeing him?'

She tidied a strand of loose hair behind her ear. 'A couple of months. I was waiting until things were more settled before I told you.'

'What does he do?'

For a moment he thought she wasn't going to answer him; insist it was none of his business.

'He runs a property development company,' she said a moment later, then adding, 'he's very successful.'

Denning remembered the shiny new Lexus parked in the drive. If material wealth were a qualifying factor for approval, Alan Marsden would pass with flying colours.

At some level, Denning had known this point was always going to come, as inevitable as it was unavoidable. Ever since their divorce four years ago, he knew it was only a matter of time before Claire found someone else. That someone would be more than just a new partner: he would fulfil a fatherly role in Jake's life, whether Denning liked it or not. It would mean awkward conversations and perpetual compromise, but he was prepared to jump through any hoops if it meant keeping Jake in his life.

'I'm always here for Jake,' he said. For the briefest of seconds he thought about reaching across the table and taking hold of her hand, but quickly decided against it. Claire was vulnerable at the best of times, and a well-meant gesture could so easily be open to misunderstanding.

He stood up and walked over to the French windows. Jake had grown bored with the cat now, and had returned to his football, banging it over and over against the fence that bordered the neighbour's garden. The neighbour, a widow in her seventies, was tolerant and understanding, but that tolerance would only stretch so far...

'Why don't you let him play with the other children in the street? I saw two or three of them when I pulled into the close.'

She looked away and shook her head. 'He doesn't like them. They used to bully him, and one of them accused Jake of hitting him. It was a lie, but the boy's mother kicked up merry hell. Threatened to call the police.'

In all probability it wasn't a lie. It was likely Jake *had* hit the boy, possibly provoked by childish name-calling, but the damage had been done: Jake was already branded an outcast simply for being different.

After a few seconds Jake noticed him standing in the kitchen. He abandoned the football and ran to his dad. Denning opened the sliding doors and crouched down to greet his son.

Jake threw his arms round Denning's neck and shouted in his ear, demanding his daddy give him a piggy back ride round the garden. Denning kissed Jake on the head and gently unwound his arms from his neck. 'It's great to see you, little fella, but Daddy can't stay for long.'

'Aww...'

He looked at his son. In so many ways he reminded Denning of himself when he was younger: a loner from an early age, preferring the company of books and computer games to spending time with other children. Unlike his older brother, Tom, who got on with everyone he met, and sailed through life without any effort. At least Jake had friends now that he'd joined a new school, albeit with other children who society had deemed as being 'different'.

'Do you want to beat Daddy at one of your computer games?'

From behind him in the kitchen he could hear Claire clicking her tongue in disapproval. 'It'll be time for his lunch soon.'

'Ten minutes. No longer.' He followed Jake through to the living room and waited until he switched on the telly and loaded up his PlayStation. After a few seconds the screen filled with images of zombies and aliens. 'I want to be the aliens,' Jake said, and who was Denning to disappoint his son?

After Denning had spent ten minutes trying unsuccessfully to stop an alien apocalypse, Claire appeared in the kitchen doorway, announcing that lunch was ready.

'I don't suppose you want to stay?' she asked Denning. It was clear from her tone that the anticipated answer was 'no'.

Denning got to his feet, ruffled his son's hair and playfully punched him on the arm. Jake recoiled and pulled a face. 'Daddy's got to go back to work, little fella, but we'll go out together soon. How would you like to visit the Planetarium?'

Jake nodded his approval, though Denning suspected he had little idea of what the Planetarium was.

Claire told Jake to go into the kitchen and wash his hands. Once he was out of earshot, she turned to Denning. 'You shouldn't wind him up like that,' Claire said sullenly. 'He'll be counting the days now until you next take him out.'

'Well, that'll make two of us.' He took a deep breath and waited for his shoulders to untense. 'Look, Claire, I don't want an argument. I just want Jake to know I'm part of his life, despite all the other shit that might be happening at the moment. I want him to know he's got a daddy who loves him.'

'What can I say?' She leant against the kitchen doorway. 'You walked out on us. It's just possible he may never forgive you for that.'

Back in his car Denning felt his chest tighten. Thinking about Marsden, and the role he might have in Jake's life, he considered running a PNC check on his wife's new partner. But was this bordering on paranoia? Marsden seemed decent enough; smarmy and up himself perhaps, but maybe that said more about Denning's own prejudice than he cared to admit.

He no longer had any claim to Claire's affections: she was a free agent and could see whoever she liked.

Jake, on the other hand…

Chapter Sixteen

Molly poured herself a black coffee and took it back to her desk. Although she tried to keep her workspace tidy, it somehow managed to act as a magnet for clutter. The present assortment of debris included a smattering of Post-it notes; a selection of A5 writing pads, some of which contained pages of scribbled notes she had yet to transfer to her computer; a stack of old Tesco's receipts; an unopened box of staples; a broken stapler, and a crumpled tissue. The only personal touches consisted of a miniature cactus plant in a bright yellow pot and a framed photograph of her and Jon on holiday in Vegas three years ago. Happy times.

She remembered a primary school teacher once telling her class of fellow ten-year-olds that a tidy desk was a sign of a tidy mind. She hadn't appreciated the significance of the comment at the time, and if she was honest, probably didn't see the significance of it now. A cluttered desk, she believed, was more likely the sign of an over-worked police officer.

She blew some crumbs off her keyboard and logged on to the Police National Computer database, tapped in her username and password, then entered the name 'Anthony John Ferguson' and the date of his arrest.

When his file came up, she clicked on the photo. There were several pages devoted to Ferguson and his murder spree, the greater and gorier details of which were now pretty familiar to her.

She took a sip of acrid coffee and wished it was time for another cigarette.

Within minutes of her slipping into the office that afternoon her DI had pounced; he wanted to know if there was any progress regarding Gregor Kane, and any likelihood of an imminent arrest. She'd fobbed him off as best she could with a half-truth about pursuing an active line of inquiry and something about following up a useful lead. It was the kind of tosh they fed the press whenever there was nothing noteworthy to share during a stalling investigation, and DI Broomfield wasn't an idiot: at some point she would be expected to deliver the goods.

Molly felt bad. She had intended to phone the hospital first thing that morning to see if there was any progress with Adam Sloane, but it had slipped her mind. Another thing to add to her guilt list.

She skimmed over the pages, scanning the prosaic text for the piece of information she wanted. And there it was, a couple of sentences buried in a long, dull section about Ferguson's defence:

> Ferguson claimed that on the night of the last
> murder on 21 July, he was in the company of
> a friend: Derek James Rodman of Darbly Road,
> Camberwell, SE5. When questioned, Rodman
> proved to be an unreliable witness.

She sat back in her chair and let out a long, deep breath through her nose. It seemed the Bermondsey Ripper case wasn't quite so cut and dried after all.

–

'I've spoken to Leanne's best friend from school, Samantha Haddon. She reckons Bailey didn't just teach Leanne, he was shagging her as well.'

Denning had literally just walked into the MIT suite when Neeraj came running over with the news, like a child keen to impress one of the older kids.

'Shagging?' Denning sat down at his desk and tried to shift his focus from Alan Marsden back on to Daryl Bailey. He spotted a yellow Stick-it note with a message in what looked like Trudi Bell's childish scrawl, saying that she'd found something interesting on the CCTV footage, but he decided to take one thing at a time. 'Can you be a bit more specific, Deep? Is Samantha Haddon saying Daryl Bailey and Leanne Wyatt were having an affair?'

'Not an affair exactly, boss. She just said they were "shagging". Apparently everyone knew about it.'

'Including the school?'

Neeraj shrugged. 'Don't know about that. But she says all their mates knew what was going on. It seems our Mr Bailey was quite popular with some of his female pupils.'

'Whilst she was still at school?' He was thinking aloud. 'So that was at least five years ago. Leanne would have been, what, sixteen, possibly younger.' Denning forced his brain out of neutral. The friend could have been lying. But if she was telling the truth, then it told them Bailey was a liar and possibly a paedophile, depending on how old Leanne was when the alleged sexual relationship had started. He would be having another conversation with Daryl Bailey very soon, and this time he'd forgo the kid gloves approach. He thought for a moment. 'I understand Bailey's got an ex-wife out there somewhere. Get hold of her. Let's hear what she has to say about her pervert of an ex.'

Neeraj nodded and headed back to his desk. Denning caught Trudi Bell's eye and waved her over. 'Trudi, I understand from your scrawled note that CCTV has come up trumps.'

Trudi smiled. 'The footage from the street outside the Fleur de Lys shows Leanne getting into a taxi with an older man. Looks to be in his late thirties, possibly early forties. Certainly fits the description of the man she was seen chatting to at the bar the night she was killed. I'll ping it over to you. You can clearly see that it's Leanne.'

'And the man?'

'Hard to say. There are no clear shots of his face and he's wearing a baseball cap.'

'OK. Email me the footage.'

She turned to head back to her desk. 'Trudi, whilst you're here: any luck with the mysterious white Transit van?'

'Nothing yet, boss. I'm still waiting for the tech department to clean up the footage from Haggerston Park.'

'Let me know as soon as they forward it to you.'

A couple minutes later, Denning was staring at the images. Luckily the CCTV on Upper Street was digital rather than the now virtually obsolete analogue, which was notoriously poor. However, even allowing for that, the images were rarely one hundred per cent clear, especially if the footage had been recorded at night as too much extraneous light inevitably got in the way. The man with Leanne had been clever enough to keep his face away from the camera, or maybe he was just lucky. He was the wrong build for Gregor Kane, but the right general shape and age to pass for Daryl Bailey. Denning was sure the man in the CCTV footage climbing into the back of a taxi alongside their murder victim was the same man who'd lied to them the previous day. He noted the time stamp on the image: 23:12.

As the taxi drove off, he could just make out the name of the cab firm on the side of the car. He jotted down the number and reached for his phone.

Chapter Seventeen

The hospital corridor stank of pine disinfectant and antiseptic handwash. And something sickly sweet that Molly couldn't define.

Adam Sloane was in a private room on the second floor. He was still wired up to a portable machine that made various bleeping sounds at irregular intervals. According to the nurse Molly spoke to when she arrived, there was no change in his condition, nor was there likely to be.

She looked at his pale face. A thin dotting of post-pubescent stubble ran under his chin, and his hair had been brushed flat against his forehead. In the photos his mother had shown Molly his hair was gelled and spiky, his smiling face bursting with life. Lying comatose in a hospital bed, a tube protruding from his mouth, he looked like a ghost of the fun-loving boy he had once been.

The soulless room was decorated with a splattering of Get Well Soon cards and an Arsenal scarf, which hung over the bed like a pendant.

It was hot, the sun searing through the south-facing window with a view of nothing in particular. Molly went over to the window and pulled down a blind so it half-blocked out the sun. The room cooled slightly, as long shadows spread over the floor by the bed, casting awkward shapes across the polished linoleum.

She looked over at Adam. Even if he recovered from the coma, he would be irreparably brain-damaged to the point where he would require permanent care for the rest of his life.

His mother would do her best for as long as she could. Adam's father, it seemed, was now living with a woman he'd met on a dating site and had little or no contact with his children. Molly had shared many conversations with Debbie Sloane over the past few weeks. There were times she'd felt more like an extended family member than a police officer. Debbie worked long hours as a secretary for a pharmaceutical firm and didn't have many close friends. Molly had become part confidante and part counsellor in the short time she'd known Debbie, constantly promising to catch the person responsible for turning Adam Sloane from a lively, active teenager into a vegetable.

Adam was seventeen. She remembered what she had been like at seventeen: wild and headstrong to the point of bloody-mindedness. But she'd learned the hard way that life could punch you in the guts when you didn't expect it, especially if you pushed your luck too far; a lesson Adam Sloane was learning now. Only perhaps for him it had come too late.

–

The taxi driver hadn't been much help. He told Neeraj he recalled picking two people up from the Fleur de Lys on the night in question: a young woman and an older man. He remembered them because the girl seemed to be drunk and he was worried she would throw up in his cab. When presented with a photograph of Daryl Bailey, he'd been unable to confirm whether or not he'd been the male passenger in the taxi that night. 'About as helpful as soggy toilet paper,' Neeraj had said.

What he could confirm, however, was where he'd dropped them off: a house on the borders of Highgate and Crouch End. Neeraj gave Denning the address.

Denning despatched Ryan Cormack to the Fleur de Lys with a photograph of Bailey to show to the bar staff. Hopefully this would give them the confirmation that Bailey had been the man in the bar with Leanne the night she was killed. He wanted something concrete before he spoke to Bailey again, and proof he was seeing Leanne Wyatt despite claiming he hardly knew her would do very nicely.

He parked the Focus on Hadley Drive, and headed to number 24.

The street had a mixture of house types: a row of terraced cottages ran down one side, with larger, semi-detached 1930s properties lining the other side. There was a gastro pub at one end of the street, and an abandoned church at the other end.

He wondered why Bailey would take Leanne here; his own house wasn't so far away if he really wanted to impress her.

Denning walked up the tidy gravel drive and rang the doorbell. The garden was alive with colour. He nearly whacked his head against a hanging basket chock-full of begonias and trailing trumpet plants, which hung precariously from a rusting bracket beside the front door. After a moment the door was answered by an elderly man with wispy strands of white hair floating around his balding head like a fluffy halo. He looked to be well into his eighties, maybe older, and was dressed in a fraying beige cardigan with leather patches at the elbows, and a checked shirt with a thin, polyester tie, complete with egg stain just below the knot. He eyed Denning suspiciously, nodding slowly when Denning showed his ID.

'Sorry to bother you, sir, but I was wondering if you were at home on Monday evening, say around 11:30 p.m.'

The elderly man continued to look at Denning's ID for a moment or two before he answered. 'Sorry? What did you say?' He fiddled with a hearing aid in his right ear. Denning repeated the question. 'I was in bed,' the old man replied slowly. 'Asleep. Why do you want to know?'

Denning explained about the taxi. He showed him a photo of Daryl Bailey and another of Leanne Wyatt, but the old man just stared blankly at them and shook his head.

'Could I ask your name, sir?'

He stared at Denning for a moment, rheumy eyes blinking at the sunlight. Denning thought he was going to have to repeat the question again, but the old man suddenly spluttered back into life. 'Andrews,' he said. 'Brian Andrews. Who did you say you were…?'

Denning explained his identity again, slowly and loud enough for a passing dog-walker to hear. 'A taxi dropped a man and a woman at this address at around 11:30 p.m. on Monday evening,' Denning repeated. 'Did you see anything, or—' He was going to say 'hear anything' but realised that was unlikely. 'Do you recognise either of the two people in the photographs, Mr Andrews?'

Brain Andrews looked at Denning and thought carefully for a moment. 'What two people in what photographs?'

Denning felt a thin bead of sweat trickle down his back. Was Daryl Bailey using the old man's house as an illicit love nest without his knowing? It seemed unlikely. 'Is your wife at home, Mr Andrews? Maybe I could speak with her?'

Brian Andrews fiddled with his hearing aid again. 'She's gone to stay with our daughter in Basingstoke. She won't be back until Sunday.'

Denning thanked the old man and apologised for disturbing him. Brian Andrews muttered something under his breath and retreated inside his house, firmly closing the front door behind him. Denning heard the rattle of a chain being slotted into place.

After speaking to some of the neighbours and eliciting a similarly negative response as that of Brian Andrews, Denning concluded it was possible the taxi driver had made a mistake. Either that or he had deliberately misled them for some reason. Whatever the case, it seemed nobody had seen anyone fitting the description of Daryl Bailey or Leanne Wyatt in the vicinity of Hadley Drive on the evening in question.

Chapter Eighteen

'Seriously? Sound like someone's taking the piss.' Denning couldn't fail to detect the note of derision in Neeraj's voice when he told him about Brian Andrews. 'Are you sure he wasn't having you on, boss? I mean he could have been in league with Bailey and the pair of them are using the house as a knocking shop.'

Denning ignored the inane sniggering that followed, allowing Neeraj to get it out of his system. 'I want that taxi driver checked out,' he said. 'Either he's an idiot, or he's lying. Whilst I wouldn't rule out the former, I'd be happy to put money on the latter. In the meantime, Trudi, any luck with Daryl Bailey?'

'No one who's at West Ham now was there when he played for them. I spoke to someone at one of his other clubs up north, but apparently there was never any scandal whilst he was there. There may have been plenty of rumours doing the rounds about Daryl Bailey, but that's all they were: rumours.'

He turned to Neeraj. 'What about the former Mrs Bailey?'

'No luck there either, boss. Seems she remarried, but as to her present whereabouts…' Neeraj offered another shrug.

'Then keep digging. If Bailey lied about his relationship with Leanne, then what else has he been lying about?'

'What first?' asked Neeraj. 'Taxi driver or continue digging for dirt on Bailey?'

Denning decided to overlook the slightly impertinent tone in Neeraj's voice. If he had more energy and less of a throbbing headache, he might have commented on it. 'Bailey's our priority at this stage. So you and Trudi keep looking into Bailey's background. There has to be something dodgy there: it can't all be rumour and speculation.'

'What about Gregor Kane, boss?' Kinsella asked.

'His name stays on the board until we rule him out.' He nodded towards the far end of the office, where a photo of a smirking Gregor Kane was pinned on the whiteboard next to one of a serious-looking Daryl Bailey.

'Is there anything else anyone wants to add?' He cast his gaze around the open-plan office and was greeted by a general shaking of heads. Only Neeraj had a hand half-raised in the air.

'Sorry, boss. I forgot to tell you: the DCI wants a word.'

–

The cyclamen in McKenna's office now looked like it was awaiting a priest to deliver the last rites. Denning shot it a pitying look and sat down opposite the DCI.

McKenna was leaning back in her chair, fixing Denning with her steely stare, a guilty whiff of malt whisky faintly discernible on her breath. 'What's the story with Daryl Bailey?'

'He lied about knowing Leanne, so he's a person of interest.'

She sat in silence for a moment, chewing matters over in her head. 'This is according to one of Leanne Wyatt's former school friends, yes? Although the school has yet to confirm it?'

'To be fair, it's in the school's interests to keep quiet about any possible liaison between a pupil and a member of staff, especially one as high-profile as Daryl Bailey. If it were to become public knowledge, it wouldn't do much for their reputation.'

McKenna offered up a watery smile. 'OK, what about Gregor Kane? Where does he fit into this?'

'Kane's not off the hook, not yet, not by a long chalk. But, for the time being, he's on the back burner.'

'You know CID are after him for dealing? Well, him and about half-a-dozen other scrotes, but he's on their watch list.' She shuffled uncomfortably in her chair, and Denning wondered if she suffered from back trouble. It was so easy to think of Betty Taggart as some kind of Terminatrix: indestructible and devoid of emotion; sometimes he had to remind himself she was as subject to human frailties as everyone else.

'If any evidence puts Kane back in the frame, then we'll go after him. CID will just have to suck it up. I get that dealing is serious, but so is murder. Under the circumstances, I think that takes priority.'

'All right, Matt, get back in your pram. I'm only saying try not to piss on their parade, that's all.' She began subconsciously picking at a blackhead on her chin. 'Do you have anything else on Bailey, besides the vague rumours about his possible paedophile tendencies?'

'We're still looking into Bailey's background, and I plan to speak to Bailey again tomorrow. We have evidence to suggest Bailey was with Leanne the night she was killed.'

'Do we have enough to charge him?'

Denning shook his head. 'That's still a long way off, unfortunately. We still need proof he was the man with Leanne the night she was killed, let alone anything that can directly link him to her murder.'

'Any luck with forensics?'

'Still waiting on their report coming through. They're as overworked and short-staffed as the rest of us, but I'll chase that up as a matter of priority.'

McKenna's hand dropped from her chin and she began drumming her fingers on the desk, a sure sign their meeting was coming to a close. 'Just remember, Matt: the clock's ticking on this, and an early result will be a definite bonus, for everyone.'

'Once we have that proof, we can go after Bailey hammer and tongs. But we'll need something solid before we can even think about touting this before the CPS.'

She stopped the finger drumming and leant forward in her chair. 'There is another possibility...' She waited until she had his full attention. 'Someone else is involved. Someone other than Gregor Kane and Daryl Bailey. Someone we don't yet know about.'

This wasn't something Denning wanted to hear. He could feel the vein in his temple throb again, a pulsating beat like a metronome that seemed to get louder with each beat.

Chapter Nineteen

The bar was busy with after-work drinkers but Molly found a table at the back near the toilets. A few minutes later Trudi sat down opposite her, dumping her handbag and sunglasses on an empty chair.

'Bacardi and Diet Pepsi, as requested.' Molly pushed the drink across the table towards Trudi, then took a long, welcome sip of her pint.

'Cheers. Good day?' asked Trudi.

She told Trudi about her visit to Adam Sloane and her frustration about the lack of progress with the case. 'Gregor Kane's luck has to run out at some point,' she concluded.

Trudi knocked back her Bacardi. 'You've got that right. He's a prick. And it's possible he might have more than just your little drug victim on his conscience, assuming he's got one.'

Molly wrinkled her brow. 'Really?'

Trudi twitched and shuffled in her seat. She finished the rest of her drink in one eager gulp, then swirled the melting ice cubes round the bottom of the glass. 'I needed that. Cheers, babe.' She tipped her empty glass in Molly's direction. 'Do you want another?'

Molly nodded at her nearly-full pint of Kronenbourg. 'I think I'm probably fine for now, but thanks anyway.'

Trudi headed to the bar and returned a few minutes later with another Bacardi and Diet Pepsi and half-pint of Kronenbourg, which she placed in front of Molly. 'You can top it up when it runs low,' she said, nodding at Molly's pint.

Trudi started talking about her girlfriend, who, according to Trudi, was seeing another woman. This didn't seem to be based on anything other than rampant paranoia on Trudi's part, but Molly smiled supportively when she felt Trudi needed it. She was curious about Trudi's reference to Gregor Kane... She could wait and choose the right time, or she could just cut to the chase and jump straight in with it. She decided on the latter approach.

'What did you mean about Gregor Kane having more on his conscience than Adam Sloane?'

Trudi placed her drink on the table and rubbed a hand through her blonde bob. 'Sorry. Forget I said anything. Me and my big gob: I'll get meself hung one of these bleedin' days.'

'Is it something to do with the murder inquiry? Leanne Wyatt? Is Gregor Kane a suspect?'

An awkward silence followed. Trudi looked like she wanted to change the subject. Eventually she said, 'Gregor Kane knew Leanne Wyatt. He *is* a suspect, but and swear you'll keep this under your hat − it now looks like someone else could be in the frame.' She took another sip of her drink, and then wiped a thin sliver of sweat from her top lip. 'Look, I shouldn't be telling you any of this, at least not while the case is still ongoing. Denning's got us running round like blue-arsed flies chasing up some dodgy bloke who knew Leanne. He reckons he's a more credible candidate than Kane. Personally, I'm not so sure, but you know me: I turn up, smile, do the job, and keep me mouth shut.'

Molly chewed her bottom lip. 'You think Kane did it?'

'He's certainly capable.'

She thought about this before she answered. Gregor Kane would have been a child twelve years ago, which would rule him out of being the Bermondsey Ripper, but she couldn't voice that thought aloud to Trudi. Her brain was whirring. If Kane *was* a suspect, then this could be a way into MIT for her. 'Why the cross carved into the victim's forehead? That has to mean something.'

Trudi offered a casual shrug. 'Who knows? Something drugs-related, maybe. Perhaps she threatened to grass on him and this was a warning to others not to try the same.'

After a pause, Molly asked, 'Who's the new suspect?'

'You know I can't tell you that, Moll. Betty Taggart will have my tits in the mincer if it gets out that I've been chatting to someone about the case who isn't on the team.'

'I can help you, though, if Gregor Kane *is* involved. I've been watching the guy for the best part of a month. I know things about him that might be useful to the case.'

Trudi stared at her Bacardi for what felt like a lifetime. 'I dunno, Moll. Like I said, Denning's chasing his tail with this other suspect. There's even CCTV footage of this guy with the victim, well, as good as. Kane could be out of the running by now for all we know.'

'Is Kane still officially a suspect? As far as Denning's concerned?'

'Until he's formally ruled out, then yes, he's still a suspect.'

'Maybe I should speak to Denning?'

Trudi nodded. 'I'm still not sure. You just said you didn't think Kane did it. Besides, Denning would want to know how you heard about Kane's involvement, and if it gets back that it was me who told you...'

'I can keep your name out of it. I know Broomfield had a meeting with Betty Taggart today. I could ask him what it was about. It's more than likely got something to do with the murder investigation. It would be too much of a coincidence it was about anything else.'

Trudi drained her glass. 'Let me have a word with Denning. I can suggest he speaks to you, then take it from there.' She a paused for a moment and looked at her phone. 'Look, I'll speak to Denning tomorrow. I have to go now. I said I'd do some shopping for my old mum after work.'

She waved her hand and smiled at Molly, slung her handbag over her shoulder, put her sunglasses in her top pocket, and headed towards the door.

Molly watched Trudi thread her way through the crowded bar and out onto the street, attracting second glances from men as she weaved past them. She was on the point of finishing her pint and starting on the half when she noticed something on the floor. She bent down to pick it up and realised it was Magda Kilbride's business card. It must have fallen out of her bag when she took her purse out to buy the drinks. As she put the card back in her bag, she remembered there was something she needed to speak to Jon about.

Chapter Twenty

Jon was watching television when Molly got back. He was wearing his dressing gown and his faded Led Zeppelin t-shirt with the rip in the neck. An open can of Stella sat on the floor by his feet.

'How was your day?' he asked.

'Interesting.' She headed into the kitchen and poured herself a glass of orange juice. She wasn't in the mood for cooking, and there was little chance of Jon offering. She removed the takeaway pizza menu from the fridge door and wandered back into the living room.

'Dinner,' she said, tossing the takeaway menu at Jon. He gazed at it half-heartedly before chucking it onto the coffee table.

'I'm not hungry. Order whatever you want for yourself and I'll have what you don't eat.'

She took her mobile phone out of her bag, selected the number for the local pizza restaurant and ordered a twelve-inch meat feast. It would be there in ten minutes.

'I spoke to Kenneth Walters today,' she said.

'Who?' Jon seemed half asleep. She worried that he was now smoking so much dope it was causing his brain to atrophy. Then she thought about Adam Sloane lying in his hospital bed, only being kept alive by machinery and maternal will power, if anyone could describe that as being alive...

'He's the detective who investigated the Bermondsey Ripper case,' she said. 'He's retired now, but still as sharp as a tack.'

'Not this again.' Jon slumped back into the old leather armchair that faced the telly. He was watching a documentary about the Rolling Stones on one of the satellite channels, but with the sound tuned down low, as though he was only half interested. 'I thought you'd have got this out of your system by now.'

She sat down on the chaise longue, shoving a pile of dusty magazines onto the floor. The room smelled fustier than usual: stale tobacco mingled with marijuana, mixed with stale sweat; only this time she couldn't be bothered to open a window. 'Jon, I think it's possible they could have got it wrong about Ferguson.'

'You are joking, aren't you?'

'No.' She sighed. 'It would be nice if you could back me up on this. Offer me a bit of support, like you used to.' She thought back to when they'd first got together. He'd bumped into her coming back from the beer tent at a music festival in Brighton, causing her to spill her drink down her front. He'd apologised and insisted on buying her another, and then another. They'd spent the rest of the night chatting, discovering they shared a passion for hard rock and left-wing values. She'd barely clocked the age difference at first, and even when she did it hadn't mattered. Within a week they were officially a couple. Within a year they were living together. Whatever else they agreed or disagreed on, Jon had always been there for her. He'd encouraged her to apply for CID and had supported her ambition to join MIT, or so she'd thought. But things had changed after he'd lost his job. Now he no longer had his own career, and his own purpose in life, it was almost as though he resented her having one.

'Look, I'm just saying be careful.' He drank some more Stella, swilling the liquid round in the can to gauge how much was left. 'You go poking around into a possible hornets' nest from years back and suggest that the Met could have fucked up on a major murder inquiry, then what? It's not exactly going to help your long-term career plans, is it?'

Molly bit her tongue. 'Maybe, but the very least you could do is take me seriously.'

Jon switched off the television. 'OK. What did this geezer have to say?'

'Ferguson had an alibi for one of the murders. I've checked it out.' She told him about Derek Rodman and the straggly loose ends that had been left untidied by the original investigation.

'Granted, it sounds like there might have been some short-comings during the investigation into Ferguson, but I imagine that's par for the course on a major murder inquiry. This still sounds pretty tenuous. What have you got to go on? Ferguson had a dodgy alibi, and you think that proves he's innocent. The alibi was dismissed in court, you said so yourself. Then some half-baked theory about this poor cow in Haggerston Park having a cross carved on her forehead. It could have been anything. And let's just say you are right, what then? What exactly do you plan to do with this information?'

'I'm not sure yet.' She was unwilling to get into a fight, but she was determined to stand her ground and not be readily dismissed. 'But there's clearly something dodgy about the investigation into Ferguson. A cover-up maybe? I don't know yet.' She thought back to Ken Walters. He seemed decent, honest; not the sort of detective to knowingly go along with a miscarriage of justice. But it was possible she had read him wrong.

She looked over at Jon; he finished his can of Stella, scrunched the can in his fist, and threw it in the overflowing waste-paper bin beside the fireplace. 'I'm worried that you're going to get yourself into trouble over this.' He sighed. 'This isn't even your investigation. I know you want to join MIT, but chasing shadows that probably aren't even there isn't the best way to go about it. My advice, for what it's worth, leave well alone. This could backfire and bite you on the backside big time.'

She picked at a loose thread on her blouse. She tried to snap it off, but instead the thread grew longer until she ended up biting it off with her teeth. 'I also spoke with an old friend of yours.' She watched his face twitch with interest. 'Magda Kilbride. She's got her doubts too.'

If Molly had expected a flicker of recognition from Jon, then she was disappointed. 'Who the fuck is Magda Kilbride?' he asked.

'She says she worked with you at the *Echo* a few years back.' Molly described Magda, the dyed-red hair, the boots and the attitude.

Jon half smiled as a distant memory seemed to gestate in his brain. 'Oh, you mean Mags. I remember Mags.' He nodded slowly to himself, then after a moment said, 'but she was bonkers. You really can't take anything she says seriously. She was always chasing her tail to get a story. That was when she wasn't making stuff up.'

'We had a good chat.' Molly tried not to sound defensive. 'She's an interesting character. I liked her.'

'Yes, I remember Mags,' he repeated, still smiling to himself, before adding, 'You know you can't trust her.'

Molly still wasn't convinced she could – or even should – trust Magda Kilbride, but Jon's reaction seemed harsh. Mags hadn't said anything to suggest there had been any animosity between them. She wondered if there was something else at play: professional jealousy perhaps, or something more…

'An interesting character,' said Jon. 'Yes, that's certainly one way of describing Mags Kilbride.'

–

Sarah was out when Denning returned home. He vaguely remembered her saying something about going to a leaving do for someone after work. She'd even asked him if he wanted to come along.

He always struggled to get on with Sarah's work colleagues: hedge-fund managers and investment bankers whose conversation revolved around second homes, skiing holidays and the tax breaks available for private health care. He tried hard to avoid using the word 'wankers' whenever he thought of them.

He thought back to his conversation with Claire that afternoon. She was right about him having no say in how she led her life now, even though they would always share a constant bond through Jake. But what if Claire were ready to move on; move on and take Jake with her? He was with Sarah now and, he kept reminding himself, they were happy.

He looked over at the picture of Jake and felt a sense of doors closing.

Chapter Twenty-One

Denning called a briefing for 9 a.m. the next morning.

Progress was too slow for his liking. It wouldn't be long before the media would be snapping at their heels, salivating for something more substantial than a few discarded scraps. And then there was Betty Taggart. He knew she'd be watching events unfold from behind the dusty venetian blinds in her cramped and sweaty office.

Trudi Bell kicked things off. 'It seems you were right about Leanne keeping herself to herself. She rarely posted on Facebook or Twitter, and didn't do Instagram or Snapchat, or any of the half dozen other social media sites that have popped up over the past few years. Her last post on Facebook was just over two weeks ago: a picture of her and Charlie at the beach in Margate, taken by her mum. It's got half a dozen likes. Apart from that, there are a couple of emails to various former school friends where she mentions that she was seeing someone, but she doesn't say who. One of her friends asked if she was still seeing Gregor Kane, to which she replied "sometimes". There's nothing else worth noting, and no mention at all of Daryl Bailey. Of course,' she added, 'it would help if we had her mobile phone.'

'Any luck there?' Denning asked.

'Her service provider reckons it's probably switched off as it's not transmitting a pulse,' said Ryan. 'However, they've said that the last known location they have is somewhere around the Highgate/Crouch End area, as was picked up by their mast on

Highgate Hill. They can't be more specific than that unfortunately.'

'That's where the taxi driver says he dropped them off,' Neeraj offered.

Denning nodded. 'In which case we talk to him again, and find out exactly where he dropped them off. We now know we're looking in the right areas, but we still need to narrow it down further.'

'What about Kane? Is he still in the frame for this?' It was Dave Kinsella, leaning back in his chair, a cup of Costa coffee in his hand, a light dabbling of sweat on his moustache.

'He was never out of it as far as I'm concerned,' Denning said. Out of the corner of his eye he spotted Trudi Bell briefly raise her hand, then lower it again. 'However, Kane's alibi checks out. CCTV footage confirms he was at the Cat in the Hat on the night in question. Witnesses, including the door staff, claim he arrived around 9 p.m. and left after 1 a.m. the following morning. We know Leanne was still alive at 9 p.m., so, for the time being, Kane's in the clear.'

'He could have left unobserved,' Ryan suggested. 'Nipped out a fire exit for instance.'

'Agreed, it's possible, which is why his name stays up there for now. But let's focus on Bailey for the moment.' He pointed to Bailey's photo on the whiteboard. 'Ryan, any joy at the Fleur de Lys with Bailey's photo?'

'The manager couldn't say for certain. One of the women who was working that night says she thought he looked like the bloke who was with Leanne on the night in question, but she couldn't swear to it.'

Denning nodded. 'OK. Deep, what about the former Mrs Bailey? Have we had any luck tracking her down?'

'Seems she remarried and moved to Canada about eight years ago,' Neeraj said. 'I've spoken to the Canadian police to see if we can get any contact details for her, but nothing so far.'

'Well, give them time, Deep. They are eight hours behind us.' There was a spluttering of suppressed laughter from the team. Denning patted the air with his hands and the laughter fizzled away to nothing. 'OK, everyone, can we have some quiet.' He held up a brown manila folder. 'We've now got the forensics report through. As expected, it confirms what we already suspected, that our victim was killed elsewhere, then dumped in Haggerston Park sometime in the early hours of Monday morning. Also, there's a surprising lack of DNA, which suggests our killer is either very thorough or very lucky. Unfortunately, it means we have even less to work with than we'd hoped. We need to find the murder location. With a bit of luck, our killer's left DNA there.' He looked over to Neeraj. 'Deep, you and I are going to have another word with the taxi driver. Let's put a rocket up his backside until he tells us where he really did drop them off that night. Until we hear otherwise, he was the last person to see Leanne alive, so that makes him our best witness.'

'You're convinced the bloke she shared the taxi with is our killer?' asked Kinsella.

McKenna's words from yesterday bounced round Denning's brain: *what if there's another person involved?* It was something he didn't want to think about, not unless he had to...

He ended the briefing and returned to his desk. He was about to check for any new emails before heading out the door with Neeraj, when he was distracted by the sight of Trudi Bell sauntering towards his desk.

'Could I have a quick word, boss?'

He indicated for her to sit down, and she perched half a buttock on the edge of his desk. He could smell her perfume: *Jezebel*, he thought; it had been Claire's favourite.

'What is it, Trudi?'

She shot him a warm smile. 'I've got some good news about the Transit van, boss. We've got a partial reading from the number plate. Can't quite make out if the first letter is an R or a B, but we've got something to work with. I'm going to do a Vehicle Online Description Search on the PNC in a minute and see if it throws anything up.'

'Good. Well done.' He looked blankly at her, not sure why she hadn't brought this useful gem of information up during the briefing. 'Is there something else?'

She leaned in close, her cleavage inches from his face. 'Look, I know this is probably slightly against the rules, boss, but there's a detective constable with CID, Molly Fisher. She's been keeping obs on Gregor Kane for a while now; she's familiar with his movements, his contacts…'

'OK, Trudi, thanks for telling me, but I'm not sure why I need to know this.'

'She could be useful.'

Denning pursed his lips. 'To be honest with you, Trudi, unless she has any evidence that can directly link Gregor Kane to the murder of Leanne Wyatt, I can't see what use she could be.'

Trudi lowered her voice. 'I accept this is asking you to go out on a limb, boss. But I know Molly: she's a good officer, and to be blunt, she's wasted in CID.'

The aroma of Jezebel was boring a hole in his sinuses. 'Sorry, but I don't see what any of this has got to do with me.'

'She wants to join MIT. This might go in her favour next time she puts in an application.'

'You mean she's already been turned down?'

Trudi shrugged. 'A bit of mutual back-scratching, sir, that's all I'm saying.'

Denning sighed. The last thing he needed right now was to humour some wannabe raw recruit to MIT. But she might, just *might* have something useful to offer. If nothing else, she could rule Kane out of their inquiry, if she had any evidence that even indirectly supported his alibi. Christ, there wasn't much else to go on at the moment, and Kane had yet to be officially stood down as a suspect.

He made a note of her name and told Trudi he'd think about it.

Chapter Twenty-Two

The taxi driver was enjoying a bacon sandwich when Denning and Neeraj walked into the office flashing their ID.

He was a fat, balding man in his fifties, with at least a couple of days' growth round his double chin. He barely looked up from a copy of *The Sun* when he saw the two officers standing in the doorway.

'Barry Haynes?' Denning asked. It was hot and stuffy in the pokey cab office: little ventilation and no air conditioning meant the room smelt of stale tobacco and bacon.

'Not you lot again. I went over everything with Gunga Din yesterday.' He nodded at Neeraj.

'I'd like you to go over everything again,' Denning said. 'But this time I'd like you to tell us the truth.'

Haynes folded the newspaper and threw it on the desk. He stuffed the remainder of the bacon sandwich in his mouth. 'If it's still about that girl that was murdered: I've told you where I dropped her and the bloke off. As for what happened after that, I can't help you.' He spoke through mouthfuls of bacon sandwich. Denning noted the look of disgust on Neeraj's face. There was something unpleasant about Barry Haynes, and Denning would have been quite happy to drag him down the station for questioning if that's what it took.

'Perhaps you could tell us *exactly* where you dropped them?' he said coldly. 'The elderly gentleman who lives at the address you gave my colleague knows nothing about any couple being dropped off on the evening in question.'

Hayes swallowed the last of the sandwich. He rubbed a hand over his front, smearing bacon fat and butter over his grubby shirt.

'What is this? The fucking Spanish Inquisition? I didn't do that kid in.' He picked up his newspaper and opened it. 'Why are you giving me a hard time?'

Denning grabbed the newspaper and threw it on the table. 'Could you just answer the question, Mr Haynes? Rather than continuing to waste our time. I need you to give me the exact address where you dropped them off.'

There was a sudden pause, with only the chattering from the other end of a two-way radio filling the silence.

'OK, maybe I was a bit vague when he asked the other day. I'd been busy that night. Look, I was tired and my shift was due to finish at midnight. They wanted me to do another job. They're always short-staffed here.'

Denning could feel his limited patience wearing thin. He cast a disparaging eye round the shabby cab office, with its hard, plastic seating and wood-chipped walls. 'Could you come to the point, Mr Haynes. Otherwise we'll continue this conversation back at the station.'

Hayes looked at a spot on the floor. 'The bloke asked me to drop them at the end of the street. By the junction with Highgate Road. That suited me as this other job had just come in back in Islington.'

'So it could have been Highgate Road, Hadley Drive, or any one of the half dozen or so streets in that area?' Denning struggled to keep the anger from his voice. Thanks to the laziness or sheer stupidity of Barry Haynes, the murder location could be just about anywhere in north London. He could feel his shoulders tense. 'Can you give me a description of the man?'

He shrugged. 'Like I told your mate yesterday: tall, smart, well-spoken but not posh. He certainly wasn't short of cash.'

'Really?'

'When he opened his wallet it was stuffed with twenties.' Haynes rediscovered his fascination with the spot on the floor. 'He gave me a twenty as a tip,' he said sheepishly.

Denning suspected the generous tip was intended as an incentive for being deliberately evasive should the police come asking questions. He showed Haynes a photo of Daryl Bailey. 'Was this the man?'

Haynes stared at the picture for a few seconds, before offering another shrug. 'I dunno. I suppose it could be. To be honest with you, I didn't really take that much notice of him. I was more interested in her: she was a looker.' He glanced back at the scrunched-up copy of *The Sun*. 'Real shame what happened to her. If he's the bastard responsible, then I hope you catch him.'

'Well, with help from people like yourself, Mr Haynes, hopefully we'll do just that.'

The sarcasm seemed to be lost on Haynes.

Once they were back outside Neeraj said, 'You still want it to be Bailey, don't you, boss?'

Denning was about to reply when his phone rang: it was Ryan Cormack. He answered it, nodded, sighed, then turned to Neeraj.

'Problem, boss?'

'Another body's been found.'

Chapter Twenty-Three

Molly had struggled to find Derek Rodman. He didn't use social media, and an internet search failed to throw up anything useful.

She'd told her boss she had a hospital appointment that morning and wouldn't be in until lunchtime. It was another fib. She was getting very good at lying, something that concerned her. Usually she was honest to the point of virtue, but somehow she'd turned into someone who could bend the truth whenever it suited.

She remembered Jon's words from the previous evening, accusing her of being obsessed with Anthony Ferguson. Maybe he was right, perhaps this was becoming an obsession, albeit not for the reasons Jon thought.

The Ferguson case files included an out-of-date address for a bedsit in a house in Camberwell long since converted into luxury apartments. None of the neighbours recognised the name Derek Rodman, and the estate agents had no idea what had happened to the previous occupants prior to the conversion two years previously. She'd asked in a nearby pub, but had no luck there either. It was only when she popped into a convenience store on the next street to buy twenty Silk Cut that she thought it might be worth asking the elderly shopkeeper if he'd remembered anyone called Derek Rodman. He'd scratched his greying beard and mentioned a part-remembered conversation with someone who'd told him she'd bumped into Derek a year ago, and that he was off the booze and working in a community centre somewhere in Kilburn.

It had taken her the best part of an hour to phone round all the community centres listed in Kilburn and the surrounding area before she eventually struck gold. The Hazel Kerr Day Centre on Brondesbury Park Road catered for children and adults with behavioural problems. Derek Rodman was one of the support staff.

She'd been expecting some life-ravaged ex-alky with halitosis and attitude, but instead was introduced to a polite and softly spoken man in his early fifties. He was dressed in mustard-coloured shorts and a faded blue t-shirt. Both his face and arms were tanned, and apart from a few broken veins on his cheeks, there was nothing to suggest this was someone who had once struggled with the demon drink. He smiled when she introduced herself, offering her a warm handshake.

'How can I help you, miss?' The room was painted in bright primary colours, and the walls were adorned with prints of animals and flowers. An avalanche of children's toys poured out of a cupboard at one end of the room. Derek Rodman gestured towards a couple of padded armchairs next to a wide window which overlooked Brondesbury Park. She declined his offer of tea or coffee, knowing it would just mean she would have to stop off somewhere for a wee later.

'I'd like to talk to you about Anthony Ferguson.' She caught a look of unease twitch itself around his face. 'Don't worry,' she reassured him, 'this isn't in any official capacity.'

He seemed to relax at this and tried hard to smile. 'It was all a very long time ago,' he said. 'I'm not sure I can add anything beyond what I told the police twelve years ago.'

'Ferguson claimed he was with you on the evening of the last murder. That would have been the 21st of July. It was a Friday evening. Can you confirm that?'

He scrunched his face up and slowly nodded. 'I told the police this at the time. They didn't believe me then, I don't see any reason why they would believe me now.'

'But you definitely told them Anthony Ferguson was with you on the evening of twenty-first July twelve years ago?'

He nodded again. 'Yes.'

'I'm sorry to sound pushy, Mr Rodman, but can you be sure?'

Derek Rodman blinked and slowly nodded his head. 'You mean because I was an alcoholic and couldn't have told you if it was Christmas or rice pudding most days…?' His voice was deep and calming; he spoke without any emotion, just stating facts. 'I accept I was in a bad place back then.' He sighed. 'I would start the day with a can of strong cider, then work my way through several more before lunchtime. Evenings, it would be spirits – whisky preferably, but I was never fussy. I can understand why the prosecution found it so easy to discredit me.' He looked directly at her, not aggressively but with a mix of sorrow and repentance. 'But I got myself sorted out.' He opened his mouth to speak again, but no words came out. He closed his eyes, shook his head, and started again. 'I had a heart attack a week before my forty-fifth birthday. I should have died, but they managed to save me. It was enough to convince me to give up the booze for good. With a lot of help and support, I managed it. I turned my life around. I've been dry for nearly eight years now.'

Molly was sympathetic. Sometimes it *was* possible for people to sort their lives out before they disappeared forever beneath the cracks in society. Sometimes people were saved from self-destruction by fate or luck or the kindness of strangers. And she knew all about that.

'To answer your question, miss: yes, I'm sure Anthony Ferguson was with me that night.' He lowered his voice as a couple of children appeared. 'Tony was a strange character, difficult to like; he didn't have many friends. I suppose I felt sorry for him. His gran and my old mum had been friends for years, and I kind of took him under my wing.' He dropped his gaze for a moment and looked at the floor, searching his brain for a half-forgotten memory. 'Tony came round to my bedsit around ten that evening. I'd had flu so I hadn't been drinking as much as usual. I got the impression he wanted to talk. He didn't say so, but he clearly had something on his mind. I thought maybe it was something to do with his gran, but whatever it was, he kept it to himself. We ended up playing cards and drinking into the small hours. He slept on the floor and left early the next morning. He was working on a building site at the time. Apparently the boss had it in for him and was looking for any excuse to give him the boot, so he had to make sure he got to work on time every day. The next thing I knew, he'd been arrested for murder. I have to admit, I was shocked.'

'You don't think he did it?'

He looked at her, grey eyes twinkling, happy to feel he was being useful. 'Well, yes and no.' A child came over to him and handed him a toy aeroplane with a one of the wings broken off. Rodman slotted the wing back into place and handed the toy back to the child. 'There you go, Billy. Just be careful with it now.' The child ran off laughing. Rodman turned back to Molly, keeping his soft voice low, ensuring no one – especially young ears – could overhear what he had to say. 'In a way I wasn't *that* surprised he killed someone. I mean, there was a viscous, nasty side to him, and he had some serious issues with women.' He shook his head. 'I suppose he never forgave his mum for abandoning him. And well, to put it bluntly, he wasn't exactly a looker. Women tended to give him a wide berth. Even so...'

Molly wanted to shake him, insist he came to the point. Instead, she just smiled. 'Go on, Mr Rodman.'

Rodman sighed and shook his head again. 'Whatever the case, and irrespective of what you might think about him, I promise you, miss, Tony Ferguson was with me the night of that last murder.'

Molly couldn't avoid the thought that if they were wrong about the last murder, could they have been wrong about all of them?

Chapter Twenty-Four

'Body of a female, around mid-to-late thirties. Victim of a prolonged and particularly brutal assault.'

They were standing in a car park behind a fast-food restaurant at the far end of Dalston Way, less than a mile from where Leanne Wyatt had been found. Blue police tape had already been wound round the crime scene, hanging heavy in the limpid air. Uniformed officers and crime scene investigators busied themselves. A white forensic tent was in the process of being erected behind two industrial-sized rubbish bins. The rancid smell from the overflowing bins was almost overpowering.

'What have we got?' he asked.

A red-faced man in his sixties came over to join them. He was dressed in a pair of heavy-duty blue coveralls.

Gorton introduced them; 'This is Dr Ian Bevan. Home Office pathologist.'

Denning shook the older man's gloved hand. Bevan dropped his face mask and began to remove the blue coverall. He was grey-haired, with a full beard and jowly cheeks. He wore a pair a pair of old-fashioned horn-rimmed glasses, and seemed to have trouble breathing.

'Mid-to-late thirties?'

Bevan nodded. 'At this stage we've only done a preliminary examination, but I would say no older than forty. Obviously we'll know for certain after the post-mortem.' He took a handkerchief from his trouser pocket and loudly blew his nose. 'Sorry,' he said, 'hay fever. I'm a martyr to it this time of the year.'

Denning smiled politely. 'When was the body found?'

'Earlier this morning,' Gorton said. 'A couple of homeless guys were scavenging for food.' He jerked his head in the direction of the two giant metal rubbish bins in the far corner of the car park. 'They spotted her lying behind one of the bins. At first they thought she was a shop window dummy.'

'Where are they now?'

'Being interviewed by two uniformed officers in the restaurant,' Gorton said. 'We thought it only fair to offer them something to eat. They've had a shock.'

Denning could see Neeraj itching to ask the obvious question.

'Was she killed here?' Denning asked.

Bevan sneezed and followed it up with a cough. 'Early indications would suggest that's the case. Blood splatter has been found in the alleyway that leads onto Dalston Way, and there are signs of a scuffle. The body was dumped by the bins, presumably in an attempt to conceal it. The clothing doesn't look like it's been disturbed, so at this stage we can likely rule out sexual assault. The post-mortem will confirm it one way or another.'

'Approximate time of death?'

Bevan sneezed again. 'At this stage it would only be a guess. It was another warm evening, so the heat would have speeded up rigor mortis, but probably not by a lot: it's still in its fairly early stages.' He wiped a bead of sweat from his forehead. 'I'd say between ten and twelve hours.'

'So, around midnight…?'

'Or an hour or so either side.'

'What was she doing here?' Neeraj asked.

Denning thought about this. 'Good question.' He turned to Neeraj, 'Speak to the restaurant staff: find out what time the place shuts, and who was on duty last night. Get uniform onto that. And get hold of any CCTV.'

Neeraj nodded. He opened his mouth to say something else, then changed his mind. Denning already knew what Neeraj was thinking. There were some similarities between this and Leanne Wyatt's death that couldn't be ignored, but Denning wasn't going to jump to conclusions, at least not yet.

He watched the white-suited CSIs entering and leaving the sealed-off crime scene. 'Do you mind if I have a look?'

'Fill your boots,' said Gorton. 'Unless Dr Bevan has any objections.'

'I'm all done for now,' Baker said. 'I prefer to do a more thorough examination on a mortuary slab rather than a public car park.' He began to remove his forensic suit. 'I'll let your DCI have the post-mortem report as soon as I can.'

Denning thanked him and then climbed into a forensic suit for the second time that week.

The body lay splayed between two overflowing food bins, legs akimbo and arms outstretched almost like a crucifix. He could feel himself start to sweat. The stench was unbearable: rotting food and rotting flesh, both crawling with maggots, combined with a sickly-sweet aroma of something acidic, something that made Denning think of bile.

The victim was smartly dressed, in an expensive-looking red jacket and tight black skirt. Her tights were torn, and one of her black shoes was missing.

The face was as Bevan had described it: bruised and bloodied like a rotten plum; uncannily similar to Leanne Wyatt. He checked the face, in particular the forehead, but although there was extensive bruising, there was nothing that looked like a cross. Her hair was straggly and unkempt, seemingly at odds with her otherwise smart appearance. It looked at first glance like a blonde wig. There was something strange about her, something Denning couldn't quite put his finger on…

He returned to Gorton and climbed out of the forensic suit, wiping a bead of sweat from his forehead with a flick of his hand. He watched Bevan get into a large estate car parked beyond the police cordon and drive off. 'Have we used Dr Bevan before?' he asked Gorton.

'Technically he's retired,' she replied. 'He's doing us a favour coming out at all.'

Denning looked around him. The car park was bordered on one side by the brick arches of a railway viaduct. The rear of the restaurant was L-shaped and took up another two sides. An eight-foot high wire mesh fence ran along the final side, beyond which lay a small scrap of derelict land. A short driveway connected the car park with the Hackney High Road, and a narrow alleyway – the likely location of the murder – ran down one side of the building leading to Dalston Way.

'Was anything found with the body?'

Gorton shook her head. 'No handbag, no phone. But she was wearing this.' She handed Denning a clear plastic evidence bag containing a thin sliver necklace with the name 'Tanya' engraved on it.

At least this time they had a name.

Chapter Twenty-Five

'There's no evidence to suggest it's the work of the same man. I accept there are some superficial similarities, like the level of violence involved in the murder, and the location of the body, but so far there's nothing to link this victim with Leanne Wyatt.' Denning was sitting in McKenna's office, trying not to look at the near-dead cyclamen. She sat opposite him, drumming her nicotine-stained fingers on the desktop, fixing him with her gimlet stare, probably unaware she was doing either.

'Tanya,' she said, after a gap. 'Has anyone called Tanya been reported missing?'

He shook his head. 'Missing Persons haven't come up with anything. Though it would be helpful if we had a surname.'

The finger-drumming continued for a few more seconds, then abruptly stopped. 'Has the name come up during enquiries into Kane and Bailey?'

Denning had to confess it hadn't.

'Mid-to-late thirties...?' She thought for a moment. 'Do we know what Bailey's ex-wife was called?'

'As far as I know she's called Joanne and now lives in Canada. We're still waiting for our Canadian counterparts to get back to us with contact details, but it would help if we knew whereabouts in Canada she is.'

'Mid-to-late thirties,' she repeated. 'Roughly the same age as Bailey.' She looked directly at Denning. 'I'm guessing Joanne Bailey would be of a similar age?'

Denning shook his head. 'We don't know. We don't know much about her at this stage.'

McKenna sat back on her chair and ran her hand through her hair, unconsciously tugging at a clump with her fist. 'Theory: what if the former Mrs Bailey wasn't in Canada after all, but actually here in the UK? Daryl Bailey murders his teenage mistress after she threatens to tell his ex-wife about their affair, then he murders his ex because she found out anyway – threatened to tell the school what a sleazebag he is, maybe even threatened to tout the story round the press?' She released the clump of hair, which splayed like a raven's wing on the top of her head. 'OK, I know it sounds insane, but it's a theory?'

Denning pulled a face. 'Until we ID the body, it's all just speculation. And why kill her in a car park?' He looked back at McKenna, met her gaze, refusing to be intimidated by any gimlet stare, conscious or otherwise. 'It's a bit of a leap of faith to assume this is Bailey's ex-wife.' He rubbed his chin. 'I'm still not convinced there's any connection with Leanne Wyatt's murder. The MO's similar, but there are significant differences. Leanne Wyatt's murder seemed organised, this feels more opportunistic. Random. Plus there doesn't seem to be a sexual motive here.'

McKenna pursed her lips. 'Have we ruled out a robbery-gone-wrong scenario? Her bag and phone are missing.'

'But not her necklace. It looked like solid silver to me. No mugger's going to leave that behind.'

McKenna clasped her hair again. 'But we're not ruling Bailey out for this yet, are we?'

He shook his head. 'Definitely not. He's good for Leanne Wyatt, and he's a possibility for this.' He wrinkled his brow at her. 'Should we bring Bailey in for questioning for Leanne Wyatt? Make things official?'

She shook her head. 'Not yet. Wait until we've ID'd our latest victim. If there's anything, and I mean *anything* to link Daryl Bailey with this "Tanya", we bring him.'

Molly had been surprised to get a phone call from Magda Kilbride suggesting that they meet, and saying she wanted a chat. Molly's initial instinct was to fob her off with an excuse, but curiosity had got the better of her.

The Pig and Whistle was a trendy gastro pub beside the river in Battersea, not far from the monument to utilitarian architecture that was the former power station. The whole area, it appeared, was undergoing some major urban regeneration.

The pub was busy with a lively throng of lunchtime drinkers: a heady mix of business-people and tourists, all enjoying the summer sun.

Mags was sitting in the beer garden at the back of the pub, which overlooked the river. She was chatting on her mobile phone, but abruptly ended the call as soon as she saw Molly approach. 'What do you want to drink?' she asked before Molly's backside had even made contact with the chair. She was dressed in black, just like the first time they'd met. This time her hair seemed to be a different shade of magenta; lighter and less aggressive, but perhaps the intense sunlight had somehow tempered its fury.

Molly asked for a pint of Kronenbourg. Mags barked their drinks order at a passing waiter: a pint and a sparkling mineral water for herself. Molly briefly wondered if she should have requested something non-alcoholic too: she imagined a clear head might be wise when dealing with someone as slippery as Magda Kilbride.

The beer garden was large and airy and decorated with colourful plants in ceramic pots. Sweet-scented honeysuckle wound its way round a decorative trellis beside their table. Beyond the low wall lay the Thames, snaking its way through the city with a casual indifference.

The waiter returned and placed their drinks on the table. He smiled and asked if they wanted anything to eat. Molly spotted menus on the table. She felt her stomach rumble but suspected Magda Kilbride's largesse was unlikely to extend as far as lunch. However, she didn't get the chance to find out as Mags dismissed the waiter with a curt nod of her magenta-topped head.

She raised her glass at Molly. 'You've been rattling cages from what I hear.'

Molly wrinkled her brow. 'Sorry...?'

'Rumour has it your visit to Kenneth Walters has stirred up more than just his Sanatogen.'

'Really?'

Mags stared at Molly in silence for a moment. She took a sip of mineral water and offered up a vulpine smile. 'Word is, he's been in touch with a couple of his old cronies to ask if there's any truth in whatever tale you told him. I hope you kept your story simple.' She continued smiling at Molly. 'I believe he also asked about you.'

'What about me?'

The vulpine smile remained fixed on her face. 'Well, that's what we'd all like to know, isn't it?'

Molly drank some of her pint: it hit her empty stomach like a boxer's punch. Molly hoped word hadn't got back to her DI about her informal investigation into the Ferguson case, and the awkward explanations that would involve. 'What do you mean by that?' she asked.

She sensed Mags was playing games with her; hoping to find the right buttons to push.

Mags took another sip of her drink. She looked directly at Molly from over the top of the glass. 'What's the real reason behind your interest in Anthony Ferguson?'

Molly shrugged, trying to make it look casual. She couldn't believe she'd already drunk more than half her pint, and was beginning to regret not having asked for a soft drink. 'I told you last time we met.'

'Oh yes, something about new evidence coming to light.' The vulpine smile returned. 'Retired old fools like Ken Walters might buy that old tosh, but some of us are cynical enough to know bullshit when we smell it.'

Another silence fell upon the table like a mourner at a wake. After a few moments Molly asked, 'Who told you about Ken Walters?'

This time it was Mags's turn to shrug. 'I have my contacts. And as I'm sure Jon's told you, a good journalist never discloses her sources.' She circled a manicured finger round the rim of her glass. 'Let's just say I have a mate who owed me a favour.' That smile again. 'I presume you mentioned me to Jon? What did he say about me? Was he happy to reminisce about the good old days?'

Molly stared out at the river. It looked blue and clear in the blinding sun, and the word 'opalescent' sprang to mind. There were people rowing up the river, heading west towards Maidenhead, where her Aunt Mim lived. On the distant bank builders were encasing another over-priced apartment block in a skeletal cocoon of scaffolding.

Normal things in a normal world.

'Jon remembers you,' she said after a moment, then added, 'he also said you were a fantasist.'

Magda Kilbride threw out her half-cackle, half-bray that passed for a laugh. 'Ouch. Well that hurts. I mean, I wasn't expecting him to do cartwheels at the mention of my name, but surely our dalliance meant *something*.' She gave another laugh. 'Well, you can tell Jon I'm disappointed. I thought I meant more to him than that.' She paused. 'Does he still have that tattoo of a dragon on his... well, let's just say, in an intimate area?'

Molly could feel her heartbeat quicken. The alcohol was now swimming round her brain as well as her stomach. Her gut reaction was to get up and walk out. Or rather, throw what was left of her drink in Mags's smug face, call her a fucking liar, then get up and walk out. But her glass was almost empty and Mags would doubtless claim the gesture as a victory. Instead she took a deep breath and said, 'Jon's an adult. I don't own him any more than he owns me. Besides, we all do things we regret, and I don't see why I should condemn him for one lapse of judgement, however long ago.'

Magda smiled again. 'Just one…?' She held up her drink to her lips as though about to take another sip, but instead just held it there, poised in mid-air. 'I don't suppose he's told you about Melanie Harris…?' She wobbled her head from one side to the other. 'No, I didn't think he would have. In all fairness, it was a long time ago, just after his second marriage went tits up, and she was young and pretty, in a naïve kind of a way. But that didn't stop your boyfriend mooning round her like a lovesick poodle: sending her flowers, hanging round outside her flat… I mean nobody actually used the word *stalking*, but you get the picture…' She gave an indifferent shrug. 'The paper intervened before the police got involved and the whole thing was hushed up. She was persuaded to drop the harassment case she planned to bring against the paper. Jon kept his job, but he got his wings clipped.'

Another silence followed. Molly was tempted to order another drink simply so she could have something to throw over Mags, but she didn't want to waste the energy, or the drink. Instead she stood up, grabbed her bag, and said, 'Well, he was right about one thing: you are a fucking fantasist.'

As she left the bar she was convinced she could hear Magda's cackle follow her down the street.

Chapter Twenty-Six

'Christ, I've known pathologists miss stuff before, but failing to spot a pair of knackers and a Johnson has to be a first.'

Denning was back in the airtight vacuum that passed for McKenna's office, sweat trickling down his neck. The air in the office seemed to be getting thinner, as though McKenna had had the room hermetically sealed off from the rest of the building.

'I suppose it was easy to miss at the crime scene,' he said. 'The pathologists usually only do a basic examination of the body in situ, and we were all keen to get away from there as quickly as possible. The stench from the bins was rank, to put it mildly.' He looked at McKenna and rubbed his hand over his right temple. His mouth felt uncomfortably dry.

'Don't get me wrong, I'm not excusing Bevan. This *is* incompetence on his part but, to be fair, I could have done a more thorough check myself. Or at the very least, ensured he'd done a more detailed examination at the time.'

He glanced at the pathologist's report sitting on McKenna's desk: the folder was open and the first sentence of the first page revealed the startling news that their victim was a thirty-eight-year-old man. Denning realised now what had struck him as odd when he'd looked at the body, besides the wig-like hair: the hands had seemed too large for a woman.

'You'll get no argument from me. But the fact is we've all fucked up. Fortunately we held back on the press release, otherwise we really would look like a bunch of twats.' She sat back in her chair and he could feel her gimlet stare bore into him. 'So, what are we talking here? Tranny? Pre-op? And is it relevant to why he was killed?'

Denning shrugged. 'Until we have a name, and I mean an *actual* name, we can only make guesses.' He paused. 'However, we can rule one thing out.'

'What?'

'This wasn't Joanne Bailey.'

'Unless Bailey was married to a transvestite,' McKenna said dryly.

'I think the term is "crossdresser" these days,' Denning said, ignoring the icy look she shot him. 'And apparently Joanne Bailey is alive and well. We've just heard back from the Canadian Police. Seems she was on holiday in New Zealand and only got back last night. But she can't shed any light on Bailey's alleged affairs, claiming it was all a long time ago and she's moved on. She claims she knows nothing about any flings with underage girls. It looks like we might be back to square one re Daryl Bailey.' He tried to keep the disappointment out of his voice. 'I think we're now looking at two entirely unconnected murder investigations.'

McKenna sighed deeply 'Fucking bollocks.' She shot Denning a wry look. 'No pun intended.'

–

As soon as Molly arrived at the hospital she could sense something was wrong. Adam Sloane's mother was sitting in the waiting area just behind the nurses' station, her face drained of colour. She was clasping a plastic cup of what looked like tea, staring at it without appearing to register what it was.

'Mrs Sloane.' Molly said softly. 'Debbie...' She sat down next to her, clinging to the desperate hope that she wasn't about to hear the news she'd been dreading.

'He suffered a fatal coronary embolism about an hour ago.'

Molly saw that tears had dried on Debbie Sloane's cheeks. Her voice was raw, the words leaden and empty.

Molly placed a hand on her arm. 'I'm so sorry. I'm sorry for what you're going through and I'm sorry we haven't managed to bring anyone to justice for this. But we will. I promise you.' But even as she spoke the words she knew they'd be of little comfort.

She nodded. Molly could only imagine her pain. She knew what it felt like to lose someone close, but not a child. That was something beyond her understanding. That kind of grief was something she couldn't comprehend. How did a mother assimilate that agony?

'Is there anyone I can call?'

Debbie just shook her head. She seemed in a daze, as though the reality of what had just happened had yet to sink in.

Molly glanced into the room where Adam Sloane had been lying for the previous two weeks. It was empty, the sheets already stripped from the bed. Adam's body would already be in the mortuary awaiting a suitable slot for a post–mortem. A young life had been snuffed out before he had even had a chance to make his mark on the world. 'I will need to take another statement from you,' Molly said gently. 'But that can wait.' She looked at the traumatised woman sitting on a hospital chair staring into a plastic cup of cold tea, barely aware of what was happening around her. 'I'll ask someone from the family liaison unit to get in touch with you. It'll be some support.' Debbie nodded again, like a puppet being pulled by invisible strings.

'You've got my number. If you ever need to talk, just call me.'

There was nothing more Molly could say. It was likely Debbie had already stopped listening to her. What she needed now was time and space to grieve.

Molly headed outside. She reached into her top pocket for her cigarettes, dug her lighter from her bag, lit up, leaned against a wall and inhaled, relaxing her shoulders as she felt the welcome nicotine kick hit her system.

It was difficult to suppress the guilt she felt. If she hadn't allowed herself to be distracted chasing the ghosts of the past, they might have brought someone to task for this by now. A young man was dead, little more than a boy, and she had failed in her duty of care.

Chapter Twenty-Seven

Lucy Russell was in her late teens, possibly early twenties, blonde and willowy, with sad eyes and a firm handshake. She led Denning and Neeraj into the compact flat she shared with two other art students in an Edwardian block not far from Wandsworth Common. The living room was decorated with joss sticks and candles, and abstract photographs of children and animals filled the walls. Lucy Russell was dressed in a washed-out man's checked shirt and a pair of torn dungarees; the front of which was adorned with splashes of dried paint.

'We knew about Dad,' she said, sitting opposite them on a squishy beanbag. Denning and Neeraj sat on a faded leather sofa that looked like it had once belonged in the back of a Ford Cortina. Someone had written 'K+L' in Tippex on one arm of the sofa.

Lucy Russell flicked a loose strand of blonde hair from her pale face. She'd reported her father missing earlier that afternoon. When she couldn't get an answer from his mobile phone, she'd rung one of his neighbours. She'd gone round to his flat, but there had been no answer at his front door. Then she'd contacted the police. It was, she'd told them, very out of character for him not to be in touch.

Tony Russell was an unemployed divorcé who had lived in Islington. He was also a crossdresser whose alter ego went by the name Tanya.

'Mum was cool with it,' Lucy added, 'or as cool as anyone can be about these things.'

'How long had he been doing it?' Neeraj asked. His tone suggested that he equated transvestism with paedophilia in the list of life's perversions.

She looked at Denning when she answered. 'I don't know; a while. Possibly from before they were married. It wasn't something we discussed much.'

'When you say your mum was "cool" with it, how much did she know about his other life?' Denning kept his voice, neutral; trying to sound non-judgmental.

'She knew about "Tanya". She even helped with his make-up sometimes; suggesting a softer blusher, or a subtler eye-liner. Mum used to joke that it was one thing being a transvestite, it was another thing looking like one.' Her shoulders dropped. 'I mean, don't get me wrong, it wasn't plain sailing. She was always concerned about friends and neighbours finding out, but I think that was because she worried they wouldn't understand and would make my dad's life difficult.' She threw a glance at Neeraj, sitting uncomfortably on the car seat of a sofa. 'Some people think cross-dressing is weird, but that's mostly to do with their own issues rather than other people's.'

Denning suppressed a smile 'Did it play a part in your parents splitting up?' he asked.

She shook her head. 'No. Looking back, I suppose it didn't help, but they split up because of the usual stuff: money, work. They'd been together since they were teenagers, so it wasn't an easy decision. Mum's remarried now.'

'Lucy, I know this may seem like a tactless question, but I have to ask it: was your dad gay?'

She looked from Denning to Neeraj and back to Denning. 'Most people make that assumption, but no, my dad wasn't gay.' She sat back on the beanbag and offered them a weak smile. 'It's hard to explain, but...'

'Try to,' Denning suggested. 'Take your time.'

She picked at a loose thread on the beanbag. 'When he was Tanya, it was like a different personality took over. Tanya enjoyed the company of men. She liked flirting, and enjoyed the attention men paid her. She liked men buying her drinks, and I suppose, deep down, she revelled in the idea of them finding her attractive.' She shrugged. 'Maybe it's something in all of us: the need to satisfy the masculine and feminine sides of our personality.' She fixed Neeraj with a kind smile, which he didn't return. 'I honestly don't think it was anything to do with sex,' she said.

'You're sure?' Denning asked.

She nodded. 'I'm pretty sure my dad never took things any further than flirting.'

'But he might have done?' Denning fixed her with a reassuring smile. He didn't want to make things any harder for her than they already were, what with losing her dad and having to talk openly about private and personal matters, but he had to determine why Tanya Russell had been killed. If Tanya had been picked up by someone who had expected one thing and got another, it could be a strong motive for murder. He'd seen *The Crying Game*. He knew how easy it was to mislead someone, even innocently.

Lucy Russell stopped plucking at the loose thread. She placed her hands on her lap, and Denning saw tears prickle in her eyes. 'I'm not entirely sure I can explain it. I think, maybe, it was a self-esteem thing. Dad was...' she dabbed at her eyes, shook her head and continued, 'he was a lovely guy, but he wasn't the sort of person who'd stand out in a crowd. It's not that he was shy exactly, more reserved. He came from a very conservative background; he'd worked in banking and had few very close friends. Tanya enabled him to become someone else: someone attractive and glamorous, even though it was a lie.'

Neeraj shuffled his feet awkwardly. Denning asked, 'Where did Tanya go to meet men?'

'She would hang around bars – straight bars – and sometimes clubs. I think she belonged to a website for men who were attracted to cross-dressers, though I don't think she ever actually had the nerve to meet up with anyone she chatted to online.'

'Websites…?' Denning tried to keep the surprise from his voice.

She smiled at him. 'Yes, it came as a shock to me too, but apparently there are straight men out there who get turned on by transvestites.' She sighed again. 'I suppose it takes all sorts.'

'Did any of the men he met ever turn violent?' Neeraj asked.

She shook her head. 'He never said if they did, but I don't think so. Usually the men were either totally oblivious, or too pissed to care.' She smiled again, happy memories overtaking the sadder ones. 'Tanya was very convincing, even close up. Especially with my mum's help. She always said there were times even she found it difficult to tell.'

'Was there a particular bar Tanya liked to frequent?' Denning asked.

She shook her head. 'I honestly don't know. I never really enquired. It's not an easy conversation to have with your dad. Don't get me wrong, I loved him and I didn't have a problem with what he did, but like I said, it wasn't something we discussed much.'

'What about last night?' Neeraj asked. 'Do you know where he went?'

Again she shook her head. 'I'm sorry, I wish I could help you more.'

'Perhaps your mother might be able to throw some light on his movements?'

'Mum remarried about four years ago. She hasn't seen my dad in all that time. My sister lives in Wolverhampton, and she and my dad were never close.'

'Was there anyone else in his life? A partner? Friends?'

She wiped away another tear with the back of her hand. 'My father was a very private man, Inspector. There was so much I didn't know about him. Perhaps it's only now that I fully realise that. But, no, he wasn't seeing anyone after he and my mum divorced. I don't know about friends, but I'm pretty sure what friends he had knew nothing about his other life.'

She paused, as though unsure about saying anything more.

'Anything you tell us, Miss Russell, will be treated in absolute confidence,' Denning soothed. 'And anything, no matter how trivial or seemingly irrelevant might be useful in catching your father's killer.'

Lucy Russell nodded and cleared her throat. 'Dad was very clean-cut; he rarely drank and never took drugs.' She clasped her hands together and tried to squeeze her body into a tight shape. 'Tanya, however, did use recreational drugs from time to time. Cocaine mostly, but only sometimes, and usually when needing a bit of a confidence boost.'

'You wouldn't know where your dad… I mean, where Tanya would have got her drugs from?' Denning asked.

Lucy Russell shook her head, but Denning was sure he could hazard a fairly accurate guess.

Chapter Twenty-Eight

Tyler Rabas lived in a fourth-floor flat of a tall, soulless high rise on the Ashbrook estate, about half a mile north of Hackney. At first his mother refused to let Molly in, insisting that her son was out and defying Molly to suggest otherwise. It was only when Molly told her Adam Sloane was dead that she finally and reluctantly allowed Molly across the threshold.

The flat was neat and homely, decorated and furnished on a budget Molly surmised, but not without a nod towards creativity. A wooden sofa and matching armchairs were arranged around a low cabinet, on which sat the telly and some family photos. There were plenty of pictures of Tyler Rabas and his mother and young sister, but no suggestion of Tyler's father.

Tyler padded through to the living room when his mother called him. He looked sulky and petulant as though she'd interrupted something important, like his PlayStation, or a session chatting to mates on social media.

His mother introduced Molly as a police officer with the drugs' squad, and told him she wanted a word about Adam Sloane. He sat down on the edge of the sofa, looking for all the world like a little boy lost.

'Ty,' Molly began, keeping her voice level and calm. 'Adam died this morning.' She let the words sink in. She watched as he looked over to his mother before staring sullenly at his feet. Tyler Rabas was a teenage boy, so he wasn't going to show any emotion in front of a police officer, especially a female police officer, but she suspected he was struggling to take in the news about his best friend.

'I'm sorry,' he mumbled, still fixated on his feet.

'I'm sure you are, Ty. And I really don't want to intrude on your grief any more than I have to, but I need to know who supplied Adam with the drugs. I need you to tell me who's responsible for killing him.' She was being deliberately blunt, trying to shock him into telling her what she needed to know. 'As you can imagine, his mother is devastated.' Molly looked at Tyler's mum, who sat tight-lipped on the other armchair, arms folded across her chest. She slowly shook her head at the mention of Adam's mum, doubtless imagining herself in Debbie Sloane's shoes.

Tyler looked up from his feet and glanced over at his mum. 'I don't know,' he muttered, refusing to meet Molly's gaze.

'I think you do, Ty. And I think you owe it to Adam to tell me.' She looked at him, her voice still calm and sympathetic; her body language neutral and unthreatening. She wasn't going to get anywhere bullying the lad. 'You were Adam's best mate. You were with him the night he took the Ecstasy. You were going to a friend's party, that's right, isn't it? You wanted to have a good time. You knew how to get hold of drugs.'

He nodded slowly. 'It was Adam's idea,' he said, a slight catch in his voice. 'I said I'd get some booze. I knew where I could get some vodka, but Adam said he wanted something harder.'

'I'm not judging you, Ty, and I'm certainly not blaming you.' She pulled herself forward on the sofa so that she was only inches away from Tyler's face. 'We all do silly and impulsive things sometimes, things we later regret. And sometimes we wish that we could go back in time and do things differently. But we can't. However, we can do the right thing if we're given the opportunity to do so.' She was so close to him, she could smell his sweat. The redness in his eyes told her she was getting through to him. 'Ty, this is your opportunity to do the right thing now, and tell me who sold Adam the drugs.'

He looked up at his mum again. She reached out and put a hand on his arm. 'Ty, if you do know anything, you need to speak up.'

He shook his head again.

'Ty, was it Gregor Kane?' Molly asked. 'Was he the person who sold Adam the Ecstasy?'

She waited for an answer. He didn't speak, just continued to stare intently at his feet. Eventually he nodded.

It was the admission she'd been waiting for, but she needed to be certain. 'You're sure, Ty? Gregor Kane provided Adam with the Ecstasy?'

'Yes,' he replied. 'It was Gregor. He used to hang round the school. Everyone bought gear off Gregor.' His voice was blank; sticking to cold, bare facts; keeping emotion at bay.

Molly thanked him. He would have to come down to the station and make an official statement confirming what he'd just told her, but that could wait. It was likely they would have to offer the family police protection once it was made formal: grassing on a member of the Kane family wasn't going to make their lives easy in the Ashbrook estate, or anywhere in east London for that matter.

Once she was outside, she phoned her boss. 'Boss, we've got Gregor Kane,' she said. 'We can bring him in at last.' But even as she spoke she had a feeling this was just the beginning of their problems rather than the end.

Chapter Twenty-Nine

'Tony Russell, otherwise known as Tanya Russell. Cause of death: a fractured skull, causing a bleed on the brain. His badly beaten body was found in a car park behind a KFC earlier today. Motive, as yet unknown.' Denning addressed the group. There was a photograph of Tony Russell on the whiteboard, next to one of Tanya taken from the website his daughter had mentioned. If he looked closely, it was possible to see Tony Russell hiding behind Tanya's made-up face and slicked blonde wig. But Lucy Russell was right: Tanya was convincing. The other photo, taken post-mortem, showed a face twisted out of shape by repeated blows. The level of violence suggested that whoever had done this had revelled in the sheer brutality of it.

'We've got a tranny-basher out there now too, as well as a psycho killer,' Dave Kinsella said. He shook his head; Denning wasn't sure if it signified disgust or despair.

'Like I said, Dave: no known motive as yet, so let's try not to jump to conclusions. And can we please avoid using expressions like "tranny-basher". Tanya Russell is a victim and will be treated with the same respect as all victims. We're not here to judge either the victim or how she chose to live her life. The victim identified as female and that is how we will refer to her.'

The room fell silent. Denning was sure he spotted Kinsella's face redden as he exchanged a glance with another officer. 'The good news is that forensics got some DNA this time. Unfortunately the DNA database drew a blank.'

'So whoever it was has no previous?' Kinsella asked.

'Looks that way, Dave. But it does mean that when we do finally arrest someone for this, we have something solid in the way of evidence.'

'Are we definitely ruling out a connection with Leanne Wyatt?' Trudi asked.

'At this stage, Trudi, yes.' Denning was determined to treat the two cases separately. There was still nothing concrete to suggest an obvious link. Trudi and Ryan had been going over Tanya Russell's laptop, checking the details of anyone who had visited Tanya's profile on the dating website. It was going to take time to get names and addresses as, perhaps understandably, most of the site's users were keen to maintain their anonymity. It was also possible that this was an entirely random attack: transphobic crimes were on the rise in the capital and cases like Tanya Russell's were becoming depressingly common. 'However, we know that Tanya was an occasional cocaine user. We don't know who supplied her, but we do know who the main dealer is in this area.'

'Gregor Kane,' Trudi offered.

'More than likely, but I can't see Kane admitting anything. And besides, this doesn't look like it's drugs-related, at least not on the surface.'

'Russell could have owed Kane money. That's a motive,' Neeraj said.

'Again, that's a possible avenue worth exploring,' Denning said. 'However, according to the post-mortem there were no traces of cocaine or any other drug found in Tanya Russell's system when she was killed, and speaking to his daughter, I get the impression she was only a light user.'

Kinsella said, 'Maybe he found out Tanya was a bloke and went for him. I don't reckon Gregor Kane's much of a tranny lover.' He looked round the room, then added, 'Sorry, lover of people who cross dress.'

Denning waited a moment before he replied. 'That's not Kane's style. He's living in his daddy's shadow, a wannabe gangster. Beating someone up if they get in his way, perhaps, but this is in a different league. Anyway, at this stage, any connection to Gregor Kane is tenuous.'

'Sorry if I'm being naïve,' Ryan Cormack said, 'but are we sure we want to rule out a connection between this and Leanne Wyatt? I mean the manner of the murders is very similar...'

'Except "Tanya" wasn't raped,' said Kinsella, 'for obvious reasons.'

'It's possible whoever did it didn't know about Tanya...' Ryan said, ignoring the sniggering that rippled round the room. 'All I'm saying is, maybe we're being a bit hasty in assuming the cases are unconnected.'

'Tanya didn't have a cross engraved on her forehead,' Trudi said.

'Maybe he only does that after he's sexually assaulted them.' Ryan Cormack seemed determined to push the point. 'Perhaps it's some kind of marker.'

Denning looked at the two whiteboards: one for Leanne Wyatt, another for Tanya Russell. Similar, but different...

'OK, so if we're saying there *is* a connection, what are we talking about?' He looked around the room. 'I'm not sure that's a route any of us wants to go down unless we have to.'

There was a general murmuring from the room. He saw Dave Kinsella shake his head again. Denning raised his hands until there was calm. 'For the time being, we treat the two cases separately. As soon we get any evidence that points us in a different direction, then we'll start exploring other options. Until then, let's find out all we can about Tanya Russell, also known by the name Tony Russell: talk to colleagues and anyone who frequented the same bars and clubs as Tanya. Speak to anyone who might have seen Tanya with someone on the night she was killed. Let's go over any CCTV footage from the area. Unlike Leanne Wyatt, Tanya Russell was killed where she was found. Whoever's responsible has to have been spotted. Which means we put out an appeal for eye-witnesses, and plough over CTTV.'

'There's no CCTV at the back of the restaurant,' Neeraj said. 'There's some in the restaurant itself, and covering the staff entrance at the rear, but it doesn't cover the car park. We're checking the CCTV from the main road, but it's going to take time.'

'OK. We keep going over the CCTV footage. If Tanya shows up, then there's a strong chance her killer will be there too.' Denning noticed Dave Kinsella looking twitchy. 'Dave, is there something you want to add?'

'Where does this leave us with the Leanne Wyatt investigation? Are we putting it on the back-burner to focus on Tanya Russell, or does finding her killer remain a priority?'

'Both cases are being treated as a priority, Dave. Irrespective of whether or not there's a connection.'

There was another ripple of murmured chatter from the group. Denning understood their frustration at the slow progress. He understood it and took full responsibility for it. 'Look, I know it's frustrating. We have two suspects and no evidence to connect either one to Leanne's murder. But we will find Leanne Wyatt's killer, just as we'll get whoever did this to Tanya Russell.'

'And just how close are we to getting anyone for Leanne Wyatt?' Kinsella asked. 'Or even to finding out exactly where she was killed?'

Denning looked at Leanne's photograph on the whiteboard. Her innocent smile made her look much younger than twenty-one. 'Our taxi driver swears he dropped them off at the junction of Highgate Road and Hadley Drive in north London.' He pointed at the map on one of the whiteboards. 'We need to get uniform out knocking on doors in that whole area, and have a look at any CCTV.'

'We've been down there already,' Neeraj argued. 'We didn't get anything last time.'

'We focused on Hadley Drive last time, Deep, because that's where we thought the taxi dropped them off. We need to cover a wider area now. Speak to anyone who saw or heard anything suspicious on the night in question.'

Denning was on the point of adding something further, when he spotted DCI McKenna's office door opening. McKenna marched over to the front of the room and nodded at Denning. 'Sorry to interrupt guys, but I thought you might like to know: CID have got Gregor Kane downstairs. They're charging him with manslaughter. Apparently he wants to talk to someone about Leanne Wyatt's murder.'

Chapter Thirty

Kane was being questioned in Interview Room One on the ground floor. Denning was asked by a uniformed officer to wait in the corridor whilst he notified the detectives that he wanted a word. A few moments later the door to Interview Room One opened and a man and woman approached him.

'DI Denning?' the man asked, extending his hand in Denning's direction. 'I'm DI Broomfield, this is Detective Sergeant Fisher.' He indicated the short, mousy-blonde woman standing on his right.

Denning shook their hands. 'What's he said so far?'

'Nothing more than a stream of "no comments",' Broomfield said. 'But the interesting thing is that his father has refused to appoint the usual family solicitor, Tom Gracey from Gracey & Co. He's the smooth-tongued bastard we usually deal with whenever Kane's been pulled in. This time round he's been appointed a duty solicitor, but apart from advising Kane to say nothing until we produce any hardcore evidence, she's done very little.'

'What evidence have you got?'

'A written statement from a friend of the victim claiming Kane sold him the gear. We've got a warrant to search the Kane residence in Chigwell, but as you can imagine, Alfie Kane is kicking up a stink.'

'Why did he refuse to send the family solicitor?'

Broomfield shrugged. 'It seems daddy Kane has a thing about drugs. I mean he's quite happy to burn someone's house down, or kneecap their dog if they cross him, but even he appears to draw a line at selling dodgy gear to kids. I imagine Gracey is round at Château Kane now, trying to make life as difficult as possible for our team.'

Denning tried not to laugh. It would be ironic if Gregor Kane were to be brought down by his own father. 'So what's the story with him and Leanne Wyatt?'

This time it was DS Fisher's turn to pipe up. 'He claims he was with her the night she was killed. He says he has information that might be useful to your murder inquiry.'

'Looks like he wants to do some kind of deal,' said Broomfield. 'He knows we really want him to name the big boys: whoever it is who's supplying him so we can set Trident on them. If he plays ball, he'll talk, he might need some inducement.' He smiled at Denning. 'You may well be that inducement.'

Denning scratched his chin. 'Do you think he's genuine? I don't want to waste my time with that little twat if all he wants to do is play silly sods.'

'We know he's connected to Leanne Wyatt, and we know you still haven't got anyone for her murder, so it might be worth a try.' It was Fisher again. There was a hint of impertinence in her tone, and Denning wondered how come she knew so much about the Leanne Wyatt case, but he decided to let it lie.

'He's facing a manslaughter charge and his daddy's dropped him in the shitter. He's desperate,' Broomfield said. 'DS Fisher's right: if he knows anything about her murder, now's the time he's going to play his hand.'

Denning nodded. 'Fair enough.'

Broomfield paused before letting him pass. 'There's just one thing.' He looked at Denning; his stony face easing itself into a slow smile. 'DS Fisher would like to sit in on the interview.'

'Leanne Wyatt's murder is an MIT matter. You can finish interviewing Kane after I've spoken to him.'

Broomfield's expression softened slightly. 'I appreciate it's slightly irregular, but it was DS Fisher who got us Kane, after months of little or no progress. The slippery bastard was always one step ahead of us. She's a good officer: she wants to work in MIT. As a favour, would you let her sit in on the interview? She won't speak, just observe.'

He wasn't happy. This went beyond impertinence and bordered on being unprofessional. But he got the distinct impression Broomfield was implacable. DS Fisher stood next to him, a defiant look in her eyes.

'OK,' he said after a moment. 'But she keeps her mouth shut.'

—

Kane had lost the swagger which had been so on display at their previous meeting. He sat back on the creaky plastic chair with his arms folded defiantly in front of him, but the posture looked more defensive than anything else, as though he was trying to protect himself. He looked up at Denning as soon as he walked into to the interview room and Denning thought he saw the briefest traces of a smirk on his face.

Denning sat down opposite Kane, Fisher sat beside him. Fisher clicked the tape recorder back on and they both gave their names, Denning adding that he was from the murder squad.

'You have some information about the murder of Leanne Wyatt?' Denning said. 'Care to share it?'

Kane looked at his solicitor, a bored-looking woman in her late twenties with neatly ironed hair and a face like a smacked backside. 'Before I say anything, I want some assurance it'll be taken into account with this bollocks charge of manslaughter.' The diamond stud in his ear flashed as it caught the light.

'I advise you to say nothing until the police can provide proper evidence to—' his solicitor started to say.

'Shut it!' Kane barked. She immediately fell silent.

Kane looked uncharacteristically worried. The smirk that had greeted their arrival had quickly disappeared. Denning suspected that without the protection of his father, he was nothing more than a little boy lost in a world of grown-ups.

Kane's solicitor rolled her eyes and looked at the tape machine, pursing her lips together and slightly grinding her teeth.

'Well, go on,' Kane said. He was staring directly at Denning, exuding faux arrogance like a bad smell.

'That'll be up to CID,' Denning told him. 'It's their case, not mine.'

'Then no deal,' said Kane.

'If you know anything that helps us catch Leanne's killer, then it will go in your favour, Gregor.' It was Fisher this time; so much for agreeing to keep quiet.

Denning shot her a look. However, he knew there was little he could say to challenge her: the manslaughter charge was their call, not his.

'I promise you anything you can tell us about Leanne Wyatt will help your case,' she continued.

Denning bristled at the mention of 'us': Leanne Wyatt was nothing to do with Fisher or her chums in CID. He was beginning to regret agreeing to let her sit on the interview.

Kane looked at Fisher, then turned and looked at Denning. Just for a second Denning thought he saw something pass across Kane's face that might have been fear, or at least the realisation that there was a good chance he was heading for jail. Kane wasn't an idiot; he knew the minute he was off the scene some other lowlife would fill the void. Even a short spell inside would see his reputation dented and his patch taken over by a rival. He could fight his way back in, of course; he was Alfie Kane's boy and that carried some clout. But was it worth the aggro... Would Kane be willing to take the risk?

'All right,' Kane said, after a gap. 'Here's how it is: if I tell you what I know about the night Leanne was killed, you agree to drop the manslaughter charge, and forget any thought about doing me for dealing.'

'That's not up to me, Gregor,' Denning said. 'I can't promise you anything. But if you *do* know something, it really is in your best interests to tell us now. If we later find out you deliberately withheld information, it won't look good for you.' Denning could see Kane's solicitor pursing her lips together even tighter; there was a danger she was going to explode any minute. She opened her mouth for a brief second, then closed it again before any words had the chance to escape.

A heavy sigh ruffled the solicitor's papers on the table. Kane unfolded his arms and sat forward on his chair. 'All right, I met Leanne that night, just before I went to the club. She wanted to buy some gear, just some uppers. She told me she was meeting someone. She thought he was going to finish with her. She was pretty cut up about it. She'd been feeling shit. She said she wanted something to give her a lift, so I sold her a bit of whizz.'

Denning waited for him to finish. 'Is that—'

'Did she say who the date was with?' Fisher asked, before Denning had a chance to finish what he was saying.

Kane rubbed his hands over his face in a swift move. 'She gave me some tosh about wanting to get back with me. She kept reminding me that Charlie was my kid. I told her to piss off. I didn't want anything to do with her or him. I've only got her word that Charlie's mine.'

'When was this?' Denning asked.

He shrugged. 'Just before I went to the club. About nine-ish, maybe slightly before.'

Denning leaned in closer. He could smell Kane's aftershave: something expensive, naturally, though somehow it smelt a little sickly, like it had been mixed with something toxic. 'Did she tell you anything about the man she was planning to meet?'

He looked up at the two detectives. 'Yeah. She said it was Daryl Bailey.'

Chapter Thirty-One

'Claire phoned,' Sarah said, as soon as Denning entered the flat. 'Apparently her new man friend wants to take her and Jake to Paris for a few days next week. She didn't think you'd mind as you're so busy working this case.'

There was an open bottle of Sauvignon Blanc on the dining table and the smell of Moroccan chicken wafted from the kitchen area. Sarah was sitting on one of the sofas, listening to Classic FM and sipping a glass of Sauvignon.

He took off his jacket and hung it on the back of one of the dining chairs.

'When did she phone?'

'About half an hour ago. I told her you'd be back in a bit if she wanted to speak to you herself.'

Denning knew Claire would have found it easier to talk to Sarah. Although the two women were hardly friends, Claire knew there was less chance of Sarah being confrontational when it came to Jake.

He tried not to let his annoyance show. He wanted to see Jake. He wanted to go somewhere normal as a father and son; remind himself that there was a life beyond ongoing murder inquiries. But it looked like family time was a luxury he was going to have to defer for the foreseeable. It was fair enough that Claire wanted to spend time with Jake and her new man, but Denning couldn't escape the feeling that Alan Marsden was taking over his role as a father to Jake, and there didn't seem to be much he could do about it.

He remembered the name of Marsden's company and made a mental note to call round the next day. It was time he had a chat with the man who now seemed to be part of his extended family, whether he liked it or not.

—

Molly closed the front door behind her. She was mentally and physical shattered, and wanted nothing more taxing than a large glass of Shiraz and a takeaway.

She shouted for Jon but no answer came.

Heading into the living room, she flopped down into Jon's old leather armchair that faced the telly, and kicked off her shoes. A heavy fug of heat clung to every corner of the room, but she couldn't be bothered opening the French windows.

It had been a hectic day.

In the end, despite his hollow attempt at doing a deal, they had charged Gregor Kane with manslaughter as well as supplying a Class A drug. He'd refused to say who'd supplied him with the gear; name whoever it was who was higher up the chain of command. Understandable. If he'd grassed, it wouldn't matter who his father was, he'd end up yet another grim statistic in the London drug gang wars. It was likely he would be looking at seven years, out in four, assuming a jury could be persuaded of his guilt – and that couldn't be taken for granted.

She had wanted to talk to DI Denning after the interview, ask him what bearing Kane's information would have on the murder investigation into Leanne Wyatt, but Denning had retreated back upstairs the minute the interview was over without even acknowledging her presence.

Trudi had been right about Denning being attractive, in an ageing boy-band member kind of way, but there was a hint of arrogance about him. She'd got the impression he'd resented her presence during the interview, and not because it wasn't standard procedure but because she was a DS with regular CID rather than one of the sexy players from MIT. But then, maybe she'd imagined it. He was clearly under pressure, maybe her presence had added to that pressure.

She knew she should probably have kept her mouth shut during the interview with Kane, but she felt connected to the murder case; she couldn't just sit back and say nothing. Denning had evidently not mentioned her outburst to Broomfield. She had fully expected an official reprimand: a summons to Broomfield's office followed by a dressing-down, but none had come.

She wasn't even sure Kane's information, assuming he was telling the truth, amounted to anything useful; a random name, possibly uttered to keep his own out the frame. There was something familiar about the name Daryl Bailey but she struggled to put a face to it. Perhaps she'd do an internet search after dinner, or maybe Jon would know.

Jon…

Her mind turned to Magda Kilbride. Molly knew she should mentally delete everything Mags had told her. She suspected Mags was someone who took pleasure in watching others squirm, like a scrawny cat playing with an injured bird. But somehow, deep down, she just couldn't dismiss what Mags had said quite as readily as she'd like to.

There was so much of Jon's life that remained a mystery to her. She knew he had a history before they'd met; they both had. She knew about the previous marriages, all of which had ended in divorce. She knew he could behave like an idiot when it came to women, and could be impetuous and silly and totally dick-led at times. But even so, she didn't recognise the picture of her boyfriend that Mags had so vividly painted.

Molly wanted to get up, go to the kitchen and open some wine; dig out her phone and call for a Chinese, or an Indian or anything that didn't involve having to stand in front of a stove in this inexorable heat, but her feet felt like lead weights embedded in quicksand.

She heard the key scraping in the lock on the front door. After a moment Jon appeared in the living room, carrying two

Tesco's bags full of food. A couple of bottles of wine poked out the top of one of the bags.

'All right,' he said, seemingly surprised to see her. 'When did you get back?'

'About five minutes ago,' she replied.

He headed into the kitchen with the groceries and she heard the clink of wine bottles being taken out of the carrier bags and placed on the worktop.

'Do you want a drink?' Jon shouted from the kitchen.

She told him she'd like a glass of wine. She could hear him clattering around in the kitchen; opening wine, pouring out two glasses. A few minutes later he entered the living room and handed Molly a glass of red wine. He placed the other glass on the coffee table and sat down on the ancient chaise longue.

'Another bitch of a day, huh?' he asked.

Molly took a sip of wine. She wanted to ask him about Mags, but instead she said, 'Do you know the name Daryl Bailey?'

'The footballer?'

She shrugged. 'I guess so.'

'What's he done?'

'I'm not sure he's done anything.' Her big toe toyed with the rim of her left shoe. 'His name came up today.' She paused. 'Does he still play football?'

'Nah, retired years ago. He was... well, let's just say he had a bit of a reputation. Why?'

'What kind of reputation?'

Jon pulled a face. 'First Anthony Ferguson, now Daryl Bailey. What's this all about?'

'What kind of reputation?' she repeated.

He smiled, but it quickly faded. 'There was a scandal, years back: something to do with him and an underage girl.'

'What happened?'

Jon scratched the stubble round his chin. 'He was rumoured to have been sexually involved with a teenage fan. Apparently Daryl Bailey likes women who haven't had too many birthdays.

Don't get me wrong, nothing was ever proved, and the matter was never made official, but it was rumoured that it cost him his job.' Jon gave a cynical laugh. 'Whatever the case, Bailey hasn't worked in professional football since.'

'I don't remember reading about this.' She took another sip of wine. 'When did it happen?'

He stretched out on the chaise longue, resting his head on its arm. Molly could hear the elderly settee creaking beneath his weight. 'About ten years ago, or thereabouts. The club paid everyone off: the girl in question, her parents. Even the press.'

'The press were paid off?'

'Either paid off or threatened with libel.'

'Libel? How could it be libellous if it was true?'

He laughed again. 'Don't be naïve, Molly. If no one is going to corroborate the story then legally the press were on dodgy ground.' He knocked back some wine. 'You'd be surprised how often that happens.'

'Why didn't the girl report the matter to the police?'

He gave another throaty chuckle. 'You'd have to ask her that.'

Molly thought the whole thing stank of something rotten. She wasn't sure who she blamed more: Bailey for being a pervert; the club for covering it up; the press for going along with it, or the girl herself – either she had deliberately lied to extort money from a gullible fool with more cash than brain cells, or she had betrayed herself and every other female victim of sexual exploitation by selling out. In much the same way, she couldn't stop herself from thinking, as Melanie Harris had sold out by agreeing to drop her harassment case against Jon: the same Jon who was sitting opposite her now, whose attitude seemed to suggest that the idea of older men harassing young women was a source of amusement.

'What was the girl's name?'

Jon's voice rose an octave. 'You really expect me to remember? It was years ago and I wasn't involved with the story.' He cast her a teasing smile. 'You could always ask your mate

Magda; she worked that particular story at the time. I'm sure she'll be able to recall the specific details.'

Mags. He'd mentioned the magenta-haired elephant hiding in full view in the middle of their living room. Molly was tired and her head was throbbing because of the heat and the wine and the dozen crazy thoughts currently bouncing round her over-worked brain.

'Who was Melanie Harris?' The words were out of her mouth before she'd had a chance to consider their impact.

'What the fuck…?' Jon sat up abruptly. The sudden change in weight distribution caused the chaise longue to creak to near breaking point. 'Why do I suddenly feel like I'm being interrogated, DS Fisher? I thought you left the job at work.'

'According to Mags, Melanie Harris was a young woman you harassed when you worked at the *Echo*, around twelve years ago.'

Jon laughed, but it sounded slightly forced. 'I don't know what this shit is about. I told you not to believe a word that lying bitch Magda tells you, but clearly you want to believe her. Or, I dunno, maybe you want to impress her. "Yes, Mags: let's slag off Jon behind his back because he's a man and men are easy targets." Especially when we're not there to defend ourselves.' He shook his head then looked over at her; his puppy-dog eyes searching her face for an apology. 'Molly, I don't know anyone called Melanie Harris. And even if I did, I certainly never "harassed" her, as Mags puts it. Why are you so willing to believe this tosh Mags has been filling your head with? Christ, Molly, if you really want to make it into Homicide and Serious Crime you're going to have to recognise when someone's playing you for a mug.'

It was a viscous and fulsome rebuttal; cruel and personal, but Molly wasn't prepared to walk away from this fight with her tail between her legs. 'OK, why would she lie?'

'Isn't it obvious? She's jealous. She's jealous of what we've got and wants to split us up.' He took a deep breath and held his head in his hands. After a moment, he looked up and said, 'Mags is a bitter woman. All right, I admit, we had a bit of a fling years ago and I binned her off because she was bonkers. She's obviously never got over it, and this is her pathetic way of trying to get her own back.'

He climbed off the chaise longue and padded through to the kitchen. She could hear him clattering around in there, taking plates out of cupboards and banging them down on the worktop with a heavy thud. She was sure she heard the sound of glass breaking.

She'd been unfair, throwing the accusation at Jon without first getting the full story, or at the very least his version of it. She'd put money on Mags having lied, no doubt pursuing her own nasty agenda, and maybe Jon was right about it being all borne out of spite. But she was thrown by Jon's reaction: part indignation and part something else… guilt? He had lied about his fling, as he called it, with Mags. What else was there?

There was more banging and crashing from the kitchen, then silence. She heard the back door open and close.

She asked herself what had happened to her relationship. What had happened to the man she'd fallen in love with, who used to make her laugh and make them breakfast in bed on rare days off? Losing his job had changed him, as it did for so many men who suddenly lost their purpose in life and then struggled to find a place in the world that ensured their role in the pack. But perhaps it was more than that? Perhaps *this* was the real Jon, and it was only now that the rose-tinted spectacles had dropped that reality was glaring back at her.

She briefly considered packing a bag and leaving, but why should she leave her home, and besides, where would she go? The last time she'd heard from her brother, he was living in Clapham, sharing a flat with five others in what had to be insanitary and probably illegal conditions. She had few close friends, apart from Trudi, but even that would be calling in a favour too far.

And anyway, why should she leave? It was her home, even though it was in Jon's name. Sitting back in the armchair, she finished her wine with a large gulp and thought through her options. With a heavy heart, she felt a sense of doors closing.

Chapter Thirty-Two

Sheldon House was a modern office block of soft brick and tinted windows which sat in the shadow of the angular, glass monolith that was the Shard. According to the polished brass nameplate by the front door, Marsden Developments was on the fourth floor.

Denning pressed the intercom and announced himself to the disembodied female voice that answered. A moment later he pushed open the glass door as soon as it buzzed.

He'd done his homework: Marsden Developments had started up just over two years ago. Marsden himself was a former builder who renovated derelict properties as a hobby before realising just how lucrative such a hobby could be. He now specialised in turning unused and derelict buildings into stylish homes for the very rich. The Marsden Developments website gave little away about Marsden himself; with the exception of a couple of photographs of him smiling for the camera, dressed in an expensive suit. There were few details beyond the basic biography. A PNC check had failed to throw up anything of interest, not even a speeding fine.

Denning took the lift to the fourth floor. The building felt new and clean and totally impersonal. A bit like Marsden himself, thought Denning. He chided himself for being unfair. He wanted to keep an open mind when it came to his ex-wife's new boyfriend, or at least try to.

The lift doors opened on the fourth floor. A frosted glass door directly opposite the lift had the words 'Marsden Development' engraved on it.

The outer office was a small but tastefully decorated reception area. A couple of Italian leather sofas sat in the corner by the window, and large, abstract pictures adorned two of the walls. There was a decent-sized blond-wood desk opposite the door, behind which an attractive young brunette sat tapping away at a keyboard. She looked up when Denning entered the room and greeted him with a friendly smile. 'Mr Denning, is it? I'll just let Mr Marsden know you're here.' It was the same voice that had buzzed him into the building a couple of minutes earlier: light and cheery with a hint of estuary. She knocked on a door opposite her desk, announced his name, then, with the same anodyne smile still pinned to her face, asked Denning to go through.

Marsden's office was smart and well-appointed. It occupied a corner of the fourth floor, with two large windows. The view from one of them was dominated by the Shard; light dancing off its spire. The office was decorated in a similar manner to the reception area though occupying more space, with trendy, Scandinavian furniture and another large Italian leather sofa beside one of the windows. Marsden sat behind a large glass desk, on which there was only a laptop, phone and black angle poise lamp. He stood up and shook Denning's hand. 'Can Alison get you anything to drink: tea, coffee?'

Denning declined. He didn't want this to feel like a social visit.

'Take a seat.' Marsden indicated one of the padded chairs on the other side of his desk.

Denning sat down. He tried to appear relaxed, casual, but he could feel his heart thumping more than was comfortable.

Marsden, by contrast, looked unflappably cool. He was dressed similarly to the first time they'd met: a pale grey linen jacket, expensive jeans and a Ralph Lauren black and grey shirt, open at the neck.

'I take it this is about Claire,' he guessed. 'Unless you're thinking about buying a new flat...'

He smiled, and pointed at a large board on the wall behind the office door, which Denning hadn't noticed when he'd entered the office. There were shiny photographs of warehouses, pubs and a former hospital, all now transformed into luxury apartments, not too dissimilar to the smart warehouse conversion Denning now called home, courtesy of his second wife's income. There was even a photograph of an old church, next to which were some computer-generated mock-ups of what Marsden had planned for the building: sleek and trendy flats, with state-of-the-art kitchens, wooden floors and lots of exposed brickwork.

'It's about Claire,' Denning said, 'but it's also about Jake. I don't want him being used as an emotional football between myself and Claire.'

Marsden offered a cheesy grin. 'You want to know if my intentions are honourable?' He smiled again; showing even, white teeth that were more than likely capped. 'Seriously, Matt, you don't have anything to worry about. I'm very fond of both Claire and Jake, and whatever happens, I've got no plans to take your son away from you; that's just not what I'm about.'

He sounded plausible, but there was still something about him Denning just didn't feel comfortable with. 'What exactly are you about, Alan?' It felt strange calling him by his first name, as though they were old friends, but Marsden clearly felt comfortable calling him Matt.

If Marsden was taken aback by Denning's abruptness, he didn't let it show. 'Look, Matt: I'm very fond of Claire. OK, it's still early days, but I think we've got a future together. And I accept she had a life before we met. Two people don't get together at our ages without there being some baggage, but I have no problems with that.'

Denning bristled slightly at being referred to as 'baggage', but he didn't let it show. 'What about yourself, Alan? What "baggage" do you bring with you?'

There was a ping from Marsden's laptop, suggesting an email had come through. His eyes briefly left Denning to glance at the screen. A slight furrow momentarily wrinkled his forehead, before his steady gaze returned to Denning. 'I'm an open book, Matt: divorced, childless... hard-working.'

'Why did your marriage end?' Denning knew the question probably sounded impertinent, and he expected Marsden to tell him it was none of his business.

Instead, Marsden offered him another smile. 'It seems my ex-wife Angie preferred youth over experience: she left me for a younger man. After my ego got over the bruising, we agreed to be grown up about things. I let her keep the house, while I decided to focus on building up my business. Meeting Claire was fortuitous but not planned.' Marsden leant on the glass desktop. 'She told me very early on that she was divorced with a young son. I've always wanted kids, so having Jake in my life is a bonus.'

A bonus, thought Denning; his son was more than that.

'You know about Jake, don't you?' Denning asked.

Marsden nodded. 'ADHD, right? And mild autism? Yes, Claire told me. He's a good kid. OK, sometimes he plays up, and it took him a while to fully accept me being a part of his mum's life, but we're good now. I love Jakey like he's my own kid.'

The words bit into Denning. Jake was *his* kid, and Jakey *his* pet name for him. He could feel his temple start to throb very slightly. Part of him wanted to reach over the glass desk and punch Marsden's smug, tanned face, but the man was guilty of nothing more than acting *in loco parentis* for Denning's son when he wasn't around, which was more often than Denning would like.

'Look, I'm not entirely sure why I came round here today.' Denning could feel the throbbing in his temple slowly start to recede. 'I just want to make sure Jake is OK with everything. He doesn't like change.' He paused, before adding: 'And I suppose I want to make sure Claire isn't going to get hurt.' He nearly added *again* but that would have meant acknowledging his own role in his ex-wife's hurt. But no doubt Claire had already filled Marsden in on the reasons that lay behind their divorce; likely dumping most of the blame on Denning's doorstep, perhaps not unreasonably…

Marsden's eyes briefly flicked back to the laptop screen, this time lingering there for a good couple of seconds. 'I don't want to be rude, Matt, but I've actually got quite a lot on today. And you must have your hands full, with two murders to deal with. But, yeah, we should all go out for dinner sometime. Obviously bring Sandra along too.'

'Sarah,' Denning corrected. He had an uncomfortable feeling Sarah would get on well with the uber-smooth, financially successful Alan Marsden: they'd likely spend the evening discussing their investment portfolios.

'Sure,' Marsden replied, 'somewhere expensive. On me.'

Denning smiled and made his way out of the office. He glanced round at Marsden before heading through the door, but he was engrossed in the contents of his last email: the time he'd allocated for Denning was already up.

Chapter Thirty-Three

Molly googled the name Daryl Bailey, but there was no mention of him and any underage girls, just a rather bland Wikipedia page outlining his sporting achievements and how he had missed out on playing for England whilst still in his twenties. There were a couple of tabloid features from years back, and a stream of photos of Bailey in his prime, all designer stubble and white teeth. There was little about his private life beyond a passing mention that he was divorced. According to the Wikipedia article, Bailey now worked with 'youth football teams in east London'.

She suspected that if the internet had ever contained anything incriminating about Daryl Bailey, he would have had it removed by now. There had been a number of cases where people had requested internet search providers to remove any information they didn't want in the public domain. Anything controversial, like links to underage sex, would certainly have been damaging to his career, assuming there was any truth in the rumours. And if the rumours were true, then what else could he be guilty of?

The obvious answer was to speak to Mags again.

She dug her phone out her bag and scrolled down the contacts list until she came to Magda's name. But did she really want to speak to Mags? Did she even trust her?

Her finger hovered over the call button for a moment before she made the call.

Part of her was relieved when it went straight to voicemail. She left a message asking to meet, but even as she spoke she felt her stomach grip with self-doubt. Magda Kilbride was a hornets' nest that was best left unpoked. Contacting her again would likely lead to more trouble; more lies about Jon; more arguments.

She was startled when, a moment later, her phone tinkled a giddy tune indicating a text message: Magda Kilbride had agreed to meet her.

–

McKenna was doing her desk-drumming thing again. Denning suspected she was unaware she was doing it; a subconscious action that expressed some internalised anxiety she would never dream of expressing openly. It was almost endearing.

'Can we officially rule Kane out of the Leanne Wyatt murder now?' she asked.

'Even if he's telling the truth about meeting her to sell her some gear, there's nothing to say that he didn't meet her again afterwards,' Denning said. 'And he's pretty keen to point the finger at Bailey, almost as though he's trying to throw us off the scent.'

'Doesn't mean he murdered her though. Where's his motive?'

Denning gave an exasperated shake of the head. 'OK. I'm beginning to think Kane may be innocent of this. But until we have concrete proof to the contrary, he's not completely off the hook.'

McKenna shrugged. 'My honest opinion, Matt: forget Kane. He's trouble and he's nasty, but I don't think he murdered Leanne. I don't want him becoming a distraction. It's likely he's going down anyway: hopefully for manslaughter, certainly for dealing. Either way, let CID clean this particular mess up. We've got enough on our plates with two unsolved murders crying out for attention.'

Despite the seriousness of the situation, Denning's mind kept returning to Marsden; his smooth-tongued confidence and general air of ease. There was something about him he just couldn't put his finger on.

After a moment Denning became aware that McKenna had stopped talking and it was his was his turn to speak. *Two unsolved murders...* Like he needed reminding. 'If we believe what Kane says about Bailey, then that as good as put him in the frame,' he said. 'Of course, Kane could be lying, but Bailey's looking tasty for this. I think we need to bring him in, officially.'

McKenna nodded. 'And what about Tony, sorry, Tanya Russell? Are we making any progress there?'

Denning thought back to Marsden's glass-topped desk. OK, he liked a tidy desk himself, but Marsden was taking it to an extreme: nobody's desk was ever *that* tidy, not if they actually used it to do any work... 'My money's on a hate crime,' he said after a second. 'We need to keep checking CCTV in the area. We know Tanya Russell used dating sites. Forensics are going over her laptop to see if there's anything useful there, but I can't help thinking this was simply a random attack on someone who found themselves in the wrong place at the wrong time.'

'You don't think this is down to some hairy-arsed bastard she met online who freaked out the moment he discovered his date for the night came with a bit more than he bargained for?'

Denning shook his head. 'According to her daughter, the men who met her through the websites she used knew Tanya was a crossdresser so it's not like it would have come as a shock to anyone she met.'

The finger-drumming stopped. 'Two murders, Matt. Both in the space of a week. We don't want to look like we're on the back foot here.' Again the gimlet stare: not at him, but through him. 'I'll talk to the media on this, Matt. Due to the... sensitive nature of the situation, we need to tread carefully. We'll have the LGBT brigade over us like a nasty rash if we fuck this up. Any flack, best it comes my way.'

'I'm sure you'll handle the situation with kid gloves.' Although said with sincerity, he couldn't help feeling it came across as sarcastic. The comment was lost on McKenna, whose eyes remained fixed on his.

The implicit threat hung heavy in the tepid air: the clock was ticking and it was down to him to unravel this mess. He just wished he had something concrete to offer.

He left her office and returned to his desk, an unnerving sense of foreboding nagging away at him.

Chapter Thirty-Four

Mags was sitting at an outside table overlooking the river, scrolling through something on her phone. She glanced up when she saw Molly approach, threw the phone down on the table and sat back on her chair, cocking her head at Molly in a gesture that was one part greeting and two parts threat.

'This is becoming a bit of a habit, DS Fisher. Anyone would think we enjoyed each other's company.'

Molly sat down opposite Mags, dumping her bag on the table, like it was some kind of impromptu barrier. 'I need to ask you about Daryl Bailey,' she said. 'There's a rumour doing the rounds about him and a teenage girl. Do you know if there's any truth to the rumour?'

There was the briefest flicker from Mags, nothing more than a twitch of an eyebrow and a tiny pulse momentarily beating in her cheek, but enough to let Molly know she had pricked her interest.

They'd arranged to meet in the same bar as before. This time it was quieter; the lunchtime crowd had dispersed and the evening drinkers were yet to arrive. The Thames offered up a welcome breeze as the sun bounced off its shimmering surface. Molly had thought about apologising to Mags for how their meeting had ended last time but she knew the words would choke in her throat. Besides, she suspected Magda Kilbride had the hide of a rhinoceros.

Mags cocked her head to one side. 'So, Daryl Bailey's being flagged up on the radar now? Interesting.' She screwed her eyes into narrow slits. 'But you don't really think he's the

Bermondsey Ripper, do you?' She smiled at Molly. 'Or maybe you do...? Professional footballer by day, serial killer by night. Stranger things have happened.'

Molly chose to ignore her sarcasm. 'I only need to know if there's any truth in the rumour that Bailey had a fling with an underage girl. And if so, why it was never reported to the police.'

Mags was drinking mineral water again, and Molly wondered if she had a drink problem. She'd bought herself a half pint of Kronenbourg, but hadn't felt the urge to offer Mags a drink: she didn't want either of them to pretend this was in any way a social meet.

She placed the glass back on the table. 'What does Jon have to say about this? Is he still humouring you, or has he told you you're on to a loser here?'

'Let's keep Jon out of this.'

She laughed. 'So he has told you you're wasting your time. I thought he would.'

Molly could feel her shoulders tighten. She rubbed a hand over the back of her neck, massaging away the tension. 'I'm not interested in playing your silly games, Mags. I just need to know about Daryl Bailey. For the record, Jon and I are rock solid. I'm sorry if that pisses you off, but I really couldn't give a shit. He ditched you and moved on, now get over it.'

She circled the glass with her finger, slowly and with a sense of purpose. Then it stopped. 'It's lies,' she said after a moment. Mags pushed her sunglasses off her forehead and onto her face, pressing them against the bridge of her nose with her middle finger. 'The girl as good as admitted she'd made it up. She'd met Bailey at some charity football gig; he'd flirted with her, he admitted that, but he didn't take it any further. Daryl Bailey might be a sleazebag, but he's not a paedophile. At least not as far as I know.'

'What happened, exactly?'

Mags shrugged indifferently. 'The girl went to the press, not us, one of the nationals, but it did the rounds: we got to hear about it. I looked into it to see if it was worth wasting shoe leather on, but it was a non-story. The girl claimed she'd slept with Bailey. She was fifteen, and to be fair, she looked it. Bailey was contacted, naturally, but he denied everything, initially saying he'd never even met the girl. She came back with proof they had met: it seemed someone had taken a photo of them flirting at the charity match. Bailey then claimed the girl had approached him asking for money, he'd told her to go fuck herself, or words to that effect, and she'd cried rape. Just as it all looked like it was going to turn nasty, his club got involved and threatened us all with libel if anyone ran the story. Naturally, there wasn't any proof of an affair, just her word against his, so we had to back down.'

'Why weren't the police informed of all this?'

There was a cynical laugh from Mags. 'Get real. This kind of thing goes on all the time. If a celebrity ran to you lot every time someone tried to blackmail them they'd have no time for anything else. Besides, I suspect neither Bailey nor his club wanted the publicity. If you keep things off the record, you can generally keep a lid on it; but the minute you lot get involved there isn't a hope in hell of keeping it under wraps.'

'I meant why did the paper not report this to the police as soon as the girl made the accusation? There could have been some truth in the claim.'

Mags twisted her mouth into a tight smile. 'You know how it works: the victim has to make it official. Besides, I believe someone did suggest she went to the police: just to give the story a splattering of credibility if nothing else. She refused. Or was talked out of it.'

Molly wanted to say something, but couldn't find the words. The bold assumption from everyone concerned that a young girl had lied, rather than giving her the benefit of the doubt rankled with her. She knew people made up lies for all sorts of reasons, financial gain being a big incentive. When she'd first joined the police she'd been told to keep an open mind about everything: the guilty were not always guilty, and victims were not always innocent. But still, this stank of something rotten. She opened her mouth to speak, but Mags jumped in before the words had a chance to come out…

'I don't need a lecture on morality, not from you or anyone. That's not my responsibility and you're not dumb enough to believe it is. The girl learned a useful lesson about life, Bailey dodged a bullet. Everything was kept out the press, more or less.'

'But the rumours persisted? Bailey's club sacked him. They must have suspected something had gone on.'

'Bailey had earned himself a reputation over the years. OK, so it goes with the game: egos need feeding, and there are plenty of desperate people out there to feed them. But Bailey was always high maintenance, and his philandering and near brushes with scandal, real or otherwise, began to impact on his game. That was the real reason his club dropped him; not because of his wandering dick but because he stopped scoring goals.'

Molly finished her drink. 'Something tells me there's more to it than what you've just told me.'

Mags shook her head. 'Like I said, you don't seriously think Daryl Bailey was the Bermondsey Ripper, do you? I mean it's just possible someone might have spotted a high-profile figure like Bailey acting suspiciously at the time. Trust me: even if you lot didn't, my lot would have been all over it like a nasty rash.'

Molly didn't think Bailey was the Ripper; she wasn't stupid. But if Bailey had killed Leanne Wyatt, then it would prove she was wrong about there being a link between Leanne's murder and the Ripper's killings. She wanted to be a hundred per cent sure of her facts before she approached Denning in any official capacity. 'OK, so Bailey wasn't the Bermondsey Ripper, but there's something you're not telling me.'

Mags shrugged again. 'Believe what you like. You seem to do that anyway.'

'What does that mean?'

Mags' thin ruby lips tilted upwards in a twisted parody of a smile. She leaned in closer. 'I told you the truth about Jon and you chose not to believe me. He fed you a ton of shite about his past, about him and me, and you decided you were going to buy it, because I imagine it's easier than accepting the alternative: that the man you live with is an unstable liar. You're happy to believe the crap about Daryl Bailey, but not your own boyfriend. But that's your problem, not mine.'

Molly had had enough. 'I told you I didn't want to talk about Jon, but you seem obsessed. If you continue with your lies about my boyfriend, I'll have you charged with harassment.'

Again, that raucous laugh that bordered on something feral. 'A threat! Really? Why can't you accept I'm simply trying to do you a favour here? OK, I'm not one for sisterly solidarity, but even I don't like to see another woman being taken for a mug.'

'I'm not interested any more, Magda. I'm happy to leave you to wallow in your own little vat of poison.' She stood up and turned to walk away.

'OK, but before you go, perhaps you can tell me one thing? Something that's been bugging me since you first got in touch asking unofficial questions about a decade-old murder inquiry.' She looked at Molly, waiting for a reaction. 'Why are you really so interested in Anthony Ferguson?'

Chapter Thirty-Five

Bailey sat opposite them with a pathetic look nailed to his face like a wet flannel. His solicitor sat beside him, piercing blue eyes bouncing from Bailey to Denning to McKenna, then back to Bailey.

The solicitor was a young man, not more than early thirties: he was blond and tanned, and spoke with a Home Counties accent. He wore a stylish silk tie with swirly patterns on it and sharp grey suit that didn't look like it had ever hung on a department store rail. He gave his name as James Collins from Grammond and Harvey solicitors, and had insisted from the off that the police had no case against his client. Denning guessed he charged more per hour than a teacher earned in a day.

Bailey had said very little. A string of denials harmonised with Collins' continued insistence that there was no evidence to support the allegation that his client was in any way responsible for the murder of Leanne Wyatt. Denning was slowly coming to the realisation that there was probably more than a grain of truth in that.

What evidence they had was circumstantial: the figure on the CCTV footage from outside the Fleur de Lys bore a faint resemblance to Bailey but, even though the images had been digitally enhanced, it was still impossible to tell for certain that it was Daryl Bailey who'd left the bar with Leanne Wyatt that night. Bailey still had no alibi for the time Leanne was believed to have been killed, but as his solicitor wasn't shy to point out, he wouldn't need one if he hadn't done anything wrong. As if to support this, Trudi Bell had informed Denning that the allegations about Bailey and an underage girl had come to nothing. It seemed that even what little they had on Bailey was slipping like sand through their fingers.

Denning sat opposite Bailey, McKenna was on his right. She'd told Denning she was going to sit in on the interview and it wasn't as if he could have refused. She sat so close that he could feel her perfume burning a hole in his sinuses.

'My client has told you all he knows,' Collins argued. 'He's admitted to having had an affair with Leanne Wyatt. The relationship started after she'd left school and not whilst she was still a pupil at Dalston Academy, as has been alleged. They had been in a casual relationship off and on for just under a year. Miss Wyatt was also seeing someone else during this relationship, though she informed my client the relationship with this individual was, and I quote "pretty much finished". Mr Bailey agreed to meet with Miss Wyatt on the evening of the 23rd in order to tell her their relationship was now over as he suspected she was still involved with this other individual, despite her claims to the contrary. He left the Fleur de Lys bar at approximately 9:30 p.m. on the evening in question. Miss Wyatt was still alive when he left, and CCTV in the bar *should* have been able to confirm that. The bar manager has admitted that the bar was busy that evening, and he can't confirm whether the man he saw talking to Leanne Wyatt after 9:30 p.m. was Mr Bailey, or someone else. He claims he simply assumed it was the same man. Mr Bailey did not hear about Miss Wyatt's tragic death until the following afternoon, when Detective Inspector Denning and Detective Sergeant Neeraj informed him that she had been murdered. He admits he initially panicked and lied about his relationship with Leanne, but subsequently acknowledged this.' Collins was clearly reading from a prepared script. When he'd finished, he sat up straight, closed the folder on the table in front of him, and locked eyes with Denning. 'There is no proof, no probative evidence that links Mr Bailey to the murder of Leanne Wyatt. My client should be free to leave.'

'Why did you lie to DI Denning and DS Neeraj when they first spoke to you, Mr Bailey?' McKenna asked. There was a slight edge to her voice and Denning wondered if she'd locked horns with James Collins on a previous occasion.

'I have already explained that, DCI McKenna: my client panicked. He realised the kind of assumptions your officers would make if he admitted he'd been in a relationship with Miss Wyatt.'

'And what would that assumption be, Mr Collins?' McKenna was cool and steady in her questioning, but Denning suspected she was fighting back the temptation to reach over the metal table and stub out a cheroot on Collins's forehead.

Collins sighed. He and Bailey exchanged glances, but Bailey's gaze dropped to the floor as soon as Denning looked at him. 'A teacher in a relationship with a former pupil: society likes to make judgements, DCI McKenna. I expect the police are no different.'

Bailey sat there like a chastened child on the naughty step. No doubt Collins had told him to keep schtum and speak only when spoken to. The tactic seemed to be working.

Denning decided it was time he contributed something to the conversation, reminding himself that this was his gig and not McKenna's. 'I suspect your moral reticence stems more from guilt than concern at society's censure, Mr Bailey, but the fact is you lied to us. You deliberately withheld important information at a time when it was vital we were in possession of all the facts. Your lies could have jeopardised our investigation.'

Bailey didn't reply. Denning thought if he looked any more sheepish he would actually start baaing. It was down to Collins to offer comment: 'You are very welcome to charge my client with wasting police time, inspector, but equally, my client is well within his rights to bring a charge of wrongful arrest and police harassment against the Met, and I would say, he would probably have a very strong case.' He fixed his gaze on Denning. 'It's up to you, inspector.'

Denning was conscious of McKenna sitting next to him: the stale whiff of cheroot and the faint aroma of Glenmorangie assailing his nostrils. They would have to let Bailey walk. They didn't have enough charge him, and everybody in the room knew it.

He was just about to tell Collins his client was free to leave when Bailey suddenly piped up: 'It's all my fault. I'm to blame for what happened.' His outburst earned him a stern look form Collins but he continued unabated. 'We'd argued that night, at the bar. She didn't want to end things, claimed she loved me. She insisted it was over between her and Gregor Kane. She told me she hated him. She seemed different: like she was agitated, wired...' He shook his head. 'She even used her little boy against me, saying Charlie saw me as a dad. I said I didn't want that: I wasn't going to play daddy to someone else's kid.' He looked at his solicitor, who gave a sharp shake of his head in the hope of preventing his client from saying anything potentially incriminating. Bailey ignored him and continued. 'Leanne was just too clingy. She wanted a father for her child, and I don't blame her for that. But the truth is I was only looking for a bit of fun. Girls like Leanne... It's not as if they're for keeps.'

–

McKenna caught up with Denning by the lift. 'Well, that was a load of old wank.'

Denning pressed the button to summon the lift. 'We had to let him go. We had nothing on him and that super smooth solicitor knew it.'

'So we had one suspect and now we've let him walk out of here. It doesn't look great, does it?'

The lift doors slid open and they both got in. As soon as the doors closed Denning felt a sudden tightness in his chest: McKenna's fiery breath, exacerbated by the lack of air in the claustrophobic space. 'We've examined every area of Leanne Wyatt's private life. She had no enemies that we know of, and the only people in her life that might have had any motive for wishing her harm either have a solid alibi or there's insufficient evidence to convict them. We're running out of options.'

McKenna stabbed the button for the fifth floor and the lift doors closed. Denning felt the claustrophobia grow stronger. He needed some fresh air, or strong coffee: ideally both.

'There is one option we haven't yet looked at,' McKenna said. 'Maybe Leanne Wyatt didn't know her killer.' She let the words hang in the air for a second, then added, 'Maybe it's time we explored the possibility that she was killed by a stranger. In which case, we really are up shit creek.'

Chapter Thirty-Six

The path ran tight along one side of the Regent's Canal in Hoxton. It was a disparate landscape: breezeblock factory units and tired looking council flats sat adjacent to stream-lined modern apartment blocks and trendy bars. Tall buildings reflected their elongated shadows onto the canal's glassy surface. Parts of the path were overgrown with untamed foliage, thick and verdant in the summer heat. Other parts had been cultiv-ated, adorned with wooden benches and surrounded by neatly cut grass. Local gangs had graffitied their tags onto the sides of walls and buildings.

The body had been spotted by a couple of joggers. Half-submerged in the water not far from a bridge, they'd first assumed it was a binbag full of rubbish. Then one of them thought he saw an arm sticking out. Curiosity had encouraged them to take a closer look, and it was only then that they realised they were looking at a decomposing corpse.

Denning was trying not to sweat in the close-fitting snugness of the plastic forensic suit. It was unbearably hot that afternoon, and the lack of air wasn't helping. A police cordon had already been positioned around the scene, offering a flimsy protection barrier. A line of onlookers snaked along the parapet of the bridge, gazing down on the scene below with a mixture of horror and excitement. A white forensic tent stood by the water's edge.

The body had been pulled onto the canal bank by the CSIs. It was a young woman. Denning would have said she was older than Leanne Wyatt, maybe late twenties to early thirties, but it was difficult to tell from the state she was in: her face was bloated and swollen, blackened around the eyes and with extensive bruising around the mouth. It was impossible to say how much had been caused by being in the water and how much had been inflicted just before she died. Damp, dark hair clung to her scalp like an otter's fur. There was dried blood behind one ear and an ugly scratch mark on her forehead. Decomposition had already started, and the skin had a withered and puckered look about it.

Inside the forensic tent, Elizabeth Gorton was in conversation with the pathologist; not the same pathologist as last time – who had no doubt been kicked into touch after his staggering failure to tell male from female – someone Denning didn't recognise. Denning removed his forensic suit and quickly wiped his forehead with the back of his hand.

'Detective Inspector Denning, this is Dr Baker,' Gorton said, nodding in the direction of the pathologist. Baker was in his early fifties, his mostly jet-black hair looking like it was the result of a partially successful dye-job. He had a ruddy complexion and was sweating considerably as he climbed out of the pale blue forensic suit. 'Body's been there for a while, I'd say,' he commented, cursing momentarily as the elasticated ankle cuff of the plastic suit got caught on the heel of his shoe. 'At least a few days, possibly as long as a week.'

Gorton smiled at Denning. 'Never rains but it pours, inspector. I have to say, this must have all come as something of a baptism of fire for you.'

Denning smiled a curt response at her, and turned to Baker. 'Surely she would have been spotted before now? This path is popular with walkers and joggers, especially in the middle of summer. Half of east London must have been along here over the past week or so.'

Baker had climbed out of his forensic suit now, and was folding it neatly into a large briefcase. 'A body can stay immersed in water for weeks in some cases. It all depends how long it takes for decomposition gasses to bring it back to the surface. In reasonably warm water such as this,' he gestured towards the smooth, dark water of the canal, 'it won't take that long for the decomposition gases to form once the internal organs start to disintegrate. That would cause the body to rise to the surface sooner or later. It is possible it was initially weighed down with something, in which case it could have been down there a lot longer, though there's nothing to indicate that was the case here.'

'We've ruled out accidental death by drowning?' Denning asked. Even as he spoke he knew the chances of this death being anything other than suspicious lay somewhere between slim and non-existent.

'A precursory examination reveals extensive bruising to the neck as well as further bruising to both forearms,' said Baker. 'I can't say for certain at this stage, but I suspect the body was already dead when it entered the water.'

Denning nodded quietly. 'What about that mark on her forehead?'

Baker shrugged. 'Could have been caused post-mortem; she could have hit something when she went into the canal. A more detailed examination on the table will give us a clearer picture.'

'The injuries don't look as extensive as those on Leanne Wyatt,' Gorton offered, as if reading his thoughts, 'but if what Dr Baker says is right, then it's likely this young woman was killed before Leanne Wyatt. Possibly anything up to a week before.'

'You think this is the work of the same man?' Denning asked. They were only a few streets away from where Tanya Russell had been attacked, and less than a mile to the east, Haggerston Park basked in the afternoon sun. He was hoping for an answer in the negative, but he wasn't holding his breath.

'Well, I wouldn't like to fall into sexist generalisation, DI Denning, but yes, my professional guess would be that it looks very likely the same person was responsible for both murders.'

Denning gave this a moment to sink in. He didn't want to think it, but it looked like Betty Taggart was right and they had been looking for their murderer in all the wrong places.

'How certain are you?' he asked.

Gorton nodded slowly and deliberately. 'There are too many similarities for this to be just coincidence: the extensive facial bruising for one thing, the extreme use of force for another. And, again it looks as though the victim was killed elsewhere and then the body dumped somewhere public. If we find evidence of sexual assault, then I'd say it's too much of a coincidence. It's certainly a direct link with Leanne Wyatt. Possibly Tanya Russell too.' She looked up at Denning, trying to offer him a sympathetic smile. 'It looks like you've got a madman out there killing women.'

Chapter Thirty-Seven

Denning took a sip of lukewarm coffee from a paper cup. He swallowed the tepid liquid and tried not to grimace at the acrid taste. He couldn't dodge the inescapable feeling that Gorton was right, and there was a killer out there they hadn't considered, especially when combined with Betty Taggart's comments about the likelihood of Leanne Wyatt having been killed by someone other than Gregor Kane or Daryl Bailey. Added to that, there was now the real possibility that Tanya Russell could have potentially been part of that mix too, though there wasn't much to connect those killings other than the sheer brutality.

He could see the looks on the faces of his team; a team already tired and despondent from two murder investigations, now facing the unwelcome prospect of a third.

The only tiny glimmer of light this time was that it looked as though they had an ID for the victim.

'Sandra Blake, twenty eight, a secretary at Queen Mary University.' Denning addressed the room. 'According to Missing Persons, she was reported missing by her flatmate, Wendy Latimer, just over a week ago. As yet, there's nothing to connect Sandra Blake with Tanya Russell. However, there are marked similarities with the murder of Leanne Wyatt: too many for this to be a coincidence. We also have to consider the possibility that Tanya Russell was similarly targeted by our killer, even though the circumstances are slightly different. The fact that all three victims were, to all intents and purposes, single women is a likely connecting factor in all three cases.'

'Are you saying there's someone out there targeting single women?' Trudi asked.

'A serial killer?' It was Kinsella this time. His face seemed to morph into a parody of Munch's *The Scream*.

The room broke into a series of muttered conversations punctuated by the sound of someone's mobile ringing. Denning raised a hand to hush them. The mobile stopped ringing, and all eyes were back on him.

'OK, I appreciate this isn't something we want to consider, and at this stage it's nothing more than a possibility, but there's a strong chance all three murders are the work of the same person.'

Denning nodded at the whiteboards. There were three sets of photos there now: three victims with their names scrawled above their images in black marker pen. The only photo they had so far of Sandra Blake was one taken post-mortem: it would have to suffice until they could get something showing what she looked like when she was alive – pretty, Denning reckoned, just like Leanne Wyatt. The scored cross was clear on her forehead.

A map of east London pinned to the board had red stickers indicating the locations where the bodies were found, all depressingly close together. Next to the map was a jumble of photos showing pictures of the sites: they were all open spaces, accessible to members of the public and easily overlooked. The first two victims had been killed elsewhere, then dumped in a public place; Tanya Russell was killed out in the open, suggesting their killer was getting bolder, or more desperate.

Denning felt like they were being taunted; as though whoever was responsible was playing a sick game with them.

'If we work on the assumption that whoever killed Tanya Russell was unaware she was a crossdresser, then this does look like someone is targeting single women.'

'With respect, we don't know that our latest victim was single,' Ryan said.

'Agreed, but she was reported missing by a flatmate rather than a husband or partner, so until we know otherwise, it's a fairly safe assumption that she was single. And if that's the case, we need to find out how he's finding them and where.'

'The Fleur de Lys in Islington is a good place to start,' Trudi said. 'We know that's the last place Leanne Wyatt was seen.'

'What about Tanya Russell?' someone else asked.

'Tanya's last known whereabouts are still not known,' Denning said. 'CCTV footage shows her walking down Dalston Way shortly after midnight, then she disappears. Presumably that's when she was dragged into the car park behind KFC. It's probable her killer followed her and waited for a convenient opportunity to strike.'

'So we're assuming Tanya didn't know her attacker?' Neeraj asked.

'It does look to be more opportunistic than the other two murders,' Denning said. 'But I still think she was deliberately targeted. It is possible she'd met her attacker earlier that evening in a bar or club somewhere and was followed as far as the KFC car park where she was then attacked. By all accounts Tanya was quite lonely, but enjoyed male company whenever it came her way.'

'Something she shared with Leanne Wyatt,' Trudi said.

Denning looked at the photos on the board. That was a good point: both women were lonely and didn't have a wide circle of friends. They didn't yet have much information on Sandra Blake's background, but he was willing to bet she'd fall into the same category.

'Focusing on our latest victim for now: there's limited CCTV on the footpath beside the canal, and some on the bridge that overlooks the canal. The footage is being emailed over ASAP, but until we know exactly when she was dumped in the canal, we could be looking at hours and hours of CCTV. Also, we need witnesses. We need to speak to everyone who uses that path regularly: joggers, dog-walkers, even people who fish the canal. Then there are the flats that overlook the canal: get uniform doing door-to-door in the area.'

'What about the press?' Trudi asked.

'DCI McKenna is going to issue a press release this afternoon, but at this stage we're not officially linking the murders. Until we get the results of the post-mortem, the latest killing is being classed as suspicious but nothing more. We need to try and keep a lid on this, and not create a full-scale panic.'

'Shouldn't we warn women that there's a serial killer out there and they might be at risk?' The question came from Ryan. Denning had to admit that it was a good point, but McKenna had already stamped her mark on this, insisting they weren't going to start talking serial killers until they were one hundred per cent sure of their facts. It seemed the Assistant Commissioner was breathing down her neck, as much as she was breathing down his.

–

Molly was sitting at her desk. She was tying up the loose strands that needed clarifying before the CPS would proceed with the case against Kane, when Trudi texted suggesting she join her for a fag break. Molly had gone almost twenty-four hours without a cigarette and was hoping she could now claim to be on top of her addiction. But if anyone could put any truth to the rumours she'd heard about a serial killer on the loose, it was Trudi.

The sun wasn't as strong as previous days, but it was still warm in the station car park. Trudi was half leaning against the cool brick wall that ran the length of the ground floor. She raised a hand in acknowledgment when she saw Molly approaching.

'Is it true?' Molly asked. She took a cigarette from her top pocket and looked at it for a moment or two, before deciding to have one last final puff before giving up for good.

'Is what true?' Trudi asked. She was already halfway through a B&H, dropping ash onto the ground with an indifferent flick of her fingers.

'That there's a serial killer out there. Leanne Wyatt, that bloke the other day, and now this body that's turned up this morning.' She was aware she was speaking quickly, like an overexcited child. She tried to relax, drop her shoulders and take a deep breath. 'Is it true that they're all the work of the same man?'

Trudi stared at her cigarette. 'I can't discuss that with you, Moll.' She tried to offer a conciliatory smile, but it came out more like a nervous twitch. 'We're all stressed to the eyeballs up there trying to get on top of things. I can't discuss it.'

'He marks them with a cross on the forehead. The killer, I mean. There's a cross on the forehead. Just like there was twelve years ago.' She looked at Trudi. 'It's the same man.'

Trudi opened her mouth to speak, but no words came out.

'So it is true...?' Molly didn't even need to ask. She could tell from Trudi's reaction that she was right. That she had been right all along. 'Trudi, I have to speak to DI Denning. There's something he needs to know.'

Chapter Thirty-Eight

Wendy Latimer lived in a two-bedroomed maisonette in an area estate agents liked to call 'Crouch End borders'. In reality it was part of a bland seventies block that overlooked the railway line just north of Finsbury Park. The flat itself was tidy, but slightly soulless, as though its occupants only lived there for part of the time.

'Thanks for coming,' Wendy Latimer said, showing them into a square, white-walled living room on the first floor. Modern furniture filled the space, and the open windows allowed a cool breeze to enter. 'I'm guessing you're here about Sandy.'

She indicated for Denning and Neeraj to sit down. They both declined her offer of tea, and sat on a low wood-and canvas sofa that faced the large picture window with a view of her neighbour's back garden.

'I saw on the news about the body found in Hoxton. I'm guessing it's not a coincidence that you're here.'

Wendy Latimer was dressed in a plain white t-shirt and a pair of dark grey Levi 501s. She was in her mid-thirties, with dark auburn hair, smooth olive skin and a toned physique, suggesting she was no stranger to a gym. Her hazel eyes bounced between the two detectives, twinkling with concern.

Denning nodded, and confirmed that they were there in connection with Sandra's murder. 'Can you tell us about Sandra?' Denning asked.

She nodded, sitting forward on a smart wooden armchair, her hands clasped in front of her body. 'We used to work together at Queen Mary. I left last year to join a PR company in the city, but I kept in touch with Sandy. When my marriage ended at the start of the year, I asked Sandy if she wanted to move in. She was always looking for a place to stay and I thought it would be nice to have a bit of company. And, of course, the rent came in handy.'

Denning smiled at her, trying to encourage her to continue.

'She didn't have many friends; she was a bit shy.'

'What about family?'

'She'd moved down here from Macclesfield when she was seventeen. She told me she didn't get on with her mother and stepfather, and she hadn't seen her dad for nearly ten years. She didn't really seem to be close to anyone, and, to be honest, I felt a bit sorry for her.'

Denning nodded. The family would have to be notified, naturally, as they were still her next of kin, irrespective of any lack of closeness over the years.

'Do you have a photo of Sandy?' he asked. He tried not to think of the one pinned to the board back in the office.

She shook her head. 'No. That was what Missing Persons asked when I reported her missing a week ago, but she didn't have any photos of herself lying around the place. There should be a photograph of her on the staff page of the university's website. She worked in the Faculty of Arts.'

Denning made a mental note to check it out when he returned to the office. 'Why did you report her missing, Miss Latimer?'

Wendy Latimer clasped her hands even tighter and stared hard at the floor for a second. 'When I came home from work last Monday, she wasn't here. That was very unlike Sandy; she nearly always came straight home from work, especially on a week day. If for any reason she was going to go anywhere, she would have either told me or texted to say she'd be late. I thought at first she might have been working late, but that's pretty unlikely: it's the holidays and there are hardly any students around at the moment. I left it until after dinner then texted her. When she didn't reply I began to worry. I still hadn't heard anything by midnight; that's when I phoned the police.'

'When was the last time you actually spoke to Sandy?' Denning asked.

She thought before answering. 'Saturday, just before lunch. I stayed over at my boyfriend's that weekend, and went straight to work from his place on Monday morning. He lives in Fulham and works in the City, so he gives me a lift in on a Monday.'

'So the last time you saw her was on Saturday morning?' Neeraj asked.

She nodded. 'I left for my boyfriend's just after breakfast. Sandy was still pottering around in her dressing gown; she liked a lie-in on a weekend, whereas I'm always up and about early. She always called me a lark. Sandy was more of a night owl.'

'Did she say anything to you about her plans for the weekend? Was she meeting anyone? A boyfriend? A friend from work? Anyone?'

She shook her head. 'No. Sandy didn't have a boyfriend. I mean, she was very attractive, but she lacked confidence.'

'Was there anyone else in her life? Anyone she was close to?'

Another shake of the head. 'As I said, she was very shy. Apart from myself, she didn't have a lot of friends. If she'd arranged to meet someone, she'd have said. I'm sure of it.'

Denning felt there was something they weren't being told. 'Is there anything else, Miss Latimer? Is there anything you can tell us about Sandy that might help us find her killer?'

Wendy Latimer's hands were still clasped in front of her. She stared quietly at the oatmeal carpet for a couple of seconds before saying, 'I don't like speaking about her behind her back, but Sandy did like a drink. I'm not saying she was an alcoholic, far from it. Well, not exactly, but…'

Denning broke the awkwardness. 'When you say she "liked a drink", just what are we saying?'

She fidgeted uncomfortably in the easy chair. 'It was mostly at home. Don't misunderstand me, I'm not judging. I mean

I like a glass or two of wine in the evening, especially after a tough day at work, but with Sandy it was most evenings. And sometimes a bottle rather than a couple of glasses.'

'Are you saying she had a drink problem?' Denning wasn't sure how this might be relevant, but something told him it was a line of enquiry worth pursuing. 'Did she just drink with you? Or did she ever drink by herself?'

'Well, that's the thing. Sometimes she would go to the pub on a Sunday afternoon, especially if I wasn't around. She would sit in a corner, have a few glasses of wine and either read a book, or listen to music, or just people-watch. She liked glimpsing into other people's lives. She wouldn't speak to anyone, and she usually preferred quiet pubs, or at least ones that weren't too busy. I suppose, in a way, she just liked a bit of company without having to physically socialise with anyone.'

'Do you know which pub she usually drank in?'

She nodded. 'The Gilded Drake, on the Broadway. She liked it because it was mostly an older clientele that drank there, so they tended not to bother her.'

Denning thanked her. 'There's just one last thing, Miss Latimer, would you be prepared to identify the body? I know it's not pleasant, but it would help to have it formally confirmed that this is Sandy.'

She bit her lip again, then nodded. 'I suppose so. I mean, I think I was the only friend she had. Perhaps if I'd noticed she was missing sooner...' She let the words trail away to nothing, already knowing they were meaningless. 'I can take some comfort from knowing she's in a happier place now.' She paused. 'That's the awful thing: Sandy was a lovely girl, but she was so unhappy.'

'Unhappy?' Denning asked. 'In what way?'

She sighed. 'I think, deep down, she was desperately lonely.'

Chapter Thirty-Nine

The Gilded Drake sat on the corner of The Broadway and Heron Road where Finsbury Park eased itself into Stroud Green. The streets were leafy enough to give the area more of a suburban feel than an inner city one.

The pub was a testament to Victorian architecture: tall and imposing from the outside, slightly dated on the inside.

Trudi had texted to tell them she'd spoken to Sandra Blake's boss at the university, who confirmed she hadn't turned up for work the previous Monday, and nobody had seen her since. It seems she'd been owed some holiday entitlement and everyone had assumed she'd taken it without saying anything. It was only when her flatmate had contacted them to say she'd gone missing that they realised something was wrong.

Denning asked Trudi to email him a copy of Sandra Blake's photo from the university website. He could easily see the resemblance to the bloated corpse they'd pulled from the Regent's Canal earlier that day. She had certainly been pretty in life: raven-haired with deep, almond eyes hiding behind large, square glasses. She was smiling professionally for the camera, but although her smile was warm, it hinted at the shyness of which Wendy Latimer had spoken.

Wendy was at the mortuary now, identifying her former flatmate, an experience that would probably stay with her forever.

The Gilded Drake had tried hard to retain its Victorian ambience without actually turning itself into a relic from a bygone age. The seating was liver-red leather, suitably worn and scratched in places, while the bar was all polished brass and mahogany. There was a gloriously faded grandeur about the place, and Denning could see why Sandra Blake would have come here on a weekend afternoon to sit and read by herself, or to quietly observe the passing milieu of human life without being expected to fully engage with it.

The young man behind the bar was dressed in a white shirt and black tie, and looked about the same age as Sandra Blake. Denning showed him a photo of Sandra on his phone and asked if he recognised her.

'Yeah,' the barman said. 'She used to come in here now and again. Sat in the corner by herself. Liked her wine. Bit sad really.'

'Was she here on Sunday the 15th?' Denning asked.

The barman shook his head.

'Can you be certain?' he asked. 'It's important.'

'Sunday 15th,' the barman repeated, 'we was closed for a private function. One of our regulars was celebrating their ruby wedding. Sweet, really.'

'Was this all day?'

He nodded. 'Yup, all day.'

–

'Nice pub,' said Neeraj as they headed back out onto the pavement. 'I could almost see the appeal of alcohol if they were all like that.' Denning offered up a weak smile as he unlocked the car.

'Doesn't help us much though, does it? If she wasn't there on Sunday, then where did she go?'

Denning's Ford Focus was parked a few yards from the pub. He'd parked the car in full sun, and in the brief few minutes they'd been in the pub, the car's interior had warmed up considerably. Denning started the engine and switched on the air conditioning.

'We don't know for sure that she did go out on Sunday, or if she did, that she was killed then. It could have been Saturday evening after the flatmate last saw her.'

Denning pulled out into the heavy traffic on the Broadway. 'The pubs would be busy on a Saturday, especially in the evening. Besides, Wendy Latimer said she only drank in pubs on a Sunday afternoon. We have to assume she went somewhere else if the Drake was closed.'

Neeraj chomped down another Extra Strong Mint. 'Yeah, but where?'

'That's a very good question. Assuming she did go somewhere else, it could have been anywhere.'

Chapter Forty

Molly had tried to call Denning, only to be told he was out and wouldn't back until later that afternoon. She'd wanted to head off early as she'd arranged to meet someone after work, but she had to speak to Denning first.

But her mind had only been half on it. She'd seen the press release they'd put out about the latest murder and it had convinced her she needed to speak with Denning, and to do so as a matter of urgency.

She was on the point of giving up hope when Trudi texted to say that Denning had just returned to the MIT suite.

Molly took the lift up to the fifth floor. She spotted Denning chatting to Betty Taggart. His shirt sleeves were rolled up exposing tanned arms.

Betty Taggart was saying something about a meeting with the Chief Superintendent, and Denning was nodding, a joyless look on his face. It felt like it was a bad time. She thought about leaving it until the next day, but there was no guarantee there would be a good time tomorrow either. She waited till their conversation ended and Betty Taggart headed towards the lift. 'DI Denning, could I have a word, please?' she asked as he was about to sit down at his desk.

Denning looked blankly at her for a second, as though waiting for his brain to come into focus, then he said, 'Is it important? I'm kind of in the middle of something.'

She stood in front of his desk for a second or two, aware of a dozen pairs of eyes boring into her; one or two people no doubt wondering who she was. Although it was a small nick, and people would readily chat to one another, even just to exchange idle small talk, it was easy to be anonymous in the station.

'It's about the murder inquiry… Leanne Wyatt, and the others.' She was struggling to speak with a confidence she didn't feel. 'I think there's something you need to know.'

She suddenly felt a spasm of insecurity grip her. What if she was wrong about all of this? But deep down she knew she had to go with her gut and share what she knew with them.

'OK,' said Denning. 'We can talk in DCI McKenna's office.'

She hadn't expected that. In fact, it she was slightly back-footed by his response. She nodded at him, then followed him into the DCI's office.

Denning sat behind Betty Taggart's desk. Molly couldn't help noticing how at home he seemed to look in the DCI's chair. She suspected Denning was destined for better things one day.

'It's DS Fisher, isn't it?' Denning said.

He wasn't smiling, but his facial expression had relaxed from the heavy look he'd had when he'd been speaking with Betty Taggart.

'Actually, it's Molly.' She smiled at him, gradually convincing herself he wasn't quite the arsehole she'd initially thought.

'OK, Molly. What can you tell me about Leanne Wyatt, beyond her connection with Gregor Kane?'

Molly took a deep breath. 'Have you heard of a man called Anthony Ferguson?'

She watched as Denning crinkled his brow.

'He was known as the Bermondsey Ripper…'

Denning rubbed a hand over his eyes, massaging them ever so slightly. 'I remember it, but it must have been a good ten years ago. How's it relevant to Leanne Wyatt, Tanya Russell and Sandra Blake?'

She explained about Ferguson, and her doubts about his conviction; her meeting with Ken Walters and how she was sure he was keeping something from her. 'I think Ferguson is innocent and whoever committed those murders is also responsible for the recent spate of killings.' She watched Denning, trying to ignore the look of incredulity that spread across his face like a nasty rash. 'I realise that rules out Gregor Kane, and probably Daryl Bailey too, and I know it sounds mad, but there are distinct similarities between the Bermondsey Ripper murders and these recent ones: too many for it to be a coincidence.' Even as she said it she knew it sounded bat-shit crazy; *she* sounded bat-shit crazy. And judging by the bewildered look on Denning's face, he was probably thinking the same.

A heavy silence clawed its way round the airless room.

After what seemed like an age but was probably only a few seconds, Denning said: 'I'm sorry, but where's this coming from? Do you have any proof to back any of this up?' He rubbed his hand over his face again, massaging his eyeballs with his thumb and index finger. He looked like he hadn't slept for a while. 'And how do you know there are similarities between the murders? We've only released limited information so far, and we've certainly said nothing publicly about the three murders being linked.'

'People talk. A station like this thrives on rumours.' She wasn't going to drop Trudi in the shit unless she had to.

Denning stared at a space slightly above her head for moment, then said, 'Thanks, DS Fisher. This has been interesting, but I'm afraid I can't base a murder investigation around rumours and fantasy. We need hard evidence. Unless you can prove Anthony Ferguson didn't do it, and whoever did has decided to start killing again, then I'm going to have to dismiss your wild theory. But thanks for your time.'

He stood up and headed to the door, holding it open.

'The crosses,' she said, blurting it out without really knowing where she was going with the conversation. 'There were crosses on the victims' foreheads. The Bermondsey Ripper marked his victims in the same way. You can check. It'll be in the post-mortems.' She caught her breath, then continued. 'The recent victims. The killer does that. He marks them. With a cross.'

Molly sat there dumbstruck for a moment, convinced she'd just handed in her notice from a job she loved. She could feel Denning standing behind her, the door open, waiting for her to go through it and do a walk of shame through the MIT suite back to CID downstairs, where, if she was lucky and managed to hold on to her job, she would remain forever.

Instead, he closed the door and sat back down in the big chair behind Betty Taggart's desk. 'Who told you about that?'

'It's true though, isn't it? It links the most recent murders. And it connects them to the Ripper's murders.'

Denning didn't say anything. She wondered what was going through his head. Did he think she was crazy and should be chucked out of the Met for making lunatic suggestions in front of a senior officer? Or did he believe her?

'I need to talk to DCI McKenna about this.'

She didn't know what else to say. He hadn't thrown her out the office, which was a good sign, but he still didn't seem convinced.

She thanked him for listening to her and made her way back to the CID suite three floors below.

Once she was back at her desk, DI Broomfield came over and asked for a word. She was sure Denning had reported her this time. But it seemed not.

'We've heard back from the CPS.' His face was stony, not its usual smiley self. She didn't like the direction this was heading in. 'They've decided there is insufficient evidence to prove that Gregor Kane provided the Ecstasy tablet that was responsible for Adam Sloane's death. They'll charge him with supplying, but when it comes to manslaughter, he'll walk.'

–

Denning knocked on McKenna's office and she waved him in and nodded for him to sit down.

'Any news, Matt?'

He sat on the squeaky chair opposite the DCI. McKenna stared impassively back at him. She seemed cool and relaxed, as though having a serial killer on the loose in London was something she just took in her stride. Perhaps, he thought to himself, after thirty years in the police force nothing fazed her. Perhaps once he reached the giddy heights of Detective Chief Inspector he'd have found a way of adopting McKenna's laid-back detachment and made it his own.

'Antony Ferguson,' he said coldly. He'd spent the past twenty minutes studying Ferguson's files on the PNC: they were detailed and specific. Molly Fisher had been right: there *were* similarities between the Bermondsey Ripper murders and the more recent ones. Similarities which were too blatant to ignore.

He told McKenna what Molly Fisher had told him and what he'd just read on the PNC.

McKenna nodded, but her face remained impassive. 'Most violent murders bear comparable hallmarks,' she said. 'Extreme violence bordering on sadism, the dehumanising of the victim. It's not to say that all brutal murders are linked.'

'There are specific links here,' he said. 'The crosses on the victim's foreheads. That information was never made public.'

McKenna nodded. 'From memory, they held back on one or two details at the time,' she said.

'That's not to say someone hasn't managed to get hold of those details.'

'You think this might be a copy-cat killer?'

That certainly made more sense than Fisher's crazy story about the wrong man being jailed for the crimes eleven and half years ago. 'It's a very real possibility,' he said. 'There are too many similarities for it to be a coincidence, but I can't say for certain. At least, not yet.'

'So we have to look at who and why. Let's start with anyone Ferguson shared a cell with, or who was in prison at the same time as him. Maybe he discussed details with some psycho who liked the idea and thought they'd try something similar just for the hell of it. Or to gain the same sick celebrity status afforded to nutters like Ferguson.'

'On the other hand, it could just be someone who's read about the case and it's sparked some depraved primal urge inside them.'

She looked at him with a faintly withering expression. 'Has Ferguson been in the limelight recently? A book out? Or one of those godawful real-life-crime porn shows that keep popping up on the telly?'

'I don't know. I can look into it, but I don't think that's going to lead us to the answer.'

'Well, now you've brought it up we can't ignore it.' She sat back in her chair and pulled at some loose hair in the nape of her neck. 'I vaguely remember the so-called Bermondsey Ripper case. And yes, granted these recent murders do bear a faint similarity to Ferguson's killing spree, but then so do half a dozen others over the past decade if we were to look hard enough. Killers marking bodies is nothing unusual.'

'But not with something specific like a cross,' added Denning.

'Do we know for sure our killer is doing that?' she asked.

Denning waited before he answered. 'I've just spoken to the pathologist who did the post-mortem on Leanne Wyatt. He says that on first inspection, and bearing in mind the mess her face was in, it looked as though the marks on her forehead *could* have been caused by a fox, or some other wild animal, but after she'd been cleaned up, a more detailed inspection suggested they were deliberate. They're deeper, more pronounced. He reckoned they were caused by a knife or similar bladed instrument. He agrees that the marks do resemble a cross.' He paused, giving McKenna a chance to digest the information before he continued. 'We haven't got the post-mortem results back for Sandra Blake, but there were marks on her forehead too. It was difficult to be certain because of the state the body was in after more than a week in the canal, but I'd say it looked like a cross.'

'Shit.' McKenna clasped the hair until her scalp started to strain. 'The Chief Super wants this whole thing dealt with before the press start running wild. At the moment we've managed to contain the worst of it, but we're firefighting here. As soon as the media get a whiff of anything about possible serial killers, they'll be all over this story as if their Christmases had come early.'

She didn't need to spell it out. He knew the pressure they were under... the pressure *he* was under. 'One more thing – and I know this is slightly against procedure – but there's a DS in CID who seems to know quite a bit about the Ferguson case – Molly Fisher. To be honest, she was the one who put me onto this. Apparently she's keen to join MIT. OK, it might all come to nothing, but God knows we're short handed and could do with a bit of extra support right now.' He looked at McKenna. 'I wondered if we could ask CID if she could be seconded to the case.'

McKenna released her hair from its vice-like grip. 'You do seem convinced there might be something in this Ferguson story.' She folded her arms across her chest and sighed. 'OK, it's a bit unorthodox, and we don't want to give the impression we're a bunch of amateurs in MIT, but I'll get on to CID, see if they can spare her.' She wrote the name on the notepad on her desk. 'One more thing, Matt: it might be worth speaking to Ferguson himself, see if he can, even indirectly, offer up anything that might be useful.'

Denning smiled and nodded. Right now, any options were worth grabbing with both hands.

–

Molly was about to pack up for the day. It was Friday evening and it was late.

She looked up from her desk to see DI Broomfield approaching. She tried to read his face to see if he was the bearer of good or bad news, but it was hard to tell.

'Gregor Kane is pleading guilty to possession. He claims any drugs he had on him were purely for personal use and that, being a generous and gullible kind of person, he was happy to share them with friends.'

'Adam Sloane was no friend of Kane's,' Molly said. 'Nor Leanne Wyatt for that matter.'

'That's for a jury to decide. We've done all we can at this end. The CPS thinks that at best we'll get a fine for possession, but the manslaughter charge is dead in the water. It's not the result we wanted, but it's something.'

'So the bad guys win again.'

He placed a hand on her shoulder in an almost paternal way. Molly knew the gesture was well meant, even though she found it slightly patronising. 'It's the way it goes, Molly. Sooner or later Kane will slip up and we'll get him.'

She tried to smile; clock it up to experience and move on, but it rankled with her. All that work for nothing. All that sweat and grief and Kane would likely get off with little more than a caution. She could feel hope and optimism trickle away into a great void of nothingness.

'On a more positive note,' Broomfield said, his lips offering a smile, 'I've just had DCI McKenna on the blower.' His smile grew into a broad grin. 'She's asked if you'd like to be seconded onto an ongoing murder inquiry. It would only be until this investigation is completed, and obviously if anything serious comes up down here we'd need you back pronto, but this could be your chance, Molly.' His hand still resting on her shoulder. 'If you play your cards right, this could turn out to be the opportunity you've been waiting for.'

They agreed that another DS would take over her caseload for the time being and she could join MIT straightaway. She thanked him and waited until he removed his hand from her shoulder.

Molly could feel her heart thumping in her chest with a mixture of excitement and apprehension. If Denning had actually believed her, then perhaps the past few days hadn't counted for nothing after all. Perhaps her dream of finally joining MIT was about to be realised.

Chapter Forty-One

Molly wanted to head straight to the pub and celebrate her news over a couple of pints of lager. Instead, she headed to Cricklewood. She turned left as soon as she exited the tube station, carefully following the directions she'd been given.

The house was about a five-minute walk from the station, along a street consisting mostly of terraced houses and larger, post-Victorian villas, most of which had now been converted into flats and bedsits. It didn't take her long to find number 24. She pressed the buzzer for Flat C and after a moment a voice crackled over the entry phone. 'Yes…?'

She paused before she answered: she still wasn't sure she was doing the right thing, and after the day she'd had, this could potentially turn out to be the icing on the turd.

'It's Molly,' she said after a gap. 'I emailed you earlier.'

There was another brief pause, as though the occupant of the flat was having the same reservations as she was, but then the door buzzed. She pushed it open and headed up the tatty staircase to Flat C on the second floor.

There was a figure standing in the doorway of Flat C, partially silhouetted against the light that was coming from inside the flat. It was a woman, probably the same age as herself, with hair loose around her shoulders and a tired look on her face.

Molly reached the top of the stairs and shoved a hand in the figure's direction. 'Hi. Thanks for agreeing to meet me.'

The figure gave an indifferent smile and stepped back from the doorway, allowing Molly to enter.

The flat hadn't been decorated for a while. It had the same grey woodchip wallpaper as the communal hallway, and a faded chintz patterned carpet, though the pattern was mostly worn away.

Melanie Harris wasn't as she'd expected. Not that she was sure what she had expected. Taller than average and painfully thin – whether through anorexia or drugs, Molly couldn't be sure – she was dressed in a pair of men's pyjamas, a belt of thin orange rope tied round the waist.

She showed Molly into the living room. A brown three-piece suite from the 1970s took up most of the space, with a cane and glass coffee table taking up the remainder. Molly waited until Melanie asked her to sit down. There was no offer of a drink, for which Molly was grateful.

'You want to know about Jon Cavanagh,' Melanie said. She stood by the narrow fireplace with its chipped tiles and observed Molly with a mixture of curiosity and disdain. Her voice had a faint trace of an Irish accent.

'I understand you had some problems with him,' Molly said. 'When you worked at the *London Echo*.' She could feel her mouth growing uncomfortably dry. Already she was regretting coming round here asking questions about her boyfriend to a woman she didn't know, all on the word of someone she didn't trust.

Melanie Harris gave a dry laugh. 'I wouldn't exactly say I *worked* there. No, not worked exactly.' She sat down on the brown sofa and crossed one skinny leg over the other. 'I was there on a placement from college. I'd told them I wanted to be a journalist, and someone knew someone who worked there. He got me an eight-week placement there one summer.'

'What happened?'

'I decided journalism wasn't for me. I became a secretary instead.'

Molly gently bit the inside of her lip. 'I meant with Jon.'

She laughed. 'Oh, yeah, Jon. Well, he was sweet at first: helped me out. Quite a few of them were really up their own backsides – I'm sure you know the sort: thought I was just there as an unpaid skivvy to make the coffee and fetch their sandwiches and massage their oversized egos. Jon was nice, at first. He actually took an interest. Encouraged me to learn about how a tabloid newspaper works. He asked me out for a drink one evening, and I agreed.'

'Go on.'

'He knew I'd recently split up from my boyfriend – office gossip, I expect. He told me he was in the middle of getting a divorce, something about his wife being a bit of a harridan. Naturally I took all that with a pinch of salt. I mean, I was young but I wasn't naïve, I knew that men could lie easily when it came to women.'

And women could manipulate, thought Molly. 'Was it just the once?' she asked. 'Going for a drink?'

Melanie Harris nodded. 'He liked to drink. I mean, I suppose it goes with the job, doesn't it? Journalists and booze. But even so, he couldn't half knock them back. The drink didn't do him any favours either: he became less likeable; not abusive, like, just a bit blunt. I think he thought he was trying to be funny but really he was just being obnoxious. I wanted to leave but I didn't want him to think I was being rude.'

'Did he try anything on with you?'

'Not then, but I made it clear I wasn't interested in anything more. Well…' her voice trailed away. 'I thought I'd made it clear. Maybe he misread the signals, maybe he just doesn't like taking no for an answer… I don't know.'

Molly wondered if Melanie Harris was telling the truth. Perhaps this was all part of some elaborate conspiracy dreamed up by Magda Kilbride, but that was ridiculous. Why would she go to all this trouble? Perhaps Melanie was telling the truth, or as least her version of what she believed had happened to her.

'When did the harassment start?' she asked.

A casual shrug. 'After we went out for that drink. He kept pestering me to go out with him again. He had my mobile

206

number so he would continually text me, asking me out. I started to ignore the texts and tried to avoid him at work. I asked if I could be transferred to the paper's magazine in order to get away from him, but he would always find excuses to come and see me. After a while the texts became more and more aggressive: he accused me of leading him on, calling me all sorts of nasty names.'

'Did you mention any of this to your boss at the paper?'

She laughed. 'Naturally, but it made no difference. He was one of their top journalists; I was just some silly little girl from an FE college. There was no way they were going to take my side over his.'

'What happened in the end?'

'I left the placement early; after just a month. I'd already decided journalism wasn't my thing. Mind you, maybe if it hadn't been for my experience with Jon Cavanagh I might have felt differently. Who knows?'

'This just doesn't sound like Jon.'

She looked at Molly like she was a simpleton. 'But it didn't stop there. After I left he continued to bombard me with texts. He followed me home from college once, continually pestering me: claiming I'd lied about him, tried to poison people against him. There was a break-in at my flat. Nothing was taken, and I'm not saying it was him, but it freaked me out enough to make me move house. In the end I had no option but to go to the police. They took out a restraining order and had a word with the paper's owners. It seemed to do the trick. He left me alone after that.'

Molly left the stuffy flat and returned to the stuffier air of the street outside. She headed slowly back towards the Tube station, unsure how she felt about what she had just heard.

The evening was humid and even though the sun was low in the sky, the pavement was throwing up all the heat from the day.

She could feel a trickle of sweat make its way down her spine and gather in the small of her back where her blouse met her trousers.

She desperately wanted to believe that the Jon she knew and loved wasn't the same Jon Melanie Harris had described. But she couldn't ignore the fact that she'd recognised some of the characteristics: the way his personality changed when he was in one of his depressive cycles; his near-obsessiveness, or his inability to see when he was pissing someone off. She remembered how he'd endlessly texted her when they'd first met, after they quite literally bumped into one another at a music festival in Erith three and half years ago. At first, she'd thought it was charming. Jon was very old-fashioned, insisting on paying for everything; walking her home after a night out, or at least as far as her bus stop. The age gap between them had never been an issue: he always claimed she was mature for her age, while he was just a child at heart. She'd believed that too, and part of her still did.

He'd told her about his previous marriages, all four of them. Perhaps that should have been a warning sign: if he couldn't make a success of four serious relationships, then what were the chances of the two of them making a go of it? She so wanted to be wrong about what she was now thinking about him; blind herself to the growing mound of evidence that suggested the man she lived with was someone she didn't really know. She could convince herself the evidence was circumstantial and Jon was guilty of nothing more than poor judgement, but did she really believe that?

She arrived at the Tube station: a wave of roasting heat blasting out the entrance like opening an oven door. She tapped her Oyster card against the yellow pad on the gates, sidled through as they swung open, and headed towards the escalators. A line of sweating bodies rose up from below, standing on the escalator opposite like melting dummies in a shop window display.

She knew she had to speak to Jon about Melanie Harris's accusations – get his side of the story before she made any bold decisions.

Just before the escalator reached the platform level, her phoned pinged with a text – another couple of seconds and she would have been out of range.

The text was from Jon. It read: *I need to talk to you.*

Chapter Forty-Two

The French windows leading onto the narrow balcony were open when Denning returned home, allowing a welcome respite from the clammy mugginess of the hot summer's evening.

It had been a long day.

He could hear Sarah in the shower in the en suite next to their bedroom in the mezzanine level above the living area.

There was a copy of the evening edition of the *London Echo* on the coffee table. He picked it up and scanned the headline: *Body found in Hoxton canal.* The article was based on McKenna's carefully crafted press release stating that the death was being treated as suspicious, while suggesting that it might even be accidental and deliberately not connecting it with the earlier murders, which weren't even mentioned.

He tossed the paper back onto the coffee table. He cast his mind over DS Fisher's theory about the Bermondsey Ripper and her insistence that there was a connection with the current case. He wanted to dismiss her claims as laughable, but he couldn't ignore the facts.

He remembered the case. He was in his final year at King's when the Bermondsey murders seemed to rise up out of nowhere and embrace the capital in a bear hug of fear and paranoia. He had been too busy playing rugby and courting Claire to pay much attention to the finer details, but it was impossible to avoid the wider implications. He already had a vague idea about wanting to join the police back then, but at the time it was simply one career option amongst many others.

However, the sheer brutality of the killings had been hard to ignore. Claire had been reluctant to walk home by herself, nervous even of using taxis or public transport at night. Female friends at uni had been cautious about joining him and his mates for nights out amid the fear of becoming another grim statistic in a serial killer's sick quest for notoriety.

It was a sobering thought: the prospect of that killer still being out there killing people today.

He was suddenly aware of Sarah standing beside him, wrapped in a white cotton robe; her dark hair still damp from the shower. She smelt of lavender body wash and coconut conditioner.

'I didn't hear you come in,' she said. 'You look shattered.' She leant down and brushed his cheek with her lips.

Denning watched her, standing next to him looking and smelling seductive. He tried not to think about Claire, looking and smelling seductive for someone else. 'We found another body,' he said, nodding at the newspaper on top of the coffee table.

Sarah sat down next to him on the linen sofa, caressing his shoulder with one hand and rubbing his arm with the other. 'I know. I read it. It must be taking its toll.' The hand that had been rubbing his shoulder moved to hold his hand in a gesture that was tender and reassuring. 'Why don't we eat out tonight? It's too hot to cook anything.'

He couldn't think about food right now. His mind was jammed with awkward thoughts, mostly the inexorable fact that there was a serial killer out there killing women. Just like there had been twelve years earlier…

'Yeah,' he said. 'Sounds like a plan.'

'I'll phone Pablo's and see if we can get a table.'

Pablo's was a pseudo-Spanish eatery that had 'popped up' somewhere along Shoreditch High Street a few months back and had quickly established a reputation as a magnet for hipsters and hedge-fund managers alike. Sarah liked it. Claire would have hated it.

'I've booked a table for seven p.m.,' she said.

He smiled at her. 'Good. I've just realised I skipped lunch.'

–

Jon was waiting in the kitchen when Molly got back. She could smell the remains of a roach lingering in the fuggy heat.

'Where have you been?' he asked. His voice seemed laced with genuine concern, and for a moment it was like the old Jon was back in the room, the one who cared for her and wanted everything to be all right. 'I expected you back ages ago.'

'I had to meet someone after work,' she said. 'Why?'

He sat down at the kitchen table, moving a couple of dirty mugs to one side. 'Mags phoned. I haven't spoken to that bitch for years. She hasn't changed: still as vindictive as ever.'

Molly sat down opposite him. There was a sticky patch on the table, where something had obviously been spilt and not cleaned up properly. 'Why is Mags phoning you? I thought you hated her.'

'I didn't ask her to phone. I don't even know how the bitch got hold of my number.' He looked at Molly as though she was the guilty party.

She suspected a former work colleague had passed it on; she didn't really care. 'What did she want?'

Jon looked over at Molly for a moment, his eyes twinkling either with tears or anger, she couldn't tell. 'She says you've been asking questions about me. She claims you've been asking her about my past, whether I was ever violent, that sort of thing.' His eyes continued to gleam and there was a slight tremble to his voice. 'Why would you go behind my back like that, to *her* of all people? I *told* you what she was like. You can't trust a word she says, but still – you would rather talk to her than ask me myself.' He shook his head. 'Why do I feel like you've betrayed me?'

She waited until he'd finished. She could feel anger swell up inside her like a balloon inflating inside her stomach. *Her*

212

betrayal: that was rich. That was very rich indeed, after what she'd just heard earlier that day. 'Why don't you ask me about who I was meeting this evening? Because she had some very interesting things to say about you, Jon. Very interesting and very alarming.'

He splayed his hands and shrugged. 'What are you talking about?'

'I've been to see Melanie Harris. You remember, the intern you harassed. You terrorised that poor girl, Jon. She was just a kid.'

She watched his expression change from shock to anger to something that looked like total bewilderment. 'You've done what? You tracked down someone I worked with decades ago and talked to her about me! And did she tell you what you wanted to hear? Did she tell you I was some kind of sicko who did... what, exactly? What did she tell you about me?'

Molly tried to keep her voice level. 'She told me you pestered her, intimidated her. She had to go to the police, Jon. That's how desperate she was. That's how *frightened* she was.' Her voice was rising now; all efforts to remain detached and impassive, professional almost, were evaporating. 'In fact, she pretty much supported everything Magda Kilbride told me about you.'

Jon stood up quickly, knocking one of the mugs onto the tiled floor, where it smashed into several pieces. He went to the sink and ran the cold tap, splashing tepid water onto his face.

She felt a pang of guilt prickle at the back of her neck. Was she being unfair?

Jon turned to face her. 'It's all lies, Molly. All of it. I asked Melanie Harris out for a drink a couple of times, but only because she led me to believe she was interested in me. I texted her a couple of times after she left – because she hated the job, not because of me – and asked why she'd lied about me. It wasn't harassment. This is all shit stirred up by Mags because she's jealous of us and bitter because her life is empty and the only pleasure she can get is to try and make other people's lives as depressing as hers.'

There was water dripping off his face. Or maybe it was sweat, Molly couldn't tell.

He leaned against the sink, his hands gripping the worktop either side of it. 'But what really hurts, what I struggle to forgive, is that you went behind my back. You believed these lies enough to track down some silly bint I worked with years ago who fed you a ton of shit about me and you believed her. Why, Molly? I mean, just… *why?*'

She couldn't answer. Words formed in her head but got stuck in her throat. She hadn't meant it to be like this – this confrontation between them. She'd wanted to be cool, calm and collected, but instead found herself shaking inside; her stomach twisting and her mouth dry.

'Jon, I so wanted not to believe that girl, but nothing you've said has convinced me otherwise.' She could feel tears prickling behind her eyes. 'What happened back then? What was going on inside your head?'

He was red in the face, either with sadness or fury, it was difficult to tell. He looked at her, his face still damp, just staring at her. Then he said, 'I can't do this. I need some air.'

He charged past her, out of the kitchen and a moment later she heard the front door slam. She just sat there, her whole body trembling very slightly. Somewhere in the background she could hear tinny music playing, probably a neighbour's radio.

She tried to convince herself she'd done the right thing confronting Jon: she was a police officer and confronting people with difficult facts was part of her daily life. She'd developed an almost intuitive sense of knowing when someone was lying to her, but when it came to her own boyfriend, she couldn't be sure.

How could she tell if she was living with a monster?

Chapter Forty-Three

It wasn't that Denning didn't want the food; the grumbling in his stomach was proof of that. It was more that he just couldn't concentrate. It was like the act of eating was just too much effort.

The restaurant was air-conditioned and not very busy, but he felt uncomfortably warm. Their fellow diners consisted mostly of cool young couples looking bright and trendy and trying hard to look bored. Sarah was doing her best to keep the conversation going: talking to him about anything other than work, anything to keep his mind off the very thing he wanted to focus on.

'I've seen a couple of properties online I think we should have a look at,' she said, smiling at him over a roasted pecan and avocado salad. 'One's in Hertfordshire, so it would be a bit of a trek into work every day, but it's been on the market for a while and they've just reduced the asking price by twenty thousand. If we were to put in a cheeky offer…'

He looked up from his plate of chorizo sausage and cucumber salad, suddenly aware that she was waiting for him to speak.

'Did you hear what I said?' she asked.

'Sorry, I was miles away. Something about a property in Hertfordshire.'

'Well…?'

He took a sip of iced water, hoping it would help to cool him down. 'Yes, I think we should look at it. This weekend maybe.'

'Matt, is anything the matter? You've barely touched your food.'

He threw his fork down on the table. 'I'm just not as hungry as I thought.'

'Do you want to order something else?'

He shook his head. His phone pinged with a text, from Claire. *Can we meet?*

His first thought was to ignore it; she probably just wanted to mess him around over Jake again. But he wanted an excuse to get away from the restaurant and away from Sarah and her incessant chatter about buying houses.

'I need to pop out,' he said, getting to his feet. 'I'll see you back at the flat. I won't be long.'

'What about your dinner?' Sarah asked, her voice rising an octave above its usual level. 'You can't just leave it.'

'I told you, I'm just not that hungry.' He took three twenty pound notes out of his wallet and placed them on the table next to Sarah. 'Tell them to keep the change.'

–

Twenty minutes later, Denning was knocking on Claire's door. The minute she opened the door, he could tell she'd been crying: her puffy eyes were tinged with red.

'What's happened?'

She ushered him into the compact sitting room at the front of the house. The walls were painted an off-white and a cream sofa and two matching armchairs sat on a pale carpet. The only punctuation of colour was a blue and beige rug beside the faux marble fireplace. Denning sat in the armchair that faced the television, where he always used to sit when he lived there.

Claire sat down on the sofa, folding her body around herself.

'Where's Jake?' Denning asked.

'He's in bed,' she replied, although it was much earlier than his usual bedtime.

'What's happened?' Denning repeated.

'Alan and I have had a massive argument.' She said it very matter-of-factly. 'I think it might be over between us.'

'When was this?'

'A couple of hours ago. Jake was playing up and I said he couldn't go to LazerWorld tomorrow. He had a massive tantrum and started throwing things. Alan just snapped. He said he'd had enough of us living like this.' She rubbed a hand over her eyes. 'He's not been himself lately. I think he's stressed about work. That and the fact his new place is taking so long to finish. I've texted him a few times in the last couple of hours saying we need to talk about it, but he hasn't replied.'

For a moment Denning thought this might be down to him, that maybe he'd come across too heavy when he'd confronted Marsden that morning: the overprotective father and ex-partner scaring off the competition... 'It doesn't follow that it's over just because you've had an argument. Maybe he just needs a bit of space to get his head together.'

She shook her head. 'No. Things haven't been right for a while. I think he resents Jake. I mean, he's never said so, and they seemed to get on well together, but God knows Jake can be difficult when he wants to be.'

He couldn't deny that Jake could be a handful, even though he'd calmed down since his GP had changed his medication to Equasym XL. However, Marsden had assured him Jake wasn't an issue, despite what Claire might think. 'You need to speak to Alan, Claire. Before you start jumping to conclusions.'

'I know when a relationship is dead in the water, Matt. I knew with us, didn't I?'

He sighed. 'This isn't about us though, is it?' He looked over at his ex-wife, sitting crumpled and pathetic on the pale sofa. He couldn't help feeling responsible for the mess her life had become. Part of him wanted to go over and give her a reassuring hug, tell her everything would work out all right. But there wouldn't be any point: neither of them could turn back the clock.

'Look, if you want my advice, call him tomorrow. Tell him you want to meet up somewhere neutral, and talk things through. Sarah and I can look after Jake for a while if the two of you need some time to yourselves.'

Claire's face contorted into a tight fist. 'Is that why you came round tonight? It's not about me at all: you just want to take Jake from me.'

'Now you're not being rational, Claire. I came here because you texted me. You wanted to see me, so here I am.'

She shook her head. 'I'm sorry. I'm not thinking straight. I don't even know why I texted you. I just needed to talk to someone.'

'There's always your mum.'

'My mum doesn't want to know. She's never forgiven me for agreeing to divorce you. She thinks I should have worked harder at the marriage. She blames me.'

Again, he felt another twinge of guilt. 'That's not true. She's never taken sides.' He'd always got on well with his former mother-in-law; obviously she'd saved her censure of their divorce for Claire's ears.

'Speak to Alan, Claire. Sort this out. If you want him back in your life then do something about it.' He stood up to leave. 'I'm sorry, but I just don't have the time or the energy to deal with this right now.'

-

Molly waited up for Jon. She'd tried reading a book, tried watching some rubbish on television, but nothing seemed to sink in. She'd thought about calling him, but realised his mobile phone was sitting on the table in the sitting room.

She didn't know how she felt. She knew she loved Jon, despite everything, but she couldn't commit herself emotionally to a man she couldn't trust. She couldn't take the risk of getting hurt again.

It was after midnight when he returned. She'd assumed he'd been down the pub, getting pissed out his mind, but he was sober. Sober and surprisingly calm.

'I think I owe you an explanation,' he said, sitting on the chaise longue. He rubbed a hand over his head. There were sweat stains on his t-shirt and a faint smell of vomit about him.

'Jon, I—' she began, but he cut her off.

'It's true, about Melanie Harris. Not the way she puts it, but basically she's right about me behaving badly. I'm not going to gloss over it, but I was in a bad place, mentally. I'd just split up with Marguerite, my head was all over the place. Melanie was all friendly and flirty at first; she clearly enjoyed having someone chasing round after her like a prick. She got off on me making a twat of myself over her. But, I admit, things probably went too far.' He paused, staring at his feet and slowly shaking his head from side to side. 'She was just a kid, she didn't know what she was doing. I was in my thirties, twice divorced, I should have handled the whole thing better. But, like I said, my head was scrambled; I was drinking too much, taking too much white powder. I didn't know my own backside half the time. I was desperate and I thought she offered a way out.'

'So you did harass her? Is that what you're saying?'

He rubbed his palms into his tired eyes. 'No. Not "harass". She's wrong. I just... I suppose I did get slightly obsessed. I thought if I could pull an attractive young girl like Melanie, then I could convince myself I wasn't useless and past it.'

Molly struggled to take all this in. 'You deliberately intimidated a young woman just to prove to yourself you weren't past it? And you think it's OK to behave like that?'

'No, of course I don't. I'm not trying to excuse my behaviour.' He reached out to touch her but she flinched, backing away instinctively.

'Really? Because it sounds to me like that's exactly what you're doing.'

He rubbed his hand over his face, wiping away sweat and tears and snot. 'I don't know what else I can say. It was a long time ago. I was a fuck-up back then.' He shot her an imploring look. 'I was a different person then. You have to believe that.'

A silence filled the stuffy room. Molly didn't know how to respond. If Jon had been capable of that, what else was he capable of?

'I'm going to move my stuff into the spare room,' she said, 'at least for now.' She couldn't think about the long term. She didn't even know if she and Jon had a 'long term'. She wasn't sure about anything any more.

–

The digital clock display read 02:43.

Denning had been awake for at least half an hour. Knowing sleep was unlikely, he eased himself out of bed carefully and quietly so as not to disturb Sarah who lay next to him, her deep breathing giving way to the occasional light snore. There was a coolness about the flat, helped by the fan standing at the foot of the bed, circulating unruffled air around the large, open space. His skin was itchy and the t-shirt he slept in was drenched with sweat.

He padded downstairs to the living room and headed to the French windows. Outside, London slept the sleep of the just. Except it didn't. London never fully slept: there was always a lack of stillness about the city, even at night.

Claire's cry for help still echoed in his ears. He knew that he and his ex-wife would be forever bound together by their love for Jake. But sometimes it felt like more than that. Marrying so young, both barely out of university, it had felt as though their lives were destined to be eternally entwined. Claire was going through a bad patch, again, and he was going to have to shoulder some of the blame.

Then there was the unavoidable reality of there being a serial killer out there somewhere…

A stubborn pain gnawed at the base of his neck. He tried rubbing it away, but it stayed there, throbbing like a pulsating dagger. He scratched at his skin, trying to erase the itchiness that just wouldn't go away.

He thought about Fisher and her wild claims; maybe not so wild after all – maybe more like pieces of a puzzle that didn't quite fit at the moment, but could somehow if someone were able to slot them together correctly.

Chapter Forty-Four

Molly pushed open the door to the MIT suite. The room felt stuffier than the CID offices downstairs, but the layout was exactly the same: a large, open-plan office with metal desks arranged in pairs. Although it was a Saturday morning, there were already one or two detectives tapping away at keyboards as though this were a normal working day for them. She hadn't had time to take it all in the other day, when Denning had ushered her into Betty Taggart's office, only to promptly usher her out again a few short minutes later.

She noticed three mobile whiteboards at one end of the room, on which were posted an assortment of photos and a mass of scribbled notes, connected by arrows and with certain words encircled. The atmosphere felt heavy and slightly intimidating. CID seemed friendlier somehow, or maybe she just knew everyone better.

Molly was trying to be positive. This was what she'd waited such a long time for. But the timing couldn't be worse.

Jon was still asleep when she'd left for work that morning. She'd briefly thought about knocking on his bedroom door to ask how he was, but everything still felt too raw for her to go prodding that particular wound. Part of her wanted to run a PNC check on Jon: if Melanie Harris had reported Jon's harassment to the police then there would be a record, combined with their respective statements. But what would be the point? Jon had as good as admitted that Melanie Harris's claims were true. And there was always the possibility the PNC would tell her something she didn't want to know.

The first person to speak to her was Trudi. She arrived a few minutes after Molly and greeted her with a warm smile. 'Molly, hi. What you doing here?'

'I'm joining the team,' she said, feeling slightly awkward, realising she should have let Trudi know beforehand, rather than just pitching up unannounced. 'Temporarily,' she added. 'It's been OK'd by Betty Taggart.'

Trudi seemed momentarily taken aback, but smiled and said, 'Oh, right. Great. Well, good luck. We could certainly appreciate a bit of help. I mean I know it looks like we've got a multiple murderer out there, but dragging us in on a weekend really is taking the piss.'

Molly wasn't sure if she was joking but smiled anyway.

A few moments later, Denning appeared, carrying a cup of Costa coffee and looking slightly distracted. He placed the coffee on his desk and nodded a professional smile in her direction. 'DS Fisher,' he said, 'thanks for agreeing to help. You can use DS Myers' desk whilst you're here. He's on sick leave for the next couple of months.' He pointed at a desk at the far end of the office near what looked like a metal stationary cupboard. 'But in the meantime,' he dragged a swivel chair over from the corner beside the whiteboards, 'perhaps you and I could go over everything you know about Anthony Ferguson.'

She sat down next to Denning. His desk was neat and tidy; just an A4 pad and a photograph of an East Asian woman she took to be his wife. 'I've seen the case notes,' he said. 'I'm willing to accept there are significant similarities between the two cases. We're working on the assumption that this is a copycat killer; someone who knew Ferguson, possibly someone who was in prison with him and is now looking to bask in some of his glory.'

'Maybe,' she said. 'However, I honestly think we need to look at the possibility that the wrong man was sent down for this eleven years ago. I know all the evidence points to Ferguson being the guilty party, but there are questions.' She told him what she'd found out about Ferguson so far. There was something empowering about sharing this information with a senior officer, even one who had been so dismissive of her the day before. 'OK, I know it's mostly circumstantial,' she concluded, 'but it does cast doubt on Ferguson's guilt.'

Denning still seemed unconvinced. He nodded politely when she spoke, but she couldn't escape the feeling he was simply humouring her.

'If that is the case,' he said, 'then it raises serious questions about what the real killer has been doing over the past twelve years. We also have to ask, why now? Why start killing again?'

Molly shrugged. 'I don't know the answer to that. But Ferguson clearly had an alibi for the night of the last murder.'

Denning looked at his notes. 'Rebecca Owen. OK, but his alibi is far from watertight.'

'I'm not so sure,' Molly said. 'I spoke to Rodman. He seemed convincing.'

'Then why that one night? Why didn't Ferguson offer him up as an alibi for all the other murders if he knew Rodman was willing to lie for him?'

Molly sighed. 'I can't answer that.' Denning reached out for his coffee, but changed his mind, leaving it untouched on his desk. 'You need to speak to Ken Walters,' she said. 'he knows more than he's letting on.'

Denning nodded. 'Maybe. But first things first, I have to call a briefing as soon as everyone gets here.'

She waited until the room filled up. Once they were all seated and the general hubbub had died down, Denning rose to his feet to begin the briefing. 'First off,' he said, 'apologies for dragging you all in on a Saturday, but as we are now in the midst of a multiple murder investigation, days off are a luxury we can't afford.' There was a muttered cacophony of grumblings from the detectives, which Denning ignored. 'Next, I'd like to introduce DS Molly Fisher to the team. She's joining us temporarily from regular CID to help with the investigation. I'm sure you'll all make her very welcome and those of you who don't already know her will find time to make your introductions at some point.' He turned to face the whiteboard. 'In the meantime, Trudi has been collating the CCTV footage from the bridge next to where Sandra Blake's body was found, so our priority is to go over that in detail and look for anything that might be of interest to us. We're still waiting for the post-mortem report to get here, but we can safely assume we're looking for the same person who was responsible for Leanne Wyatt's murder and likely Tanya Russell's too. Uniform are due to visit every pub within a couple of miles of the Gilded Drake, but let's be honest, it's the longest of longshots to assume they'd hit the jackpot. Sandra Drake could have gone anywhere, assuming she'd even gone to another pub at all.'

Denning looked over at Deep Neeraj, who was chomping on an Extra Strong Mint and staring at something on his computer screen. He looked up when he saw Denning was speaking to him. Molly noticed Neeraj had heavy bags under his eyes, suggesting he too had been struggling with sleep.

'Deep, get on to the PNC,' said Denning. 'And find out everything you can about a man called Anthony Ferguson.'

'The Bermondsey Ripper.' Neeraj said with a note of derision. 'That was years ago.'

'I know. But can you just do it, please.' Denning was snappy and Molly wondered whether tempers in the MIT suite were frayed because of the heat, or the stress of the case, or a combination of both. This was either the worst time to have joined an on-going murder investigation, she thought, or the best time. She wasn't entirely sure yet.

—

Ken Walters didn't seem particularly surprised to see Denning when he knocked on his front door later that afternoon. Denning had left Fisher back at the office, compiling a list of people who'd been in prison with Ferguson over the past twelve years and who had been released in the past few weeks. It was a long list. She wasn't happy about it, and had made her feelings clear to Denning. She wanted to be where the action was, and that meant accompanying him on his visit to Walters. He didn't quite know what to make of Fisher, at least not yet. She was bright and sparky, and very keen. But she was also rough around the edges, like an uncut diamond.

'Come in, come in,' said Walters, ushering Denning into his small but tidy bungalow. 'Why don't we sit out in the garden as it's such a lovely day?'

He led the way through to the patio at the rear of the house, beside pretty flowers in ceramic pots. The garden was partially shaded by a large willow tree that sat on the slightly parched lawn surrounded by a bed of bright roses. 'Can I get you something to drink?'

Denning shook his head. 'No thank you, Mr Walters.' He wondered if he should call the old man 'sir'; officers of Walters' generation expected deference, even after they'd left the job. But the moment passed, and Walters said. 'I'm going to have a glass of beer. Are you sure you won't join me?'

'Well, OK. I don't suppose one would do any harm.'

Walters headed back into the house. He reappeared a couple of minutes later with two glasses of chilled Guinness. Denning hadn't drunk Guinness for years. He appreciated the cool, rich taste as he took a sip. 'Cheers,' said Walters, raising his glass at Denning as though it were some languid social occasion. 'I believe Liz McKenna is your DCI. I worked with her ex-husband for a number of years. She has quite a reputation, so I hear: balls of steel.'

Denning smiled. 'I'll pass on your regards.'

'Do they still call her "Betty Taggart" behind her back?'

'About Anthony Ferguson,' said Denning, ignoring the attempt at small talk. 'I believe you spoke to a colleague of mine last week. She said there might be some doubts about aspects of the original investigation. She mentioned something about Ferguson having an alibi for one of the murders? Is that true?'

Walters sipped his Guinness, licking a thin sliver of foam from his top lip with a flick of his tongue. He eyed Denning cautiously. 'Oh yes, the delightful Detective Sergeant Fisher.' He stared momentarily at his glass. 'She lied to me, which I didn't appreciate at the time. Some cock and bull story about re-examining an old case as part of some Met training scheme. I suppose in hindsight I should have appreciated her ingenuity. But I never like being lied to.' He chortled to himself. 'She must have thought me a silly old duffer. After all, if I can't tell when a slip of a girl is telling me fibs, then I couldn't have been much of a copper back in the day, could I?'

Denning tried to reassure him with a sympathetic smile. 'It was a bit unorthodox, and I accept that she should have been honest with you. However, I can confirm that DS Fisher is now an official part of the ongoing murder inquiry.'

'Ferguson was a liar. His alibi was lies. It was obvious he'd asked a friend to lie for him.'

'OK. For argument's sake, let's accept that the alibi was false. But DS Fisher seemed to think there was something else. Some other doubts about the case.'

Walters watched Denning with wary eyes. 'What's this really to do with? You can't think Ferguson is in any way involved with these recent murders, can you?'

'It's possible,' Denning said, 'that someone Ferguson knew is behind these recent killings. But, taking on board what DS Fisher has told me, along with what I've read about his case, we can't ignore the possibility Ferguson *may be* innocent. I have an obligation to explore all the options before I completely rule anything out.' Credit to Neeraj, he'd been thorough when collated everything of interest the PNC had on Ferguson and the Bermondsey Ripper case.

A sudden gust of wind blew across the patio and caused the flowers in the ceramic pots to nod as though they were agreeing with Denning's words.

'Yes,' said Walters. 'Yes, I think you'd be very wise not to rule anything out when it comes to Anthony Ferguson. It's just possible things weren't quite as clear-cut as they seemed at the time.'

–

Molly had wasted an hour searching through the list of names she was compiling for Denning. Most were petty criminals who had been sent down for drug-related crimes, violence or robberies and break-ins. Others had been in for fraud, deception or handling stolen goods. One man had served two years for perjury. Only four murderers had been released within the last month: two of them were over sixty, one had moved back to Glasgow to be with his elderly mother, and the other had been recalled over a breach of his parole within a week of being released. Two men had been released early from rape sentences, but it was a big leap from rape to murder. Or was it? The truth was: she didn't know what she was looking for.

She didn't entirely buy Denning's copy-cat killer theory. It was too neat, too convenient. It felt to her like he was retrofitting the facts and trying to form them into a tidy shape. She should have been with Denning at the interview, after all she was the one who'd flashed Walters' name up on the radar in the first place.

But instead she was sitting at Denning's desk, looking over a list of ex-cons, one of whom might be a serial killer. She looked up to see Trudi waving a packet of B&H in her direction and gesturing towards the door. Molly shook her head and pulled an exaggerated sad face. There was nothing she would have loved more at that exact moment than to go for a fag break and a gossip with Trudi, but she had to plough through this crap. She would run the names through the PNC to see if anyone had attracted police attention since they'd got out, but if they were devoting their spare time to killing women then it was likely they'd be keeping as low a profile as was humanly possible.

The PNC was unable to yield anything useful, as she'd expected. She was tempted to look up the name Jon Cavanagh, even if it meant unearthing a whole heap of nasty shit she'd rather not know about. She still couldn't escape the gnawing worry that there was so much more about Jon's life and personal history about which she was ignorant. For the sake of her sanity, perhaps it was better left like that. She still had to ask herself some hard questions about her future, and whether or not Jon featured in it. Moving her belongings into the spare room was only one step off moving out altogether. She didn't yet know if that was what she wanted. She didn't really know much right now, not even if she wanted to work in MIT, especially if most of the work was as tedious as conventional CID.

At some point in the near future she was going to have to have a serious conversation with herself as to where her future lay, both personally and professionally.

Denning took another sip of Guinness. It was particularly welcome on this hot day. A wasp buzzed around his head; he tried swatting it away but it kept returning, lured either by the Guinness or by the scent of his aftershave.

'There was always something about Anthony Ferguson,' Walters said. 'I told all this to your colleague, but I'll say it again: he seemed to exude something evil. Prior to meeting him I don't think I'd ever *truly* known evil, not in an almost physical sense. I'm sure I don't need to tell you, Mr Denning, but with most killers there's a clear purpose behind why they do what they do: greed, lust, revenge. Most killers kill for a reason.' He scratched his beard, and stared at the glass of Guinness on the garden table as though mesmerised by it. 'Ferguson killed because he enjoyed the act of killing. I don't think it mattered to him: animals, people. He took pleasure from watching others suffer.'

Denning already knew this. He'd done his research: Ferguson was a cold-blooded psychopath, who'd never shown a shred of remorse for his actions. But none of this was proof of either innocence or guilt. 'But you have doubts about him?' Denning asked.

'About his guilt? No, no doubts at all.'

'DS Fisher seems to think you had doubts about certain elements of the case. If you do have any doubts, Mr Walters, now would be the time to share them.' He tried hard not to sound aggressive, but there was an edge to his voice that said he had neither the time nor the energy to fuck about. 'I need to conclusively rule any link with Ferguson out of this investigation, and time isn't exactly on my side here.'

'I think you can safely rule Ferguson out of these recent murders,' Walters chuckled. 'As far as I'm aware, he's still locked up.'

Denning looked at him, trying to fix him with the same gimlet stare that McKenna so often used on him, but Walters seemed impervious; no doubt he'd crossed swords with scarier DCIs than Betty Taggart back in his day. He decided on a more direct approach. 'Like I said, time isn't on my side. We've got a killer out there and I need to put him away before the body count rises.'

The directness seemed to do the trick. Walters dropped his shoulders and sighed. For a moment he looked like a shrunken old man rather than the strong-willed, sharp-minded ex-cop that had greeted Denning on the doorstep.

'Ferguson was an unfortunate individual. One of life's inadequates: a loser, I suppose you'd call him. I'm no psychiatrist, but I reckon murdering those women was the only successful thing he's ever done in his life.'

'Go on.'

'Well, that's it really. Nothing more than a niggling doubt. But we didn't have time for niggling doubts twelve years ago: we were up against it, as I very much imagine you are now. Time was of the essence, as it always is. And it wasn't as if Ferguson wasn't guilty. We all knew he did it.'

Denning scratched his head. The wasp was buzzing around Walters' head now, though he seemed oblivious to it; lost in his own memories.

'What, exactly, was that niggling doubt?'

'It was the murders. They were so well-planned. Everything – from how those poor women were snatched from the streets, to where and how the bodies were left for us to find – was planned with an almost military precision.' He looked at Denning, pity lining his face and sadness welling in his eyes. 'It took us months to solve those murders. Months of solid hard-core policing. We even drafted officers in from other divisions, and still we struggled to find a lead.'

Denning was confused. 'I already know this. It's in the files. I still don't see what it has to do with Anthony Ferguson.'

'That's just it, Mr Denning. We were dealing with a clever killer. Anthony Ferguson was many things, but he wasn't clever.'

'I don't see…' Denning was struggling to follow Walters' reasoning. 'Are you now saying Ferguson *didn't* do it…?'

Walters shook his head. He took another drink of Guinness. He looked momentarily crestfallen as though he'd finally been caught out and knew it was time to confess. 'No. I'm saying, deep down, I always suspected there might have been two of them.'

Chapter Forty-Five

Molly didn't want to believe what she was reading. Despite her reservations, curiosity had got the better of her and she'd decided to have a look on the PNC. She'd convinced herself she'd rather know than not know; that whatever the outcome, she would deal with it.

And there it was, flashed up on the computer screen.

The harassment claim made by Melanie Harris about Jonathan Andrew Cavanagh. He'd received an official warning, but nothing more.

However, there was a second entry under his name. She thought she was going to throw up when she read it: an arrest for assault dated almost exactly twelve years ago. But it was the name of the victim that made her scalp prickle. The person on the receiving end of Jon's violent outburst was Magda Kilbride.

It explained so much. The underlying animosity between the two of them, and the one-woman vendetta Mags seemed to be waging against Jon.

She read the report for a second time.

The officers who'd been called out had labelled it a 'domestic'. *Domestic?* Did that mean Jon and Mags had been living together...?

The details were vague, just the basic facts: a report had come in at approximately 22:30 p.m. on the evening in question. It seemed there had been an argument between 'a couple' resulting in a female being thrown against a wall causing her injury. Despite some significant bruising, the female had declined to go to hospital, insisting she would stay with a friend.

The male had been arrested, cautioned and held in custody until the following morning. The male was described as having been drunk and aggressive. Ultimately, the victim had decided to drop the charges and the case never got as far as court.

Molly felt a stab of nausea rip through her stomach.

Part of her felt disgusted at the actions of Jon, a man she'd let into her life in the misguided belief that he was a decent guy. But another part of her felt angry; angry at the thought of having been taken for a fool. She'd somehow become a pawn in a sick game of hate being played out between her boyfriend and his ex-lover, and cursed herself for contacting Mags in the first place. More worryingly, she'd *let* them take her for a fool. She ran to the ladies' toilet beside the lift and flung open the door of the first cubicle. Dropping to her knees she threw up into the toilet bowl.

–

Denning had finally swatted the wasp. It had landed on the table roughly halfway between the two glasses of Guinness and he'd thumped it with the heel of his hand. It now sat squashed and dead on the table. He stared at its crushed corpse for a minute, trying to process the bombshell Walters had just exploded in his lap.

Walters sat opposite, staring blankly at his feet. Perhaps he regretted saying what he'd said: fearing it could prize open a decade-old can of nasty worms resulting in some kind of post-career disciplinary case for gross misconduct, or dereliction of duty, or simply failure to protect the public from a potentially very dangerous man. However, Denning suspected that deep down what Walters mostly felt was relief. Relief that he'd finally had the chance to unburden himself of all the guilt and regret that had been building up since the day Anthony Ferguson was sent down. Whatever the case, he had now presented Denning with a major conundrum. On the one hand, he should haul

Walters' arse over the coals, but more pressingly, he needed to find out who this other party was.

'I know exactly what you're thinking,' Walters said. His face had taken on a waxen look, like a melted candle. 'Why didn't I speak up at the time? Why didn't I share my concerns with someone else? A senior officer, or even a fellow officer?' He shook his head slowly. 'We had our man.'

'Even though he had an alibi for one of the murders?'

'We checked that alibi. It didn't stack up, and it was only for one of the murders: there was enough good, solid evidence to link him to all the others.' Walters had raised his voice half an octave. He wasn't quite shouting, but there was a clear hint of anger in his tone.

Denning laid his hands on the table, brushing the dead wasp onto the patio. 'Mr Walters, I'm not here to have a go. Whatever you did or didn't do twelve years ago is irrelevant now. You can't change the past.' He threw the retired cop a reassuring smile. 'I need you to give me the whole story. From the top.'

Walters stood up, abruptly scraping the metal garden chair against the flagstones. 'I'm going to have another drink. Would you like another?' He nodded at Denning's near-empty glass.

'OK, just some water.' He didn't want any more alcohol – apart from the fact he'd be over the limit, he knew he desperately needed a clear head.

He watched Walters disappear inside the tidy bungalow, his shoulders stooped, his head slightly bowed.

Denning looked around the verdant garden: alive with colour and bathed in amber sunlight. The tall willow tree cast a wide and jagged shadow over the newly mown lawn, like a giant spider inching its way towards them. The garden was obviously Walters' pride and joy; the one thing that kept the insanity of creeping boredom at bay during the long, dull days of retirement. Walters had a nice life. Did Denning have the right to take that away from him because he'd fucked up a major murder investigation so many years ago? Would he have behaved any differently in Walters' shoes? *Yes*. He was damned sure he would have chased up every lead; worked the case until there were no doubts left lingering in the back of his brain saying 'what if?'. But he wasn't Walters. Walters came from a different generation of policing. He'd learned the job from the bottom up, earning his place at the top of the ladder through years of graft. Denning, as Betty Taggart had been so quick to remind him, had shot up the greasy pole aided by a psychology degree and the kind of IT skills the job required these days. Perhaps he shouldn't be too quick to judge.

Walters reappeared carrying another can of Guinness and a glass of iced tap water. He placed them on the wrought iron table and poured the Guinness into his empty glass. He took a sip and gave Denning a brief moment of eye contact, then his gaze shifted back to his feet.

'Ferguson had a low IQ. In fact, he was barely literate. His solicitor had to explain his rights to him. He was just too stupid to have planned those murders. Maybe he might have got lucky once, possibly even twice. But he didn't have the brains to get away with it for as long as he did. Not unless he had help. Then there was the description from one of the witnesses. I know, witness descriptions are never reliable: a dozen different eye-witnesses will give you a dozen different descriptions of the same suspect, each one insisting they're spot on. Even so, we had a witness who remembered seeing someone at the bus stop where the second victim was snatched. The witness was a doctor coming off a shift at St Thomas's, so hardly unreliable. But the description wasn't that of Ferguson. OK, it *could* have been Ferguson, and we just assumed the witness had got it wrong, or it was a coincidence. CCTV was no help. Whoever planned the murders had a knack of finding areas where there weren't any cameras: side roads, back streets, places where nothing ever happened.'

'The witness description?' Denning prompted.

Walters sighed. 'A tall man, late twenties to early thirties. Well built. He was seen chatting to the victim. We never managed to trace him. It just seemed easier to believe the witness had made a mistake. I mean it's possible the man in question was entirely innocent and was simply in the wrong place at the wrong time.' His gaze shifted back onto Denning. 'I know we should have made more of an effort to tidy up loose ends. And if we'd had more resources, more manpower, perhaps we would have. But like I said, this was nothing more than a gut feeling. There was no physical evidence to suggest anyone else was involved. The only DNA we found matched Ferguson. I know that if I'd taken my suspicions further I would have been told to forget it. Everyone wanted the case closed, and when Ferguson was sent down that's exactly what they got: closure, nice and neat.'

Except it was neither nice nor neat. It was scrappy and inconclusive. And it now looked like Walters' convenient ending had come back to bite them big time. Denning could feel his shoulders tense. Despite the relative coolness of the shade thrown up by the willow tree, he felt a tiny bead of sweat on his temple. 'Do you have any idea who this other man might be? Did Ferguson have anyone he was close to?'

Walters shook his head. 'Apart from Derek Rodman, Ferguson had no friends. He was a loner.' Walters drank some more Guinness, gulping it down like a man with a thirst. 'Whoever this other man was, if he even existed, there's no obvious connection to Anthony Ferguson.'

Chapter Forty-Six

Denning spent the entire journey back to London replaying his conversation with Walters in his head. If he told McKenna about Walters' suspicions, it would make the whole thing official. There might even be an inquiry about Walters' mishandling of the case twelve years ago. It would destroy his reputation and turn his peaceful retirement into a living nightmare.

And there might not be anything in it. What did they really have to work with? A questionable alibi for one of the murders; a witness statement that placed someone other than Ferguson alongside one of the victims; and Walters' claim that Ferguson didn't have the brains to qualify as a serial killer on his own merit. Since when was intellect a necessary qualification when it came to committing murder? Even if he did buy Walters' theory about there having been two killers, where was the evidence that Ferguson's mystery accomplice was the same person who'd murdered Leanne Wyatt, Tanya Russell and Sandra Blake? And even if he was, why wait until now to start killing again? There was so much that just didn't add up.

'How did it go with Walters?' Fisher asked as soon as he returned to the MIT suite. He had let her use his desk while he'd been out. There was a stack of papers littering the surface of the desk, and a couple of mugs half-filled with what looked like tepid coffee. There was also a faint whiff of cigarette smoke, which he chose to overlook.

He grabbed a chair and sat down next to her. 'Very interesting. I need to run some ideas by DCI McKenna first.' He paused for a moment. 'It might be useful if you were to sit in on that meeting.'

Fisher shot him a puzzled look, but he changed the subject before she had a chance to ask any more questions. 'That list, did anything useful come up?'

She rummaged through some untidy papers on the desk before handing him a couple of crumpled sheets of A4 with a list of names scribbled on them. One or two had an asterisk next to them, and another couple had question marks after their names.

'The ones with a star are people of possible interest. One in particular,' she pointed at a name he couldn't read, 'released a few weeks ago. Served eleven years of a life sentence for a murder committed in Brighton shortly after Ferguson's killing spree. Another,' she pointed at a different name, 'a rapist. Briefly shared a cell with Ferguson a few years back. I'm still checking some of the other names, but those are two that jumped out at me so far.'

He thanked her. He could tell that her heart hadn't been in it, but it was all the more important now to check names. 'I want a specific note of anyone who was released around the time of Sandra Blake's murder.' There was nothing to say their murderer had ever had any contact with Ferguson. There was the possibility that he had simply been inspired by Ferguson's legacy and was now trying to establish his own by acting out some sick fantasy that would leave his indelible mark on the world.

It was now dawning on Denning that the more clues they unearthed, the more questions they would raise.

Fisher looked over the list of names again. 'I'll need to check the details with the probation service. I'll get on to them straight away.' She reached for the phone on Denning's desk, lifted the receiver, then paused. 'What exactly did Walters say?'

–

'Two of them?' McKenna's voice was half an octave higher than normal. 'There were two of the bastards and Walters kept this to himself until now?'

Molly knew about Betty Taggart's reputation for straight-talking, but seeing it first hand was a new experience. She stood behind her desk, one hand on her hip, clearly looking like somebody who resented having her Saturday afternoon interrupted, even for a murder investigation. 'I don't fucking believe this.'

'In fairness to Ken Walters,' Denning offered, 'this was never anything more than speculation on his part. Unsubstantiated and certainly not supported by any forensic evidence.'

'Even so...' She looked at Molly, the wrinkle on her brow questioning her presence at the meeting. 'He should have made his concerns known at the time. We've got a maniac out there running around killing women at leisure all because Walters bungled the original inquiry. I should be demanding his arse on a stick.'

'Do we need to make it official?' Molly asked. 'I mean he's told us now, and it could yet turn out be something and nothing.' She felt guilty about dropping Walters in the shit. If she hadn't gone raking up the ashes of a cold, dead case he would have been left in peace to enjoy his retirement. Any consequences coming his way would be down to her.

McKenna shot her a look that suggested she should keep all future opinions to herself. 'Did he have any suggestions as to who this mystery accomplice might have been?'

Denning shook his head. 'We don't even know if he's still alive; if he even existed at all. And there's still nothing to link Walters' suspicions with our ongoing case. This could just be coincidence. Or, and at the moment this is the theory I'm working with, this is a copy-cat killer. Either someone who's been reading up on Ferguson and now fancies having a go themselves, or more likely someone who was in prison along-side Ferguson and sees him as some kind of celebrity.'

'Maybe…' McKenna pursed her lips together, exacerbating the spidery lines around her mouth. 'But we can't ignore the possibility that if someone was sharing the killing spree twelve years ago, they're back in action and having another go. But why now?'

'DS Fisher here is looking for anyone who's recently been released from prison, especially anyone who may have had any connection to Ferguson,' Denning said. 'It's possible our killer's been inside until recently. Not necessarily for murder, but maybe with a history of violence. I know it's all a bit of a long shot, but it would explain why they haven't been around for the past decade.'

'And you're sticking with your copy-cat killer theory?' McKenna looked directly at Denning.

He seemed to give the matter some consideration. 'Honestly? I don't know. I can't simply dismiss what Ken Walters told me, even if I'd like to.'

McKenna had stopped punching her chin. She now stood with both hands on her hips. 'I think we need to speak to Ferguson. Directly or indirectly, he seems to be the key to all this.' She turned to Molly. 'And I think we owe you a massive thank-you for pointing us in this direction in the first place, DS Fisher,' she added, and for a brief second Molly thought she saw Betty Taggart shoot a thin-lipped smile in her direction.

Chapter Forty-Seven

A slightly queasy feeling swept over Molly as the heavy metal gate slid shut behind her.

A uniformed prison officer keyed a sequence into an electronic pad on the wall beside the gate and a couple of bleeps told her the gate was now locked.

They were standing in a corridor in Bells Wood Prison in Essex on Sunday afternoon. The prison was new, built sometime in the last twenty years to house mostly Cat A and B prisoners: rapists, arsonists, and murderers. The interior was painted white. White walls, white gates, white floor. Even the furniture was white. It gave the place a slightly clinical feel, more like a hospital, Molly thought, than a prison.

The officer was a taciturn man in his early forties, with bulky shoulders and a rapidly receding hairline. His regulation black shoes squeaked noisily on the polished floor as he walked them down the corridor. The unblinking red eye of a CCTV camera let them know they were being watched. The officer had barely spoken to them since she and Denning had pitched up at the prison reception area ten minutes ago, flashing their warrant cards and having to stand there like naughty schoolchildren while the officer sitting behind the reception desk confirmed that their visit had been OK'd by the governor.

Not that it had been plain sailing organising the meeting with Ferguson in the first place. The Met's Deputy Commissioner had had to put in an official request to the Ministry of Justice directly, insisting Ferguson had information that could help the police with an ongoing murder investigation. The governor of Bells Wood, however, had been unconvinced. He had wanted to know how a man currently almost eleven and a half years into a life sentence would know anything about a series of freshly committed murders. It had taken pressure from the Ministry of Justice before he had agreed to the meeting.

And that hadn't been the only tough cajolery that had taken place. Molly had worked hard to persuade Denning to let her come along to meet Ferguson. He'd told her it should be Neeraj as he was number two on this investigation, but she'd argued that she was the one who'd led them to Ferguson and therefore earned the right to be there. Denning wasn't so sure. She suspected he thought she wanted to see Ferguson out of perverse curiosity, like looking at a caged animal in a zoo. And perhaps he was right to think that. Ferguson had dominated her thoughts for so long she knew she had to see him in the flesh and look him in the eye. Perhaps that would go some way to slaying the monster.

They were shown into an interview room off the bright, white corridor. The room was painted in slightly subtler hues of dove grey, with a plain beige carpet on the floor, and vertical blinds fighting back the glaring sun on the square, barred windows that ran along one of the walls. There was a round, wooden table in the centre of the room, with four chairs. A water cooler sat in a far corner. This wasn't what Molly had expected. Somehow she'd imagined Ferguson being incarcerated in some gothic Victorian monstrosity, like something out of Dickens.

'Take a seat, guys,' the taciturn officer said. 'Ferguson will be here in a minute.' He looked at Denning and Molly, unsmiling. 'As the governor confirmed, I'll be present throughout the interview.' He closed the door and stood between the table and water cooler, arms folded.

Denning had asked that they speak to Ferguson alone as he was more likely to be forthcoming if there wasn't a prison officer present. However, as he'd made clear to Molly on the journey up, he didn't expect Ferguson to offer up anything useful at all. They were simply doing this to keep Betty Taggart off their backs.

There was an oppressive silence in the room, interrupted by the filtered white noise of the prison that seemed to emanate through the breezeblock walls and thrum and hiss around the visitor's room.

Molly had never been inside a prison before, and it wasn't an experience she wished to repeat in a hurry. There was something intimidating about the sound of a gate locking behind you, knowing that your liberty was curtailed, albeit temporarily. Denning seemed more at ease with the situation. Perhaps he'd been to a prison before, or maybe he was good at hiding what he was feeling. During the car journey to the prison, conversation had been limited: she learned that he was married, his wife was half-Chinese and he had a degree in psychology and criminology from UCL, but otherwise they'd mostly passed occasional comments about the case as the Essex countryside had sped by. Looking at him now, she wondered what lay behind the ice-cool demeanour. There was no denying he was attractive, not quite in a male model kind of way as Trudi had suggested there was a softness about his face and his forehead was a little too high – but he was certainly gym-fit and had sexy, pale blue eyes. She wondered what his opinion was of her.

Her thoughts were interrupted by the door to the interview room swinging open.

Another prison officer appeared, a woman this time, her blonde hair scraped back into a tight bun. She was pretty, with a nice figure, but had a look that said she could take care of herself if the need arose. She wore a pair of trendy black glasses that made Molly think of a librarian. Shuffling in behind her was a shrunken husk of a man in a dirty grey tracksuit. His hair and beard were streaked with silver, and his face was mottled with the scars of childhood acne. She recognised Ferguson from his photos. He'd aged, by a lot more than twelve years, and it was more than just prison pallor: it was as though something had died inside him.

He sat down next to Molly and Denning at the round table. The female prison officer muttered something to her male colleague then left the room. The male officer stood by the door, legs apart, folding his hands behind his back, pretending he was somewhere else.

Ferguson was shorter than she'd imagined, probably a little over five feet, but stocky. She suspected this was a result of regular visits to the prison gym. He looked over at Denning, but his eyes fixed on Molly: deep-set and smouldering black, just like the photograph that had stared at her from the various websites she had perused when she first checked out the monster that was Anthony John Ferguson.

'Mr Ferguson,' Denning began, keeping his voice detached and professional, 'we need to ask you some questions about the Bermondsey murders. I realise they were some time ago and your memory might be hazy.'

Ferguson didn't blink. He stared impassively at Molly: his cold, dead eyes trying to burrow into her soul. She could feel something deep inside him desperate to burst out; something cold and sinister, something evil, and she realised at once that she had been wrong to ever question his guilt.

'We need to know if you committed the murders alone, Mr Ferguson, or, as we now suspect, you had an accomplice.'

Despite Denning's cool manner, Molly could see a slight furrow in his brow.

After a minute – that felt much longer – Ferguson shifted his gaze from Molly onto Denning. When he spoke, his voice was surprisingly high-pitched, like a child's.

'I don't have to tell you shit, copper.' He looked back at Molly. She felt slightly less intimidated by him now she'd heard him speak. His voice was so incongruous with the squat, pug-like body.

'We think your accomplice is killing again,' Molly said, dredging up a confidence she didn't fully feel. 'We'd like you to tell us who that person is.'

There was heavy silence. The muted hubbub of prison life seemed to reverberate around the grey-painted room. Then Ferguson laughed. It sounded like a small animal was dying in his throat. But the laugh sounded forced, as though he was trying to prove a point: he held the cards and it was up to her and Denning to beat him at his own game.

'You're talking rubbish.' He was looking at Molly again, fixing her with a dark stare. His eyes moved from her face to her breasts, where they lingered. She felt her heart rate quicken. She wanted to speak, but her mouth felt suddenly dry. Glancing over at the water cooler, she wondered if helping herself to a glass of water would be seen as a sign of weakness.

'Not rubbish, Mr Ferguson, rather – fact.' Denning was taking charge of the conversation now, forcing Ferguson's gaze away from Molly's chest. 'The detective who investigated your killing spree has told us he knew there had been two of you, but could never prove it.' He leant forward, resting his elbows on the table. 'It must be galling for you, Mr Ferguson, knowing you're banged up in here for the rest of your life while your mate is still at liberty. He's out there now, Tony, a free man, while you're rotting away in here. I don't think that's fair on you.' Denning sat back in his chair. His words seemed to have the right effect. Molly saw Ferguson's Adam's apple bob up and down in his throat, and his gaze dropped to the floor.

'Like I said before, you're talking crap.'

'Actually, you said "talking rubbish"; that's not technically the same thing, but as it's not true anyway I'll let it pass.' Denning smiled, knowing he was slowly managing to chip away at the granite exterior. She remembered what he had said in the car: Ferguson had a low IQ. He would be easy to manipulate. 'I just need a name, Tony. Tell us who he was and we'll go away.'

Ferguson's gaze returned to Molly. He made it obvious he was staring at her breasts again. Then he looked her in the eye.

'Do you know how many women write to me every week? Loads. They either want to marry me or save me, or shag me. Some of them even describe their sexual fantasies to me in graphic detail. You'd think the screws would destroy the letters, but they don't care. Some of them probably get as big a thrill as I do reading them.' He looked at the officer standing by the door, but if he was expecting a reaction, none came. 'Is that the real reason you're here?' He was looking at Molly now when he spoke. 'You wanted to see for yourself what I was really like?' He winked at her, a dirty, lascivious wink that made her want to retch. She opened her mouth to speak, but her throat was too dry. She was grateful when Denning spoke.

'Did he make you do it, Tony? Did he bully you into killing all those women? Because I don't think you really had it in you to do that. I don't think that was you at all. I think he made you do those terrible things to those women, then left you to take the blame. Am I right, Tony?'

Ferguson was still staring at Molly. She returned his stare, risking being swallowed up by those cold, dark eyes.

'Fuck off.'

'I'll take that as a yes, Tony.' Denning folded his arms across his chest and looked at Ferguson. Eventually Ferguson shifted his gaze from Molly to Denning.

'Just tell me his name,' repeated Denning, 'then we can go away and leave you to get on with your life. You must be due for parole soon, Tony. Tell us who this other man was and that'll go in your favour at the parole hearing. Do yourself a favour: don't keep lying for this man. Whoever he is, he's not worth it.'

Ferguson was fidgeting now; shifting uncomfortably in his seat like a bored child. Molly could almost see the cogs whirring in whatever passed for his brain.

'Nobody made me do anything. I killed those little tarts. No one made me do it. I didn't need anyone's help either. I ain't thick.'

'It wasn't your idea to carve a cross on the victim's faces, was it, Tony? Someone else did that.' Denning was talking directly to Ferguson, seemingly not intimidated by him. 'Why? What was that all about?'

He didn't answer. He looked briefly at Denning, then his gaze returned to Molly. He smiled at her and it made her feel sick.

'What about Rebecca Owen?' Molly asked. 'Did you kill her? Because Derek Rodman claims you were with him the night she was killed.' Out of the corner of her eye, she caught sight of Denning throwing her a glance, but she continued anyway; this was as much her investigation as his now, whether he liked it or not. 'You didn't kill Rebecca Owen, did you? You had an alibi for that night.'

Ferguson blinked. 'Who the fuck is Rebecca Owen?'

'The last victim,' she said, feeling anger and bile rising in her throat. 'Rebecca Owen was the name of the last person you were alleged to have murdered, but I don't think you did it.'

Denning put his hand on her shoulder. She knew she'd been shouting, losing it; bordering on being unprofessional. Unlike Denning, unlike cool, controlled Denning who was the very epitome of a professional.

Denning spoke calmly: 'I'm going to ask you one last time, Tony: who was he? Who was the man who murdered those women with you? Just give us his name.'

But Ferguson said nothing. He sat on his chair, his sick, killer's eyes fixed on the table. Then he turned to the prison officer guarding the door, 'I want to go back to my cell now. I'm getting bored.'

–

'What was all that about?' Denning asked when they were back in the car park heading towards his Focus.

'All what?' she asked, but she knew what he was going to say.

'Pressing him about the last victim? You're not still convinced he's innocent, are you?'

She shrugged off his questioning. 'No, I don't think he's innocent. But I do think he's lying.'

Denning unlocked the Focus with a double beep. 'Well there's something we can agree on.'

Chapter Forty-Eight

When Molly switched her phone back on, there was a missed call from Jon. She decided against calling him back, at least not yet. She needed time to think before she spoke to him again.

Jon and Mags. The image was ingrained on her brain. She now found it impossible to think of one without immediately thinking of the other.

Work. She needed to focus on work. Seeing Ferguson had stirred up a mountain of raw emotions in her, ranging from hatred to fear. Hatred at having to share a space with a monster that didn't give a shit about what he'd done and fear that his accomplice was still out there.

They were travelling back to London; Denning concentrating on driving as the Sunday traffic grew heavier the closer they got to the capital. He hadn't pressed her about her outburst, but she could sense that he was biding his time until the opportunity arose to bring it up again, perhaps officially in front of Betty Taggart. She would jump off that bridge when she had to.

'Was he what you expected?' Denning asked. They were approaching a roundabout just outside Brentwood. Denning drove like her grandmother: carefully and steadily; slowing for bends and going through the gears every time he slowed down or sped up. In other circumstances she would have found it amusing.

'Sorry?'

'Ferguson. Did he live up to your expectations?'

She stared out of the window at the passing urban conurbation, where Essex towns and London suburbs slowly merged. 'He's a psychotic serial killer. I'm not sure I had any expectations.'

It was a withering reply. She wasn't in the mood for small talk, even work-related small talk. It was also a lie. She *had* had expectations about Ferguson, and he'd pretty much fulfilled them. Her desire to see him face to face had been partly driven by curiosity.

Her phone pinged with a text message, from Jon again: *We can't leave things like this. Let's talk x* She slipped the phone back into her pocket.

'What about you?' she asked, trying to sound friendlier. She felt guilty for snapping at him. Denning seemed almost human now; friendly and chatty, and much less like the ice-cool arsehole she'd shared an interview room with the other day. There was a lot of shit swimming round inside her head at the moment, but none of it was caused by Denning. 'What did you think of Ferguson?'

Denning negotiated the roundabout with care, checking his mirrors before signalling, then swinging into the London-bound lane. 'I'm now convinced there was someone else. I could read his body language. Besides, despite his arrogant claims, it's clear Walters was right about him not having the brains to carry out those murders alone. Maybe the odd random attack, but nothing as orchestrated as those killings.'

'I just can't see why Ferguson won't name him. He's got nothing to lose; in fact, he's got everything to gain, so why not just tell us who he is?'

'Maybe he's trying to protect someone. Or maybe whoever it is has still got some kind of hold over him.' Denning glanced in his mirror before pulling out to overtake a slow-moving lorry. 'If someone made him do it, they probably assumed he'd be stupid enough to get caught.'

'They'd have been right then. It makes sense: Ferguson is arrested, the killings stop, everyone assumes the right man has gone down for it. If it hadn't been for Walters' niggling doubts, we would be none the wiser.'

'Not to mention the dogged determination of a rogue CID officer going out on a limb. And all entirely off her own bat. That really is commitment to the job, DS Fisher.' He smiled at Molly when he said it, but she didn't return the smile. Despite the possible breakthrough, she was beginning to wish she'd never got involved in this bloody case.

Chapter Forty-Nine

'What are we saying here?' asked Kinsella. 'The Bermondsey Ripper was two people, and one of them's started killing again?'

It was first thing Monday morning. Denning had spent the previous evening chewing the facts over and over in his head. This was no copy-cat killer: this was the real thing, coming back for another go. Walters was right about Ferguson being too stupid to have carried out a series of murders as sophisticated as the Bermondsey Ripper killings. He was guided by animal instinct and little else. The Bermondsey murders clearly bore the hallmarks of someone who knew how to stay one step ahead of the police. Molly Fisher had been right all along.

'That's how it's looking, Dave. We spoke to Ferguson yesterday,' he nodded in Molly's direction. 'We now believe he had an accomplice and that that man has never been found. Obviously we can't say for sure, but we're now exploring the possibility that whoever helped Ferguson is also responsible for the murders of Leanne Wyatt and Sandra Blake – and quite possibly Tanya Russell. The carved cross is his signature. We also believe that this man is clever, motivated and manipulative. It's likely he coerced Ferguson into committing those murders twelve years ago, and has been successfully lying low ever since.'

'Why did he wait until now before starting his recent killing spree?' Kinsella was clearly struggling to buy into the two-killer theory.

'I can't answer that, Dave. We're currently exploring the possibility that he's been inside for the past decade, or maybe living overseas. At this stage, we just don't know.'

There were the usual mutterings from the team. Denning let them get on with it for a few seconds; it was good for them to get it out of their systems.

'Where do we go now?' Ryan Cormack asked over the general hubbub.

'We need to go over every aspect of Anthony Ferguson's life. It would appear he was something of a loner, but he must have been close to someone. Close enough to let that person persuade him to become a killer.'

'What about the bloke who provided his alibi?' Trudi asked.

'Derek Rodman.' Denning wrote his name on the whiteboard. 'He's a possibility, and we'll certainly be speaking to him, but he was an alcoholic at the time, so it's unlikely he had the skills or ability to plan something like the Bermondsey murders. But we can't rule him out.'

'What about workmates?' This was Neeraj.

'Good point, Deep. Ferguson spent most of his years out of work. But he did work from time to time as a casual labourer on building sites. A lot of this was likely to have been cash-in-hand work, so untraceable. We need to compile a list of any places he worked and people he worked with.' He looked around the room. 'We have a vague description of someone who might be our man: tall, late twenties to early thirties at the time of the original murders, meaning he'll be around forty now.' He was going by Walters' description of the man seen at the bus stop talking to one of the victims. It really wasn't a lot to work with, but at the moment it was all they had.

'OK everyone, time is absolutely of the essence here. We know there's a strong chance the killer will strike again, so we need to find him. Let's get to work.'

He looked over at DS Fisher. He kept thinking about her behaviour in the prison yesterday. It was almost as though she'd had some personal vendetta against Ferguson. Maybe this was because she'd spent so much time looking into the case; had spent too much time getting inside his head. She was bright and keen, and if it was up to him, she'd get that place in MIT. But on the other hand, there was that impulsive streak that she struggled to control. If she wanted to make in the Murder Squad she was going to have to learn to keep her emotions in check.

–

Molly was aware that Denning was looking at her. She knew she looked a state. She'd stayed at Trudi's last night: she couldn't face seeing Jon – couldn't face another row. At least not yet. But it was coming. She wasn't the kind of person to run away from confrontation, but equally she wasn't one to seek it out until she was absolutely ready to stand her ground.

There had been another couple of texts from Jon, which she'd ignored. She'd discussed the situation with Trudi and her partner, Charys, leaving out the finer details. Both agreed she needed space and time away from Jon in order to get her head together. They said she was welcome to stay with them as long as she wanted. But their flat was small, and they liked their own space.

Denning had stopped looking at her. He was talking on the phone to someone, his back to her so she couldn't read what his expression. Not that she could read Denning anyway: his cards were kept way too close to his chest for that.

Perhaps he was speaking to his wife. She imagined Denning's home life was a bed of roses compared with hers, especially right now. She imagined everybody's home life was a bed of roses compared with her own right now.

–

Denning had finished printing off the Ferguson case files from the PNC. There was now a stack of paper a couple of centimetres thick sitting on his desk. He planned to take the hard copy of the file home with him that evening and learn · everything he could about Anthony John Ferguson.

Meanwhile, Molly's search of recently released ex-prisoners had thrown up nothing useful: they all either had alibis for at least one of the murders, or were too young to have been around and active twelve years ago. Besides, he had a gut feeling about the kind of man they were looking for. He would be clever; clever enough to manipulate someone else into committing murder and clever enough to ensure he stayed well out the frame. He suspected someone like that would never have been anywhere near a prison.

He was interrupted from his thoughts by Neeraj shouting over at him. 'Boss, I think you'll want to see this.'

The whole team stopped what they were doing and looked over at Neeraj. He was pointing at his computer screen.

'I just clicked on this to get the latest cricket score and this came up.' It was the front page of an online copy of the *London Echo*. The headline made Denning's blood run cold: *Serial killer loose in London: who'll be next?*

Chapter Fifty

Denning read the article twice. He skimmed over the content at first, taking on board the gist of the story, then read it again in detail. And it *was* detailed.

Below photographs of all three victims were the bold facts about the case, some of which had already been revealed to the public, most of which hadn't. A 'source' from within the Met claimed that the police suspected the same man was responsible for all three murders, but as yet were clueless as to who this might be. There was mention of a 'former Premier League footballer, now turned PE teacher', and 'the drug-dealing son of a notorious east London gangster', both of whom the article stated had been taken in for questioning but subsequently released. But it was the final sentence that was caused the skin on the back of his neck to prickle: *Police suspect there may be a link to a series of murders that gripped the capital twelve years ago, dubbed the work of the Bermondsey Ripper.* Next to this there was an old photograph of Anthony Ferguson taken at the time of his arrest, looking dark and feral.

It was damning. It was what they had been trying hard to avoid, at least for as long as they could. Panic would slowly spread like a plague, just as it had twelve years ago. They would find themselves under the most invasive scrutiny from both the press and the public. Not only that, cranks would crawl out from underneath every stone imaginable contacting them to claim they were the killer. A difficult case had suddenly become a whole lot harder.

'Has Betty Taggart seen this?' Kinsella asked.

The team were either looking at Neeraj's computer screen, or looking the article up on their own computers. But there was no escaping it: *a source from within the Met…* They were all thinking it: someone on the team had spoken to the press.

He caught sight of Trudi shooting a look in Molly's direction. He hoped the press leak and Molly's arrival on the team were purely coincidental.

'To answer your question, Dave, I'm guessing not.' He looked over to McKenna's office. She was sitting at her desk tapping away at her keyboard. Had she seen the article she would have called him in by now to share some expletives with him.

'How did the press get hold of this?' Ryan asked.

'Well, it says a "source within the Met",' Kinsella barked. 'I reckon it means one of us.' He turned and looked at Molly. She sat at her borrowed desk, tight-lipped and giving nothing away.

'Let's not start jumping to conclusions,' he said. 'The press make stuff up all the time. Some bored journo's probably put two and two together and assumed there's a link between the recent murders and the old ones.'

'Correctly,' pointed out Kinsella. 'They obviously know their facts. And what about all the Ferguson stuff? We've only just found that out ourselves. It's clear that someone's opened their gob.' He wasn't going to let this drop until they had somebody's arse on the carpet for it.

There was an outburst of idle chatter in the room that quickly looked like it was in danger of getting out of hand. Denning raised his hands: 'Let's not get this out of proportion. Yes, it doesn't help us, and yes, it does suggest that someone's deliberately talked to the press, but we don't know that for sure. Most of this could have been worked out by somebody checking facts and making assumptions. Three suspicious deaths all very similar, and all within a few miles of one another occurring over the space of a couple of weeks – it doesn't take a genius to work out there's quite possibly a connection.'

'What about the Ferguson link though?' Neeraj asked. 'They couldn't have worked that out. Unless Walters told them.'

'Walters is hardly likely to go to the press with this. He'd be as good as publicly admitting that he fucked up all those years ago.' But Denning sounded more confident than he felt when it came to ruling out Walters. He couldn't rule out anyone. 'We need to work hard and fast now it's all out there. The one advantage is it will likely mean that our man will be even more careful now. He may even decide to lie low for a while, which means the chances of there being another murder are looking slimmer. But equally, it means he'll be on his guard, less likely to slip up, and therefore even harder to find.' He looked around the room. It was still uncomfortably muggy in the MIT suite, and the team were already exhausted. Tempers were in danger of fraying or snapping altogether. 'OK, let's get on with it. We need a complete picture of Anthony Ferguson's life. Something's got to connect him with this other man; it's up to us to find it, and quickly.'

He was about to return to his desk when he caught sight of Neeraj raising his hand. 'Could I have a word, boss? I think there's something you should know.'

—

Molly tried to remain calm. They were back in Betty Taggart's office. She was sitting behind her desk this time, lips clenched, face the colour of puce. Denning was half leaning against the filing cabinet. Neither was smiling.

'You never said your partner is a journalist.' Denning spoke as though they were making idle conversation at a dinner party. Her first thought was to wonder how the hell he'd found out about Jon; she'd made damn sure she hadn't shared any personal information with him on the car journey to and from Bells Wood. But then she remembered Deep Neeraj whispering in Denning's ear the minute they'd all finished gawping at the tawdry headline in the *Echo*. Neeraj knew about Jon. She,

Trudi, Neeraj and some of the others had shared the odd post-work drink over the years, which inevitably led to the occasional snippet of personal information slipping out after a couple of pints.

'*Was* a journalist,' she corrected. 'He isn't any more.'

Denning looked at Betty Taggart. Her lips remained pursed, exacerbating the lines round her mouth.

'Somebody leaked this shit to the press,' Denning said coldly. 'Somebody from my team.' They were both looking at her now, not threateningly but with a look that suggested one wrong answer would result in a small nuclear explosion going off in Betty Taggart's office. 'You can see the difficult position this puts me in. I need people I can trust.'

He was being reasonable. Almost too reasonable. She'd rather he just shouted at her. She would shout back, naturally, and not let concerns about deference to senior officers cloud her reason. It would instantly kill stone dead any hopes she had of ever gracing the MIT suite again, at least in this division, but it was her default response mechanism. Her dad had ingrained that in her from an early age: *never let anyone walk all over you, because if you do it once, they'll make a habit out of it.*

'It wasn't Jon,' she said. She felt her voice falter slightly as she spoke and she hated herself for it. Not because it suggested she was lying, but because it made her appear weak. 'It's just not his style,' she added. But if she was honest, she didn't know what Jon's style was these days.

'We're not saying it was intentional.' It was Betty Taggart's turn now. Like Denning, her voice was cool and level and dripping icicles. 'Perhaps you and he shared some pillow talk, "how was your day at the office, dear", that kind of thing, and you mentioned something you should have kept to yourself. He's not appreciated the... the sensitivity of the information, and passes it on to an old friend in the press. Next thing...' She threw a paper copy of the *Echo* onto the desk in front of her, where it landed with a heavy thud, its front page headline shouting up at her. Molly didn't know how she'd come by it. Had someone just nipped out to the nearest branch of WHSmith and bought a copy, simply so Betty Taggart could make this overly dramatic gesture?

'Jon's not an idiot,' Molly argued. 'Besides, I haven't spoken to him about this. At least not in any detail.' She wasn't sure why she was defending Jon, especially when she couldn't swear they were still a couple. But in reality she was defending herself rather than him. Even if Jon had leaked the story to the press, it would be her neck in the noose rather than his. They would assume she had given him the information and that, like a dog with a stick, he had only done what any good journalist would do with a juicy story.

'Look, this wasn't Jon.'

'So you've already told us, Molly, but you can see where we're coming from here, can't you?'

She looked imploringly at Denning. 'I swear; this' – she jabbed a finger at the newspaper lying accusingly on the desk – 'has got sweet fuck-all to do with me. I'm telling you the truth.'

A heavy silence fell on the room. Betty Taggart sighed and looked at Denning. 'It's your call, DI Denning.'

Molly watched as a frown lined Denning's face. 'OK, I'm willing to give you the benefit of the doubt. But if anything like this happens again, you won't find me so accommodating.'

Chapter Fifty-One

The building site was a sea of mess and noise. A massive crane loomed high and ominous over a breezeblock shell, destined to become yet another luxury housing development that would be priced beyond the pockets of the average Londoner. Men in hard hats and orange vests sweated in the heat. The whole area was contained behind a white wooden wall, its blinding starkness punctuated with the occasional computer-generated mock-up of how the expensive apartment block would look when finished: three brick and glass rectangular boxes positioned around a concrete and gravel forecourt, with a granite fountain as its centrepiece.

'Nice,' said Neeraj.

'Really,' replied Denning. 'I think it looks ghastly.'

He parked the Focus next to a grubby Portakabin that housed the site's office.

Barry Thomas was the site foreman. He greeted Denning and Neeraj with a half-smile and a vice-like handshake. Thomas was in his early fifties, with a thick neck and a fuzz of salt and pepper on top of his head. His cheeks and forehead were red from too much exposure to the sun.

'How can I help you guys?' he asked, removing a couple of manila files from an orange plastic chair, and indicating for Denning and Neeraj to sit down. Denning brushed some grit off the seat before sitting on it.

'It's about Anthony Ferguson,' Denning began. 'I believe he used to work for you, about twelve years ago.' It had been Ryan Cormack who'd made the connection: Ferguson's employment history had been patchy, with many years spent on the dole. However, at the time of the murders, he'd been employed on a building site and had been overseen by Barry Thomas.

Thomas sat behind a wobbly metal desk, its surface smothered with papers and folders and general rubbish. Denning spotted a copy of the *London Echo* tucked under a pile of glossy brochures, but couldn't tell if it was today's. 'That little runt. Yeah, like I could ever forget him.' Thomas's had a strong hint of West Country about it. 'But I wouldn't exactly say he worked for me. We used to subcontract a lot of the work in those days. I mean you think there's a shed-load of building work going on in London now, well you should have seen it back then, before the credit crunch. We couldn't throw them up quick enough.' He paused briefly when a young lad popped into the scruffy office to ask Thomas to sign something. He scribbled a barely legible scrawl on to the paper – some kind of chitty – and the young lad left the office, throwing Denning a curious glance as he did so. 'Sorry about that,' Thomas continued, 'it never stops.'

'Anthony Ferguson,' Denning urged. 'What was the nature of this contract work?'

Thomas relaxed his bulky shoulders and stretched his spine, which made a series of clicking noises. Denning thought he heard him fart. 'He was employed as a general labourer, but had had some basic training as a plasterer. Not that he was a very good one, mind. We often had to get another couple of lads to go over his work again, sorting out all the bits he'd botched.'

'Why didn't you get rid of him?' Neeraj asked.

Thomas shrugged. 'If he hadn't been arrested, I probably would have eventually.'

'Oh, yes,' remembered Denning. 'He got into a fight. What happened?'

'Something and nothing. One of the other guys was winding him up about something, nothing unusual in that, but whatever it was he said he got Ferguson riled. He hit the bloke with a claw hammer.' Thomas ran a hand though his wavy hair. 'Don't get me wrong, Ferguson was provoked, but the guy needed stitches. It could have been very nasty. That's when your lot were called in. He was questioned over the assault, then the next thing I know he's been arrested for murder.'

'And that was the first time Ferguson had been violent, to your knowledge?'

'Yeah. At the time I thought it was out of character. Ferguson usually wouldn't dare say boo to a goose. Looking back, I realise it was probably only a matter of time before he turned nasty. Though getting a bit tasty with a bunch of hairy-arsed builders is a totally different ball game to attacking women.'

'Why did you keep using Ferguson if you weren't happy with his work?' Neeraj asked.

'Good question. Suppose I felt sorry for him. Besides, he may not have been very good, but he was reliable. He'd turn up for work on time, and usually not hungover. I can't say that for a lot of these boys. Admittedly, that may have had something to do with me putting a boot up his backside and threatening him with the push if he was ever late.' He laughed at the memory. 'Besides, he was only ever on short-term contracts, so it's not like we was stuck with him. To be honest with you, if we hadn't been so desperate for workers, maybe I wouldn't have used him, but we had such a high turnover of men back then, it was easier just to put up with him.'

'Was there anyone he was particularly close to?' Denning asked.

Thomas gave another throaty guffaw of a laugh. 'No chance. Like I said, most of the lads used to take the piss out of him on a regular basis.'

'So he was unpopular?' asked Denning?

Thomas thought for a moment. 'I wouldn't exactly say he was *unpopular*. It was more a case of victim mentality. If something went wrong on the site, he'd usually get the blame for it, even if it wasn't his fault, like. He just put up with it, stupid sod.

He used to get the piss taken out of him too. Sometimes it was just harmless banter, but sometimes it could be quite nasty.' He reached over and opened the door of a small fridge that sat on a shelving unit beside the desk. He took out a can of Coke and pulled back the ring. 'Would you guys like one?'

They both declined, then Denning asked, 'So he had no friends that you knew of?'

Thomas took a swig of Coke, draining most of the can in one long, continuous gulp. 'Look, mate, I employed him to do a job; his private life was no concern of mine. I certainly never knew he was out killing women in his spare time.' He finished the Coke, scrunched the can in his fist and tossed it into a bin in a corner. He folded his arms across his large chest. 'Do you mind telling me what all this is about? I told the police everything I knew at the time, which wasn't much.'

Denning offered him a propitiatory smile. 'I just need to know if Ferguson was close to anyone while he worked for you. Did he speak to anyone? Was there someone who didn't treat him like something they'd stood in?'

Barry Thomas belched loudly. He sat staring at Denning and Neeraj as though he was trying to suss out if they really were a cops, or just some random blokes who'd walked in off the street to ask a load of dumb-ass questions about somebody who didn't matter any more, if he'd ever mattered at all. He scratched at a large red spot on his neck. 'There was one bloke. I wouldn't exactly say they were friends. Prior to the incident with the hammer, there had been a bit of aggro one day, nothing physical, just a slanging match. Probably some banter had got out of hand. We were already behind schedule on a job, so tempers were strained. A couple of the lads were having a go at Ferguson about something or other. Ferguson just sat there and took it, as he usually did, and a few of the other lads joined in. It was a bit like a sport for them really: goading the poor bastard until he cracked. Anyway, this other bloke got involved. He started sticking up for Ferguson. Told the guys to leave him alone. Well, it did the trick: they backed down. Don't get me wrong, it wasn't long before the piss-taking started up again. A few months after this incident, Ferguson decides he's grown a pair of balls and goes off on one like Rambo's uglier bastard brother.'

'Who was this bloke?' Denning asked.

Thomas shrugged. 'That's just it, I can't remember. He was only with us for a few weeks while we were finishing off a job. Another contract worker: ran his own business, I think. That wasn't uncommon − if were behind with a job and it was nearing completion, we'd often contract smaller jobs out to local firms. Mostly it was just tidying up and finishing off: putting in kitchens and bathrooms, ironing out any little kinks. These were high-end properties. When people are paying top rouble they expect quality. It's more cost-effective than going over schedule.'

'But you must have records?' asked Denning.

Another shrug. 'The accounts department might know. I mean, I could get onto them, like, and ask, but it was yonks ago. The bloke might have gone out of business by now.'

'It's worth a try, and I would really appreciate it.' Denning handed Thomas his card.

Thomas said, 'OK. But you're still not going to tell me what all this is about?'

Denning stood, pushing the plastic orange chair back with his legs. 'Just get in touch as soon as you've got the name and any contact details for that contractor.'

Chapter Fifty-Two

'I know it's a load of old tosh, but it doesn't make us look good.'

Denning had just returned from talking to Barry Thomas when McKenna had beckoned him into her office. She wasn't shouting, but her voice was audible enough to be heard beyond the thin partition wall that separated her office from the rest of the MIT suite.

The Chief Superintendent had summoned her with an irate phone call: Daryl Bailey, ex-professional footballer – and probably soon to be ex-PE teacher – was suing the Met for releasing his name to the press in connection with an ongoing murder inquiry. Of course, the story in the *Echo* had been careful not to name Bailey, but social media had not been so reticent.

The official line was that he had never been anything other than a suspect: questioned and released without charge. But the implications were clear.

McKenna had already been on the phone to the editor of the *London Echo* to ask how they had come by their information, and roasting his nuts over the irresponsible article and the damage it would cause an ongoing police investigation, but tabloid newspaper editors had thick skins. He'd got his story, anything else was her problem, not his.

'Has Bailey got a case?' Denning asked.

'Who knows? The Met lawyers are on to it now. In the meantime, muggins here has been ordered to give a press conference about this shit.' She jabbed a finger at the folded copy of the *Echo* still sitting on her desk. 'This, I could really do without.'

'The timing's not great.'

McKenna tugged at her hair. 'Are you sure that girl's got nothing to do with it?'

Denning wanted to believe Molly was innocent, but doubt lingered at the back of his mind. Nothing like this had ever happened before she joined the team.

'Look,' he said, 'the damage has been done now. We can't undo it. OK, it adds to the pressure, but maybe that's a good thing.'

'Sorry?'

'Now we have an added incentive to find this nutter. We'll be under greater scrutiny and if we fuck up it'll be all over the tabloids.'

She made a clicking noise with her tongue. 'Personally, I can't see how that helps.'

'OK, so maybe it won't, but we have to try and salvage something out of this mess.'

'I agree with you there.' There was a pause, which Denning took as his cue to leave. He was just about to get up from his seat when she said, 'keep an eye on Fisher. I have a gut feeling there's something she's not telling us.'

Denning looked puzzled. 'You don't believe her about leaking the story?'

She threw a smile in Denning's direction. 'Call it feminine intuition, but there's something about that girl I just don't trust.'

–

Molly was still poring over the CCTV footage from the bridge overlooking the stretch of canal where Sandra Blake's body had been found. It was a frustratingly slow and tedious process, not helped by the fact that she was sure she could feel a dozen pairs of eyes boring into the back of her head. Whispered conversations had abruptly ceased the moment she'd left Betty Taggart's office. Trudi had shot her a sympathetic glance, but she'd ignored her and headed straight to her desk.

It had taken all her inner strength not to tell Denning and Betty Taggart to go and fuck themselves. Did they really think she was capable of selling them up the river like that? She might be new to the team, but she was a good detective; a team player. And Denning had stood there looking at her with his condescending attitude, like she was sitting on the naughty step.

She'd got as far as drafting a text message to Jon but had pressed delete before sending it. She needed to calm down first. She was tempted to ask Trudi if she wanted to go for a fag break, but maybe it was better to focus on work. It would serve as a good distraction if nothing else.

Shortly after their bruising encounter, Denning had buggered off to chase up a lead. She'd wanted to go with him, but knew there would be no point in asking. She'd have to keep her head down for a while, prove herself to the team. Denning was back now, sitting in Betty Taggart's office with a pained look on his face.

Several hours' worth of footage had been painstakingly scanned already, without yielding anything useful.

She stared at digital images of people walking across the bridge, one or two stopping to look at the canal below. Cars and vans crossed sporadically, the frequency decreasing as night began to fall. She fast-forwarded the footage, watching the images become even more blurred and indistinct. This felt like a waste of time: she should be out there with Denning, speaking to people, trying to find that elusive lead instead of being stuck inside this sweaty office marking time. The footage whizzed past: lots of nothing, with the occasional person swaggering over the bridge. Then suddenly there was something there. She paused the video, and rewound slightly: it was a van, a Transit. It was impossible to make out the colour, and she couldn't make out the registration number. It stopped in the centre of the bridge. The timestamp said 01:27. Someone got out and opened the back doors. After a couple of seconds they removed something from the back, slung it over their shoulder, then dropped it over the parapet into the canal. She couldn't be one hundred per cent sure from the haziness of the footage, but it looked like a body.

Chapter Fifty-Three

Molly showed the footage to Denning. He peered closely at a freeze-frame of the suspect. 'Looks like he's got his face covered by a scarf or something, and he's wearing a baseball cap.'

'The suspect seen leaving the bar with Leanne was wearing a baseball cap,' Molly said. 'Could this be the same man?'

Denning continued staring at the shady image on the screen. Poor street lighting had resulted in dark shadows pooling across the screen. 'Possibly.' He rubbed a hand over his chin. 'Get onto traffic: trace the route of the van. If we're lucky, we might get a clear shot of the number plate this time. I'd lay odds on this being the same van that Trudi spotted on the CCTV at Haggerston Park.' He turned to her and smiled. 'Let's face it, we're due a lucky break.'

There was warmth in his smile. It was a marked contrast to the ice-cool, professional Denning who'd made her squirm in the DCI's office that morning. She still couldn't get the confrontation out of her head. It was gnawing away at her, punching her brain. She felt like someone was drilling a hole in the side of her skull.

'Can't argue with that,' she said.

'This is good work, Molly,' said Denning. 'Well done.'

She returned to her desk feeling slightly vindicated. She should have felt buoyed by Denning's encouragement: it was clear that, despite whatever reservations he may have had, he didn't blame Molly for what had happened earlier after all. Or he had, but he'd since forgiven her. It was hard to read Denning.

She suspected he would have made an excellent poker player, if he ever played poker.

But the banging in her head was growing worse. She searched in her bag for some paracetamol but realised she'd used the last two at lunchtime. She could ask Trudi for some, but there wasn't much point. She glanced at her watch: it had already gone five, and the end of a long, hard day. She was tempted to ask Trudi if she and any of the others wanted to head down the pub. But there was something she had to do first.

Chapter Fifty-Four

The hospital reminded Denning of Bells Wood Prison: white-walled and sterile, except without the locked gates and unnerving sense of despair.

He exited the lift on the second floor and spoke to the first person he saw wearing a uniform. An attractive young nurse showed him into a private room off a long, white corridor. The room was small but clean. The window framed a shimmering east London landscape, a view dominated by the monoliths of Canary Wharf and the fringes of the City. A local radio station chattered away in the background.

Daryl Bailey was lying on a hospital bed, dressed in an unflattering grey and blue gown with a slight tear on the shoulder. A wire ran from a plastic clip on his middle finger to a portable monitor beside his bed, which gave off an intermittent bleep.

Bailey's face was a mass of red and purple; his right eye swollen shut and a crust of dried blood caked to the base of his nose. One of his arms was encased in a plaster cast.

According to the nurse Denning had just spoken to, Bailey was lucky it wasn't worse. He had a couple of broken ribs, a fractured wrist and a ruptured spleen. They'd managed to stem the bleeding to the spleen, which meant, luckily for Bailey, they wouldn't have to remove it. Otherwise, the injuries were mostly superficial. He'd look a mess for a while but he'd recover.

Bailey looked up when Denning entered the room. As soon as he saw who it was, he turned his gaze towards the view from the window.

Denning pulled a chair over from the corner of the room and sat down. 'Mr Bailey?'

Bailey continued to ignore him. He kept looking out the window. The blind was pulled part of the way down to keep out the sun, but there was still a brilliant whiteness glaring through the glass. 'Who did this to you?' Denning asked.

He'd been found by a road cleaner in a side street beside a trendy bar in Shoreditch just after lunchtime. According to the paramedic who tended to him at the scene, the smell of booze suggested his lunch had been of the liquid variety. His extensive injuries had resulted in a call to the local constabulary.

Ordinarily, this would have fallen within the remit of regular CID, but under the circumstances, McKenna felt it would be prudent for Denning to speak to Bailey.

'Mr Bailey, I'm not going to leave until you tell me what happened and who's responsible. I can stay here all day if I have to.' It was a lie, of course, but it seemed to have the desired effect. Bailey shifted his focus onto Denning.

'Do you want to know who's responsible for this?' His voice was hoarse, as though the very act of speaking seemed to drain the energy from his body. 'Do you really want to know? Then I suggest you look in a mirror, Denning.' He coughed suddenly, his whole body shuddering. Denning poured him a glass of water from a jug on the cabinet beside his bed. He offered it to Bailey, who batted it away with a swipe of his hand. Some of the water splashed onto the bedclothes as well as Denning's sleeve. Bailey looked at Denning. His right eye might have been out of action, but his left eye was red and bloodshot and full of anger. 'If you hadn't tried to nail me for Leanne's murder, I wouldn't be lying here now. And I'd still have a fucking job. You've destroyed my life.' His gaze returned to the window.

'Maybe if you'd been honest with me in the first place...' Denning tried to sound sympathetic; there was no point in antagonising Bailey further. 'Look, if it's about that newspaper story, you can sue the arse off them. OK, maybe they didn't actually name you, but they weren't exactly discreet.'

The bloodshot eye flashed back onto Denning. 'I'm suing the arse off *you* lot. And my lawyer reckons I've got a strong case. You had no real evidence linking me to Leanne's murder, Denning, and no reason to arrest me. According to the local news, there's a psycho out there, and you wasted time chasing after me when you should have been out there looking for him. You've fucked up, and you know it.'

'We had evidence that placed you with Leanne the night she was killed. We know you lied about having had a relationship with her. We strongly suspect, but can't prove, you had been involved with her whilst she was still a pupil at Dalston Academy.' He looked despairingly at Bailey. 'We had enough evidence to justify going after you, but I'm sorry it came to this. If you tell us who did it, we'll go after them and you can get your life back.'

Bailey didn't reply, and Denning let a silence fall between them. From outside the room there was the distant sound of an alarm followed by the clatter of running feet. Somewhere in the hospital someone's life was about to be saved. Or end, depending on the outcome. But he knew he'd done nothing wrong. Even if Bailey wasn't bluffing and he did sue, Denning knew he'd done everything by the book. And he would rather that than end up like Walters and be silently eaten up by a decade's worth of regret at having let a killer off the hook because it made for an easy life.

'I told you, I've lost my job.'

'The school have told you this, have they?'

'They want to see me as soon as I get out of here. And it's not because they want to offer me the head's job.'

'You don't know that. Even if they do try and sack you, you'd have a good case against them for unfair dismissal.'

His one working eye shot Denning a dark look. 'You are having a laugh, aren't you? Did you not read that fucking story

274

in the paper? They as good as accused me of being a sodding paedophile. What parent is going to let their kid go to a school with a nonce on the staff?'

'Then sue the paper, not us. They're the ones who printed the story and put all this in the public domain.'

'What's the bloody point? The damage is done now.'

When Denning had first met Daryl Bailey, he'd put him down as another arrogant tosser who thought the rules didn't apply to him. Now, looking at Bailey lying battered and sore in a hospital bed, he actually felt sorry for him. Whatever he was, he didn't deserve this. 'Tell me who did this to you, Daryl.'

But Bailey remained tight-lipped. 'That's up to you lot to find out. I assume you can get it right some of the time.'

–

Denning sat at the dining table and poured himself a glass of German beer. He needed to soften the rough edges off a bad day.

Bailey's words had hit home. He refused to feel responsible for what had happened, but there was a part of him that had felt at least a pang of guilt when he'd seen Bailey lying in that hospital bed.

There was a yellow Stick-it note stuck to the front of the fridge-freezer. In Sarah's barely legible scrawl it read: *Gone for a drink with Miles and Victoria. Hendry's Bar, Shoreditch – we'll be there anytime from 7 p.m. onwards. Drop round. x* Miles Crawford was a friend from uni, now working for one of the major banks. Miles and his wife Victoria had introduced him to Sarah at a dinner party five years ago. Ordinarily, he would have enjoyed catching up with them, even in somewhere as pretentious as Hendry's, but he wasn't in the mood for socialising tonight. He just wanted to chill and watch some rubbish on the telly.

Although it was another warm evening, the flat was pleasantly cool. It should have felt empty without Sarah, instead he found himself enjoying the peace and quiet. He checked his phone for missed calls: there was another one from Claire, and a new message indicating he had a voicemail. He didn't have the energy to listen to whatever minor drama was playing out in her life today. He'd call her tomorrow, if he remembered.

Chapter Fifty-Five

Jon was in the kitchen when Molly let herself into the house. He was sitting at the kitchen table staring into space. There was a half-eaten plate of pasta on the table along with a can of Stella.

She'd opened and closed the front door quietly, trying to make as little noise as possible. Already this no longer felt like her home.

He looked up when she walked into the kitchen. A smile briefly flitted onto his face, but quickly faded when it wasn't reciprocated.

'Molly... How are you?' He pushed the plate to one side and pulled out a chair, urging her to sit down. 'I was worried about you.'

She sat down opposite him. She wanted a glass of water, but the sink was full of dirty dishes. Her headache was getting worse.

'I think we need to talk.' She took a copy of the *London Echo* from her bag and dumped it on the table in front of him. 'Have you seen this?'

He picked up the paper, scanning the front page. 'Shit, but...' He threw the paper onto the table. 'You don't think I gave them this, do you?' He looked pleadingly at Molly. 'You think I'm selling stories to the media about you and your police mates?' He shook his head. 'You couldn't be more wrong.'

Molly could feel bile rising in her throat. 'I've been behaving "strangely" because you lied to me about your relationship with Magda Kilbride.'

She watched his mouth open and close, but without any words coming out. 'What are you talking about? What *relationship*? That's shite.'

'I know it for a fact, Jon.'

A vein began to pulsate in his temple. He was wearing a shabby blue and black checked shirt that badly needed an iron, with a stain down the front that looked suspiciously like pasta sauce. 'We had a brief fling, nothing more. It was ages ago and it wasn't serious.'

'The two of you were living together. I'd say that was pretty serious, wouldn't you?'

She watched as his face flushed crimson, either with embarrassment at being caught out, or anger because she'd found him out. She couldn't tell which, and she didn't really care.

'How do you know all this?'

She dropped the eye contact. 'I did a PNC check.'

His jaw fell towards his chest. 'You've been checking up on me? Spying on me! That's great. I mean, that's really great.'

She didn't want to tell him that she'd done more than that. She'd gone over and over the events of the week that Leanne Wyatt and Tanya Russell had been murdered, trying to remember what Jon had been doing and where he'd been. The night Leanne was killed she'd gone to bed early. Jon had stayed up late to watch a film, or so he'd said. But had he waited until she was asleep and crept out in the early hours? She couldn't remember what time he'd come to bed. And then there was the night of Tanya Russell's death. That was when she'd first mentioned Mags; flagging up an unhappy reminder of his past. Had that sparked something rotten inside him? She knew his personality changed when he was in the pits of one of his black moods, but did that despair turn him into something ugly? And what about twelve years ago? He had been in a bad place then too; the break-up of his marriage having sent him to the brink...

She hated herself for thinking this. It was paranoia of the worst kind. Or so she desperately hoped. She was a good detective; she'd know if she was living with a murderer, wouldn't she? She knew Jon wasn't capable of killing anyone, let alone a bunch of random women, and yet, did she really know him well enough to make that assumption with any real certainty? He'd lied to her about his relationship with Mags, and the violence. What else had he lied about?

'I trusted you, Molly,' he said, tears smarting his eyes. 'I let you into my life, open my heart and soul to you, and you go behind my back and rake up all this shit about me. Shit that was dead and buried.'

Molly took a deep breath. 'She alleges that you assaulted her, Jon.'

'That's bullshit. If you'd bothered to check your facts, DS Fisher, you'd know she dropped the charges. And the reason she dropped the charges is because she lied. I never assaulted her. We argued and she hit her head against a bookcase to make it look like I'd smacked her. I thought you would have twigged by now: Magda Kilbride is a serial fantasist. She wouldn't know the truth if it slapped her on the arse. She's taken you in and played you for a twat.'

Molly stared at the plate of half-eaten pasta. It looked like it had been reheated in the microwave, possibly more than once. Jon was pathetic and hopeless and could no more manage to look after himself than he could fly to Mars and back in a Cessna aeroplane. What had once seemed endearing now seemed annoying. But what was worse, what really rankled with her, was that he hadn't thought she'd deserved to know the truth about his relationship with Magda Kilbride. It was as though she didn't matter.

'I think you're the one who's playing me like a fiddle. You've lied to me and that hurts. What else haven't you told me? I want to know what else you've kept from me.'

'What the fuck is this? I didn't tell you about me and Mags because it's irrelevant; *she's* irrelevant.'

'*Irrelevant?* You had a relationship with her and now you're saying it was irrelevant.'

'Jesus, Molly. This is taking the piss.' He blinked at her, fighting back his tears, trying hard to remain in control.

Jon, who so easily lost control... Jon who may or may not have assaulted Magda Kilbride during an argument... Jon who hated Mags, *who hated women...? Hated them enough to kill them...?*

She could feel her head spinning, the room blurring. Jon's voice was inside her head now, shouting accusations through tears and snot.

'I've only come back to collect my stuff,' she heard herself say. 'I'm moving out. I'm going to stay with a friend until I can get my head sorted.'

'Molly, this is ridiculous. I'm sorry I lied about Mags, and I swear I didn't leak that story to the press. Get this in proportion. If we split up, it means she's won. It means Mags has got what her twisted little mind wants and it's the end of you and me.'

Molly tried to stand, but her legs seemed to belong to another body. Her head was awash with noise and light. She grabbed hold of the kitchen table and pulled herself to her feet. She turned towards the door into the hallway, but as she did so the world seemed to swim around her. She heard Jon's voice shouting out her name, then the whole kitchen began to spin a dervish, getting giddier and giddier. She felt Jon's hand on her shoulder then her knees buckled and the floor tiles raced up to meet her. The last thing she remembered was the side of her head connecting with the corner of the kitchen table.

Chapter Fifty-Six

'DI Denning? It's Barry Thomas. I think I've found the name you're looking for.'

Denning had only been at his desk for less than half an hour when Thomas phoned.

'Go on.' He scribbled the name on a piece of scrap paper: Daniel Placzek.

'He ran a small outfit based in Lewisham,' Thomas continued. 'I can't remember the company name, and we haven't used him for years, and I've got no idea if he's still around. Sorry I can't be more helpful.'

Denning thanked him and ended the call. He entered the name into the Police National Computer database, but nothing came up. Next he did a QUEST search – Query Using Extended Search Technique, despairing yet again at the Met's obsession with silly acronyms. He entered a general description, with what few details he had about Placzek, hoping something might have been flagged up that would point him in the right direction. Still nothing. Whoever Daniel Placzek was, he didn't have a criminal record. He decided a more lateral approach might work. He logged out of the PNC and clicked onto the internet. The Met had recently introduced a monitoring system to ensure officers weren't misusing the internet in work time, but trying to identify the whereabouts of a possible killer was hardly a misuse of his time. He typed 'Daniel Placzek, Lewisham builders' into the Google search box. No website came up, suggesting the business was no longer active, but a couple of sites listed the name along with a phone number and an address in Lewisham. Denning tried the phone number but the white noise from the other end suggested the number was no longer active. He wrote down the address: 5 Catford Road, Lewisham SE13.

His team had begun drifting in shortly after he'd arrived at 8:30 a.m. He noticed that Molly Fisher hadn't turned up yet. So much for trying to make a good impression. He needed to know if there was any progress with the Transit van from the CCTV footage. Someone needed to get onto traffic as a matter of urgency and get it followed up.

A van, a van used by a builder...?

He was about to head out of the office when Trudi Bell grabbed him. 'It's about Molly,' she said, her face tight with tension. 'She's had an accident.'

Chapter Fifty-Seven

Molly rubbed the bruise under her left eye. It still felt sore to touch. The harassed young doctor who'd treated her in A&E last night told her there would likely be a mark there for a good few weeks. She'd tried not to grimace when he'd told her.

But there was no serious damage. A blood test had shown that she was slightly anaemic. That, combined with a lack of fluid intake over the past couple of days, had resulted in her dizziness. She'd been advised to rest and take things easy, and make an appointment with her GP for the next day.

Her remaining memories of the previous evening were still slightly hazy. It seemed Jon had phoned for an ambulance as soon as she'd hit the deck. She half-remembered him staying with her in the ambulance, sobbing his apologies for how he'd treated her, for lying to her, and for being a general shit. He'd offered to stay with her once they'd reached the hospital, but she'd asked him to call Trudi. To his credit, he had. Trudi had arrived fifteen minutes later, full of concern, and throwing recrimination at Jon.

Some strong painkillers and a good night's sleep had helped. Although she still felt sluggish this morning, she felt confident enough to head into work later.

And now she was waiting. Counting the slow-moving minutes with a mixture of apprehension and self-doubt.

Her voicemail was clogged with messages from Jon: a heady brew of further apologies and promises to change his ways. He begged for another chance and wanted her to move back in. But she needed time to think about where her future lay and whether Jon was going to be a part of it. In her heart, she didn't want to end it, but there was so much to consider.

She checked her watch again. Another hour and she could take some more ibuprofen.

It was another warm and sunny day. The heat showed no signs of abating. The forecasters said it could last for another week, with a possibility of thunderstorms in the south. There was already talk of hosepipe bans, and the supermarkets were running out of bottled water. Molly had spent a number of years living with her father in Sydney, where hot summers were par for the course and rarely made the news.

'That looks nasty.' Molly looked up. Silhouetted against the sun, Magda Kilbride was dressed in her standard garb: black Levis, black boots, a black and grey striped blouse and, despite the heat, a black gent's blazer. The silver dagger brooch was on her right lapel. Her voice was emotionless. It reminded Molly of the voice at a self-service check-out dispassionately informing you that there was an unexpected item in the bagging area.

'I wasn't sure you'd come,' Molly said. She'd been surprised when Mags had agreed to meet her so early; there was something about Magda Kilbride that made Molly think she wasn't a morning person.

Mags sat down next to her. They were sitting on a bench in Hyde Park, overlooking the Serpentine; sunrays dancing brightly on its surface. It was early, and the park wasn't busy: a couple of joggers and a dog-walker were the only other people she'd seen since she'd got there.

'What do you want this time?' The voice was still cold, devoid of anything faintly human. But Molly didn't care. She no longer feared Magda Kilbride and her little bottles of poison.

'I want to tell you you're a bitch. And I wanted to say it to your face.'

Mags laughed, not the usual half-cackle/half-bray that signified her amusement, but a rather forced titter. She pushed her sunglasses onto her forehead and Molly noticed her eyes were bloodshot. She suspected Mags was on some sort of comedown from the night before.

'You could have texted me to tell me that. You don't need to drag me out here to tell me something I couldn't give a shit about.'

'I've been digging around, Mags. You've got a pretty colourful past: arrested for drug-dealing when you were seventeen; cautioned for assault when you were twenty, possession of cocaine six years ago. Then there's the soliciting. Don't get me wrong, we've all got a living to earn, and Christ knows I'm not one to judge, but it's a bit of a career change from hooker to journalist.'

The journalist's face remained impassive. 'What can I say? I'm a woman of many talents.'

'And then there's the real reason you were sacked from the *Echo*. A costly libel case concerning a story about a pop star and a rent boy, which you as good as admitted in court had been nothing more than a product of your disturbed imagination.'

An elderly cyclist in a Panama hat smiled as he passed them. To the casual passer-by they doubtless looked like nothing more than two friends having a morning catch up.

'Is that all?' she said. 'I thought you were at least going to mention Jon. I mean he's the real reason you're here. I expect you've worked it all out about me and him: that little brain of yours whirring away like a demented hamster on its wheel, trying to connect all the dots; finally realising Jon's been playing you for a fool all this time. I take it he's responsible for *that*.' She jabbed a finger at Molly's cheek. 'Well, get it off your pathetic chest then. Have a little rant. And try and find something more original to call me than a bitch, for Christ's sake. In my line of trade, that's practically a compliment.'

'Why did you do it, Mags? Why did you give that story to the *Echo*? You knew we were trying to keep it quiet.'

Her blood red lips made a little moue. 'How did you know it was me?'

'I was obviously meant to think it was Jon, but he wouldn't do that. He might have the morals of a dog but, like a dog, he values loyalty. This was the work of someone bitter. Someone who enjoys stirring shit simply because she likes watching people squirm.'

Mags made a noise that sounded like 'Pah'. She turned to face Molly, the sun bouncing a searing glare off her shades. 'Jesus. You only know about Ferguson because I pointed you in the right direction. If it hadn't been for me you'd still be struggling to find your own backsides with two hands. You owed me, and I always collect.'

'I owe you jack shit, Mags. I should arrest you for disclosing confidential information about an ongoing police investigation to a third party.'

She laughed again, still not quite her usual animalistic ejaculation, but with more conviction than the previous lame titter. 'You are having a joke, aren't you? I'm a bloody journalist, it's my job. Besides, this isn't schedule D or anything, and there's nothing to suggest this information isn't in the public interest. Besides, some hack would have put two and two together sooner or later. Three murders, all within a few weeks of one another. The press aren't stupid, you know.'

'Later would have suited us.' She shot Mags a sharp look. 'You've jeopardised a major investigation, and for what? To try and split up me and Jon? If that's the case, then better luck next time. Not that there's going to be a next time, because if you try anything like that again, we'll come down on you like a ton of bricks.'

'When will you get it into your thick skull? I couldn't give a stuff about you and Jon. He's nothing to me. He was a rubbish shag then and I expect he still is now. We only got it together back then because we were both in a bad place at the time. Trust me, I wouldn't have gone near the twat otherwise.'

'And vice bloody versa, I'm sure.' Molly stood up. She'd had enough. She had said what she'd come to say. Now she'd find a café, buy some water and take another two painkillers. Then she'd head into work and do her job. 'I feel sorry for you, Mags. I have a job I love, a man I love and a life I love. What have you got?'

She turned to leave.

'Before you rush off on your merry way, you ought to know: I've been doing some digging myself.' She waited a second, just enough to let the words sink in. 'I know all about you, DS Fisher. I know what's driving your obsession with Anthony Ferguson.'

Molly stopped in her tracks. She wanted to turn back and face Mags, but she wasn't sure if she could stop herself from punching her in the mouth. Instead, she decided to walk away. But she could still hear Mags shouting at her back. 'I know the truth, and I think it's time DI Denning did too.'

Molly was trembling as she walked. She hurried her step until the voice became too distant to hear. She hated Mags, but she hated herself even more. Hated herself for being naïve and trusting. Of course Magda had given the story to the press: that was the main reason she'd agreed to meet Molly in the first place. She'd as good as admitted that: the tape recorder on the table had been evidence of her intent. But Molly, blinded by her own crusade, had ignored the implications.

She needed to find some water and take the ibuprofen; something to numb the pain.

Chapter Fifty-Eight

Catford Road was a mixture of residential properties, shops and office blocks in south east London. Denning had been based in Lewisham when he'd first joined the Met over ten years ago. Back then the area was still trying its damnedest to resist all and every attempt at gentrification. Poor transport links had always made parts of south London less appealing to the professional classes, but the inexorable upward movement of London house prices, combined with the extension of the DLR had seen the area become more desirable. As a result houses once divided into tiny bedsits had since been returned to their original purpose as family homes and once dingy pubs had been transformed into trendy gastro pubs. Smart, sparkly estate agents offices had replaced betting shops and convenience stores along Lewisham's High Street. It wasn't quite Shoreditch, but it was getting there.

The space where Daniel Placzek's builder's yard used to be was now occupied by a second-hand car showroom. Denning was casually admiring a three-year-old BMW convertible on offer at a very respectable £14K when a ferrety-looking man in a neat grey suit approached him with a cheesy smile. He had sandy blond hair, which was cut slightly too short for his long face. 'Only one previous owner. Sold it when she relocated to Japan.' He shook Denning by the hand. 'We offer credit, if you'd like to take it for a test drive.'

Denning flashed his warrant card. 'Tempting, but I'm here on business.' He watched the man's face drop. 'I understand this site used to be a builder's yard around twelve years ago.

Just wondering if you know what happened to the bloke who owned it.'

He blinked at Denning for a couple of seconds as though unsure what he was talking about. 'Before my time, mate. But you could ask the owner, Mr Jackson. He's popped to the bank, but he should be back in about half an hour.'

Denning looked at his watch: it wasn't worth driving back to Stoke Newington then schlepping all the way back down to Lewisham. He spotted a coffee shop across the road.

'OK, I'll come back at eleven. If you could let him know I'd like a word.' He handed the man his card, who stared at it, as though it would give him the answers to all the mysteries of the universe.

Chapter Fifty-Nine

Trudi looked up from her desk as soon as Molly walked into the MIT suite.

'What are you doing here? I told Denning you wouldn't be in today.'

'Where is Denning?' Molly asked, ignoring Trudi's concern.

'He's gone to Lewisham to follow up a lead.' She grabbed Molly's arm. 'You should be at home with your feet up watching *Loose Women*.'

Molly was aware of the bruise on her cheek. Aware, too, that people were looking at her.

'I'm fine,' she lied. Besides, she'd rather saw her own head off than watch *Loose Women*. She looked around the office. 'I need to speak to Denning. Do you know when he'll be back?'

Trudi shrugged. 'I dunno. You could text him if it's urgent.'

Molly thought about it. She was certain Mags was bluffing about contacting Denning, and even if she did, would Denning believe her? It was unlikely, but she couldn't take that risk.

She put the thought out of her head and switched on her PC. Since the story had appeared in the press, the other media had run with it. Consequently, the team were now inundated with calls and emails, some from people who thought they had important information that could help with the case, but many from cranks who simply wanted to share their theories about how the murders were the work of everyone from Jack the Ripper to Dirty Den. They all had to be checked, even the crank calls. It was time-consuming and it was frustrating.

She wanted to do something useful.

There were still hours of CCTV footage to pore over. The white van that had been spotted on the bridge over the canal at Hoxton had been traced as far as a junction with Green Lanes and Collins Road, just before Clissold Park to the north of Islington. The trail had gone lukewarm after that. She clicked on Google Maps, and typed in 'Collins Road, N5'. The map showed a maze of residential roads and side streets connected with Collins Road, all with little or no CCTV coverage. To anyone who knew the area it would be the ideal place to lose a vehicle.

Local uniform had conducted extensive door-to-door in the area, even checking any CCTV from private households, but there had been nothing.

Then a thought struck her. She returned to the CCTV footage of Green Lanes, specifically the junction with Collins Road. There was little traffic at that time of night, mostly the occasional night bus, taxi or delivery vehicle. She sped the video up, and saw that about ten minutes after the van had disappeared down Collins Road, it reappeared on Green Lanes, travelling south back towards Islington. The driver had obviously doubled back, assuming the police would only check CCTV on the northbound lane. She followed the course of the van for another few minutes, and watched as it turned left into Foresham Grove. Foresham Grove didn't have any CCTV, but it led to Albion Road, which stretched from Islington to Stoke Newington. The CCTV footage from Albion Road didn't show any sign of the van. It had disappeared in Foresham Grove. Cross-referencing back to Google Maps, she clicked on Street View. The date at the bottom right of the screen said Monday 23 October 2017, so it was recent enough to ensure that little would have changed.

There was nothing significant about Foresham Grove: a row of two-up-two-down Victorian terraced houses ran along one side, a disparate mix of modern flats and tall, thin townhouses along the other. The street looked like any other quiet residential street in north London. If the driver was clever, he could have waited, then double-backed along Green Lanes assuming the police would only check vehicles travelling in one direction. On the other hand, would someone really go to that much trouble at that time of night?

She headed over to Neeraj's desk. In the absence of Denning, he was in charge. 'Deep, the van from the first murder. Whereabouts did we lose it?'

Neeraj had been going over witness statements from the most recent murder. There were files stacked on his desk. He dug behind them and pulled out an A5 notepad, searching back over several pages. Eventually he found what he was looking for. 'Here we are.' He scanned his notes. 'Somewhere on Green Lanes. Uniform have been down there, but nobody saw anything suspicious. It's likely he used it as a through route to get to somewhere else. We're still waiting for the outstanding footage from the surrounding streets. Apparently there's a hold up because someone's been off sick. Let me get on to traffic and chase it up.'

'Don't bother,' said Molly. 'I think our killer lives in Foresham Grove.'

Chapter Sixty

Simon Jackson was in his late forties, with a heavy frame, which he'd successfully managed to squeeze into an expensive designer suit. His hair was unnaturally blond, and Denning suspected the assistance of a bottle. Jackson greeted Denning with a firm handshake and a professional smile. 'What can I do for you, Inspector?'

Denning told him about Daniel Placzek. 'Anything you could tell me about him would be useful.'

They walked to Jackson's office at the back of the showroom. Denning sat on a comfy leather sofa, while Jackson sat opposite on a leather bucket chair. There were framed photographs of expensive cars on the walls: a couple of Porsches, a Lamborghini and a bright red Ferrari. A silver-plated model of 1950s Rolls Royce Silver Ghost sat on his desk. Jackson clearly liked cars.

'You're going back a bit,' Jackson said, 'I mean I only took over the lease on this land. I didn't have anything to do with his building firm.' He unbuttoned his jacket and his stomach swelled in his shirt. 'He had hoped to sell the building firm as a going concern, but it was just the land I was interested in. It's a great site: loads of passing trade, and the whole area's come up in recent years.'

'Why did he sell up?'

'He'd gone bust, or so he claimed. A number of larger firms that he did contract work for had been slow in paying him. He needed to sell what he could to keep the receivers off his back.' Jackson flashed an awkward smile. 'He was also going through an expensive divorce at the time, which didn't help matters.'

Denning nodded slowly, knowing all about expensive divorces. 'What was Placzek like?'

Jackson wrinkled his brow. 'He seemed perfectly normal: friendly, honest. I felt a bit sorry for him, if I'm honest. I got the impression he didn't want to sell up.'

'But he had no choice? He was in financial difficulty?'

'Yes. Well, that's what he told me. It's just...' Jackson paused, chewing his next words over in his head. 'I met some bloke at a trade do a few years after I'd bought this place, a big-time property developer: he claimed he often used Placzek's firm and there were a load of big jobs in the pipeline. As far as he knew, business was going great guns. Mind you, so much is about keeping up appearances. The reality could have been very different.'

He looked at Denning. 'Can I ask what this is in connection with?'

'We think Placzek might have had a connection with Anthony Ferguson.'

'Ferguson? The bloke who murdered those women?' He let the surprise work its way over his face. Even now, thought Denning, after all these years, the name Ferguson could still evoke something akin to revulsion. 'You think Placzek knew him?'

There was a pause before Denning answered. 'We believe they worked together.' He was reluctant to give too much away.

'Does this have anything to do with that story in the papers the other day?' Jackson asked.

Denning ignored the question. 'Do you know what happened to Placzek after he sold this place?'

'Not a clue. Sorry. Once the deal went through I never heard from him again.' He rubbed a hand over his belly as if he had a stomach ache. 'You could try his ex-wife, though. She might have an idea.'

'I don't suppose you have an address for her?'

Johnson smiled again. 'If she's still living at the same address Placzek was when he sold me this place, then yes. My solicitor should have the details.' He looked at Denning. 'Let me give him a bell, then I'll email it through to you.'

Denning thanked him, and stood to leave. He was about to head out of the office and back into the showroom when Jackson said, 'Doug mentioned you were interested in the Beamer in the forecourt.' He flashed Denning another professional smile. 'Are you sure I can't persuade you to take it for a spin?'

Chapter Sixty-One

Foresham Grove was quiet at that time of day. There were a few cars parked outside the row of terraced houses, and one or two outside the flats, but mostly the street had an empty, abandoned feel about it. Like so many residential streets in London, its liveliness would come in the evening when its residents returned from work, or at weekends when neighbours would chat to one another while putting the bins out, or washing their cars.

When she'd told Neeraj what she was doing, he'd sucked his teeth and made a tutting noise, as though he was uneasy about her going off on her own bat. He reminded her that uniform had already done door-to-door down the street and come back with nothing to report.

But they hadn't been looking for what she was looking for.

Not that she knew what that was yet, not exactly. But the van had to be here. Unless the CCTV was lying, there was nowhere else it could be. Maybe uniform hadn't thought to ask the right questions. Or maybe they'd been too willing to accept whatever the householders had told them.

She looked along the street, from one end to the other. It didn't look any different to what Google Street View had shown her. There was a 'To Let' sign attached to one of the bland, modern townhouses, and one of the terraced houses had had scaffolding up on Google Maps, which had since been taken down, but otherwise there was nothing remarkable about the street at all. Except something didn't feel right.

If their killer did live on Foresham Grove – and it was still a very big if – then it could easily be any one of these houses, or even one of the flats in the modern, square block opposite. Uniformed police officers would have spoken to every single resident, any suspicions noted and flagged up with MIT. But according to Neeraj there had been nothing.

Then a thought suddenly hit her. What if he didn't *live* here? What if he just parked his van here and then walked to wherever he lived? But surely someone would have mentioned a parked van during the door-to-door enquiries? Unless...

She crossed the road to take a closer look at the house that was To Let. It was tall and thin, and had an integral garage. She peered through the letterbox: there was a scattering of junk mail and leaflets for local supermarkets lying in the empty hallway. A flight of carpeted stairs rose off to the right, and there looked to be a door at the end of the hallway leading to a sitting room at the back of the house. There was a fusty smell about the place, as though it hadn't been aired for a while. She wondered how long it had been To Let for.

She twisted the handle of the garage door but it was locked.

Stepping back on the kerb, she looked up at the empty house. There was an agent's name on the 'To Let' board: Newbold and Stradling. She made a note of the number. With a bit of luck their office wouldn't be too far away.

The girl sitting behind the desk introduced herself as Bernice and looked like she'd probably just left school. She threw Molly a confused look when she asked about the townhouse on Foresham Grove.

The Islington office of Newbold and Stradling was laid out more like a trendy restaurant than an estate agency. There was a counter in one corner, with fridges stacked with drinks behind it, and a comfy seating area by one of the floor-to-ceiling windows. Molly had been greeted by a large computer screen opposite the front door as soon as she'd walked in, which flashed up images of expensive properties and their price per calendar month.

'Oh, here it is,' Bernice said. 'I'd forgotten we still had it.' She turned the computer monitor round to show Molly. She touched a thumbnail image of the property and the details flashed up on the screen. 'Three-bed, two bath, one en suite,' she read, 'kitchen, two receptions and a garage. There's also a lovely patio garden.' She pointed to a picture of a tiny courtyard space, bedecked with tubs and climbing roses. 'It was on for £2500 pcm.'

'Was?'

'We let it about six weeks ago. The sign should have been taken down by now. I'll get someone on to that.'

She had a sweet sing-song voice and wore too much make-up for someone so young. Molly suppressed the urge to advise her that less was more when it came to applying the war paint, unless she wanted people to think she was a transvestite. Instead, she said, 'I need to know who it's been let to.'

Bernice swivelled the screen back round to her side of the desk, and peered curiously at the details on the screen. 'It says Lance Grady.' She looked at Molly. 'I'm sorry, I don't remember him. There's a contact mobile number and email address for him, but not a lot else I'm afraid. I could check his file; that might tell us more.'

Molly indicated that she would appreciate it if she could. Bernice picked up the receiver, pressed a button and asked for someone called Marge. She nodded and said 'hmm' a couple of times, then put the receiver down. 'We can dig out his file and email through scanned copies of the paperwork, if that's any help.'

Molly took a note of the contact details for Lance Grady, and asked if the file could be emailed through that afternoon. Bernice nodded her assent. 'Can I ask what it's about?'

'We think Mr Grady may be connected to an ongoing murder investigation,' Molly said.

Bernice's mouth opened to form an O. 'Gosh,' she said, 'I'm sure if we'd known that, we'd never have agreed to let the property to him in the first place.'

Chapter Sixty-Two

Denning found the address Jackson gave him. It was a tree-lined street not far from Greenwich Park. The houses were mostly large detached and semi-detached properties set slightly back from the road. Late Victorian or early Edwardian, Denning reckoned, with large gardens and off-street parking. It was the kind of place Sarah wanted them to move into, assuming their combined incomes could manage to meet the massive mortgage payments necessary to own such a property.

14 Weston Avenue was one of the semi-detached properties. The driveway was large enough to contain two cars comfortably, but it was bereft of cars. It was possible Placzek's ex-wife no longer lived there – she may well have remarried and moved away.

He rang the doorbell and waited for an answer. After a moment a woman in her early forties answered the door. She eyed Denning curiously before he flashed his warrant card and explained who he was.

'Mrs Placzek?'

The woman did a double-take at the mention of the name. 'Jesus, I haven't been called that in years.' She shot Denning a quizzical look. 'What's this about?'

'Can I come in? I need to talk to you about your ex-husband.'

She glanced in the direction of her neighbours, seemed happy that nobody was watching, and let Denning in.

The house was airy and well-furnished, with tasteful Chinese rugs on the floor and gilt-framed pictures on the walls. She showed Denning into the sitting room.

'I'm Angela Patterson now,' she said. 'I went back to using my maiden name.' She sat down on one of the two large sofas, which were arranged around an ornate marble fireplace, and indicated for Denning to do the same. 'If this is about Daniel, I'm afraid I haven't seen him in years.'

Angela Patterson was well dressed, in a light summer frock with a silky scarf draped over her shoulders. She had a pair of Jimmy Choo sandals on her feet: Sarah had several similar pairs in her wardrobe. She smiled a lot when she spoke, flashing immaculate white teeth.

'Do you know where he might be?'

She gave a light shake of her head. 'Not a clue, sorry.' She shot Denning the same quizzical look she'd given him when she'd opened the door to him. 'I don't think you said why you want to see him?'

He liked her directness – not aggressive, just straight to the point. 'It's in connection with an ongoing murder inquiry.' He paused before continuing. 'Do you know if he had anything to do with a man called Anthony Ferguson?'

She looked shocked, her hand going to her scarf, tugging at it unconsciously. 'The name sounds vaguely familiar, but to be honest with you he knew so many people, especially in connection with the business. I'm afraid I can't place him.' She stopped fiddling with her scarf. 'What has Daniel got to do with a murder inquiry?'

Denning didn't think there would be any harm in giving her the whole story. When he had finished she looked blankly back at him. 'I don't believe this. Daniel never had anything to do with those murders. Don't get me wrong, we didn't exactly have the happiest of marriages, but he was never violent. And I can't imagine he would have associated with someone who was capable of that.'

'We know that Anthony Ferguson and Daniel worked together at the time of the original murders. We also now know there were two men involved.'

'And you really think Daniel was this other man?'

Denning shot her an imploring look. 'That's why we need to speak to him as a matter of urgency. We need to eliminate him from our enquiries if he's innocent.'

'And if he's not...?'

Denning left the question unanswered. 'What happened to him after you divorced?'

She gave an easy shrug. 'How the hell would I know? I was just glad to be shot of him,' She looked at Denning. 'Don't misunderstand me, I didn't hate him, not really. It was just that he changed. Well, I suppose we both changed, but in Dan's case it wasn't for the better.'

'Go on.'

Her face dropped. He noticed she was no longer smiling at him.

'When we met he was just a normal builder. He worked for a firm in Kent, worked wherever they sent him. I'm an accountant, so we had a good life. We weren't loaded, or anything, but we were comfortably off. But Dan wanted more. He set up on his own; I did the books and sorted out all the paperwork that goes with running a small business, while he went out and got the contracts. Then everything changed. *He* changed. He became more... I don't know – ruthless, I suppose. Money and status suddenly became important to him. We bought this house with a mortgage that was way too much for us. He began chasing bigger and bigger orders. Unfortunately some of these big boys are slow to part with their cash. We ended up with a cash-flow problem, for which he blamed me. I told him I was an accountant not a bloody magician: if these bastards weren't going to pay up when we asked them then there was bugger all I could do about it.' She began to fidget, twisting a ruby ring on her middle finger, turning it over and over as the memories poked through the barricade she'd erected to keep them out. 'It wasn't a good time for us. Not just professionally, but on a personal level too.' She looked awkwardly at Denning, who smiled and nodded, encouraging her to continue. 'Dan always wanted children, but I didn't. We used to argue about that, and with the business getting into difficulty, one thing led to another.' She continued to twist the ruby ring as though she was unscrewing a bottle top. 'I had an affair and Dan found out. He went ballistic: I'd never seen him in such a rage. But he was never violent; it was all just shouts and the odd threat, but nothing physical. He just wasn't that kind of man.'

How many times had Denning heard that phrase? Rapists whose wives insisted their husbands weren't violent; neighbours who swore blind the paedophile living next door was a paragon of virtue, or the workmates who insisted there was no way the quiet bloke who sat opposite them every day could be a terrorist. He'd learned that people who were guilty of criminal behaviour rarely advertised what they were.

'Did you notice anything strange about his behaviour around this time?'

She pulled a face. 'Are you kidding? Business going up the Swannee, marriage going down the toilet? Yes, he was pretty strange. But do I think he was out killing women with some nutter he knew from work? No, that's mad.'

There was a real danger they were going to end up going round in circles without making any progress. 'What happened when you divorced?'

She dropped her gaze for a moment. 'He walked out.' She continued to stare at the carpet. 'I came back from Sainsbury's one day and he'd gone. Just left a note saying he needed time to get his head together. And that was it: I never heard from him again.'

'Did you try and contact him?'

'I tried phoning him, but there was never an answer. None of his friends knew where he was, and what family he had left had had no contact with him for years. Eventually I received confirmation from my solicitor that he wasn't contesting the divorce and I could keep the house.'

'Didn't your solicitor know where he was?'

'Apparently not. He dealt with Dan's solicitor and that was that. There was no suggestion of us meeting up. It was all done through third parties. We'd already transferred the deeds of the property into my name in case Dan were to be made bankrupt, so there wasn't too much left to discuss.' She smiled at Denning. 'That was the final contact I had with him, albeit indirectly.'

'So you've heard nothing from him in ten years?'

She shook her head. 'Nothing. Not a card, not a phone call.'

Denning glanced round the spacious living room. 'Do you have any photographs of Daniel?'

She shook her head again. 'I chucked them all after he left. In fact I got rid of everything of his: clothes, golf clubs, anything that reminded me of him. I even had the house redecorated from top to bottom. I wanted him deleted from my life entirely.'

'I know this might seem like a strange question, Ms Patterson, but was your husband religious at all?'

She offered him a curious look. 'Yes. Well, his mother was. Devoutly. Dan was more lapsed, though he did go to church when we were first married. Is that relevant?'

Denning wasn't sure yet. He stood up to leave. 'One last thing, Ms Patterson: what do you think happened to your ex-husband?'

She gave him a thoughtful look. The smiles that had greeted Denning on his arrival had vanished now, replaced with a slight creasing in the forehead and a stony expression. 'If you want my honest opinion, Inspector, he topped himself. I mean, it's the only explanation.'

Chapter Sixty-Three

'What happened to your face?' Denning asked.

Molly put a hand to her cheek, wincing as a stab of pain bit into her. She'd forgotten about the bruise.

'Nothing,' she said. 'I had an accident, that's all.' She was aware that she sounded defensive, probably making him jump to all sorts of conclusions. But she didn't really care.

Denning was about to lead another briefing. The MIT suite gradually began to fill up with detectives.

Molly sat at her desk at the back of the vast room. She felt like she was on the periphery of the action; still an observer or at best, a bit-part player rather than one of the team.

'What's the score with Daniel Placzek?' Dave Kinsella asked before Denning had even started the briefing.

'He's dead,' Denning said abruptly. He waited until the room fell silent before he continued. 'Or at least that's what his ex-wife believes.'

'Do we have any way of proving that?' Kinsella asked.

'Unless we chance upon his corpse, Dave, then no, at this stage we can't prove it. His wife seems to think he topped himself after his business and his marriage both went tits up at the same time.'

'Does that mean we're ruling Placzek out of this?' Ryan Cormack asked.

'We can't regard him as a suspect if he's dead,' Kinsella said abruptly.

'Until we know for certain, Ryan, no, we're not ruling him out; at least not officially.'

Molly could sense the tension in Denning's voice. Up until now she'd kept quiet. She still wasn't sure there was anything in her theory about Lance Grady; she didn't want to open her mouth and make a fool of herself until she was one hundred per cent sure of her facts. However, Deepak Neeraj wasn't going to give her the luxury of choosing her moment.

'I believe DS Fisher has something to say,' he said.

All eyes in the room swung towards Molly.

'It might be nothing.' She took a deep breath and told them about her visit to Foresham Grove and the empty house.

'Lance Grady?' Denning screwed his face up. 'Have you run the name through the PNC?'

She looked sheepish. 'Yes. There's nothing. And according to the electoral roll, there's no one registered at that address.'

'Sounds like a made-up name,' said Neeraj.

'But at least it's a name.' Denning seemed to give the matter some thought. 'You're sure the house is empty?'

'It didn't look like anyone lives there, but I couldn't swear to it.'

Denning nodded. 'OK. Let me know the minute the estate agents send you through their file on this Lance Grady. Also, if the place is unoccupied, let's get hold of a set of keys and have a good look inside the house. It may throw up something.'

Denning scribbled the name 'Lance Grady' on the whiteboard.

'Are we sure this bloke's a suspect?' Neeraj asked. 'DS Fisher said the house was empty. It's possible he just uses it as a London address.'

'It *looked* empty,' Molly said. She avoided Denning's eye when she spoke. 'That doesn't mean he isn't living there.'

'And he lets his mail pile up behind the front door?' said Neeraj.

'So he hasn't been there for a while,' Trudi butted in, 'doesn't mean he wasn't living there at the time of the murders.'

'OK,' said Denning, 'until we know otherwise, Lance Grady stays on the board.'

Chapter Sixty-Four

Half an hour later, Denning was walking past Molly's desk when she grabbed him.

'Lance Grady checks out,' she said. 'He's based in Bahrain and works for an engineering company. But he does visit the UK from time-to-time.'

She showed Denning the scanned paperwork from Grady's file, which had been emailed through less than ten minutes ago and now formed a neat pile on her desk. There was a photocopy of his passport, proving he was who he claimed to be, as well a copy of his references from both his bank and his employer.

'Do we have any contact details for him?' Denning asked.

'There's a phone number,' she said, flicking through the paperwork, 'and an email address for the company he works for.'

'Get hold of him. Ask him if he knows the name Daniel Placzek,' Denning said. 'It's a long shot, I know, but let's make sure we cover all our bets before we officially write Placzek off as a dead end.' Denning thought about Ken Walters. He didn't want any unanswered questions lingering over this investigation only to blow up in his face a decade down the line.

He looked at Molly. She was rubbing a hand over her forehead. She looked tired. They all looked tired: hot and tired.

Denning headed back to his desk. He was struggling to hide his frustration. Not only had the PNC failed to throw up anything useful regarding Daniel Placzek, but none of the utility companies had any record of a Daniel Placzek for the past ten years. The DVLA had confirmed that their records for him had ended around the same time. It looked like Angela Patterson had been right: Daniel Placzek was dead.

But despite this, Denning still wasn't entirely convinced.

It wasn't unheard of for people to disappear completely: to top themselves in some obscure location, lying undiscovered for years, sometimes forever. If Placzek had been Ferguson's accomplice then it was possible he'd killed himself shortly after Ferguson was caught. It made sense. He would have been constantly looking over his shoulder, counting down the days until there was a knock at his door followed by some awkward questions. Ferguson's arrest combined with his ongoing business and personal problems would have been enough to push him over the edge.

However, no body had ever been found. He'd checked the PNC for a list of unidentified bodies that had been discovered over the past decade and none of them fitted the description of Daniel Placzek. But to disappear so completely, without leaving any kind of trace, just felt too convenient: too neat. According to Angela Patterson, Placzek hadn't left a suicide note, simply telling her he needed time to get his head together. Again, this wasn't unheard of for suicides; sometimes the act was spontaneous and unplanned. But it was unusual, and taken together with everything else, Denning couldn't help wondering if Daniel Placzek was still alive.

He was about to shut down his computer for the night and head home, when the phone on his desk rang.

'DI Denning.'

'Front desk here, sir. There's a woman downstairs who says she needs to speak to you.'

Denning sighed. It was late and he was tired. 'Can someone take a statement from her?'

'She's says it's to do with the murders. She says her name's Magda Kilbride and she has some information about one of your officers.'

Chapter Sixty-Five

The following morning Molly arrived at work with a numbing headache. She'd already taken two paracetamol, which had so far failed to kick in. She hadn't even had a chance to switch on her computer when Deep Neeraj appeared beside her desk with the news that Denning and McKenna wanted to see her in McKenna's office.

She knocked on Betty Taggart's door and entered.

McKenna was sitting behind her desk. Her face was inscrutable, as always. Denning was sitting on her right. It all looked terribly formal. She had a feeling in the pit of stomach that she knew what this was about. She hoped she was wrong.

'Sit down, Molly,' McKenna said. Her voice was cool and impassive, like a lady vicar at a summer tea party. 'First of all, I'd like to say you've been a major help with this murder inquiry, and we're very grateful for your input.' McKenna sat back, folding her arms in front of her chest. 'If you hadn't flagged up the link to the Anthony Ferguson murders, we'd probably still be playing blind man's buff with these recent murders. As it is, we now have a solid lead, and it's only a matter of time before we catch the man responsible.' She paused, letting the words sink in before she continued. 'Remind me again why you took such an interest in this case in the first place.'

Molly tried to make eye contact, but instead focused on a dead cyclamen on top of a filing cabinet. 'I've always wanted to join MIT. I've never made any secret of that.'

'Hmm.' McKenna nodded slowly. Denning remained silent. 'I don't doubt that. So many detectives see MIT as sexy, or at

309

least beneficial to their long-term career. And then some of us fall into it almost by accident.' She unfolded her arms and leant forward over the desk. 'And then there's you.' She let a silence fall. 'The Bermondsey Ripper case was more than just a link to the present day murders for you, wasn't it?'

Molly felt her heart thudding in her chest, but she was determined to brazen it out for as long as she could. If this was the end, she was damned sure she'd go down fighting. 'I don't know what you mean.' She looked at McKenna and then at Denning. Denning refused to give her eye contact, keeping his gaze firmly fixed on McKenna.

'Rebecca Owen,' McKenna said. 'She was Anthony Ferguson's last victim.' McKenna waited until her words had sunk in. If she was hoping for a reaction, Molly was determined not to give one. 'She was killed shortly after leaving a nightclub in Brixton almost exactly twelve years ago to the day Leanne Wyatt's body was found,' McKenna continued. 'And she was your best friend. You were with her the night she was killed. You left her outside the club and took a taxi home. Rebecca subsequently came into contact with Anthony Ferguson and his accomplice and they killed her.'

'Sorry, but I don't know what you're talking about.'

'It's all in the witness statements, Molly.' It was Denning's turn to speak. Like McKenna's, his voice was cool and dispassionate. 'It took me a bit of time to confirm the details because you were Margaret Milne then. I had to do some digging, but I can confirm that Margaret Milne and Molly Fisher are the same person.'

Molly tried to read his face but it gave nothing away. Her headache had just got a lot worse. After a moment she spoke. 'Fisher is my stepfather's name. I started using it when I moved back from Australia ten years ago.' Her throat was dry and scratchy. 'My brother couldn't say "Maggie" when he was little: he always called me Molly and it just stuck. I've always been known as Molly.'

'I think you're missing the point,' McKenna said calmly. 'We're not too bothered about what you call yourself. I'm more concerned about the fact that you failed to disclose your connection to the earlier murder inquiry.'

'Magda Kilbride.' She continued to look at them. They didn't need to say anything; she knew who'd spoken to them, and why. 'She's a fantasist. She just wants to cause trouble.'

'Again,' said McKenna slowly and deliberately as though talking to a child, 'I think you're missing the point.'

'We've looked into what she told us,' said Denning. 'And whilst I don't doubt she may well have an agenda, we now know what she's told us is true.'

Another silence hung in the air like a bad fart. Molly knew it was her turn to say something. She should offer up her side of the story, but she wasn't even sure what that was. What could she tell them? That she'd had a breakdown after Bex's death? That she'd blamed herself; run away to Australia to stay with a father she barely knew? That she'd tried hard to block it all from her mind for the past twelve years, only for it to bubble back to the surface the minute another young girl had been found murdered in circumstances that bore an uncomfortable resemblance to Bex's?

'I'm a good detective,' she said. There was a ball of something hard and uncomfortable stuck in her throat. 'I didn't tell you about Bex because I didn't think it was relevant.' She looked imploringly at her senior officers. McKenna was tight-lipped with a face carved from flint. Molly thought Denning was looking pityingly at her, as though he felt the need to apologise on her behalf.

'I'm afraid that won't cut it.' McKenna's ice-cool voice again. She fixed Molly with a look that seemed to burrow into her soul and linger there like a stab wound. 'I'm going to have to ask you to return to regular CID. Your secondment here was only ever intended to be temporary so it's not as if there will be any loss of face. We'll tell your DCI you're no longer needed on the case, now that we have a tangible lead.' She leaned in closer until Molly could smell her coffee breath – coffee laced with something sweet. 'This isn't a major fuck-up, but with the press crawling all over this case like the maggots they are, especially this Magda woman, I can't risk any more stories getting out there.' She offered an attempt at a smile which failed to travel from her lips to her eyes. 'Maybe you should take the rest of the day off? You've already put in some serious hours on this case.'

Molly opened her mouth to speak. She knew she had to say something to try and save face. 'I want to stay around. I can still help.' She looked at Denning. 'The house on Foresham Grove: it could throw up something useful.'

McKenna folded her arms across her chest. 'Go home, DS Fisher. You're now officially off the case.'

Chapter Sixty-Six

Molly logged off her computer and grabbed her bag. She told Trudi she was going home because she had a splitting headache, which wasn't a million miles from the truth.

Just as she reached the lift, Denning caught up with her.

'Molly, I'm sorry about what happened in there. You know I had no option but to go to DCI McKenna.'

Molly pressed the button for the ground floor. 'Don't blame yourself.' She turned to face the lift doors, willing them to open.

'I meant it when I said I appreciate your input with this case. But you've got to see that there's no way we could let you stay on the team. You're personally involved. And if this Magda woman is out to get you, then that's going to be a serious distraction.'

'You didn't have to listen to her,' she said. 'Mags, I mean: you could have told her to piss off.'

'On the other hand, you could have been honest with me from the start.'

'Would it have made any difference?'

There was a beat before he answered. 'I don't know. Maybe we could have worked around it.'

The lift arrived; the doors glided open and a couple of MIT detectives whose names Molly couldn't remember brushed past them and disappeared into the MIT suite. Just as she was about to step forward and enter the lift, Denning placed a hand on her shoulder. 'You can always reapply. When this is all over and things have settled down, you can put in an official transfer request to MIT. I'm sure your application will be looked on favourably.'

She entered the lift and pressed the button for the ground floor. 'At least think about it,' she heard Denning say as the lift doors slid shut. By the time the lift had reached the ground floor she'd already drafted a resignation letter in her head.

–

Half an hour later she let herself into Jon's house. The curtains were still drawn, in a vain attempt to keep out the day's heat. Jon was in the sitting room, listening to The Clash on his stereo system. She'd heard it as soon as she'd walked up the front path.

He switched it off as soon as he saw Molly standing in the doorway.

'Sorry, I didn't hear you come in.' He stretched his arms out to give her a hug, but changed his mind and let them hang by his side instead. 'How are you?'

She wasn't even sure what she was doing there. She just knew she needed someone to talk to, and Jon seemed the obvious choice.

'I've been kicked off the murder investigation.' She could feel tears gathering in her eyes.

He came over and gave her a hug. She hated herself because it felt good. It felt like old times, before Magda Kilbride had come into their lives and nearly destroyed everything. 'I really need to talk to you, Jon. I think I've fucked up big time.'

He led her over to the wonky chaise longue, gently pushing her onto it, keeping an arm round her shoulders. She was struggling hard to keep the tears from coming, trying to remain as calm as she could.

'I'll make us some tea,' he said, then disappeared into the kitchen.

When he returned a few minutes later, she'd tried hard to compose herself.

He handed her a mug of tea, and sat down next to her. 'What happened?'

She told him about her meeting with Denning and McKenna; the humiliation of having to return, tail between her legs, to regular CID. She told him, too, about Bex, and the guilt she'd carried inside her for over a decade. 'It was during the trial. I went there every day, listened to all the evidence, that's how I knew about the crosses.' She fought back tears as she spoke. 'I watched Ferguson standing in the dock looking ugly and pathetic. But I remember him saying he had an alibi for the night of Bex's murder. I always wondered, deep down, if it could be true. I kept asking myself if he really was innocent and the man who killed Bex was never punished for it.'

When she'd finished, he put his arm round her. 'You can't keep blaming yourself,' he said gently. 'None of this is your fault. You need to know that.' He kissed her cheek. 'Why did you never tell me any of this?'

She wiped her eyes with the back of her hand and sniffed back some snot. 'I was thirteen when we moved back here from Sydney. We had no money: Mum walked out on our dad when she found out he was having an affair with a nineteen-year-old barmaid. Bex was the first friend I made at school. I still had an Australian accent then, I mean not strong, but enough to make me stand out. Bex used to have a go at anyone who took the piss. She was like that: mouthy. After Bex died, I was in a state of shock. I tried to shut everything out of my mind. As soon as the trial was over, I went to stay with my dad and his bitch of a girlfriend in Sydney, but that didn't work out. She resented me, and he and I had never been all that close. I came back to the UK after a couple of years and just drifted from one dead-end job to another for a while. It was my stepdad who persuaded me to apply for the police. He was a solicitor and had a few contacts in the Met.' She chewed at her bottom lip. 'And it helped. It gave me a focus. I couldn't do much for Bex, but I can help put away sick bastards like Ferguson.' It felt cathartic to get it all out there. For so long she'd put everything in a box and hidden it away, out of sight and out of reach.

From beyond the French windows came the sound of the neighbours' children playing in the back garden. It sounded like they were splashing around in a paddling pool. Just for a moment, she envied them.

'How the hell did Mags find out about it?' Jon asked.

She shrugged. 'Who knows? Mags has a knack of digging up shit people would prefer to keep hidden.'

He held her closer. 'I'm sorry I lied to you about me and her.' He looked her directly in the face. 'I honestly meant it when I said it was nothing. Me and Mags…' His voice trailed away. 'It was a mistake. I was so out of it back then. It sounds like bullshit to say I didn't know what I was doing, but it's the truth. I was a fuck-up. I was a fuck-up and Mags took advantage of that. As soon as I came to my senses, I kicked her into touch. She's been carrying on with some sort of vendetta ever since.'

Molly stroked his cheek. 'Including letting me think you could have been somehow involved with Anthony Ferguson.'

He relaxed his hold on her. 'You what?' Then his mouth twisted into a smile and he burst out laughing. 'Really? You seriously thought I was…'

She interrupted him before he had a chance to continue. 'She had me thinking all sorts. I know now it's because she's damaged. She's poisonous, and some of that poison seeped into me.'

'But you thought there was some truth in what she said?'

She wiped her nose with her hand. 'No. Well, I don't know. All this crap with you and Mags, it all happened at about the same time as the Bermondsey Ripper murders. I didn't *want* to believe any of it, but she made me question everything about you. I knew you'd lied about you and her. I began to wonder if I really knew you at all.'

'You actually thought I was capable of murdering those women?'

She was suddenly aware of a change in his tone, a tensing of the muscles in his shoulder and neck. From outside the sounds of the children playing had stopped. 'No. Well, I don't know.' Molly shuffled free of his body, and sat upright on the chaise longue. 'You've said it yourself; you were all over the place twelve years ago. OK, it sounds bonkers now, but I couldn't just dismiss what was in my head. Mags seemed to know so much more about you than I did. There's a part of you that always feels like it's slightly out of reach. I'm not talking about the age gap because that's not important. I'm talking about how you keep so much of your life locked away.' She waited for him to reply, but he just looked at her with a vaguely bewildered expression on his face. 'Can't we put all this shit behind us? Start again?' she asked.

He stood up and walked to the French windows, pulled back the curtains and looked out into the garden. 'I wish,' he said. 'But I'm not sure how easy that's going to be. It's not like we can just put a sticking plaster over this and hope it heals.'

'We can if we want it to,' she argued, but already she could feel everything slipping away. 'This doesn't have to be the end, Jon. If we split up, then it means she's won.' She joined him by the French windows, placing a hand on his shoulder.

'I think it's you who's obsessed with her rather than the other way round.'

She removed her hand from his shoulder. There was nothing more she could say. She slipped out of the sitting room and walked to the front door. She closed it quietly behind her and began walking down the street. She didn't know where she was heading, just that she needed to walk.

Chapter Sixty-Seven

Denning tried to fight back the niggling guilt. He felt bad about how they'd treated Molly: about the way *he'd* treated Molly...

He stared at his phone, considering whether to ring her and apologise, but it wouldn't do any good: the decision couldn't be unmade. McKenna had never been entirely happy having Molly on the case in the first place, and she wasn't in any mood to have one of her decisions challenged. Once the dust had settled he would try and persuade McKenna to let them give Molly another chance. However, until then the best thing she could do would be to keep her head down.

He shifted his attention back to Daniel Placzek. There was still nothing to suggest Placzek was alive, even though Denning's gut feeling was telling him otherwise.

A search of Placzek's accounts at Companies House had shown his building business had been profitable for a number of years, but had suddenly begun to lose money around the time of his divorce. Somehow that seemed to be the key to it.

But if Placzek was out there, where was he? Unless something tangible came their way, it would be like searching for the proverbial needle in a haystack.

He looked up the CCTV footage from the night Leanne was killed. The footage had been noticeably cleaned up now and it was just about possible to make out the features of the man seen leaving the bar with Leanne. There was something familiar about those features. Denning couldn't say what it was, but he was certain he recognised the man in the blurry footage talking to Leanne. She was smiling and clearly drunk: totally oblivious to what fate had cruelly planned for her.

He froze the picture at the point where the footage of the man was clearest, and studied the image hard. There was certainly a superficial resemblance to Daryl Bailey: similar age, similar build, but it was possible to see that it wasn't Bailey.

It would make sense: they knew Leanne had a date with Bailey the night she was killed. Bailey said he'd left her around 9:30 p.m., after they'd had an argument. The CCTV from the street outside had been able to confirm this, even though the bar manager had insisted he'd seen them talking until after 11 p.m. But the bar had been busy. What if the bar manager had been mistaken, and Leanne was actually talking to someone else? What if she'd met another bloke at the bar who looked like Bailey: older, smart and flashy; just the kind of man she'd go for. If this man had witnessed the argument between Leanne and Bailey, he could have waited for his chance and offered her a drink and a shoulder to cry on. But was this mystery man Daniel Placzek, back from the dead?

Denning was about to get up and grab himself a coffee from the machine beside the lift, when Angela Patterson rang. 'Sorry to bother you with this when I'm sure you're up to your eyes, but you did say to get in touch if I found any old photographs of Daniel…' There was a slight pause from the other end of the line. 'Well, actually, I've found his old passport in the bottom of an old desk in the study. It's a few years out of date, but it's got his photo on it.'

'That's very helpful. Can you scan it and email me a copy?'

'I don't have access to a scanner, but I could drop it off later today if that's any help.'

Denning gave her directions to the station, and instructed the front desk to inform him the moment it arrived.

–

Neeraj cursed. The key didn't fit in the lock. The girl at the estate agent's had insisted he sign some silly indemnity form before they agreed to release the keys for the house. He'd told her that this was part of an important police operation, but she'd stood her ground. Not that it mattered; it wouldn't be his dangly bits on the chopping block if this all went tits up. Not that he'd believed for a moment they'd find anything. He couldn't understand why Denning had taken Molly Fisher so seriously. She was a nice girl, Molly, but she just didn't have what it took to hack it in the murder squad. He wasn't surprised they'd let her go.

He tried another key; this time it fitted. He unlocked the garage and lifted the metal door.

Parked in the garage was a slightly dirty white Transit van: an exact match for the one on the CCTV.

He phoned Denning. 'You're not going to believe this, boss.' He could barely keep the excitement from his voice. 'I think this it. We've finally nailed the bastard.'

–

Molly had had no intention of walking away from the murder inquiry, at least not entirely. She meant it when she'd told Denning and McKenna that she still had plenty to offer the investigation. Besides, it would be a welcome distraction from Jon.

She'd returned to Trudi's tiny flat in Limehouse. The flat was on the ninth floor of a converted council block. It had two small bedrooms, a compact lounge-diner, and an impressive view over the Thames to Bermondsey.

She was camped out in the back bedroom that served as an office, guest room and wardrobe overspill. She was grateful to Trudi and Charys for putting her up, but she knew she couldn't stay forever.

Jon wasn't answering her calls. The situation had bounced from one extreme to the other: after days of feeling like she was being stalked by him, now he was ignoring her. She couldn't blame him, and she didn't.

Whilst it had been good to finally get everything out in the open and tell someone about Bex, it looked as though that honesty had come at a price.

Molly shoved Jon to the back of her mind, booted up Trudi's laptop and remotely accessed her work email. Before she'd been so unceremoniously taken off the case, she'd sent an email to Lance Grady, and if he replied she was morally obliged to pass that information on to Denning.

And there it was in her inbox: a reply from Grady.

Chapter Sixty-Eight

'We lifted some prints,' Neeraj said at a briefing the following morning, 'but they don't match anything we have on record.'

There was a photograph of the white Transit van pinned on the board. It was the same van as the one in the CCTV footage. It was now just over a week since Leanne Wyatt's body had been discovered in a children's playpark in Hackney and her killer was still out there.

'The crime scene bods also found some DNA samples in the van which match both Leanne Wyatt and Sandra Blake,' he continued. 'They're going over the house now.'

Denning nodded. 'Do we know where the van came from?'

'It was purchased for cash from a dealer in Barnet just over a fortnight ago,' Ryan said, looking at his notes. 'The purchaser gave the name Lance Grady. We've got a description but it's vague: smart, well spoken.'

'This bloke's obviously covered his tracks,' Trudi added. 'Assuming he isn't Lance Grady.'

'I think it's safe to say this whole thing has been carefully planned from the off,' said Denning.

'And you still think he could be Daniel Placzek?' Trudi asked.

'He remains a definite possibility,' Denning said. 'We need to speak to him. And sooner rather than later.'

'How do we know we're not wasting our time looking for a dead man?' Kinsella asked. 'You said it yourself, boss: his ex-missus thinks he topped himself.'

'At the moment,' Denning said, 'I'm keeping an open mind, Dave. Angela Patterson *thinks* he could have killed himself, but she didn't know for certain. It's equally possible he's still alive and he's out there somewhere. Maybe with a new name.'

'Let's be frank,' Kinsella said, his voice hard, 'even if we find Placzek alive and well, we don't have any real proof that there *is* a connection between the Ferguson case and these recent murders. It could be that we're chasing fucking shadows.' He sat with his arms folded across his chest.

'There's too much for it to be a coincidence,' Denning said. 'Ken Walters admitted he always suspected there were two killers at the time. Placzek is the only person to have ever had any real contact with Ferguson. If he's still alive – and I accept that's still a big if at the moment – then we need to find him. Whoever our killer is, he knows what he's doing and he's had luck on his side up until now. But his luck's going to run out at some point.'

'Let's hope so, for all our sakes,' he heard Kinsella mutter under his breath.

'OK. We've got enough to keep ourselves occupied.' Denning ignored Kinsella and quelled the murmuring that now seemed to accompany every briefing. 'Get these new leads chased up. Ryan, speak to the dealer in Barnet again, get a detailed description of the man he sold the van to. Ideally see if he has any CCTV from the day in question. Deep, get onto Forensics: see if there's anything that proves Leanne Wyatt or Sandra Blake were in that house. I want to speak to Lance Grady, see what he has to say for himself. Everyone else, keep going over CCTV footage and witness statements until we can find something that puts our man in the frame.'

Denning ended the briefing. He was about to return to his desk, when he spotted a young uniformed officer pushing open the glass doors to the MIT suite. He heard her ask for him by name and one of the detectives point him out to her. She headed over to him, smiled and handed him a medium-sized brown envelope with his name scrawled on it. 'This was just handed in at the front desk, sir,' she said. 'You wanted to know as soon as it arrived.' Denning took the envelope from her, thanked her, returned to his desk and tore open the envelope. True to her word, Angela Patterson had handed in her ex-husband's passport. There was a handwritten note attached with a smiley face at the bottom. Denning fought back an inappropriate urge to laugh.

He opened the passport and looked at the photo of Daniel Placzek. Placzek's features were unremarkable: wavy light brown hair that brushed his shoulders, a strong brow, pale eyes. The photo was over ten years old. If Placzek were still alive, he would look different now: older, greyer round the temples. But there was something strangely familiar about the man in the photo. At first glance it was possible to see a faint likeness between Placzek and Daryl Bailey, but he knew it couldn't be anything more than a passing resemblance. However, he was sure there was *something*... He stared at the picture, hoping whatever it was would jump out at him, but he was either too tired or too distracted to see it.

He put the passport in the top drawer of his desk and stretched his shoulders, trying to suppress a yawn. At least they now had a picture of Daniel Placzek. He'd have the photo scanned and put on the whiteboard beside the other photos of suspects, and alongside the three victims.

He was about to pop to the machine by the lift and grab another rancid coffee, when his computer pinged him a notification that he had received another email. He gently shook the mouse to bring the screen back up. There were over a dozen unread emails in his inbox, most of which had arrived in the last hour. Most would be a waste of time: people suggesting names for their murderer, usually neighbours or ex-partners against whom grudges were still borne; sometimes people would suggest the man they were looking for was a celebrity, or politician or member of the royal family. Occasionally someone would claim they were the murderer and challenge the police to catch them.

He'd once read somewhere that over a hundred years ago the detectives investigating Jack the Ripper had received dozens of letters from people either claiming to be the Ripper or naming random people as the killer. All of which wasted a great deal of police time. Email, he surmised, was the twenty-first century equivalent: an opportunity for lonely, desperate or disturbed people to vent their collective spleens, or just think they were being helpful...

However, towards the bottom of the page, he noticed an email from Molly Fisher. His first thought was to wonder if she was asking for her job back in MIT, but the subject box said: Lance Grady. Curiosity aroused, he clicked on the email and was grateful that she'd bothered to forward it to him. He liked to think he'd have been as generous in similar circumstances.

Denning read the email.

> Spoken to Lance Grady. He rented the house in Foresham Grove because he wanted somewhere to crash whenever he's in London – seems his sister's just had a baby so he'll be spending more time in the UK. He gave a spare set of keys to a friend so he could keep an eye on the place.

When Denning read the friend's name, it hit him like a punch in the face.

He took Daniel Placzek's passport from his desk drawer, opened it and looked again at the photo. His stomach turned a somersault. He couldn't quite believe what he was seeing; didn't *want* to believe what he was seeing. But he couldn't avoid what was staring back at him, and suddenly everything fell into place.

If he allowed for the age difference; the slightly receding hair now expensively cut and dyed blond... If he added a light brushing of stubble and a fake tan, he was looking at a photo of Alan Marsden.

Chapter Sixty-Nine

Denning rang Claire's mobile but it went straight to voicemail.

Jumping into the Focus, he reversed out of the parking space at the back of the station, turned the car round with a screech of tyres and pulled out onto Stoke Newington Road, narrowly missing an oncoming bus.

He placed his phone in its holder on the dashboard, turned the speaker on, and kept trying Claire's number. Each time he got her answering service. On the third attempt he left a message urging her to contact him as soon as she got the message. He remembered her saying something about having split up with Marsden, but he couldn't remember the details. Cursing when he had to stop the car at a red traffic light, he berated himself for having been stupid enough to let his son and his ex-wife get so close to a man as dangerous as Alan Marsden. He'd had his suspicions about Marsden the first day he'd met him; standing in Claire's kitchen looking like a dog licking its bollocks.

When he arrived at Avonbrook Close, he parked against the kerb, jumped out of the car, ran up the driveway and banged on the front door.

The Lexus wasn't in the driveway, but Claire's blue Mini was there.

There was no answer at the front door. He headed round the back and tried the French windows. They were locked. He peered through the glass: there were clothes lying on the floor and dirty dishes on the table, and he immediately knew something was wrong.

He spotted a neighbour hanging out washing in her back garden. She looked about the same age as Claire and there were a couple of young children playing at her feet. Denning didn't recognise her, but assumed she'd moved in after he'd moved out. 'Excuse me,' he shouted over the fence.

The woman looked up. She was pegging a man's shirt to a rotary drier. 'Can I help you?' Her voice wasn't unfriendly, but tempered with a note of concern at the sight of a sweaty stranger standing on her neighbour's lawn.

'I'm with the police,' he flashed his warrant card over the fence; it was easier than trying to explain that he used to be married to the woman who lived there. 'Have you seen Claire Denning today? Or her son?'

The neighbour's face briefly wrinkled with concern. 'Not today.' She finished pegging the shirt and stood with her hands on her hips, a young child tugging at her sleeve. 'I saw her yesterday, around three ish. She was heading off somewhere with her son and, well, I assume her partner. To be honest, I don't really know them. We've only lived here a few months. I think someone mentioned something about her being divorced.' She tilted her head at Denning. 'Has something happened?'

'Around three o'clock yesterday afternoon,' he said. 'You're sure?'

'Yes. They headed off in that big car of his.'

'Did they say where they were going?'

She shook her head. 'I only saw them briefly. I was cutting the front lawn at the time.'

'How did they seem?'

'Sorry?'

'Where they happy, upset?'

Her face wrinkled even more. 'Now you mention it, the little boy seemed a bit upset. He looked like he'd been crying. But then he always seems to be upset about something. He's a bit highly strung.'

Denning ignored her remark. He gave her his card and asked her to contact him if Claire came back.

He raced back to his car. Once inside, he thought about what to do next. If he was playing this by the book, he should phone it in as a potential kidnap situation; arrange for back-up and declare a personal interest. But then it was possible he was overreacting. They still didn't have any hard evidence confirming Alan Marsden was Daniel Placzek, let alone any real evidence that Placzek was their killer. Everything they had was circumstantial: a tenuous link between Marsden and the man whose garage had been used to store a van which was involved in the murders, and a ten-year-old photograph of Placzek that bore an uncanny resemblance to Alan Marsden. If he called this wrong, McKenna would have his dick on a stick.

He needed to speak to Claire before he made this official. But first he needed to find her. And Jake.

Wherever they were, his gut told him they were with Marsden. He phoned Marsden's office, but his secretary said he hadn't been in the office for a couple of days and his mobile was switched off. She wasn't sure where he was.

Denning needed to get a trace put on Marsden's mobile, which meant he'd have to contact the station. He took the phone out of its holder and dialled Neeraj's number.

'Deep, it's Denning. Listen, I need you to do me a massive favour, and this needs to be done off the record.' He heard the hesitancy in Neeraj's voice, but he gave him Marsden's number and asked if he could do it ASAP. Even if the phone was switched off, it would still generate enough of a pulse to indicate its location. There was no guarantee Marsden would have his phone with him, but it was a start. Neeraj reluctantly agreed to do this, though he made it clear that he thought McKenna should be informed. Denning spoke quickly, unsure if his phone was going to die any second. He was wasting valuable minutes trying to convince Neeraj not to take this to McKenna, at least not yet.

He thanked Neeraj, told him he owed him one. This would at least give them a direct lead to Marsden, but it would take time. It was likely that Marsden was holding Claire and Jake against their will. If he was their killer, he would know by now that they were onto him. The papers were full of the fact that they were close to making an arrest. Even if this was an exaggeration to try and reassure the public, it might be enough to make Marsden panic.

Denning made a decision: he couldn't wait for Neeraj to trace Marsden's phone. If Claire and Jake were in danger, he needed to find them now.

He gripped the steering wheel to try and stop his hand from shaking.

Where would Marsden take them…? Grady's house in Foresham Grove had just been searched; Marsden wasn't at the office; he'd been staying with Claire whilst his own house was being renovated, at least before they'd split up… His own house? Probably one of his developments. He thought back to the time he visited Marsden's office: the model of the luxury apartment block; the plans for a warehouse development; the church conversion

It could be any one of those, or even some other development Denning knew nothing about. Then he remembered something Angela Patterson had said.

He started the car and pointed it in the direction of north London.

Chapter Seventy

Molly hadn't expected to receive a reply from Denning, but it would have been nice if he'd bothered to acknowledge her email. She suspected the information she'd given him hadn't been especially relevant, but at this stage in a murder investigation any little detail could prove useful.

She was heading into work to speak to Broomfield. She'd made up her mind about resigning. Even if she stayed in CID she would have to run the daily gauntlet of everyone knowing she had tried and spectacularly failed to make it in MIT. She could live without the humiliation.

The car park at the rear of the station was quiet. Molly convinced herself that the situation justified a cigarette, to calm her nerves if nothing else.

She opened the packet and saw that there were three left. Once this packet was finished, that was it: she would give up. She would give up the ciggies, the job, and Jon. Move away and start afresh. But then she'd tried that before, after Bex was murdered. It hadn't worked then. Was there any guarantee it would work now?

'All right, stranger?'

Molly looked up and saw Trudi approaching from the door to the custody suite.

'So much for giving up.'

'This is it for me, Trudi. I've had enough.'

Trudi's raucous laugh echoed in her ears. 'How many times have I heard that?'

'Not just the ciggies.' She exhaled slowly, enjoying the moment. 'Everything.'

Trudi touched Molly's arm. 'I know you've been through a shit time lately, babe, but the worst is out there now. Just deal with it. It'll blow over.'

Molly shook her head. She took another draw on her ciggie; she didn't even like the taste any more. 'I've fucked up.' She jerked her head towards the building behind them. 'And I bet I'm the talk of the locker room in there.'

Trudi kept her hand on Molly's arm. 'Who cares what people are saying? Fuck 'em!'

'It's not just that, though, is it?'

'Jon?' Trudi stared at her cigarette for a moment or two, as though it would provide the answers to all their problems. 'I thought you two were on your way to sorting things out? Now you know he's not some serial, psycho pervert.'

Molly tried not to laugh. 'You make it seem so simple when you put it like that.'

'Well, there is one piece of good news,' Trudi said, smiling. 'Gregor Kane's screwed. Word is, it was Kane who put Daryl Bailey in hospital.'

'Why?'

Trudi shrugged. 'Looks like our boy had stronger feelings for Leanne Wyatt than he cared to admit to. We don't know if he actually did it himself or got one of his grubby mates to do it, but either way he's going down for GBH.' She smiled at Molly. 'And that's not all. A witness has come forward claiming Kane knew the batch of Ecstasy that killed Adam Sloane was dodgy. He'd been warned about it but still went ahead and sold it.'

'Where did all this come from?'

'Apparently he's had a major falling out with his gang of little boys. Seems there's some new piece of scum trying to muscle in on Kane's patch and loyalties are being bought. And now that Daddy's disowned him, the vultures are circling and someone wants Kane off the scene.'

Molly tilted her head towards the sky and blew out a plume of smoke. A thick bank of cloud had appeared from nowhere, shielding them from the sun. 'So we've got enough to charge him with Adam Sloane's manslaughter now?'

Trudi nodded. 'And that's down to you, babe. You can't seriously think about chucking all this away.' She looked imploringly at Molly. 'You're a good copper. Hang on in there. Keep your nose clean and reapply once the dust settles.'

Molly finished her cigarette, popping the stub in the metal bin on the wall beside the door to the custody suite. She threw a weary smile at Trudi. 'Don't think I don't appreciate this, but you're wasting your time. I've made up my mind. I'm going to go in there and hand in my notice. My mind's made up. Oh, and I might throw a few choice words in Denning's direction. It was me who gave him the link to the Ferguson case, and he thanks me by wrongly accusing me of leaking a story to the press, then he throws me off the case.'

'That's the other thing,' Trudi said. 'Denning's disappeared.'

Chapter Seventy-One

The church was boarded up and looked semi-derelict. It was built from mellow brick and had a late-Victorian pseudo-Gothic look about it. There was scaffolding running along one of the walls and a triangular 'For Sale' sign with the word 'Sold' plastered over it hung precariously above the main door. The building seemed abandoned, as though somebody had started work on it but had stopped before they'd got round to finishing it.

Denning parked his car in a nearby side street. He looked around, but couldn't see any sign of the Lexus.

This was where the taxi driver had dropped off Leanne Wyatt and her killer. A typically suburban street in north London with nothing out of the ordinary, except for the disused church standing incongruously at one end. It was the same church he'd spotted in a glossy picture on the wall in Marsden's office: one of the planned development projects he'd boasted about. The church in the photo had been CGI enhanced to give an indication of how it would look after the conversion, but Denning knew he'd seen it somewhere.

He approached the front door with caution and turned the ancient square handle. Nothing. The door refused to budge even when he put his shoulder to it. It probably hadn't been used for years.

There was a side door under the scaffolding, partially obscured by weeds and an untamed magnolia shrub, which he thought might be worth a try. He fought his way through the greenery and reached the door. It looked slightly newer than the one he'd just tried at the front of the building, probably a later addition. There was a brass knob, faded and green round the edges, but it turned when he twisted it, opening the door with a faint click.

Beyond lay an eerie darkness and the distant sound of rustling.

He knew he should phone this in, but the last thing he needed was CO19 charging in boots first and making a three-course meal of everything. He switched his phone to silent as a precaution, even though this would result in a rap on the knuckles from Betty Taggart.

Inside the old church there was a musty, damp smell, like an old pair of shoes that had been left out in the rain. The rustling sound seemed to be all around him. Probably rodents, or bats. Bats in the belfry, he thought. But didn't bats only come out at night...?

Other than the incessant rustling noise, the church seemed ghostly quiet. Denning began to think he'd got it wrong: they weren't here. Perhaps he'd got it all wrong. Maybe Claire had taken Jake away somewhere, to her parents, or to Alton Towers. But she'd have told him. And then there was what Claire's neighbour had said about seeing Jake looking distressed.

Gradually his eyes adjusted to the dark, helped by thin beads of light that filtered in through the boarded-up windows. He could make out a few discernible shapes: planks of wood and bags of cement that were no doubt part of the planned conversion. To his right was what looked like the framework of a wooden-studded partition wall. Loose electric wires dangled overhead like coloured spaghetti. Denning hoped they weren't live.

The rustling noise had now subsided; whatever was causing it had been driven back into the dark shadows that pooled around the silent corners of the building.

Then he heard what sounded like a muffled cry coming from somewhere above. He wasn't sure if it was human in origin, or if it was a bird trapped somewhere inside the building.

He could make out a door to the left of him that looked like it might lead somewhere. Edging slowly forwards, and using the cool brickwork of the wall on his left as a guide, he headed in the direction of the door. When he reached it he was relieved to discover it wasn't locked. Carefully, he pushed it open. In front of him was a staircase. Getting his bearings, he realised this must lead to the steeple.

Again he heard the same noise as before. He couldn't be sure, but it definitely sounded like a cry. He began to climb the staircase, as slowly and silently as he could. He grabbed an ancient metal handrail hoping it wasn't going to come away from the crumbling wall, and cautiously edged his way up, feeling his way; all the time following the direction the muffled sound was coming from somewhere overhead.

Roughly a third of the way up the staircase there was another door that opened onto a small, windowless room. There was a light in the ceiling: a 40-watt bulb dimly illuminated a sorry scene. Claire and Jake were sitting on the floor, hands tied behind their backs. Jake was whimpering, and Claire looked like she'd been crying. There was no sign of Marsden.

Claire gave a slight gasp when she saw Donning approach, her eyes squinting at him in the dim light. After a couple of seconds, recognition clicked in. 'Matt.' She blinked back tears as she struggled to try and free herself, but in vain. He could see she was shaking.

He ran over to them, telling them it would be OK, lying that help was on its way. They had both been tied to an ancient radiator that looked like it would come away from the crumbling brickwork with one sharp tug, but it held firm when he pulled at it.

Apart from being shaken and clearly distressed, his ex-wife and son seemed unhurt. It looked like he'd got to them in time. He untied Jake, trying to calm him with a reassuring smile and squeeze of his shoulders. Jake backed away, squirming slightly at his touch.

'It's all right, little fella, Daddy's here. You're safe now.'

His son looked at him like he was a stranger. As soon as he was free he threw his arms around Claire and held on to her as though his life depended on it.

'Jakey, you need to be a brave boy for Daddy.'

His son looked at him with heavy eyes.

'Matt,' Claire's face was wet with snot and tears as she spoke. 'It's Alan...'

Denning started untying Claire. 'I know. I know all about Alan Marsden.'

Jake was crying now and still clinging onto Claire. Denning struggled to untie the rope round Claire's wrists, but Marsden clearly knew what he was doing when it came to tying knots: it wouldn't budge. Denning burnt his fingers as he tore at it, but the best he could manage was to loosen it slightly. He needed a knife. It was possible the builders had left something that he could use, but it would take time to look for it, assuming he could find anything in the dark.

Claire was struggling to pull her hands free, grimacing slightly as the rope bit into her flesh.

Then suddenly there he was. Marsden, or Placzek, or whatever he was calling himself, standing in the doorway looking worryingly calm.

Claire spotted him first, giving a little gasp, attracting Denning's attention to the fact that a violent killer was now standing between them and their only exit.

Chapter Seventy-Two

The gloomy darkness of the staircase embraced him: he was little more than a solid shape in a doorway. But there was no doubt it was Marsden. The imposing self-confidence was unmissable.

Denning couldn't tell if he was armed, but even if not, he was dangerous and they were trapped.

Marsden stood there with his hands in the pockets of his designer jeans, seemingly cool and unruffled, watching them. Denning wasn't sure how long he'd been standing there.

'Give me your phone,' Marsden said. His voice was calm, level; there was certainly no hint of fear or panic. He gave the impression of being in control, but how much of that was for show?

'They know I'm here,' Denning said. 'My team. They know where I am.'

Marsden offered a snort of amusement. 'No they don't. Now give me your phone.'

Denning quickly weighed up the situation. If Marsden wasn't armed, he could probably tackle him and take him down with a blow to the stomach. Marsden was solidly built, probably the result of regular trips to the gym, but Denning's years of playing rugby had made him fast and fit. However, if he got it wrong, he'd be putting Claire and Jake in even greater danger. Marsden was clearly unpredictable.

'You might as well cut to the chase, Marsden.' He paused. 'Is it Marsden? Or do you still go by Daniel Placzek?'

'Not Placzek,' he said coldly. 'I haven't been Daniel Placzek for a very long time.'

'OK. It's Alan Marsden. That's fine with me, but whatever you call yourself now, you know this is where it ends, so why not do what's sensible and give it up.'

Marsden let out a long, deep sigh. 'I'm not going to ask you again, Denning. Give. Me. Your. Fucking. Phone.' He spoke slowly, giving heavy emphasis to the last five words. He sounded annoyed, as though the situation he found himself in was an inconvenience he hadn't planned for.

Did Marsden have any kind of plan or was he making it up as he went along, Denning wondered? If he had a plan then he was likely to be less dangerous as long as it looked like everything was going his way, but if he was reacting to events as they happened, he would be even more unpredictable. And that wasn't good for any of them.

He reached into his jacket pocket and took out his mobile phone. It was still switched to silent mode, but he could see he'd missed a couple of calls and a text. He handed the phone to Marsden, who casually threw it over his shoulder and down the stairs behind him. Denning heard it clatter down the dusty steps. He needed to keep Marsden talking. He needed to try and come up with a way to get himself and his family out of this situation alive. That meant finding out if Marsden was armed.

'You don't need Claire and Jake for this. Let them go, and then you and me can chat.'

Marsden was still standing in the doorway, most of him hidden in shadow. He could see Denning more clearly than Denning could see him.

'I'm not interested in cosy chats, Denning. I just need to think about how I'm going to get rid of you and your little family. And let's be blunt about this; I'm already in a whole heap of shit, so adding a few more corpses to my murder quota isn't going to make a whole lot of difference.'

Denning needed to lure Marsden further into the room, away from the door and into the light. That way he'd have a better chance of knowing if Marsden was armed. 'Just let them go, Alan. They don't need to be here for this.'

Marsden was leaning against the doorframe now, hands still in his pockets. He was wearing his leather jacket, which could easily contain a knife or a gun...

'I suppose you feel quite proud of yourself, Denning, thinking you've worked it all out? You sussed about me and that moron Ferguson, but I'm guessing he didn't tell you about me?' He looked at Denning, raising an eyebrow as he spoke. 'No, he wouldn't, would he? Apart from the fact that he's too stupid, he's scared shitless of me. He knows what I'm capable of. Even banged up in a high security nick he's scared I'm going to get to him. But he was amusing at the time.' Marsden gave a dry laugh. 'I had a hamster when I was a kid. I used to enjoy making it do things. Anthony Ferguson was much like that hamster, except not so bright.'

Behind him, Denning could hear Jake crying. Claire was trying to shush him, but his sobs were growing louder. 'Do you want to shut that little brat up?' Marsden barked.

Claire's shushing grew louder, but had little effect. Denning glanced over his shoulder and saw that Jake was still clinging tightly to Claire, burying his head in her shoulder, which slightly muffled his crying. Claire had her arm around him, reassuring him that everything would be all right.

'Let them go,' he said to Marsden. 'You can see Jake's frightened.'

Marsden stood firm in the doorway. He'd taken his hands out of his pockets now, and had folded them over his chest.

'I really thought me, her and him could make a go of it, you know. I actually thought I could make it work: be a normal family. I mean, I knew she hated your guts, so you were never much of a threat. I even got off at the thought of you working that murder case, knowing I was always one step ahead of you.' He smiled coldly. 'You see, Matt, I'm one of life's winners.' He cocked his chin in Denning's direction. 'I lose at nothing.'

'Why did you kill those women, Alan?'

He looked bored. 'Which ones? The recent tarts, or the ones I persuaded Ferguson to do?' He gave another dry laugh. 'Opportunity, I suppose. I was in a bad place when that sad little twat came into my life. He told me he fancied this girl who worked in a pub he used to frequent. The stupid fucker plucked up the courage to ask her out once and she got her boyfriend to smack him, or so his story went. He told me he wanted to get his own back, so I said he should teach her a lesson. He didn't take much persuading. I honestly believe if I'd told him to jump into the Thames dressed as a giant prick he'd have done it.' Marsden laughed at the memory. 'Christ, he was so easy to manipulate, I began to wonder just how far I could push him.' His voice was still calm, detached; it was almost as though he was recalling an amusing anecdote rather than describing something that bordered on pure evil. Denning felt a writhing in his guts. There was something about Marsden that went beyond repellent.

'I suggested he follow her home after work and do her. I'd tag along and watch, just for the hell of it. Silly bastard got the wrong woman didn't he? I mean, what did you expect? It was dark and he was stupid. Don't get me wrong, he still went ahead with it. And to be fair, I'm not sure he actually meant to *kill* her, but she kept screaming. Screaming and screaming. Screamed the fucking place down. Luckily we'd had the good sense to drag her into a wood so there was no one around to hear.' He twisted his mouth into a sick parody of a smile. 'I got such a fucking kick out of it. I can't describe the buzz, watching someone totally helpless, completely at your mercy. I knew I needed to do it again, only next time I wasn't going to remain a bystander. We planned it: the best places to go to find likely victims. Isolated spots were always good, parks at night, railway stations. It became like a sport.'

'Your idea to carve a cross on the victims?'

'My parents were religious. My mother wanted me to become a priest. I nearly joined a seminary when I was

340

eighteen. I've spent my whole life trying to escape religion, yet it follows me everywhere.' He gestured at the building. 'Even now, it feels like God's mocking me. This was the ultimate defiance. Sometimes love and hate, good and evil get confused. Ferguson didn't understand. He went along with it, mostly because he was shit scared of me, but also because it gave him as big a kick as it gave me. For once in his life he wasn't the one on the receiving end. Then one day he said he didn't want to do it any more. I threatened him, saying I'd drop him in with your lot, but the stupid fucker had finally decided to grow a pair. He told me I was on my own. That suited me. Ferguson had become a liability by then. Half the time he couldn't even get it up. I did the last one myself. I probably enjoyed doing that one more than all the others. Then two days later your mob picked Ferguson up. I couldn't be sure he wouldn't talk, so I legged it to Spain for a while, then France. I had nothing to lose: my marriage had gone tits up and I was up to my arse in debt. It seemed like the perfect opportunity for a fresh start.'

Denning tried to stay calm. He needed to keep Marsden talking, and try and find a way out of this situation without anyone getting killed.

'What about now, Alan? Why did you kill Leanne Wyatt, Tanya Russell and Sandra Blake?' He made sure he used their names to emphasise the fact that they were people: human beings and not *sport*.

'Fate,' Marsden said coldly. 'I'd already met Claire through a dating site, and I actually thought it might work. This was everything I'd ever wanted: a ready-made family.' He looked over at Claire and Jake. Claire was blinking back tears and struggling with the rope; Jake was quieter now; clinging to Claire, and watching the events with a mixture of confusion and terror. She placed an arm over his head, so he wouldn't have to hear what was being said.

'But as always, life has a habit of taking you in a different direction when you least expect it to. We'd had an argument,'

Marsden continued, 'about you, as it happens. I found myself chatting up some random bint in a pub. I don't even know why. She was pissed. Pissed and lonely, and very up for it. So I took her back to a mate's house... Suddenly she seemed to sober up, and started bleating on about having made a mistake. I don't even remember what happened next. Maybe I just snapped. I was already in a shitty mood, so who knows, wrong time, wrong place...?' He smiled a cold smile. 'I just remember the *buzz*. I hadn't been that turned on for years. I kept reliving it in my head, over and over.

'Then a couple of weeks later, I was in a bar in Islington. There was some young tart having an argument with her boyfriend. After he left, I offered her a drink; then another, and the next thing we're heading back here. This time I planned it. I couldn't risk using the house again in case someone saw us. She didn't take much persuading, in fact, I'd say the little bitch was gagging for it. Then she started whining about having a kid and begging me not to hurt her.' He gave a hollow laugh at the memory.

'As for the third one, well, that really was unfortunate. A spur of the moment thing. I saw her coming out of a bar one night with her skirt half-way up her arse. I followed her and when she started getting suspicious, I grabbed her and pulled her into an alleyway. But she fought back and that was when I discovered "she" wasn't a she at all. I freaked out. I decided I would plan the next one properly. I'd already decided on a suitable candidate.' He jerked his head towards Claire, still trying to comfort Jake. 'She was becoming a liability, and it would have been fun watching you trying to figure it all out — too arrogant to admit you were out of your depth, and too stupid to see what was staring you in the face.'

Denning felt sick. He hated himself for having allowed his family to get close to this monster: someone who spoke about murder as though it were little more than an amusing pastime. He remembered what Walters had said about never having known evil until he'd met Ferguson. He hadn't known the half of it.

'I decided it might be prudent to let the dust settle. I suggested to her' – he nodded his head in Claire's direction – 'that we take a break in France, let things cool down for a bit, but she wasn't keen, kept saying it wouldn't be fair on Jake. Then that story appeared in the newspaper. She must have started putting two and two together and got a bit wary, coming out with lots of questions. Perhaps that's got something to do with having been married to a copper. I don't know if she'd sussed something; I'm not sure I really care. The long and the short of it is that we had an argument. She told me to leave, even threatened to call you.'

'Why take them here?'

'I needed them out the way to give me time to think. If it's any consolation, I wasn't planning to harm them. However,' he looked coldly at Denning, 'those plans may have now changed.'

He could hear Jake whimpering. He wanted to turn round and comfort his son, but he couldn't risk taking his eyes off Marsden, not even for a second. 'Where do you go from here? Back to France, Spain? Somewhere new?' Denning was standing directly in front of Marsden now. If he were to go for Claire or Jake, Denning would get to him first. But that wouldn't be of any use to his ex-wife and son if Marsden decided to go for Denning. He was blustering self-confidence, and at some point Marsden was going to call his bluff. 'You know how this is going to end, Alan.'

Marsden laughed. 'I know I'm fucked whatever happens, so I haven't got much to lose now, have I?' He reached into his leather jacket and Denning caught a glimpse of something shiny reflecting off the dull lightbulb: Marsden was armed with a large kitchen knife. It looked suspiciously like one of the knives that belonged to part of a set he and Claire had been given as a wedding present. He must have used it dozens of times. Now it was about to be used on him.

'Don't be stupid, Alan. Drop the knife and let's be sensible.'

Marsden seemed to think about this for a moment, then shook his head. 'I don't think so.' He lunged at Denning, the knife held tightly in his right hand. Denning jumped out the way but the knife grazed his shoulder, causing him to wince. He managed to throw his entire body at Marsden, momentarily catching him off guard and causing him to drop the knife. But Denning had misjudged the move and fell to the floor. He saw the knife on the floor and reached out to grab it but Marsden was too quick for him. He aimed a kick at Denning's head, catching him on the right temple. Denning felt a sharp stab of pain searing through his skull and a brilliant white light flashed in his eyes. He wanted to throw up. He saw Marsden grab the knife. He could feel consciousness slipping from him as the light from the bare bulb in the ceiling seemed to grow brighter. He saw the knife in Marsden's hand. Mustering his last drop of energy and desperately trying to ignore the pain that was ripping through his body, he rolled himself onto his side just as the knife came down. The knife grazed his jacket, but the jagged pain that tore into his arm told him it had succeeded in again making contact with his flesh. He could hear Claire screaming, begging Marsden to stop; Jake was crying out for his daddy. Blood began to pool on the dirty floor around him as the voices and screaming merged into one cacophonous noise.

Marsden was standing over him, looking down. There was nothing in his eyes but emptiness; not fear, not panic, not anger, just bland indifference.

He was about to bring the knife down again for a final time when Denning heard shouting coming from the direction of the staircase. There was a scream then Marsden froze, collapsing on the floor beside him, the knife still gripped in his hand, his eyes white and protruding, his mouth open.

Denning could feel bile in his throat as his head felt like it was going to explode. He looked up and saw a blurry trio of figures

344

standing in the doorway: Neeraj and a couple of uniformed officers, one of whom was holding a Taser, the wires of which were attached to Marsden's chest. Then everything went black.

Chapter Seventy-Three

They were outside the church.

The air was cooler now, puffy clouds scudding across a greying sky.

Police tape was being wound round the perimeter of the church. Several police cars were parked on the street and an ambulance stood nearby, its blue lights flickering.

A couple of paramedics, one male, one female, were attending to Denning: applying bandages and cleaning his wounds. The paramedics were insisting that he went to hospital arguing that he might have concussion, and were concerned about the loss of blood from the knife wounds. He heard himself say he was OK, though he didn't feel it. He was more concerned about Claire and Jake.

'They've gone to A&E to be checked over,' Neeraj said. 'But apart from shock, they seem all right.'

'Marsden...?'

'He's gone to hospital too, just to make sure he's fit enough to be questioned. But he'll be charged with murder, attempted murder, kidnap. You name it, we'll do him for it.'

Neeraj popped an Extra Strong Mint into his mouth and smiled. Denning wasn't sure if it was because he'd saved the day or he was flirting with the female paramedic. He suspected the latter.

'How did you know where I was?'

Neeraj was still smiling; it made him look friendly and likeable. 'I finally got a trace on Marsden's phone. It seemed a bit strange that he was in a derelict church. And what with you going AWOL, I put two and two together.' He noisily crunched the mint. 'You don't need a degree in psychology to figure out how people's brains work.'

Even if Denning had had the strength to argue with him, he wasn't going to. 'Thanks, Deep. I owe you big time for saving my life.'

'Actually,' he said sheepishly, 'it's Molly Fisher you should be thanking. She said if we found Marsden we'd probably find you.'

The paramedics had finished patching him up. He agreed to go to St Mary's to be checked over, but mostly because he wanted to see Claire and Jake. He wasn't sure how much psychological damage had been inflicted on them, or what the long-term repercussions were going to be for Jake. At the very least he owed them an apology for messing up their lives.

Chapter Seventy-Four

'Alan Marsden AKA Daniel Placzek has been charged with the murders of Sandra Blake, Leanne Wyatt and Tanya AKA Tony Russell. The DNA recovered from the van found in Foresham Grove is a match, and traces of Leanne Wyatt's DNA were also found in the church,' McKenna informed them all calmly over a briefing the next morning. 'Unfortunately, there is insufficient evidence to charge him with the earlier murders. So unless Anthony Ferguson talks, there's fuck all we can do about Marsden's connection with the earlier murders, and it looks like Ferguson is going to stay tight-lipped for the foreseeable.'

'What about his confession to DI Denning?' Neeraj asked.

'It wouldn't be admissible in court. Marsden could argue he made it under duress. Though,' McKenna paused to let her words hit home, 'I believe he was telling the truth about his involvement in those earlier murders, and if anything tangible ever comes to light, we *will* have him.'

'So Marsden's going to get away with it,' Kinsella said.

'Depends how you look at it,' McKenna replied. 'He'll almost certainly get life, maybe even a full-life tariff like Ferguson. Alan Marsden isn't going anywhere any time soon.'

-

Denning's shoulder still hurt, despite the painkillers he'd been given at the hospital. They were chatting in McKenna's office; tidying up the few remaining loose threads to ensure they had a watertight case to put before the CPS. McKenna had offered him a leave of absence, and time to recover from his ordeal. Sarah had mentioned something about a break at a friend's villa in Majorca. But he'd rather focus on work. They were already down on numbers in MIT and his absence wasn't going to help. Which reminded him, 'Molly Fisher?' he said. 'We've got a vacancy in MIT; DS Myers has informed us he isn't coming back. Fisher has certainly proved her worth.'

McKenna smiled. 'I'm sure if DS Fisher were to put in another request to join us, it would be looked on favourably. However, we can't overlook the fact that she misled us.'

Denning accepted that Molly had gone against procedure, even if she'd had her reasons. But he'd put in a good word for her; it was the least he could do.

And then there was Claire. She was staying at her mother's in Devon. She'd taken Jake with her.

So far, she wasn't blaming him for what happened. He had no way of knowing if Marsden had meant it when he said he'd wanted to make a go of it with Claire and Jake. Maybe everything he'd done had all been about filling some kind of void in his life. Perhaps settling down to live as a normal family might have been enough to curb his psychotic urges. But Denning doubted it. Men like Marsden got off on the thrill of making people suffer. Sooner or later he would have killed again.

'We're checking with our colleagues in France and Spain,' McKenna continued, 'to see if there are any other similar unsolved murders that have taken place there over the past twelve years, because I don't believe for one minute Marsden waited until his return to UK shores before he restarted his killing spree.'

'You think there are other murders?' he asked.

'I'd put money on it. Marsden's a dangerous and damaged individual. I reckon there are other victims out there,' McKenna said coldly. 'Christ alone knows how many.'

It was starting to rain when Molly climbed out of the car. She was carrying a small bouquet of white lilies. White had been Bex's favourite colour. She walked the short distance from the gravel car park next to the chapel of rest and crossed the damp grass towards Bex's grave. It was well-tended; her family still treasured her memory. A bunch of white roses rested against the headstone, while a Japanese Anemone sat in a bright ceramic pot beside the grave.

Molly had never forgotten her best friend. She'd spent the past twelve years blaming herself for the part she had played that night: for walking away when she should have stayed. Maybe now was the time to finally forgive herself and lay the guilt to rest.

She placed the bouquet beside Bex's headstone, and brushed away some light moss that had started to grow along the top.

Then she kissed the headstone and told Bex she loved her.

A wood pigeon fluttered out from behind a bush and she watched it disappear into the pale sky.

She returned to the car. Jon was waiting in the driver's seat. 'Everything all right?' he asked.

She nodded. 'It will be now.'

A Letter From Graeme

A massive thank you for choosing to read *Know No Evil*. It's been a long journey from initial idea to finished novel, and a lot has changed along the way. Despite having a fairly clear plan of where I wanted to go with the book, the characters evolved and the story developed as I wrote it. The end result is a fair bit removed from the early concept, but I hope the book is all the better for it.

I'd love to know what you think about *Know No Evil*, so please consider writing a review as they can help other readers discover new authors and their books for the first time. Or maybe you can recommend *Know No Evil* to people you know.

Hopefully you'll take Matt Denning and Molly Fisher to your hearts and join me on their journey throughout future books. I wanted to create two detectives who come across as real and credible; the kind of cops you'd find working in the Met Police today, but who are also interesting and complex enough to engage with readers. Both characters are flawed, but both have many admirable qualities too.

It's always good to hear from readers, so please do get in touch via my website or Twitter page. You can also follow me on Instagram, where I mostly post cat pics.

Thank you so much for your support, I really appreciate it.

Graeme Hampton

www.graemehampton.com
Twitter: @GHam001
Instagram: graeme_hampton

Acknowledgments

So many people have helped make this novel possible and I would like to take this opportunity to thank them.

Firstly, thanks to Sarah Hull, formerly of Writers' Essentials, who first saw a glimmer of potential in the book and helped me to make it as good as I could. And thanks to Angela Blacklock-Brown for pointing me in Sarah's direction, as well as for her own numerous words of encouragement over the years.

Keshini Naidoo and Lindsey Mooney, along with everyone at Hera Books, deserve a massive thank you for their patience, skill and enthusiasm, and for giving me the opportunity to achieve my dream of becoming a published author.

A mention too for fellow crime writers Sarah Hilary and Angela Marsons for their wise words and good advice.

A special thanks to Tracey Caswell, Jessica Dyson, Gary Metalle, Annie Lacey, Walter Oskars and the late Nina Klein for providing me with either technical information or regular encouragement, and in some cases both.

Finally, a shout out to Jericho Writers for their support and advice, and Claridge House, Lingfield for offering the perfect writer's retreat.